M000208067

Beauty
is the
Beast

Beasts Among Us - Book 1
By
Jennifer Zamboni

Cover by: Mirella Santana

www.mirellasantana.com.br

Stock material used under rights from © Neostock-
model Natalia & depositphotos

Copyright © 2018 Jennifer Zamboni

All rights reserved.

ASIN: B07HZ5SR2Y

ISBN-13: 978-0-692-04284-7

To my parents who read to me every night.
And
To the librarians at Newmarket Public Library who
were so wonderful to this little bookworm.

FULL MOON

Chapter 1:
Co-Workers

"What the—" I bolted upwards in my bed, rubbing the dent in my forehead and glancing around for my assailant.

The shrieking of my cell phone beckoned my attention to the floor on the opposite side of my queen-sized bed.

"Freaking house," I growled.

My phone had been plugged in on my bedside table, and just because I slept through—I checked the time and disabled my alarm—"15 minutes!" I yelped, dashing around my room throwing on black, slim fitted jeans and a grey square neck tee, slapping makeup on my face, and throwing my wildly curly hair into a french braid ending with a bun.

Out in the sunlit hall, I ran into a slim, petite woman with sleek blonde hair, Lacey-Marie.

"You look … different," I said.

"Good morning to you too. It's fake and bake!" She spun in a slow circle. "Check it out, I don't look dead anymore."

She stopped spinning, thrust out one hip, and planted her hand on it. "You overslept."

"Yeah, that's not all that uncommon for me after a full moon." I huffed and brushed past her.

"I was thinking we could buy a spray tan booth."

She stopped me.

"Um—" I glanced down at my caramel-colored arm.

"Not for us, for the salon. I mean, of course I'll use it too, but it would be great to get paid to own it."

She did look good, especially compared to her normal corpse pallor, but she smelled like chemicals to my nose.

"You know you want the money."

I grumbled at that. "And we're supposed to use all our free time spraying people with smelly goop? Have you not noticed how busy we've been?"

"Oh, come on," Lacey pleaded, clasping her hands and thrusting out her lower lip.

Percy wandered down the hall, sticking one last bobby pin in her carefully designed updo.

"Tell her a spray tan booth is a good investment for the salon." Lacey turned her attention to our generously shaped thirty-something mediterranean friend, housemate, and business partner.

"Gretchen is right. We might experiment with a booth sometime in the future, though. Perhaps even hire a tech to run it."

Percy, always our peacekeeper, found us some middle ground.

"Come on, Gretchen," Lacey pleaded with me again. "Please?"

"Yeah, all right. Money, good. Fake and bake, good," I assented to make her happy.

I still didn't like the idea of adding yet another odor to the salon. I know, I was more sensitive than most, but I didn't think I'd ever be a fan.

I wrinkled my nose at the smell wafting from my friend.

Lacey sniffed her shoulder. "I did it this morning

before you guys got up. Do I smell funky?"

"You smell like something that crawled into a hole and died, as always. Let's get some breakfast."

"Gee, you're such a good friend. I detect grumpiness. I'm going to prescribe a dose of non-cranky tea and a big breakfast. There will be no biting the clientele. We want their money and their repeat business." Lacey shoved me forcibly enough to make me grumble. Normally a shove from a woman of her petite stature wouldn't have affected me in the least, but Lacey is a special girl.

"You love me. And I'm not grumpy, but you can feed me anyway. Or rather, Percy can feed me. I don't think I'd eat anything you'd attempted to cook. It would run squealing from the table." I shoved back, making her stagger to the side. I do have a slight size advantage.

She shoved back once more before Percy broke us up.

"Ladies, we haven't even started the day yet."

"Right, which means we don't have to be professional and shit yet. How about it? Wanna give bottle tan a whirl, Percy? I bought a bunch of different shades." Lacey wasn't giving up.

I didn't think Bahama Mama was exactly the right color match for Percy's olive skin.

"No thanks, dear. My hair's done for the day. And really, who knows what that stuff will do when it comes in contact with hairspray?"

"She's already gorgeous. We wouldn't be getting business otherwise." I yawned and stretched.

"What time is it?" Lacey-Marie glanced around for a clock.

"We've got plenty of time. A good breakfast is in order for both of you. You're so skinny." Percy prodded Lacey's waifish ribcage.

Lacey looked down at herself and pouted. "It's not my fault I never grew any boobs. I never got a chance to fill out."

"You look good," I said. "Your makeup is fantastic today. What are you hiding under all that goop?"

"You'll never find out," she promised. "I'd still rather have your boobs. And your butt. And your waist."

"Seriously?" I rolled my eyes. I'm just a product of my muddled heritage. I used to work hard to keep fit, but now it came naturally.

Lacey glared at me.

"Sounds good, Percy. I'm in the mood for eggs," I said, deliberately changing the subject.

"Eggs for you and me then, and a red smoothie for you, Lacey?" asked Percy.

"Red's my favorite color," said Lacey.

"Pink's your favorite color," I reminded her.

"Yeah, I know, but not when it comes to smoothies. You're so argumentative this morning." Lacey rolled her eyes at me.

"So are you," I pointed out.

"No, I'm not."

"Girls! Kitchen, now!" Percy came between us, and placed a palm on the smalls of each of our backs, pushing us toward the door.

My stomach growled loudly, telling me we'd spent way too long staring at Lacey-Marie.

We felt the house pulsate once, twice, as if rejecting the idea of a new piece of technology. Percy's mansion was old and living. I'm not saying it had character; I'm saying the house was alive. Mostly it just moves rooms around, but it is most definitely sentient. Like now. I had intended to follow the others to the kitchen and ended up in the pantry instead.

"Really? I'm starving."

Oh, pantry, there is technically food here, I thought then proceeded to the kitchen to join the others, used to the house's quirks after years of living with them.

I scarfed down my food so I'd have extra time to get ready for work.

Olympian's Salon was inside the enormous house we all shared and Percy owned. Lacey and I moved in not long after we started booth renting from her.

The big old fashioned vanity that served as my station only needed a cursory inspection. I usually cleaned up at night, but something always sneaked past my attention. A bobby pin here, a brush there. My combs needed attention, so I picked up my sanitation jar, dumped the soapy smelling mess in one of the shampoo bowls, and rinsed my combs thoroughly. I refilled my jar with clean solution and placed my now damp combs in a drawer.

Percy entered through the salon's back door, depositing a steaming mug of herbal tea into my hands that smelled strongly of lavender and lemon.

"Thanks," I said, then lit some lavender-scented candles, sat down in my chair, and sipped while I waited for opening.

Percy knows me well. The more mellow I start the day, the better things go.

"No problem. I left a full thermos on the table." Percy pointed at the silver monstrosity that carried the massive quantity of tea that I consumed daily. It stood on the little table we kept our drinks and a bowl of trail mix on for our personal use.

"Thanks," I repeated, sliding down in my chair so my neck and head were supported against the back, which still smelled faintly of customers and long-washed-away product.

Lacey joined us, chomping peppermint gum and reeking of cigarettes.

I wrinkled my nose at the scent, being a non-smoker.

"I know, I know. I'm just walking by." She turned around and dug in her own station, coming up with a bottle of sweet pea-scented body spray. A couple of squirts went directly onto her clothing, then a squirt into the air over her head.

"Happy?" she asked.

"Ecstatic."

The bell over the front door rang as one of our stylists, Penny, and her brand new boyfriend, Scott, dashed in.

"Made it in time today!" The petite brunette removed her jacket and fluffed her hair.

"Ready to open, ladies?" Percy didn't wait for our answer, just flipped over the 'Open' sign on the front door.

Penny gave her boyfriend a quick kiss. "Thanks for the ride, babe. See you tonight!"

"No problem. See you later. Bye, Gretchen," said Scott with a wave.

I waved in return as he headed out the door. I'd introduced Penny to Scott, who was the bass player in the band I was a member of, several months ago. They had started dating recently and didn't appear to be all that serious about each other. Or at least Scott wasn't serious. Penny seemed to be oblivious to his flirtations with other women, or she didn't care.

The bell over the double doors rang, bringing with it a rush of cool morning air, warming earth, and exhaust. All four of our heads popped to attention.

Client number one. Who was the lucky winner? Me.

I blew out my candles and followed the others to the front desk. Each of us flipped through our appointment books, mentally preparing ourselves for the day. The monster inside me was already pushing at its cage. Being cooped up wasn't my thing, but I loved my job.

The young woman closing the door was Magan Marchessault. She struggled to free herself from one of her coat sleeves, then deposited it, and her purse, onto one of the seats in the waiting area, releasing the scent of paper, laundry detergent, rose water, and nail polish.

"I'm an absolute mess. I've got a meeting at noon with a major client, and I can't, just can't, show up looking like this." Magan pointed to the inch-long roots that were barely noticeable in her light brown hair.

"Come on over, Magan. I'll get you fixed up. Just a color today, or do you did you want a trim as well?" I motioned her over to my chair. Whoever had taken the appointment, probably Lacey by the handwriting, hadn't noted a cut, but that meant absolutely nothing.

The bell over the door rang again.

"You have to get a cut, it's in your eyes. I'm the mother, you don't get a choice." Mrs. Cordwell admonished her son, Lunden.

Great, a walk-in. Lunden was one of my regulars, but I really wished they'd made an appointment.

"Gretchen, he's absolutely got to get this mop cut. Please tell me you have time," she pleaded with me.

I glanced between Magan in my chair and the eleven-year-old and his perfect looking mother.

"I'll try to squeeze you in. Give me half an hour. It's going to be tight, and I'm not guaranteeing anything." Hopefully, Magan wouldn't take me too long to foil today. Her hair wasn't particularly thick, but she was always in a hurry and liked my complete attention.

"Fine. It's got to be done." Mrs. Cordwell tugged her son's arm, wandering towards the museum to kill time.

It's not a real museum, just old salon and barber shop paraphernalia Percy has collected over the years. Fascinating to us cosmetologist types, a little frightening for the general public, especially the old perming machine that dominated the display in its own glass display cage.

I left them to it and hurried to the back room, pulling up Magan's client file on the computer and writing myself a quick sticky note of instructions. I selected two bottles of color, developer, a measuring bowl, and a color brush. I measured in natural level 9 color, with a dash of ash, then added a dollop of developer. Magan's hair tended to pull warm, so ash was needed, no matter what. The result would be an exact match for her already existing blond highlights.

Just as the strong chemicals wafted up and stung my nostrils, the house kicked the air filtrations system on.

"Thank you," I muttered, grabbing a mini whisk and homogenizing the chemicals, then dropping in the brush. I already had a pile of foils on my station, so I was good to go.

I covered Magan in a large plastic cape that resembled a spray-painted garbage bag, sectioned her out with clips, and got down to business. Once I got into my rhythm, I didn't even have to think about my foil placements.

Magan lacked a healthy social life, so we talked mostly about her work.

I sealed down the last foil with a flourish. "All right, you've got about 30 minutes. Feel free to grab a cup of coffee and catch up on the latest gossip. I'm gonna have you process in the waiting area, if that's okay with you."

"Sure." Magan got up, wandered over to one of the comfy chairs, and settled herself in.

"Come on over, Lundan. Let's get you cleaned up."

He dragged his feet, but he made it to my chair under his own steam. I admit, I hurried through his cut. I combed it this way and that, checking for anything crazy uneven. I was booked solid for the day, and I really didn't have the time.

I just finished sweeping up when my next client came in. Good timing.

Lacey and Percy were whipping out the styles as well. It happened when we all took appointments for each other.

Clippers on, squirt it down, scissor over the top, don't chop a knuckle, and it was time to rinse my highlight.

I guzzled tea in between clients, taking deep breaths to keep myself level-headed in the chaos, and kept going. Lacey was doing the same mad rush, only with caffeine. I don't do well with caffeine. I get irritated easily. Lacey, on the other hand, had no problem with it whatsoever.

Percy managed to keep us both stocked up while sipping her water. The woman was magical. She was just as busy, but still relaxed, and raking in the tips.

My last client of the day was Mem Franz, and she arrived promptly at 6:30. She was one of my favorites, a flamboyant older woman, who was a high school French teacher. She always had the best stories about her kids and she always smelled like fresh laundry.

"Gretchen, give an old lady a hand. What can you do about this?" She pointed at her dyed blonde hair.

"I think a good trim should do the trick. It doesn't look too wild, just a little shaggy," I suggested, feathering my fingers through her ends.

"Perfect. Can I get a shampoo first? That's my favorite part."

"Of course." I ushered her over to the shampoo station with a gentle hand on the back of her shoulder.

The shampoo was most people's favorite part. I suppose it's relaxing. I don't really have feelings either way about having another person washing my hair, but whatever.

She laid back, folding her hands over her ample tummy, and closed her eyes with a sigh. She didn't chatter at me until I had her seated and caped.

Hers was an easy cut. I just had to follow the same lines I'd cut the month before when I'd taken her waist length hair up to her shoulders and put in some long layers. The extra bounce added youth to her style, which better fitted her personality. At 66 or so, she was showing no signs of slowing down.

I hated when my older clients started declining. It meant that I was going to lose them. Even if I only saw them once a month or so, they became my friends.

"I chaperoned a field trip today. It was wonderful to get out of the classroom. Kids should get out more often," said Mem, sitting perfectly still as I combed and cut.

"Where'd you take them?"

"Hiking. Just some local trails. Easy stuff, but they're going stir crazy, and we've got three more months to go."

Mem's husband looked up from the newspaper he

was reading, and smiled at her in the mirror, before going back to his article.

We settled into easy conversation born of a long client/hairdresser relationship. After blow drying her hair, I had her put on the glasses that hung from a beaded chain around her neck.

"What do you think?" I asked, standing by her side with an arm around her shoulder as she inspected herself in the mirror.

"Perfect, dear." She patted my hand and smiled.

"She looks 10 years younger." Her husband stood, depositing his newspaper back onto the coffee table.

"You'll have to take her out and show her off," I said with a laugh as I cashed them out.

"Oh, I will. We're going out for a late supper," Mr. Franz promised, taking his wife's hand.

"Thank you, dear. You did a wonderful job." Mem tipped up onto her toes and gave me a dry kiss on the cheek.

"See you next month. First Tuesday, same time?" I asked, before giving her a hug.

"Sounds perfect. Make sure you call and remind me, though."

"I will. See you later."

"Good night, dear."

I watched them leave, then penciled the appointment into my planner. I closed it with a thump and shoved it into a drawer.

"Are you doing close out tonight, Lacey?" I asked, rubbing my shoulders.

"Yeah." She wandered up to the counter after sweeping up the last of the hair.

I started the millionth load of laundry for the day and folded what came out of the dryer with Percy's help.

"Percy, I'm going for a quick run. I'll be back in 20 minutes for supper." I called, before dashing up the left staircase. I need to clear my head and my sinuses from my day.

"No hurry." Percy acknowledged without looking up from her bookkeeping.

I hurried anyway. I didn't want to waste time walking.

Percy's house isn't just huge, it's a mansion she had built in the 1700s. She's lived there almost full-time ever since, selling off her other properties over the years.

My particular suite of rooms took up the west end of the house. I threw off my hair-infested work clothes as soon as I got the door shut and yanked on a sports bra and a pair of shorts, then shot back out the door. I ran on the property, so I didn't really care who saw my state of undress, and the chill didn't bother me. Part of me wanted to change completely, to become a furry four-footed monster, but there were humans about.

The moon was waning, and I'd spent the last three days as a wolf. I needed to remember how to be a human again.

The woods smelled vaguely of wolf, which I wrote off as my own scent. I ran a lot, and it hadn't rained recently.

Percy threw a sweatshirt at me as soon as I arrived back in the kitchen for dinner, and I put it on without a word. I didn't particularly care if anyone stared at me. Looking was okay, touching was not. I'd gotten used to both at a young age. I was a lady of the evening when I changed, a slave, as was my mother and my grandmother.

I got lucky and made it out alive and not-so-free nearly 200 years ago when no one else did, but I still didn't want to associate with the job.

My phone pinged, and I pulled it out to see a photo message from Mem. She and her husband, George, were dressed up and sitting so close together that their foreheads touched, each wearing a brilliant smile.

I sent her a quick reply: *Gorgeous as always :)*

She sent back: *Thanks to you, dear!*

Percy's body relaxed as she set a nearly mooing steak in front of me. Gone was the persona of the pleasantly plump Greek woman in her mid-30s. In her place was a blonde buxom goddess with a spicy warm skin tone only slightly lighter than my own, otherwise known as Persephone, as in wife of Hades and daughter of Demeter. She'd moved to Isenburge, Maine to get as far away from the Mediterranean Winterland home of her husband as she could nine months out of the year.

Her violet eyes were the most unsettling I'd ever seen. Even more so than my yellow ones, covered by brown contacts, or even Lacey's red eyes, also covered in mud brown contacts.

A big steaming mug of blood was set in front of Lacey-Marie. As a vampire, she lived off the stuff. She had a severe sun allergy and an aversion to religion.

We're an interesting bunch to be running a salon. But a job is a job no matter who or what you are. We're good at what we do. And good at hiding what we are. As far as we could tell, our clients, Penny, and my band mates suspected nothing.

Chapter 2:
Death

The dark did nothing to dampen my senses the next morning, and something was off.

I stretched my hand towards my nightstand, fumbling for my phone. *4:10 a.m.* glowed at me from the screen.

I groaned and snuggled down into my covers as I tried to figure out what had woken me up. Nothing was amiss in my suite, so I closed my eyes and took a deep breath.

The sweet coppery smell of blood assaulted me, provoking my animal side to my surface. I shoved the wolf down as best I could and sat up. My hearing sharpened, but all I could pick up was the deep, even breaths of Percy and the silence of Lacey-Marie.

Not wanting to wake anyone else, I tiptoed to my door and down the stairs, avoiding the creaky ones. I stopped at the bottom of the stairs and focused on the dark figure sitting at Penny's station. The reek of blood was wafting from our work area.

I approached slowly, my feet making no sound on the tiled floor and my blood heating in anticipation. My heart sped up, and my breath came in short bursts as the smell of prey enticed me. It was a woman, her long brown hair draped over the back of the chair, her head lolled to one side.

My muscles shook as I fought the urge to change. Slowly, carefully, I stalked around, my eyes sharpening in the dark as I took in the woman's face, and I moved closer. Now that I was right on top of her, the woman's scent under the blood became familiar.

Her dead eyes were wide open, and her jaw was slack. There were two deep slices, like gills, over each jugular and despite the overwhelming scent, there was very little blood on her. I reached out a hand and touched Penny's still warm arm.

Rage filling me, nostrils flaring, I threw my head back and howled long and loud.

In a moment, Percy was at my side, her clothes and hair rumpled by sleep, eyes alert.

"Get a hold of yourself, Gretchen," she demanded, her hands clenched on her hips.

I snapped my jaw shut and fought the animal clawing its way out of my skin once more. Deep breaths. Don't think about the smells, just breathe.

Percy picked up the phone and dialed as a few tears slid down her cheeks and dripped off her chin. I heard a muffled voice pick up. "I need to report a murder," she said, her voice steady. "My name is Persephone Pluto, and I'm at Olympian's Salon and Day Spa. I also live here." She gave the address of the salon and the phone number.

She was quiet for a moment, listening to the voice on the other side. "No, nobody heard anything. Everyone has been asleep." After answering a few more questions, she hung up and beckoned me over with a wave of her hand.

"Go wake Lacey up, then start a pot of coffee. After that, I want you to go outside for a minute and cool off. Now get out of this room until the police get here. We can't have you endangering anyone."

I nodded then raced up the stairs and pounded on my best friend's door. "Wake up, you deaf corpse!" I roared, my humanity hanging on by a thread.

"Good god, what's your problem? Do you have any idea what time it is?" Lacey answered the door in a pink, lacy, barely there baby doll.

"Get dressed," I growled.

"What's going on?" she asked, suddenly looking alert.

"Penny's dead."

"What!?" she grabbed my arms. "When? How?"

"Not too long ago by the feel of her. Someone cut her throat. Oh, and she's downstairs. Cops will be here any minute. I can't believe the smell didn't wake you up." I turned away from her, and headed down a back staircase to the kitchen.

Or at least that was my goal. Doors and stairs don't always lead where they're supposed to. I ended up in the library.

"Don't mess with me. This is not a good time," I muttered at the house as I made my way down the hall to the kitchen. Not that the house cared what I thought. It was probably its fault that Lacey didn't smell anything. It was really good at protecting everyone from a vampire feeding frenzy by absorbing the smells.

I hurried with the coffee and put a kettle on for myself. I was going to need a good dosing of tea before I could deal with humans.

Lacey followed me outside so she could smoke.

"So, who found her?" she asked, lighting up.

"I did." I waved her growing cloud away from me.

"Seriously? What were you doing up? Did you hear something?"

I shrugged my shoulders. "I don't know what woke me. But I could smell her as soon as I did."

"So, no clue who could have done it?" She took a deep drag off her cigarette and aimed the resulting stream of smoke away from me.

"Not so far. All I could smell was blood and her."

My ears picked up the sound of approaching sirens. I took a few steps away from my friend, closing my eyes and focusing on taking deep, slow breaths. The air was cool, fresh smelling, and clean. I counted backward from 10, breathing as I went. My pulse slowed, and my senses dulled as my wolf became dormant once more.

"Ready to go back inside? I think the paramedics have landed," said Lacey, taking my hand.

I let her lead me back into the kitchen. The pleasant aroma of freshly brewed coffee permeated the air, and I sniffed in appreciation. I might not be able to drink the stuff, but I could still get some enjoyment out of being around it.

Lacey pulled the large insulated coffee carafe, which was usually used for clients during business hours, from a cabinet. I selected mugs and stacked them on a tray.

The tea kettle whistled, and I poured it over sachets of tea for myself, the scent of lavender and lemon billowing upwards as the hot water hit the mixture.

"You got the coffee?" I asked Lacey.

She nodded, grabbing the bottle of fresh cream from the fridge for the coffee tray.

"Good. Let's get this over with." I followed her through a maze of rooms to the salon with my pot of tea, where Percy stood talking quietly to the police as paramedics loaded Penny into a body bag resting on a gurney.

Percy's eyes were red rimmed, and there were salty tear tracks down her glamoured cheeks. Gone was the goddess, her public face firmly in place.

An officer broke off from the group.

"I'm Officer Reynard. Ms. Pluto says you're the one that discovered the body?" He held out his hand to me in greeting.

I nodded as I shook it and took in the strong scent of German Shepherd. His K-9 partner must have been waiting in his cruiser.

"Walk me through it."

I detailed as honestly as I could, without implicating my true nature, my discovery of Penny's body. I felt like I should have been crying. I was sad, yes, but I'd seen so much death over the years that I'd become a bit callous to a single death after the initial shock.

"You heard nothing?" he asked.

"Nope. I don't know what woke me up. I just felt like something was off so I went to investigate. I screamed when I found her, and Percy called 911."

He asked for a few more details before questioning Lacey-Marie.

I poured myself a mug of tea and took a seat on one of the chairs next to Percy.

"So now what?" I asked her.

"Well, this is a crime scene, so these gentlemen and ladies will be around for a while. We'll have to cancel today's appointments and proceed from there." She waved her index finger in a circle and cast her eyes around the salon.

"Proceed?" I asked.

"Yes. Decide whether or not to remain closed for a time."

We removed ourselves from the salon as soon as they finished with Lacey and headed upstairs with our mugs. There was no way any of us were going back to sleep, so we sat in Lacey-Marie's room and pretended to watch a movie in silence.

I dozed off eventually, curled up in a deep blue armchair, as did the others.

Waking up alone I stood, stretched, and made my way down to the kitchen.

A scowl darkened Lacey-Marie's pale features as she sat in the chair farthest from the sunlight pouring in through the kitchen's big windows. She wouldn't actually burst into flame like in the movies. She told me once that in the first few seconds of exposure she'd get a blistering sunburn, then char black and crispy in a few minutes. But no actual flame, puffy dust, or spurts of blood. Never having seen a vampire burn or die before, we had a little discussion about the most practical methods of killing each other, way back during cosmetology school in the mid -80's. 1980's. Lacey wasn't alive yet, in the 1880's.

She was changed when she was in college in the 70's. Getting turned kind of put a damper on her biology major and her passion for sun tanning, poor girl. That's why she was so excited about the spray tan booth, I think.

She sampled her blood and performed a nose wrinkle worthy of me.

"What's in this?" She smacked her lips as she tried to decide whether or not she liked the taste.

"Maple syrup. I don't see why you shouldn't be able to enjoy it. It's local." Percy held up a jug of syrup with her own label. On top of being the original owner of the salon and a stylist, she also ran an organic farm. She didn't eat anything that wasn't organic, a remnant of how things used to be.

I had to agree. Organic range fed beef was so much better than cow pumped full of growth hormones, which wreaked havoc on my wolf.

In front of me, she set a plate of blueberry maple

turkey sausage she'd traded for during farmer's market.

The muffled sound of a phone ringing in the salon interrupted our quiet breakfast, and Percy immediately jumped up to get it.

"Don't even think about it, Percy. It's probably a reporter," I garbled around my mouthful of meat.

Percy understood me just fine but didn't cooperate. She was in the salon, in human form, in the blink of an eye.

It was disconcerting when she changed. I don't know how she managed to keep up the glamour all day, but she's really good at it. Glamours take a lot of energy as they 're flawless magic illusions that cover a person, or sometimes objects, with a different appearance. Lacey wore a necklace spelled with a glamour that she had to replace once a week as it wore out, and it was expensive. It wasn't much of a disguise as it just hides her fangs. The contacts that covered her blood red irises were cheaper than a glamour.

"That was a cancellation, Lacey, your 1:00. She saw it on the news. I crossed it out of your book so you'll know not to call her." Percy pushed her way back through the doors and bolted down the rest of her breakfast.

Lacey and I followed her example. If the phone was already ringing, it was just going to keep going, guaranteeing a very long day.

I ran upstairs to my room to dress for the day, wishing I'd gotten up early for a run.

I stripped off my fuzzy pajama pants and deposited them on the floor with yesterday's clothes. My top joined that, and I flung the door open to my walk-in closet, dodging my punching bag, coming to stand, hands on hips, in front of my clothes rack. I wasn't officially working, so professional clothes weren't required. I dressed quickly in tight jeans and an oversized black hoodie, opting to remain barefoot.

I threw my wild, curly dark hair up into a ponytail and decided against makeup before locking my door—a habit to keep out wandering clients—and shoving the key in my pocket.

"Seven times. The phone has rung seven times since you two went up to change. Five new possible clients and two regulars wanting appointments for this week." Percy sat on the swivel stool, staring at the salon phone. She poked it with her index finger as if expecting it to bite or ring, which is what it did.

Lacey answered, putting on her professional voice. "Good morning! Olympian's Salon, Lacey-Marie speaking, how may I help you? Uh huh, no . . . Uh, I'd have to see it . . . No, don't buy a box of bleach, come in. I'll see what I can do . . . No, I won't be able to do anything about it today, but we can discuss options . . . Yes, yes. All right, see you in a bit."

Lacey hung up the phone and joined Percy in glaring at the ringing annoyance. "That was Yvonne Sandus, one of my sometimes regulars. She let one of her friends dye it black and cut it. Apparently it's a mess."

"Lacey, we're closed. We're not working," I reminded her, leaning over the desk on my elbows.

"I'm not going to do anything today, just look at it. It's not like we're going anywhere."

The phone rang again.

My turn.

"Good morning! Olympian's Salon, Gretchen speaking. How may I help you?" I asked in my professional voice.

"Hi. I got a cut there yesterday, and it's just not right. I want my money back," a woman's voice snapped at me.

"I see…" I paused. I'm not good at these situations. "Can you tell me who cut your hair so they can—" straighten you out "—correct the situation?"

"I don't know her name," said the exasperated-sounding voice.

"Describe her to me."

"Tall, dark."

Well, that describes me as Percy is middling height with dark hair, and Lacey is petite and blonde.

"Gretchen?" I supplied with a snap of my own.

"Yes that's it, Gretchen."

She must have forgotten my introduction already.

"Your name, please?" I asked, pulling my appointment book towards me.

"Lucinda Evermont."

I couldn't remember the name, so I flipped through my schedule in search of her. I didn't have a single Lucinda listed on the previous day's page, and I write down all my walk-ins.

"I'm sorry I—we—don't have your name here in our register for yesterday."

"Well, I—She must have realized what a terrible job she'd done. I want my money back."

"Listen, lady, I'm Gretchen. And I'm absolutely positive that I didn't cut your hair yesterday. You're gonna have to find another stylist to swindle—"

Percy grabbed the phone from my hand before I could finish my tirade.

"Hello, ma'am…. Yes I'm sorry about that. Gretchen's had a tough week… Yes. I'm sorry, we don't do refunds, but if you'd like to come in, I'd be happy to fix it for you. Yes… yes… of course. .. No, you're right. Have a nice day, ma'am. You too." Percy placed the phone back in the cradle and turned to glare at me.

Just call her damage control.

"What? She's trying to steal my money. She's never even been here before!"

"You could have handled that a little better." She squinted at me in annoyance.

"I could have, but this way makes me feel better," I said crossing my arms.

"Go pour your tea. I can hear the pot whistling." She stood her ground as I glared back. "Now, Gretchen. The day hasn't even started yet, and I can't have you phasing today."

She was right, of course.

I stomped to the kitchen to remove the noisy kettle from the stove and turn off the burner.

My big thermos stood at the ready with metal balls of loose lavender-chamomile tea arranged around the opening. I poured the boiling water over them and inhaled the scented steam, leaning my forehead against the cabinets above the counter. Without moving from that position, I pulled open a drawer and selected the bottle of lavender extract that was kept there. Pulling the stopper, I placed my index finger over the top and tipped it, then dabbed the greasy feeling scent on my pulse points and ran my fingers over the loose tendrils of hair hanging around my face, hoping that would be enough.

We spent a good chunk of time on our cell phones canceling appointments that morning.

Yvonne Sandus arrived just before our usual lunch break, her hair a disastrous hack job and uneven color worthy of a three-year-old with a Sharpie and a pair of blue Crayola crayon scissors. Lacey took pity on her and helped her out, despite the fact that we were closed.

Percy and I kept busy answering calls from concerned customers, breaking for a late lunch with the rest of Percy's staff after Lacey evened out poor Yvonne's correction.

We had just sat down when a loud banging on the front door interrupted us.

"I'll go see who it is," Christina, Percy's right-hand woman, stood from her seat. When did Christina show up?

We heard a woman's raised voice, Christina trying to reason with her, and the woman not having it.

Christina returned with an apologetic look on her face. "She insists on talking to the manager. Apparently, she doesn't appreciate having her appointment canceled. She said her name is Shenna Seidl."

Percy was the acting manager, but all three of us went.

"She's one of my clients," Lacey-Marie muttered as we exited the kitchen and wound our way through the house towards the salon.

As soon as Shenna saw us, she quit pacing and beelined for Lacey, smelling of perfume and anger.

"I got a call canceling my appointment. I have to have that appointment. It's my boyfriend's birthday."

"I'm sorry, but we have to close the salon for the next few days," said Percy placing a gentle hand on her arm.

"I don't care! You can't just cancel appointments on people without giving them time to make other plans."

"Oh, gee, the next time one of our girls is murdered, we'll make sure to schedule it at a more advantageous time for you," I snarled.

She looked taken aback, as she should. It's not like

we randomly closed the salon on a regular basis. In fact, we'd never done it. None of us were ever sick, so we didn't have to worry about that, and I knew where the full moons fell, so made sure to schedule around it.

"Murdered?" Shenna squeaked out, the stench of her anger fading.

"It's not something we were looking to advertise," said Lacey, adopting my crossed arm posture.

"Oh, sorry. I, uh, I've gotta go." Shenna backed away from us and headed right out the door. She left tire marks as she burnt rubber, getting away like I was chasing her.

"I'm not too sorry about that. Her boyfriend is probably going to spend his birthday with his wife." Lacey squared her shoulders and led the way back to the kitchen.

"So it's official, we're closing for a few days?" I asked Percy as we regained our seats at the table.

"It's up for discussion, of course, but I do think it's best."

"I agree." I rested my chin on my hands and my elbows on the table.

"Me too," said Lacey.

"Good," said Percy. "I'm glad we're all in agreement."

I took a bite of my sandwich while she studied her own food.

Lacey, who didn't eat lunch, just nursed another cup of coffee.

"What do you think of bringing on another girl?" Percy asked.

"Already?" Lacey raised her eyebrows.

"I don't think we can handle the workload alone. We really need another girl. I'd like to hire a few other positions as well." Percy picked at her bread distractedly.

"Such as?" I asked, leaning towards her with interest.

"I think we could use a manicurist, and I'd love to bring a masseuse on staff."

"I wouldn't complain about either of those," I said, thinking about how nice a weekly back rub might be.

"Me either," said Lacey. "But I'm not too sure about hiring another stylist right now. I think it's too soon. Besides, I think we can handle things on our own for a while."

"Do we really need to put it to a vote?" Percy asked scrunching her eyebrows together and pressing her fingers to her left temple.

Lacey scowled and shook her head.

"Then it's settled. I'll put the word out." Percy dug into her lunch as I polished off mine.

The rest of the day was used up cleaning and airing out the salon. We should have taken it easy. It was just the beginning.

Chapter 3:
House Guest

Before we opened the day after Penny's funeral, I cleaned out Penny's station.

I sat in her spot, empty box in hand, staring down at her things. I'd promised her family I would pack it all up and mail it to them as soon as possible, so I took a deep breath and delved in.

Penny's shears were loose in her drawer, so I fastened a rubber band around the blades to keep them shut. Her razor was a flip handle with a removable guard left over from her school days. The guard slipped as I closed it, and the blade ran across the pad of my thumb. Blood welled up as I stuck the wound into my mouth.

The blade was fresh, without a single hair clinging to it, and the cut was clean, which usually made it harder to heal with no jagged edges to clot together, but the regenerative nature of my blood healed the cut within five minutes.

I stuck the razor in the box, piling her other tools on top. I opened all the drawers, making sure there was nothing left behind, then carried it to the back room in search of packing tape.

The day promised to be a busy one as it was our first open since the murder, our books maxed out with rescheduled appointments on top of the already existing ones.

It was mid-morning when the bell over the front door tinkled annoyingly and both doors swung open, inundating the salon with cold air. The man who walked in carrying a suitcase filled the room with size and presence enough to raise my hackles as the smell of testosterone and magic washed over me with the breeze.

"Can I help you?" Lacey-Marie asked, leaning her petite frame over the front desk so that her folded arms pushed up her small breasts.

"I'm here to visit my wife." He ran his hand over his thick, dark hair, staring down his nose as if Lacey were less than a gnat.

Whoever his wife was, she was either the luckiest woman to be married to such a looker, or the most pitiable for being stuck with someone so snobbish.

"Hello, Persephone," he said, his voice a gravelly bass.

I dropped to my chair, followed by my jaw and my dignity.

"Hades... what are you doing here?" Percy stopped mid-cut to address her husband, the Greek god.

"Day-amn," Lacey-Marie muttered loudly enough that pretty much the entire salon heard her.

What was Hades doing in the mortal world? I couldn't remember a tale of him leaving his kingdom. Not that I knew many myths.

"I came to see you, wife. I wanted to know what, exactly, it is about this place that makes you leave me year after year. It's . . . quaint," he said, setting his suitcases down by the front desk.

Quaint? The place was a fricking mansion. Jerk.

"I like it here. It's distinctly untainted. Ladies, this is my husband from Flor-ih-da." Percy spoke slowly, probably to nail into Hades' skull where it was he was supposed to be from.

"Right, the Pluto family of Florida," said Hades, walking over to his glamoured up wife and giving her a kiss.

Percy hugged him briefly, then pushed him away, resuming her haircut.

Not that her client minded. She was just as busy staring as the rest of us. Percy could have given her a mullet, and she would have said she loved it just because Hades was in the room.

"So, where should I put these?" he asked, pointing to his bags.

"You can put them up in my room. Gretchen, can you show him since you seem to have a moment?" Percy asked, without looking my way.

"Uh, yeah, sure. It's right upstairs to your right," I said.

"Show him, Gretch." Percy turned and gave me a look.

Fine. "Follow me." I ushered him towards the foot of the stairs, not sure how I felt about having him follow me. It was kind of like having the devil watch your back.

Percy's room was on the opposite end of the house from mine. She watched sunrises; I watched sunsets. She also left her door unlocked, so I pushed it open and showed him in.

"So this is Percy's room—your room too, I guess."

"So I surmised," said Hades, looking around with a critical eye.

"Is there anything else you need?" I asked, backing towards the door. It was only a polite question. I hoped he wouldn't respond.

"Yes. I would like a glass of wine and something to eat. I'm famished. It was rather a long trip."

I bet. I'd never been to the fae lands, but they

sounded far away. I'm not sure I'd be allowed, being of tainted blood and all. I wondered how Hades felt about people like me. I knew he let dead guys hang out at his place, but what about weres?

"Follow me," I said again. "I'll get you set up. I don't cook, but there's leftovers, so feel free to help yourself."

Does Hades normally help himself, or does he just get served? There were no minions, servants, or slaves here, and I wasn't about to play the part for him.

We made our way back through the salon, and I could feel eyes on us the whole way. I told myself to keep going, and we arrived in the kitchen without any fuss from the house.

"Plates are up there." I pointed at a cabinet. "Utensils here." I tapped the drawer. "Red or white?"

"Red. Merlot, preferably."

Ick, nasty, dry stuff. I only drink wine once in a while, but I don't like dry, dry, wines. I've got to admit, I love a good dark beer or rum. I'd had lots of years to develop my taste. I dashed down the basement stairs and picked a merlot from Percy's collection, brought it up the stairs, and hunted for a corkscrew in the junk drawer. I found it right next to the forks. Imagine that.

I stabbed the cork and started twisting. The little arms of the easy puller thing rose up like a tiny, slow cheerleader until they stood vertical, then I just had to press down. The cork slid out a half inch. Not so presto. I wriggled it carefully, not wanting to break anything, and it came loose with a hollow *pop*. I grabbed a wine glass and poured a bit into the bottom of the glass, handed it to Hades, and waited.

He swirled it around the glass a few times before going to work on his food.

I left him to it, making my way back to the salon where I was mobbed by every woman in the salon except for Percy, who was standing with her arms crossed and with an unfocused gaze.

"So, did you know he was coming?" Lacey-Marie asked me in hushed tones.

"Not a clue. Did she say anything to you indicating that maybe . . ." I trailed off shrugging my shoulders up towards my ears and shaking my head.

"Nope. I kinda assumed she was getting ready to fly south, for a visit," said Lacey.

"Fly south?" a new client asked.

"They live in Florida. Or rather, he does. They're originally from up here, but he works down there. She goes down for the winter with all the snow heads, and a vacation or two, now and then."

"Gretchen!" Lacey admonished.

"What? She does." I stomped over to my seat and flung myself in it. "I don't like him."

"Dude, he's gorgeous," said Lacey-Marie, as if that mattered at all.

"Yeah, he is, but I think he's an arrogant ass," I said, spinning myself slowly, not caring that Percy could probably hear every word.

"So is this the first time you've met him?" asked Lacey's client.

"It is. I've heard a lot about him, but this is the first time I've ever laid my peepers on him," I said, stopping my slow spin with one boot-clad foot stomped on the floor.

"Not even a picture," said Lacey. "It's an interesting marriage those two have going." She turned and looked over at Percy, who was now busily blow-drying her client, probably ignoring us. "They married young, and I guess they love each other."

"I think she's better for him than he is for her. They'll never get a divorce or anything," I said.

I wondered if fae could get divorced, or if once married they were married for life. I'd never read or heard anything about a fae divorce. Lots of philandering, though. Maybe they just didn't like to talk about it.

I mentally shrugged and collected my next client, a color, so someone else would have to wait on his highness.

I don't know why I disliked him so intensely since I'd never met him before. I'd only heard the myth, where he kidnaps Persephone and marries her.

In reality, theirs was a Zeus-ordained arranged marriage. Her mother hadn't approved, and she's the one who spread all the rumors.

Whatever it was, I hoped I could put my finger on it soon. It would eat away at me until it came out, and I just didn't have the energy to pour into Hades hating.

The front door opened, and the salon suddenly smelled like animals as five wolves in human form seated themselves in the waiting area. They all turned to look at me at once, their amber gazes intense.

What were they doing in the salon? There was absolutely no way they'd come in for haircuts. That would be too much of coincidence. There were no packs in Maine. I'd made sure of it when I moved.

The humans in the room didn't know what they were, but I could tell they were intimidated, as well they should be. I didn't think they'd cause trouble with so many witnesses, but from what I remember, wolves in packs are less human and more fae. Definitely not to be trusted on my personal hunting grounds.

They did not stand or call my attention. They did, however, watch me work.

It was a little disconcerting. Apparently they planned to stay until I acknowledged them. There was no chance of that happening, at least until all the humans were gone.

I turned my client in my chair so we were both facing the wolves. I didn't want them at my back, just in case. Also just in case, I avoided my calming tea. I needed to be on my guard for the safety of everyone in the room.

Lunch time couldn't come soon enough.

They stood from their perches as soon as the room emptied of everyone human.

Percy and Lacey flanked me as I approached them.

The wolf that came forward to greet me was unimpressive in looks, but his confidence gave away his pack status: Alpha.

"Good afternoon, Gretchen. I'd like to have a word with you. Alone." He didn't offer a hand in greeting, just assumed that I'd bare my neck to him.

Hell no, buddy. "Actually, I don't have time just now." I crossed my arms under my chest and stood my ground, nostrils flaring as I tried to catch more of their scent, and maybe figure out what they were up to.

For once, Percy didn't elbow me. Instead she flung out both arms, magically dropping the blinds over all the windows and yanking the blackout curtains shut. Her figure blurred for a moment as her glamour vanished.

"This is my house. You will not presume to discuss anything without my permission." Percy's presence grew as she spoke. She is goddess, hear her roar!

The alpha stood stock still for a moment, taken aback that two females had defied him in a matter of seconds.

"Forgive me, I did not realize Gretchen recognized

you as her alpha." The man's apology was anything but genuine. If anything it was wary, defensive.

"I don't." I separated myself from my friends. "But out of respect for Persephone, let's take a walk." I hadn't really meant to make time for them, but it was unlikely they would leave if I didn't.

"Ladies, will you tell my next client that I will be running a little late? I have some... family issues to sort out." I turned my back on the pack to face my friends. It was a deliberate act of utter disrespect to the wolves.

"Of course," Lacey-Marie said quickly, glancing behind me.

The pack hadn't moved, and the mood turned icy.

"Are you sure, Gretchen?" Percy asked, worry apparent in her eyes.

"I can handle myself." I attempted to reassure us both.

"This way." I ushered the wolves out through the back of the salon and through the kitchen, grabbing a packet of lunch meat on my way past the fridge and marching out the back door. The pack could follow or not.

The alpha caught up to me at the edge of the kitchen garden. The others hung back a moment, then followed out of hearing distance.

"I feel we've gotten off on the wrong foot. My name is Kaine, and I'm the alpha of a pack started down in Texas." He had to say 'started' because wolf packs are technically nomadic, though they tended to stay within certain distances of their alpha's changing place. He still hadn't offered me a hand to shake, but at least I had a name.

"So, what is a pack from Texas doing in Isenburge, Maine?" I'd remained under the radar, so they weren't there because I was causing trouble.

"We want you back." He spoke like I'd asked a ridiculous question.

"Wow, that's a good joke. It's only been, oh, a hundred-and-fifty years or so since I was never part of your pack." I didn't stop walking to laugh at him.

"Our alpha changer made you. That makes you mine. He told you that when he made you the offer." Kaine, though not much taller than me, looked down on me in disdain.

"Yeah. Made and abandoned me. I think he gave up any rights to my person a long time ago."

"We need females," he said, moving so close I could feel his body heat.

"I don't need a male."

"I need a mate."

That stopped me. I swung around to stare at him, taking in his skinny jeans and suit jacket hipster look that screamed 'prick.'

"No," I said, backing away from him.

"You're not supposed to say no to me." He advanced on me, back straight and arms held slightly away from his sides, trying to look more intimidating.

It didn't work. "You're not my alpha."

"I'm not your alpha." He stared me down, trying to force me to submit.

Bright boy. "Do I look like I'm cowering in your presence?" I pulled my shoulders square and raised my chin in defiance.

"You need a pack. Lone wolves don't fare well."

"I got off to a rough start, killing off everyone I knew, but I've managed just fine. Thanks for that, by the way," I sneered at him.

"You wanted to be free from your masters," he pointed out.

I wanted to cease being a slave, not trade one master for another. I didn't want to be a killer.

I'd at least been able to stop being a monster, especially after Percy found me. I might even qualify as animal now. I wanted to be human, and humans are not owned. "Great, thank you very much. I guess I owe you. But I'm not going to be your mate."

"All right, how about this: You get to know us, and you don't make any rash decisions. We're your family, and we would like for you to join us. Give the pack a chance. Give me a chance," he offered.

It was tempting. I wouldn't have to hide anymore, and I'd have a family I always wanted, a mate, and maybe pups. But I wanted to do it the human way. I wanted to be wooed. I wanted to fall in love and get married. I wanted to make my choice. Was that so wrong?

I gave in. "Fine. I'll give the pack thing a try, but I'm not leaving yet. You're not to hunt anywhere near people while you're here, and you're not to harm anyone."

"I'll agree to that, for now. Give it a little time, and you'll find that this world you are living in," Kaine motioned to Percy's house, "is not for you. Now let me introduce you to the others." Kaine yipped loudly, and they came running.

How handy.

They arranged themselves in a semicircle around us, eagerly awaiting their introductions.

The first was a tall, skinny guy who looked to be in his mid thirties. "This is Jacque, my second in command," Kaine introduced.

"Pleasure." Jacque spoke in a thick French accent, nodding at me.

"Dirk."

A lean Germanic soldier held out a hand to me. "Hi, nice to finally meet you. Alpha has spoken highly of you."

There was a moment of competing grips as we shook hands. Then we both let go. I liked him. I surmised the 'alpha' he spoke of was not the man in charge, but the actual changer. Interesting.

"Quintavious."

The nicely dressed man was obviously not a dominant. He did not offer me his hand, avoiding any sort of confrontation. In fact, he gave a little head bob that could have been interpreted as a bow.

The last was a petite, dark-complexioned woman who was very pregnant.

"This is Kisa, Dirk's mate."

"Hello," she said, her accent Russian. She looked me up and down with calculating eyes.

"These are just my public faces."

The ones who could be trusted around humans. I nodded.

"How about we take you hunting. Saturday night?"

"Saturday's no good. I'm practicing with my band at a party." I came up with a lie on the spot.

"Soon, then." Again, Kaine stood uncomfortably close.

"Soon," I agreed.

"I'll send somebody to issue you an invitation."

How formal, a second invitation that was really a demand. "I'll keep an eye out. Was there anything else you wanted? I need to get back to work."

I walked away. They could show themselves off the property. If they didn't, I just might have done it for them.

When I got back inside, I could tell the girls had questions, but I didn't have the time to answer them as

I really did have work to do.

Later that afternoon, I set some sheet music on my stand set up in the middle of my room.

I tuned Clarissa, my violin, by ear, no longer needing the tuning fork that I'd kept as a keepsake. She'd been with me since my beginning.

After a while, I memorized the sounds of the notes so well, I could pick out any note in a song, which made it much easier to play with others. I'd been playing the violin since I got out of the brothel, and could have made a career of it, had I wanted to. I didn't. I just wanted to be ordinary, or at least as ordinary as someone like me could be. Yes, I play in a band, but we'd never make it big. Two of the guys had families, and we pretty much stuck to playing bars.

The piece on my stand was by Paganini, one of the greatest violinists ever to set a bow to strings, in my opinion.

When I performed, I played an electric violin I called Lola as I don't play with an orchestra, but a band comprised of a drummer, bassist, and guitarist/lead singer. Our front man happens to have a red mohawk to top it all off, and there was enough ink on all their bodies to print a Sunday paper.

My music surrounded me, and I let it consume me, allowing my attention to wander away from my sheet music and beginning to improvise as I played for myself. The stuff I write for the band is dumbed down. It's good, and it compliments them, but it's not what I feel. I don't feel butterflies and bunny rabbits (unless I catch one) and I'm not seeing little fantasia cherubs bouncing around on clouds. It doesn't evoke sweet smells.

I was feeling raw, wild magic. Seeing tumultuous storms ripping through my mind and smelling the terrifying unknown. It was what a wild animal would have played given thumbs and ability. It was what someone who's caused pain and death needs to let loose. It was an outlet, even better than running away.

I closed my eyes, playing on. Notes bypassed my brain and flowed out of my fingers and wrist. While the last note drifted away, I was drained, calm. I'd needed to play over the past few days, but was afraid what would come out of me.

Setting Clarissa on the bed, I stopped the computer I had set up to record my practice and picked up the cords, before moving the microphone and the stand off to the side of the room.

I'm not a tech person, only using computers for research, recording my practices, and burning the stuff I like onto CDs at the end of every month. Sometimes I go back and listen to them, picking out different things that are acceptable to play with the band. I don't even own a phone with Internet access, just basic call and text.

I can't play most of my stuff in front of people as it's not human music. I am mortal, sort of. I can be killed, but my immune system is hyper-protective of me, so I heal quickly. I'm sure someday there will be a virus that can kill me, proving once and for all there is a human under all the fur.

I wiped down my instrument, putting Clarissa back in her case and away with everything else.

Lacey-Marie cornered me as soon as I emerged from my room.

"I'm going for a run before I say anything. Feel free to join me," I said.

"Yeah, sure. But munch something first. You left your lunch meat on the counter. I'm betting that means you didn't eat."

I was hungry, so I grabbed the meat from the kitchen, then headed back to my room to change.

Lacey met me outside, decked out in pink shorts and a sports bra. She was bent over, tying her laces.

I didn't wait for her, just took off at an easy jog to warm up. I made it to the back of the field before she caught up. The woods were where all the real running took place. There were no trails cleared, so there were plenty of things to hurdle over and duck under, and I found it therapeutic.

My feet pounded the ground. I didn't want to talk, but Lacey did.

"I can't believe how busy it's been. I've been making a ton of money. Do you think it'll stay like this?" she asked, darting up beside me.

I didn't answer.

"I mean, don't these people know we're going through a recession?" Says the girl who can't make it through a week without buying at least one pair of shoes. "So what did the wolves want?"

Great, now I have to talk. "They want me back in the pack," I said.

"Were you ever in the pack?" She raised her eyebrows in question.

"No, not really. But their alpha changer is the one who changed me. I guess that means I'm supposed to belong to them, since it was in their territory and all that."

We ducked under branches, swerved around trees, and leapt over the underbrush.

"Are you leaving?" she asked.

"Not yet, but they want me to." I ran a while longer before I was really ready to talk. Two desires pulled at my mind: to gain the support of a pack and love of the life I was currently leading.

"So, there's one little hitch to that plan, I think I'm more dominant than the alpha. Oh, wait, make that two hitches. He wants me to be his mate."

It was full dark when I ripped the contacts out of my eyes. They didn't last long, though I tried not to waste them, I saw much better without them in the night.

"The alpha wants you to be his mate? Oh, wow, that's huge. Would that make you, like, queen?" Lacey seemed to like the idea.

"Sort of. Did you miss the part where I'd have to be submissive to him? I can't do that. Especially to someone I could never respect."

"So what happens if there's a more dominant wolf than the alpha?"

"They can kick you out to fend for yourself, or the pack will kill you. They usually prefer the second method."

Chapter 4:
Bubble Baths, Books,
& Dinner

Percy didn't have much to say about her husband's arrival. In fact, she seemed to be avoiding Lacey-Marie and me. Every free moment she had, she spent cloistered away with Hades or busy readying the farm for nicer weather.

I hadn't much opportunity to talk to Lacey about him either. We were slammed at work, and she spent almost every free moment running. Apparently she had just as much on her brain as I, so when evening rolled around and I found myself alone with my thoughts, I decided a relaxing bubble bath was in order.

I poured myself a glass of raspberry wine, started the hot water running, dumped in a good quantity of bubble bath, and watched it foam up. I desperately needed to relax.

I undressed quickly, then sank down low in the bubbles, closing my eyes, thinking it was too bad I didn't have a book to read.

I wanted one.

I got up, wrapped myself in an oversized towel, and hoped everyone else was secluded in their rooms as I padded down the stairs and tiptoed down the hall.

A thin strip of light escaped under the library door, making me think maybe Percy was up.

Not Percy. Hades was up reading, seated in my favorite chair. He glanced up as I came through the door.

"Well, this is awkward," I said, adjusting my towel.

"I'm not bothered. Did you need something?" he asked, stretching, his book clutched in one hand.

I was bothered. I was standing in front of my friend's very fine looking husband in a ratty old towel. I would have preferred a really big, thick bathrobe to hide under. "I want a book."

"Well, there's plenty here to choose from." He waved his free hand at one of the huge bookshelves that dominated the walls.

I nodded, then padded over to the shelf, careful not to give him my back. Without much perusal, I snatched *Sense and Sensibility* from the Austen section and stalked back to the door.

"Enjoy your bath, Gretchen. You need to relax," he said, turning his attention back to his book and dismissing me without another word.

Wow, he was kind of not nice.

I carried the book out and flounced back up to my room, clutching my towel.

I locked my door just in case and cracked open the window. The cold night air was a delicious contrast to the steaming bath water. I wouldn't sweat to death, thereby not defeating the purpose of the bath.

Wine, book, bubbles. Okay, relax. I kept an ear out for Lacey but ended up dozing off. I woke up spluttering as I sank in the water. Bubbles smell good but taste nasty.

I heard the stairs creak, then Lacey's door a few moments later. I jumped out of my bath, sloshing water all over the floor, and tossed a clean towel over it, vowing to myself I would clean it up later. I threw my bathrobe on around my still dripping body and knotted the belt around my waist before marching out of my room and up to her door. I would have walked in without knocking, but her door was locked, so I pounded on it in lieu of knocking it down. Percy wouldn't be appreciative, never mind what the house would have done to me in retaliation.

"God, what!" she pulled the door open and glared up at me.

"Where have you been?" I pushed past her into the room.

"I went for a run. Do I need your permission to go for a run now?" she shut the door behind me, turned on the light, and crossed the room to her closet.

I stayed put just inside the door while I listened to her rummaging around changing out of her running clothes.

"No. Sorry, I'm just on pins and needles right now and I wanted to vent at you, and you haven't been around." I walked along the wall until I reached the section she had set up as a living room and flopped down on the puffy couch.

She poked her head around the door. "Oh, sorry, I didn't think. I just wanted to get out of the house." She ducked back in. "It's weird, isn't it, having Percy's husband here?" Her voice was muffled as she pulled a shirt over her head.

"Very weird. I'm not used to having a man in the house, especially one more terrifying than me. What do you think he's doing here?" I asked.

"Dunno. Maybe he thinks she cheats on him while she's away?"

"I doubt it. I have a feeling he has her watched.

Actually, I think he should have shown up before now. What kind of relationship can they maintain with her gone most of the year?"

"The kind a lot of military families lead." Lacey reappeared.

"Hey, nice sweater. When'd you get that?"

She picked at the plum-colored cardigan and gave me a sad smile. "Penny gave it to me."

"When was that?" I asked. "I don't remember seeing it before."

"Sorry, I didn't write down the date and time." She chose a recliner opposite me, sitting primly on the edge of the seat.

"Yeah, whatever." I sat up.

A gentle knock on the door interrupted our conversation.

"Come on in!" Lacey hollered louder than necessary.

"Hey, ladies. Hades is going to take us out for supper." Percy leaned into the room with a goofy expression I'd only expect to see on a newlywed.

Oh, great, an awkward dinner. Tell me, when do I change and do tricks?

"Where?" asked Lacey.

"I don't know, so dress nice. Gretchen, do you think you could bear to put on a skirt?" Percy's gaze lingered on my bathrobe.

"I don't know if I even own a skirt." I danced around the issue.

"You have a few. I've seen them. And no leather or biker wear." She shook her finger at me.

"I'll make sure she's presentable," Lacey promised. "What time should we be ready by?'

"Half hour?" Percy had to know that wouldn't be long enough.

"We'll try, but I'm not making any promises."
Lacey stood from her chair and grabbed my arm.

"Come on, let's get something picked out for you."
She tugged me toward the door.

"Help," I pleaded at Percy on our way by.

"Absolutely not. Now go get ready." Percy turned
her back on me and my torturer and headed for her own
room.

I let Lacey drag me all the way to my closet.

"All right, let's see what we've got to work with."
Lacey threw open the door and turned on the light.

"Ugh, horrible lighting. How can you match up
anything in here?" she asked, sneering at my single
overhead bare bulb.

"Um, I don't buy anything that doesn't match
everything else."

She wrinkled her nose at me.

Guess she didn't like my reasoning.

"Ah, so there are skirts in here!" she pulled one out,
a denim mid-thigh affair. "But not this one." She put it
back. "Or this one." She shuffled through my hangers
for a minute. "Here we go." She pulled out a knee-
length maroon crinkle skirt.

I'd forgotten I'd bought that. I wasn't sure I'd ever
worn it.

"What was this doing hanging up? This is the
perfect skirt for you. You're supposed to mash it up and
throw it in a corner like the rest of your clothes." She
indicated the piled of rejected clothes lying on the floor
under the clothes rack.

I just shrugged my shoulders and took the skirt
from her.

She grabbed down a brown, low cut tank top and a
suede dark patchwork vest.

"That's leather. Percy said no leather." I pointed

with a circling index finger.

"Yeah, but it's trendy leather, not biker leather. Put it on. If Percy objects, tell her I forced you into it. Now where are those boots?" she asked, thrusting her choices into my arms.

"Which ones?" I was partial to boots. They're my staple in footwear.

"Tall, light leather, low heel." She indicated a space between her index finger and thumb as an example.

"Oh those, under my bed."

"Wear those. Now I'm going to get myself ready, and if you even try to pick anything different, I'll rip it off and re-dress you myself." Lacey marched out, slamming my bedroom door behind her.

LAST QUARTER

Chapter 5: Interviews

My morning was less than restful. Not that my clients were difficult, there were just so many of them. I was causing myself more stress looking over my shoulder, dreading that at any moment the wolves would return.

Hades was constantly in and out of the salon, which raised my hackles. He carried around too much power. Part of me knew that it was in my best interest to bow down to him. Another part of me wanted to challenge him.

I whipped through my first few haircuts so fast that it was a miracle I didn't chop my knuckles to shreds, but my clients left happy, which was probably the real miracle.

I glanced at the clock. One hour until the dreaded interviews. There were two girls coming in for the manicurist position. We actually had some appointments for mani/pedis in the afternoon, so we called and asked if they minded letting a new girl take them. Thankfully, they didn't. The faster we got some help in, the better.

The stress was mounting, which meant lots and lots of tea was in order.

"Gretchen?" Percy appeared at my elbow during a lull, placing a soothing hand on my arm.

"Yeah. Fine." I wasn't. The knee-jerk reaction popped out.

"Are you?" Her smell was tinged with worry, as was her facial expression.

"No." I looked down at her, sucking in a few deep breaths. My skin itched as fur slowly pushed its way through my pores.

"Breath, Gretch. You're slipping." Percy pushed me down onto my chair as my bones snapped and reformed themselves.

I roared in pain.

Lacey's client whipped her head in my direction, her eyes wide with surprise, smelling alluringly of fear.

No! This couldn't happen in front of humans. It was happening in front of humans.

Lacey turned her chair so her client couldn't watch, and Percy yanked me up out of my chair, propelled me out back, through the kitchen, and out the door.

The fresh air hit me hard, and I drew in gulps of it.

"Don't hyperventilate. Here's your drink. Little sips while we walk." She kept hold of my elbow, threading her arm through mine, her steps slow, swaying, hypnotic.

I felt my heart rate drop. There was another audible snap. This one hurt worse as my adrenaline wore off, and I cried out.

"What happened?" Percy asked.

"I panicked," I replied.

"The wolves?"

"The wolves. Stress. Everything. I don't know if I can keep doing this, Percy, acting human. Maybe I should move back down south with the pack. I've been pretending for so long."

"It's your choice, but I would miss you. I think you'll be all right. Things have just been a little extreme lately. Are you all right to go back to work?"

"I think so." I pulled my arm away from her, Percy's calming presence going with it, but I managed to hold it together.

I had one client waiting for me when I got inside, and I made it through her cut and style without further mishap.

I needed to step up my wolf calming technique.

The door opened just as we were closing for lunch, and a willowy blonde walked in.

She could have been Lacey's sister right down to the fair skin and the pension for pink. Her flowered sundress, hitting just above her knee, was topped with a baby pink cardigan, paired with strappy heels.

"Hi, I'm Violet Densmore. I'm here for an interview?" She clip-clopped over to shake my hand.

I could look her in the eye, so she was definitely tall. Tall and southern by her accent, possibly from Arkansas.

This was gonna be fun.

I shook her hand and watched as she noted how dark my hand was in comparison to her own, and I got a whiff of expensive perfume.

"I'm Gretchen. Why don't you come have a seat in the waiting area," I drawled back, despite losing my Texan accent decades ago. I was doing good, keeping it professional and all that.

Percy stood as we approached, holding out her hand as well. Lacey followed our example, and the introductions were finished.

"Did you bring your résumé?" Percy questioned.

"I did." Violet dug through her suitcase-sized purse, coming up with a purple folder, which she opened and pulled out a single page of printed paper.

Percy took it from her and glanced over it before

passing it around.

"How long have you been out of school?" Percy asked, crossing her ankles primly by the leg of her chair.

"About a year?" said Violet, her reply sounding more like a question than an answer.

"And where have you been working?"

"At the nail salon in the Bangor mall."

"Why are you interested in working with us?"

"Well, this is a much classier establishment." Violet looked down and picked at her polished nails.

They were acrylics. Score one for the manicurist. You can't really trust a manicurist that doesn't have her nails done to the nines. That would be like a hairdresser with virgin hair.

"What else drew you to us?" Percy persisted, leaning forward.

Violet was quiet for a while. This wasn't that hard of a question, at least I didn't think so.

"I wanted a place where I could learn and grow as a nail tech. Most of the women I work with now are Vietnamese. I can't even really talk to them." She folded her hands in her lap and crossed her ankles, mimicking Percy.

"Are you confident you can remain loyal to this salon if you are hired?" Percy asked.

"I think so. You're one of the best salons in the area. I can't see myself going elsewhere."

"How about a change in career? Do you foresee that as a possibility in the near future?" Percy appeared to be writing on a pad of paper in black pen. I knew very well that she was doodling, but it made her look official.

"I don't think so. I love doing nails, and I like working with people."

"Do you have a portfolio?"

"I do, but it's mostly stuff I did in school." Violet dug in her huge bag again, pulling out a clear plastic report cover, tinted pink, containing a few pages of photographs.

Lacey looked through them first, then handed them to me. Most of the nails were your basic manicures with different colored tips and few stenciled designs. None of them looked like something she'd designed herself. She had potential. It was too bad she hadn't taken any pictures of recent work, though the mall probably hadn't provided her with much opportunity to accomplish custom work.

I handed the packet to Percy, who quickly glanced through it, then set it to the side.

She was just opening her mouth to speak when the door opened again. Our second interviewee was 10 minutes early. The woman was Violet's polar opposite. While still tallish, she had dark Italian looks. She was well put together in ankle boots, skinny jeans, and a dark purple untucked button down.

I darted over to greet her. "You must be Toni! We'll be just a minute if you'd like to wander around the museum for a few—" I trailed off as I led her over to inspect the antique perming machine.

I trotted back over as Violet's interview was being wrapped up, and it didn't look like things were going well anymore. Violet was glaring over at Toni with a look of disgust so blatantly splayed over her features, I thought she might burst into flame.

"You're interviewing someone else at the same time?" she asked, dropping her sweet demeanor, her scent moving from excitement to the heat of anger.

"Of course. We need to fill the spot quickly, and we'd like to have a few options. As you noted, this is a desirable place of employment. If you'd like to wait, we'll make a decision before our lunch break is over." Percy smiled, charming as ever.

"I cleared my afternoon for this." Violet's mouth turned down in a pout.

"So did we," I said, crossing my arms.

She didn't voice any more complaints.

"Do you have any questions for us?" Lacey jumped in, probably afraid I'd say something else.

"I can't think of anything," said Violet, grabbing up her purse.

"All right then. Feel free to browse the museum while we finish up all the interviews." Percy stood to shake her hand and gave me a jerk of her head, indicating that I should go get Toni.

I couldn't leave that couch fast enough. Southern belle, my ass. That girl was a viper. I really hoped the other interview would go better.

Toni was studying a wall display of old straight edge razors and curling irons. The razors we'd picked up at various auctions and yard sales. The curling irons were ones Percy and I had used on ourselves and others in the past. They didn't look like much, just two pieces of metal spooned together, marcel style. No spring loading on those babies. You stuck them right in the coals to heat up. I now owned a more modern set that utilized a heater.

"We're ready for you, Toni."

"Great! Oh, here's my stuff. I was all excited putting it together last night. My husband thought I was going nuts. More nuts than usual anyway." Toni's smile was large and genuine.

"Great." I repeated her sentiment. "Let's go have a look." I took the folder from her and took a furtive sniff for good measure. She smelled pleasantly of baked goods and mint. There was no underlying smell of nerves or aggression, which boded well.

I lead her over to the waiting area, receiving Violet-colored glares as she headed past us to the museum.

"Toni, this is the original owner of Olympian's, Percy."

Percy stepped forward to shake her hand as she'd already been standing, better to see that I behaved myself when Violet crossed my path.

"And this is Lacey-Marie. We each own a piece of the business."

Lacey stood and sized Toni up before taking her hand.

"Oh, cold fingers. That means a warm heart right? It's nice to meet everyone," Toni took a seat across from the couch the rest of us had arranged ourselves on.

I passed the résumé on to Percy and opened the portfolio. There were several sets of nails on the first page, all hand painted on acrylics. A picture on the bottom showed her bent over a woman's hand, a minuscule paintbrush held delicately in her long fingers. This was no airbrushing crap, but real artistry. It was unlikely she'd get to perform much freehand, but it was nice to know that she could. She could have been an artist, but a nail tech program is much cheaper and quicker than art school.

"So tell us about yourself, Toni." Percy placed the résumé to the side, and leaned forward, elbows on knees.

"Well, I've been married since I was 21. I went to college for six years, but then I got pregnant and had a couple of kids. I'm all done now—I've got my boy and girl. I went to school for nails while I was pregnant with my second. My mother-in-law lives down the road and babysits for me. She's finally retired—and can and wants to—watch the kids, so I've gotten the opportunity to work whenever I want."

"How long have you been out of school?" Percy asked as she accepted the portfolio from me and flipped through.

"Four years now."

"And the reason you left your last job?"

"Lack of babysitter, but that's a non-issue now." She smiled brightly.

I disengaged my attention from the current interview and glanced over at Violet. She wasn't looking at the displays. She was staring at us and listening in with the most intense death glare I'd ever seen.

Goody.

When Toni's interview was over, we all stood and shook hands, then left the two potentials alone and retreated to the kitchen to make a decision.

"Is there even a question?" Percy asked, laying her hands palms down on the table.

"I doubt it. Whoever we hire needs to play well with others. There's competitive and then there's catty. I don't get along well with cats." I flopped down on the nearest chair.

"I'm kinda catlike," Lacey protested in mock offense, her hand flying to her heart.

"You're a bit more like a snake," I retorted, giving her a gentle shove.

"Gee, thanks." She rolled her eyes at me. "Anyway, I agree. I'm all the cat this salon can probably handle. I vote for the Italian."

"Good, that's exactly what I was thinking. Not about the cat thing, about not having her as a part of this team. I'm sure she's a lovely girl, but we're not the right fit for her. Let's go break the news." Percy lead the charge back to the salon.

Toni and Violet marched over together.

"Ladies, we've come to a decision," Percy announced with gusto. "Violet, you seem like a wonderful young lady, and you show promise, but I'm afraid we can't offer you a job right now."

Percy can be so... nice sometimes.

Violet's fake smile fell right off her face. She grabbed her bag off the chair and hurried out the door without bothering to shut it behind her.

I found great satisfaction in doing it for her.

"Well Toni, I'm sure you've probably guessed, but you're hired. Are you all right to stick around for the afternoon to start your trial? We've got some nail appointments all scheduled for you." Percy waited until I returned to the group to make the announcement.

"Absolutely! Thank you so much! Do you mind if I call my husband and tell him?" She bounced up and down on her toes, reeking of excitement.

"Go for it. We'll go open back up," said Percy.

As soon as Lacey flipped the sign back over, Leiza Dostal walked in holding her mother's hand.

"But I don't wanna, Mumma. I want Rapunzel hair," she squawked at her mother, trying to tug her back towards the door.

"You can't have long hair until you learn to brush it yourself. We talked about this, baby. You're getting a haircut, and then we're going to go shopping." Her mother gently guided her in my direction.

"Can I get a toy?"

"Of course, but only if you're good," her mother promised.

The little brat was too old to be bribed like that, but

her mother was a sucker.

"Come on over, hun, and we'll get you shampooed," I said, trying to usher her over to the shampoo bowls.

"I don't wanna shampoo."

The whining, there it was.

"You don't have to, hon," her mother promised.

"I'd have a much easier time getting the knots out if I can get some conditioner in there." I was trying to be convincing, but I could tell she wasn't having it.

"No, I wanna buy a toy!"

"You just have to be a big girl and get your haircut. Then you can get your toy."

"Come on over, and we'll get started." I grabbed a child's cape, turning towards my chair instead of the sinks. Apparently she'd rather me yank instead of suds.

She complied while grumbling.

I dampened her hair with the cold water from my squirt bottle, then loaded on the silk drops and leave-in conditioner. I went to work on her tangles with a wide tooth comb, starting at the ends and working my way up. She whined and complained as I pulled the knots apart by hand.

"I have to get the knots out so I can give you a good haircut." I worked a particularly tight tangle with practiced fingers.

"But it hurts." She tried to jerk her head out of my reach.

"I'd be done combing already if you'd let me wash and condition it. Now you know for next time." I locked the chair into position by lifting up on the foot pump lever.

Did there have to be a next time? I love most of my clients—I even love most kids—but this one was getting on my nerves. It wasn't even her fault. I had to pin the blame on her parents. Bribing kids gets them nowhere with haircuts. They just wait until the bribes get good.

I thought it was too bad that spanking was becoming taboo. You can go overboard, yes, but this flaky method of raising kids wasn't working at all. Kids cannot raise themselves. They do the best they can, but they need parents, and they need limits and consequences. My opinion may have been colored by my time of upbringing.

Leiza had no clue what consequences were. Or limits.

Finally, I got her completely detangled, and I had her trimmed up in 10 minutes. No blow dry. Pay me. Buhbye.

Frederika Oser, who went by Freddie, was normally Lacey-Marie's client, but today she was Toni's. I had a moment before my next client was due, so I took the opportunity to stop out back to visit the manicure station.

The two were chatting happily about Freddie's lack of motivation as far as college was concerned. She was a smart girl who played field hockey and had a go-with-the-flow type of personality.

"I'm thinking about backpacking across Europe after I graduate. You know, take a year off before becoming a grown-up." Freddie was leaning so her forehead was almost touching Toni's, who was painting little designs on the corners of each nail.

Apparently there was a semi-formal dance at Isenburge High the next night.

It was Thursday, right? I mentally calculated the days. Yep, definitely Thursday.

"That sounds like a lot of fun. I wish I had taken the time to have some fun before committing myself to six years of school. Of course, if I hadn't gone when I did, I never would have met my husband. Other than that, I wasted my money." Toni turned Freddie's hand this way and that, inspecting her work.

"Are guys more human after high school?" Freddie admired her other hand.

"Aw, no, chicky, I'm afraid very few men grow up. And those who grow up completely are just boring. In fact, all grown ups who grow up are boring." Toni laughed. "I hope my husband and I never become adults."

The young woman laughed with her, and I quit lurking in the hallway.

Percy and Lacey were waiting for me when I got back.

"Well?" asked Lacey.

"She's great! I think she'll fit right in." I walked to the counter to call over my next client.

Percy joined me.

"Ethan?" I called.

"Ellie?" Percy called.

A teenage girl and an elderly gentlemen stood and made their way over. One much slower than the other.

"Percy, I have something to tell you." Ellie glanced over at the couches where her mother was sitting reading a magazine.

She closed in on Percy and spoke low, and I turned my ear in their direction.

"Matt and I are engaged, and we haven't told our parents yet 'cause there's no way they'll approve."

"Uh huh. Ellie, how old are you?" Percy asked, the scent of worry wafting off of her.

"15."

"And your boyfriend?"

"17."

"Don't you think you're rushing things a bit?" Percy led her to a shampoo bowl.

"No way! I can't wait to get married. I love him so much," said Ellie, bouncing as she sat.

Oh, boy. Percy had her hands full. She would feel obligated to tell Ellie's mother, without Ellie finding out that it was Percy who snitched on her.

"Goddammit, why can't I move faster?" My client shuffled along to my station.

"No hurry, Mr. Webel." I held the chair still while he sat.

"I know, I know. Don't ever get old. It sucks." He sighed as he sank down.

"I won't," I promised. No issue there. I'd never get old. I might get dead, especially if I decided not to join the pack, but I'd never get old.

I was performing close out, counting out the drawer and splitting money into envelopes, when the phone rang.

"Good evening, Olympian's Salon. How may I help you?" I spoke into the receiver.

"Hi, this is Amanda from Babe's Place."

Babe's Place was the only other salon in our town and therefore technically our competition.

"Hey, Amanda, this is Gretchen." I smiled as I spoke. I liked Amanda. She was good people.

"Oh, hey," she said.

"What's up?" I asked. I knew she didn't want to make an appointment.

"You need to watch the local news right now."

"Okay." I pressed the mouthpiece against my shoulder so I wouldn't shatter her eardrum. "Hey, guys, turn on the news."

"Why?" Lacey asked, wandering over to the waiting area television and doing as I asked.

"So what are we listening to the news for?" I asked

"You'll see. Talk to you later." Amanda hung up without giving any more information.

I joined the others on the couch for the third time that day.

A well-dressed woman holding a microphone stood outside a salon. "24-year-old Catherine Materna, a beautician at this salon, was found dead in her home. The body was discovered early this morning after she failed to show up for work."

The camera turned to an overly made-up hairdresser with mascara streaking down her cheeks. "Cathy is—was—never late. She's been working here since she got out of school. She's so talented. I can't believe she's dead." The woman sobbed, and the camera left her.

"The police aren't releasing any information about the death at this time. We know she lived alone, and the neighbors in the surrounding apartments allegedly never heard a sound."

The news turned to sports, and Percy turned off the TV. If details weren't being released, chances were it was a particularly gruesome murder. I should know, I'd killed before. I was a wolf at the time, but it was still a part of me that did it.

Lacey fiddled with her fingers, and Percy stared at the blank television.

We didn't know the dead girl, but still we felt a sort of solidarity with her as cosmetologists.

There was no motive; no one had heard an argument or anything. She was apparently well liked by her coworkers, and she was single, so no jealous boyfriends.

Lacey Googled her on the salon computer, and we found pictures of a curvy girl with punkish purple streaks and perfect makeup. She dressed cute, appropriate for a hairdresser. The page we found was actually connected to the salon, so we clicked on the link. There were some daring cuts and colors on her personal page. She was the kind of girl we would have liked to hire. What a waste.

Upstairs, alone, I played my violin, my music more melancholy than murder would normally dictate. Thankfully, it was only colored by my sadness for the girl, and not by my near change in front of clients that morning.

I stopped playing.

Why was the murder of a complete stranger affecting me like this? I had to be missing something that connected my life to hers besides our choice in careers.

I picked my instrument back up and played, trying to work out my thoughts. Maybe it was just the stress I'd been feeling lately manifesting itself in yet another new and less-than-thrilling way. I put my violin down and searched out Lacey, knocking on her door.

"Come on in," she called.

I did, flopping down on one of her love seats. My head rested on one arm, my legs hanging off the other.

"So what do you think?" I asked, kicking my toes.

"I dunno. Dead girl. No one I knew," said Lacey with a shrug. She'd changed into her pj's. I could see her heart printed pajama bottoms peeking out from under her oversized bathrobe.

"You don't think it was the pack, do you?" I asked.

There it was, my possible connection. I'd requested

that they not hunt near people or hunt humans, but who knows if they'd honored my request.

"Dunno, maybe. There weren't a whole lot of details." She sank down in her recliner.

"No, and you know that means there's something the police don't want the public to know. Like a girl's throat ripped out without any evidence of a dog."

"Nobody heard anything. I think you're worrying too much. If they were going to kill a human, don't you think they'd go after someone you knew? You know, as an example."

"Yeah, except the only people I'm close to are you guys. And neither of you are human."

"No shit, Sherlock."

"Up yours, Watson." I threw a pillow at her, then left to go think, worrying the pack was involved.

Chapter 6:
Parasols & Sparring

Fridays were for rehearsal, and Saturdays were for gigs. I loved both.

Austin's house was an unassuming white cape cod tucked away at the end of a long driveway. His dog, a huge Saint Bernard, gave me a slobbery greeting before I was allowed inside. "Nice to see you too, Sheltingham." I gave him a good scratch around the ears.

"Sheltingham, leave her alone!" Austin's wife, Denise, yelled out the door.

"No worries," I said, walking into their living room. "You know I love dogs."

"And they love you, I noticed. Still, he doesn't have to be so overwhelming," said Denise as she shut the door.

I wasn't overwhelmed. It was nice to be around another dog, even a normal one. He added to the already welcoming smell of the house.

I pulled out and plugged in Lola, my electric violin, then tuned her while the boys arrived. Austin was already set up and warming up with a snazzy jazz beat on his drums. I joined in. Jazz might not be my thing, but it was a good mental exercise.

Scott was unusually quiet. I wasn't surprised, what with Penny's death being so recent and all. Normally, I found Scott kind of obnoxious, but today his attitude subdued us all, producing a less than stellar rehearsal.

Mark, our lead singer and guitar player, grumbled at us but didn't push the issue. "I know things are rough right now, but we have a gig to play tomorrow," he said. Mark wasn't a heartless guy, but he was a dedicated musician.

"We'll be fine. I don't know about you guys, but live audiences always give me energy," I said, laying Lola back in her case.

Saturday rolled smoothly into Sunday, the beginning of the stylist weekend.

I got up relatively early and sudsed up with some extra strong tea tree shampoo, rinsing free the previous night's performance. There is nothing quite like tea tree in the morning. It's like Altoids for your head.

I followed up my shower with a bit of lazing around my room. I was utterly relaxed, which wasn't surprising, considering the new moon was fast approaching. I read some Austen in my bathrobe, then got dressed half an hour or so later.

It was too bad Lacey couldn't go for a mid morning jaunt, but I had that feeling she just might go all crispy if she went out in the sun.

There was a knock on my door, followed by a Lacey. "Are you up yet? Oh, good. I have to show you my new toy!" She pulled something out from behind her back.

"It's an umbrella," I said, looking over the bit of fluff straight out of Gone with the Wind.

"It's a parasol. You, of all people, should recognize

a parasol when you see one. They were pretty common in your century weren't they?"

"Yeah, I guess." I curled up one side of my lip. "Open it up. Let's see it."

"I got it right before your thing last night. What do you think?" She opened it carefully and twirled it over her shoulder.

It was pink, of course, and embroidered with roses and violets.

"Very pretty," I said.

"Do you know what this means?" she asked, bouncing on her toes.

"You can go singin' in the rain?" I guessed, shrugging my shoulders.

"Don't be ridiculous. It means I can go out during the day!" She closed the parasol and stuck it under her arm.

"You could go out with an umbrella. And that big black one offered more protection," I mentioned the huge thing I'd bought for her years ago that had met an unfortunate end, via wolf.

"And it was ugly. This is pretty. People will admire instead of scoff." She poked me with it.

She may have had a point. I'd seen elderly women walking down the road with umbrellas on a sunny day, but never a 21-year-old. A parasol would come off as an eccentric fashion statement instead of prematurely senile.

"So what are you up to today?" I asked.

"No plans, but I'll probably skip out on a run all the same. Too awkward." she shook her new toy for emphasis.

It was worth a try. "Spar with me?" I was ever hopeful.

"Maybe. You look like you just took a shower,

though." She pointed a finger at my half-dry curls.

"Yeah, I crashed when I got home last night, so I had to wash out the gook when I woke up. What did you think of the performance?"

"You guys were great. You looked like you were really into being up there. Looks like Scott's going to survive," said Lacey. "I mean, he didn't seem too torn up."

"He was on a stage in front of a crowd. What did you expect? Tears?"

"I just thought he'd be more emotional, that's all," said Lacey, scowling at me.

"He's dealing," I said, even though I shared her opinion.

She sighed and headed for the door. "I'll change and meet you downstairs in 15."

I smiled at the closed door. Good, something to do!

I changed into gray sweatpants, cut into knee length shorts, and a black sports bra. We liked to wail on each other, and we got hot pretty quick.

Yes, Lacey got hot even though she's dead. She didn't sweat, though. Lucky girl. She didn't have a very high water content to her body, so she had to lotion up day and night, or she got dried out and all wrinkly like a raisin. Vampires really aren't pretty creatures in their natural state.

I jogged barefoot down the back stairs, ending up in the pantry instead of the kitchen. Close enough. I gave a mental shrug and continued to my destination.

Lacey wasn't in the ballroom-turned-gym yet, so I dragged out the mats by myself. We always spar on these enormous mats, just in case. We have a special corner, padded 10 feet up, to prevent damage. Some days it worked better than others.

I unbalanced the plastic-smelling floor mats so they

fell on their own, then organized them all to fit together. I didn't particularly want to fall through a gap if I could help it.

We didn't use any personal padding as we both heal relatively quickly.

"Hey, great, you're all ready." Lacey-Marie sat down on the mat to take off her sneakers, tossing them aside.

As soon as she got up, we started circling each other. Lacey hadn't taken any martial arts training. She was a straight up girly fight scrapper, and incredibly strong and fast. Stronger and faster than I am. My only advantage was technique and knowing her well enough to guess what she was going to do next about eighty percent of the time.

I pulled my fists up into guard position and started to plan my move. She followed my movements, then struck out. I blocked, just barely. I threw a punch, which she ducked under. She retaliated by trying to scratch me with her fingernails.

Girly fighter, like I said.

She hissed as she threw her next punch. We became a knot of hissing, growling, and flying limbs. Every once in a while, we made contact. She landed more than I avoided, but I gave it right back to her. Her style was sloppy, while my attacks were more calculated.

We'd toppled each other to the floor when we heard a knock at the front door. We scrambled off the mats. I hadn't heard Percy or Hades stir yet, so the lady of the house wasn't available to answer.

We raced each other down the hall, through doors, and into the salon, skittering to a stop in front of the grand entrance as we regained our composure.

I opened the door, while Lacey hung back to avoid any accidental sun exposure.

"Good morning," the man standing outside greeted me. "I am Ulysses, Ringmaster of Treats and Freaks Circus." He bowed with a flourish, then continued, "We're going to be in town for a while, and I was wondering if I could drop off some program pamphlets for you to hand out to your customers. Perhaps I could hang up a poster? This is Olympian's Salon and Day Spa, is it not?"

"It is. We're closed for today, but I think it would be fine if you wanted to drop your stuff off. I can hang the poster by the front counter." I stared at the large man in front of me.

He was dressed to the nines in tails and a top hat. The slightly worn fabric strained around his large frame, his girth and height matched his booming voice. He sounded as if he were addressing an audience of hundreds, instead of just two. He smelled of sweat, animals, and aftershave.

"Wonderful! Here you go." He pulled a stack of papers from the plastic grocery bag he was carrying. "Opening day is Tuesday, and we're expecting a full house."

"Sounds neat," I improvised, not really knowing how he expected me to react.

"Yes, well, yes. Have a spectacular day!" He bowed again before departing.

"You too." I closed the door behind him.

"That was weird," said Lacey, peeling herself out of the shadows.

"I agree."

"Who was that?" Percy asked, descending the stairs dressed in her bathrobe and slippers.

"A ringmaster. Here." I handed her one of the fliers, then proceeded to hang the poster on our front counter with scotch tape.

"Huh, sounds less than legitimate," she commented, handing the paper to Lacey.

Lacey read it over quickly. "The circus part looks legit. There's no mention of actual freaks, though."

"Maybe they got rid of the side show because it's not PC, or some crap like that." I took one of the pamphlets off the pile.

There would be animals, clowns, and death defying acts. Kids would love it. Parents, perhaps less so.

"Well, I'll call Toni and prepare her," I said, waving the piece of paper.

Not that there was anything to actually prepare our new nail tech for, but still, I wanted to tell her about the strange ringmaster who delivered advertisements for his circus by hand.

Toni actually sounded excited to take her kids as they couldn't remember the last one that had come to town. I suspected she just wanted an excuse to get all stickied up with cotton candy.

As soon as I finished my calls, Lacey and I went back to beating the stuffing out of each other. I think she was even more into it than I. That girl had some serious aggression to work through, which was fine by me. The madder she got, the worse she fought, the more focused I became.

I picked her up and body slammed her into the wall.

Not appreciating that, she came flying at me tooth and claw.

There was the little vampy I knew and loved to torture.

I met her charge with my braced shoulder, sending her flying. Evidently, that's all she was capable of. The more I tumbled her through the air, the more pissed she became, the less she used her head.

Lacey-Marie was actually a pretty smart chicky. She wasn't only a biology major when she was changed, she was also a straight-A student, a cheerleader, and a regular volunteer at several charities.

The next time she came at me, I slammed her onto the mat and sat my full wolf weight on her chest. "That's enough! You're not sparring anymore, you're letting me beat you up. Frankly, it's boring me."

She hissed and snapped her teeth at me.

"I'm done. Go throw yourself into a wall." I removed my weight from her and walked towards the edge of the mat. Smelling her rage fast approaching, I leaned forward for balance and kicked back, catching her in the stomach. I heard the tell-tale whoosh of air that meant I'd knocked the wind out of her as I walked out the door, leaving her to recover on her own.

"She's an imbecile," I muttered at Percy as I entered the kitchen. She was dressed and accompanied by Hades, who looked out of character in jeans and a hooded sweatshirt.

I looked down at his feet.

Oh, good, he hadn't lost the combat boots. There was still order to the world.

"Morning," he said, sipping his coffee.

"It is." I grabbed a couple of eggs from the fridge, cracking them into the cast iron skillet, and started frying.

"What did she do this time?" Percy knew exactly to whom I was referring.

"We were sparing, hence the workout garb," I struck a pose then continued, "and she completely lost it. She's getting sloppy, and she's going to get figured out in an even bigger way than I might."

"I'll keep an eye on her as best I can, but I believe she'll settle. It's probably just the change in seasons."

"Probably. The pack is keeping me on edge, and I might be rubbing off on her."

"And as for people finding you out, we're not going to let that happen. You know when you're slipping, and I'm fine with covering for you. People like their privacy around here, and they'll respect ours."

She'd lived in Maine a lot longer than I had. I was used to people getting nosy about your business—ye olde time south was like that. She also had the tendency to believe the best of people.

"It'll be fine, I promise," Percy promised, taking over my cooking as I had a tendency to burn things.

Don't make promises you can't keep, Percy.

I gobbled my food and watched the gods eat at a more leisurely pace. It was weird, Greek gods eating and acting like civil creatures. In fact, it was downright disconcerting, though it made me feel better about my own predicament.

If gods, ageless and immortal, could pass for humans, then I could too. I just needed to learn their secret.

Maybe I should get a heart rate monitor, like the one Edward Norton used in *The Incredible Hulk*. I certainly wasn't safe when angry!

"Percy, where can I get one of those heart rate thingies that look like a watch?" I asked.

"Not sure. A sporting goods store, a doctor, eBay?" She ran down a mental list of suggestions. "Why?"

"Well, part of what brings out my inner wolfiness is adrenaline. Adrenaline shows up with an increased heart rate. It worked for the Hulk."

"The Hulk is a comic book character. You naturally have increased heart rate and adrenaline. You're the Hulk on steroids."

She had a point. "Can't we rewire one for my heart rate?" I tried again.

"I'm going to say no, but that doesn't mean you shouldn't look into it. Maybe you can get one specially made."

"Maybe you should start doing yoga or tai chi to help you get in touch with your inner calm," Hades suggested.

"Yeah, great. I don't have an inner calm. It got evicted about 150 years ago." I said, crossing my arms and scowling.

"Well, worrying is only going to make it worse, so stop." Percy was getting irritated. I could tell. "So, what do you think about the circus coming to town?"

I shrugged my shoulders and took a chair across the table. "Maybe it will bring in more business."

"Or it will take it away. People will hold off on haircuts to go see an elephant," Percy predicted.

"True. I'm a little worried about all the animals and performers with the wolves in the area." I hadn't included non-locals in my bargain.

"If they don't behave themselves, I'll bang a few heads together." Hades drained the last of his coffee.

"You can do that? Uh, legally, I mean?" I asked.

"Yes. Most of the weres and vamps fall under my rule, even when they're in the mortal world. Usually they're dragged down to see me, instead of me showing up on their doorstep, but that only means they should all be on their best behavior. It's not time yet to start a war."

There was going to be a time to start one? "Uh, would you please clear up that last statement for me?"

"It's none of your concern. And won't be, unless you stay with the Texas pack," he sidestepped.

"It sounds like something I should know so I can

make informed decisions. I'm on the fence right now."
I leaned forward and stared into his black eyes. Creepy,
scary eyes.

"It's nothing, really. Just when King Arthur
reawakens and takes over——"

"The King Arthur thing is true? Huh," I
interrupted.

"Yes, and when he does, there will be a war to end
all wars," said Hades.

I didn't care for that thought.

"What he's not telling you is you'll have to fight on
one side or the other, and humans will probably end up
dead when they get caught in the middle." Percy glared
at her husband.

Apparently, Hades hadn't intended on telling me
that bit, and I could see an obvious problem. If the fae
went to war, Hades and Percy would probably unite
against staying in this reality.

"Is there any way to prevent the waking of King
Arthur?" I asked innocently. I figured if he didn't wake
up, there wouldn't be a conflict.

"It's prophesied, but people have been trying for
thousands of years to find his resting place, and
Excalibur's. The sword could end his waiting life, and
he wouldn't be able to rise up and lead." Hades
squashed my idea.

"Wouldn't killing him start a war also?" My mind
spun with the possibilities as my pulse started beating
faster.

"Maybe, but he wouldn't be there to lead, so it
would probably be over quickly."

He was that powerful? Well that just gave me the
warm fuzzies. "That doesn't sound good to me either,"
I said, rubbing my now sweating palms on my shorts.

Hades shrugged his shoulders. You'd think the

possibility of going to war alongside his wife, whom he loved, would upset him just a little more.

I took my leave from the happy couple with a lot to think about. Apparently, there was a darker side to being a werewolf, apart from being a monster. I knew they weren't exactly wholesome, with the hunting and the killing, but I assumed that's where it ended. I hadn't realized there were politics the packs were involved in, outside of themselves. Pack wars, I could deal with. A fae war, I couldn't fathom. I didn't want to have to choose sides, and I was all about being as human as possible. Not to mention, I liked the world the way it was. I liked the people.

Clenching my lips between my teeth, I indulged the racing of my panicking mind. What could I do to prepare for this possible war? And what could I do to protect the people I loved?

I changed into normal clothes for the day: big baggy black jeans and an old tee. I had no plans to go anywhere, so I rejected shoes entirely.

The solitude of the attic was calling my name. I loved the smell of lavender and chamomile that was hanging to dry from the rafters. Up there, I could be myself, without fear that someone would walk in on me as I changed.

The only way up was a trap door in the ceiling on my end of the hall. I pulled the dangling rope, and the ladder slammed to the floor. The steps creaked softly as I climbed, and I heaved the trap door closed once I was at the top, pulling up the rope so I couldn't be followed.

Undressing quickly, I brought my wolf forward. So close to the new moon, I had very little adrenaline to mask the pain. My bones started cracking, and I screamed, stumbled over to the stereo, and turned up the volume. Distorted rock masked the sounds I made.

My muscles stretched and snapped like taut rubber bands. I felt the itch of fur forcing its way out of every pore in my body. My tailbone extended and sprouted sinew and fluff. The torment finally brought on adrenaline, muting the pain. The snaps and cracks came more rapidly, but I was numb to them. I sank down onto four paws and yawned. It was over.

I located my pile of blankets in the corner and crashed with my tail draped over my cold, black nose, the smell of my wolf comforting me. For some reason, I can think better like that. With my human consciousness married to the wolf, I am the most myself.

Instinct told me to go running to the pack. They offered me family and protection from the human world. I could produce and raise pups in safety and not have to worry about them sprouting a tail and eating their classmates during recess.

On the other paw, Percy and Lacey-Marie had become my pack. There was no hope that I could settle down, but maybe I could live with that if . . . I wasn't coming up with an 'if.' I loved them, but I was still leaning towards pack despite the coming darkness.

I hemmed and hawed for quite a while, and I lost track of time.

Tenebrous night had arrived, so I reigned in my beast, dressed my now human body, and climbed down the ladder.

The phone rang in the kitchen, and Percy answered it, sound muffled, so I couldn't make out the words, but her tone was upsetting.

I dashed down the stairs and made it to the kitchen just as she was hanging up. Her face was empty as she sank down to the floor, her legs giving out.

"Percy?" I ran to her, dropping to her level. "Who was that?"

"The police." She stared blankly ahead.

'The police' was never a good answer, especially then.

"What did they want?"

"There's another body. Since Penny was the first, they decided to notify us. Same MO as the others. They're officially saying it's a serial killer. Only hairdressers are being targeted."

"Who died?" Lacey joined us.

"I'm going to go tell Hades." Percy pushed to her feet, wavering as she stood.

She'd seen a lot of death in her day. So have I. This was way too close. There was a fox in our hen house.

Chapter 7:
Treats & Freaks

Pacing back and forth in the library wasn't having the effect I hoped. When people pace, they think, and they get answers, right? I wasn't getting answers—I was getting agitated.

A low growl escaped through my teeth as I threw myself into the overstuffed chair I favored.

No, I hadn't personally known the most recent victim, but I found myself feeling more and more responsible. I was a wolf. I should have been able to smell Penny's murderer, and the missing scent was driving me mental.

I wanted to talk about it, but Lacey was still asleep, and Percy was probably still cozied up with Hades.

It was awkward having a man in the house. Normally, I would have burst into Percy's room without waiting for her to answer my knock. Now, I avoided her room completely.

I'd had married friends before, but I'd never lived with them, and it sucked.

Sitting wasn't helping either. I heaved to my feet and headed to my room to change into running gear. Figuring I'd be alone, I dressed in shorts and a sports bra.

I hadn't intended on catching up with Hades, who

was going for a leisurely jog. I tried passing him, and he sped up to match my pace. I ran faster. So did he. I didn't really know how strong he was, but I was betting he could squash my full strength like a bug, and my strength was waning. I gave up and contented myself with trying to ignore him.

He wasn't having it. "You don't like me, do you?" he asked without a hint of exertion in his voice.

"It's not that I don't like you, I've yet to form an opinion. I certainly don't trust you." I was puffing a little after trying to outrun him.

We'd long since left the property, and I'd chosen to stick with snowmobile trails.

"Why is that?" he asked.

"Well, you're a dark fae."

"Winter fae," he corrected me, smiling.

"Same difference." I sucked in a deep breath of the wild smelling air.

"Perhaps, but I prefer the latter. Dark fae makes it sound as if we're all evil."

"Aren't you?" I ducked a low-hanging branch.

"We're just as capable of good or evil as the summer fae." He leapt over a log like it was a crack in a sidewalk.

That didn't exactly answer my question. "Yeah, but what do you consider yourself?"

"Neither. I've had my shining moments, like marrying Persephone. I've got darkness in my past as well, just as you do."

Great, he thought himself as on some sort of level with me. I wasn't loving the association.

"What about the whole King Arthur thing? You wanting him dead and all that."

"I've never claimed to want that. I need him very much alive."

That surprised me so much that I stumbled, and he caught my elbow. "Really?"

"Yes. I can see both sides of the argument, of course. The ones that want him dead, a group made up of winter and summer fae, feel they've grown beyond the fae world. They want this one."

"And the other side of the coin is?" I asked, glancing up at him before refocusing on the terrain.

"The fae that want Arthur alive, because he wants to remove the fae from the human world. Permanently. They feel he has the right to enforce this choice as he is equal blood fae and human. There are also those who still believe that humans and fae can coexist peacefully."

"Where, exactly, do you stand?" I seemed to be dodging quite a few more plants than Hades.

His movements were smooth, liquid, and I wondered if the plants were actually moving out of his way. I'd seen them do it for Percy, so maybe it was the same for him.

"The damage that the fae could inflict on this world would be catastrophic. Up until now, I've remained neutral, but I won't be able to remain so for much longer. We have a home that is perfectly equipped for us. That is why I rarely leave."

"Huh," I said.

"What does that mean?" he asked, slowing his pace.

"What's what mean?" I gratefully slowed my own.

"The 'huh.' You grunt like that a lot," said Hades.

I could have sworn a poison ivy plant bent away from him.

"I don't have anything else to say. It's just a noise."

"Very well. I'll try to decipher your utterances as we go. I think we better turn around before we hit a road." He dashed around me.

Vehicles rumbled in the distance. We'd come farther than I'd thought.

He didn't require me to talk to him anymore, which was fine with me. He was a hard guy to figure out and I respected him for that. People get easy to read after a while. It was actually fun to be kept guessing.

Percy had breakfast waiting for us, and Lacey had yet to make an appearance. I had a feeling she was making a hermit of herself for the day.

I spent the rest of the morning in my room playing both Clarissa and Lola. By the time I was finished, it was feeling like lunch time.

Percy and Hades had the same idea, though Lacey-Marie remained conspicuously absent.

The kitchen was fast becoming our meeting place for the day. Percy handed me a package of assorted deli meat while Hades glanced through the circus pamphlet that had been sitting on the table.

"I think we should go," Hades stated, waving the paper.

Percy looked at the pamphlet in distaste. "I don't know."

"You ladies need to get out of the house, relax a little. You're all going to burst if you don't let yourselves have a little fun." He set it in front of his wife.

"This isn't exactly the time for fun." She held it up between her thumb and forefinger and shook her head.

"I'll go," I said, surprising us all.

"Wonderful! There's a showing just after sundown, so Lacey-Marie can attend as well." Hades leaned his chair back and crossed his arms over his chest.

"What are you volunteering me for?" Lacey asked, finally making an appearance.

"We're going to the circus," I said, daring her to object with raised eyebrows.

"Really now. Who says I want to watch dancing poodles?" She hopped up onto the counter and swung her legs.

"There are lions and tigers as well, and acrobats." Percy joined in, warming up to the idea.

"Thrilling. Just how I want to spend an entire evening, watching little brats get sugar rushes."

I rolled my eyes. "You're so negative."

She rolled hers back. "You've rubbed off on me."

I stuck my tongue out at her.

She jumped down off the counter, and Hades threw out an arm to stop her.

"Ladies, be good," he commanded.

"Aw, come on, I was only going to take a teeny tiny bit out of her neck," Lacey protested, leaning over his arm and gnashing her teeth at me.

"Try it, and I'll rip your head off," I provoked her calmly.

"This is not funny, girls." Percy wasn't playing.

"Oh fine, I'll be good if she will," Lacey-Marie promised, reclaiming her spot.

"I'll try to restrain myself," I fibbed. If I really felt like going at it with Lacey, I wasn't going to let even the god of the dead stop me.

All right, so maybe Hades could have stopped us, but that wouldn't prevent me from trying. Fortunately, I think we were just playing around.

I shoved a fist full of meat into my mouth and chewed noisily.

"Gross! Make her stop, Percy!" Lacey complained.

"Gretchen." Percy gave me her best mommy look.

I closed my lips around the huge mouthful. It took a lot longer to chew it that way.

"What time will we be leaving?" Lacey asked.

"Around five, I think. I want to get good seats," said Hades.

"That's way before sundown. Are you trying to get me killed?"

"You can use that pretty new parasol of yours," I suggested.

"There you go, perfect solution," Percy seconded me, clasping her hands together.

"I'll look silly." Lacey wasn't liking it.

"We're going to a circus, not the opera. And actually, the parasol wouldn't be out of place there either," I said after I swallowed.

"Fine, I'll take the parasol. But if I go crispy, I'm holding you responsible."

If she went crispy, she'd be dead, but I suppose that was beside the point.

Hades pulled Percy's BMW up to the door at five on the nose. There was no point in taking separate vehicles.

Lacey held the parasol low over her head, and I did my best to block her from the low western sun. She made it into the car without a blister, and we threw a blanket over her head like a tent for the ride. She complained surprisingly little.

We scored a parking spot in the shade and managed to keep out of the sun all the way to the ticket booth, where a stooped elderly gentleman with horseshoe pattern baldness took Hades' large bills and handed him back some change. I wondered if he had been a performer in his younger days. It would be terrible to have an active job your whole life then become secluded in a booth because old age prevented you from having fun. It was one of those rare moments when I appreciated what I was. I would never have to feel his pain.

"Enjoy the show," he ordered us good naturedly, after stamping the backs of our hands with a five-pointed star.

"We will," Percy promised, then led the way towards the gargantuan red-and-white-striped circus tent.

"Why don't you ladies find seats. I'll be right back." Hades rested a hand on Percy's shoulder, then kissed her glamoured lips.

I wondered how he felt about how she hid her true self. He always looked like a god, he just toned down the presence now and then so people wouldn't trip over themselves to get near him. Or away.

"Of course. See you in a bit," said Percy, smiling warmly up at him.

Lacey quit twirling her parasol, closed it, and utilized it as a walking stick. She'd dressed rather impractically in a mini skirt, soft sweater, and stilettos. No one had ever accused her of practicality.

We found Mem and her husband, George, seated halfway up the bleachers. They grinned and waved us over.

It was a good view, not so far up that we wouldn't be able to make out what was going on, and not so close we couldn't view the whole thing. The smells were so overwhelming that I had to hold my breath for a moment to process."

"What a surprise seeing you here!" Mem hugged me as soon as I was seated at her side.

"Haha, yeah, we decided we wanted a night out. I hope we're not disturbing your date night." I tried not to wrinkle my nose at all the smells.

"Rubbish. Of course you're not disturbing us." She held her hand to her chest in mock surprise.

"I agree," said George, leaning around his wife with a palm on her knee. "I hate to break it to you, missy, but you've been around long enough to pretty much be family."

The happy couple didn't have children of their own, so they were always gathering strays. Like me.

"Good." I leaned across Mem to give George a hug.

Hades made his way up the row and sat next to his wife. The place was filling up as the brilliance of the lights hid the last moments of sundown.

Lacey perked up. She was the opposite of a flower, which thrives on sunlight and is depressed at the onslaught of night. Lacey was a definite night person, despite the day job. She played her part well.

"So, where did you go?" Percy asked her husband, taking his hand.

"I'll tell you after," he promised, scooting so they were touching.

"All right, but don't you forget." She leaned into him.

"Don't worry, I won't." He kissed her hair, and then turned his attention to the ring as the lights dimmed, then went black.

A spotlight swirled around, settling on the middle of the ring, showcasing a man dressed in tails and a top hat. The ringmaster's theatrical presence was much better suited to this, rather than door to door advertising.

"Ladies and gentlemen, boys and girls! I'm delighted—nay exhilarated—to present to you the Treats and Freaks Circus!" He stabbed a finger into the air.

"But first a little history lesson. In 1923, when this circus was founded by my grandfather's family, the show only consisted of a grizzly bear, a few acrobats, and a small sideshow of freaks. Now, about 90 years later, we've grown into a full-blown spectacle. We have animals of all shapes and sizes, which I promise are better treated than in the past." He said this with a wink, as if to appease those who might know the truth about animals in circuses. "We have performers of both the death-defying and the side-splitting."

"We had to let go of the so-called freaks when they became politically incorrect. They had to go find themselves boring day jobs. I remember them, from when I was growing up, and miss those particular performers dearly. But let us push such sorrow aside. Because, ladies and gentlemen, we have a show that will leave you speechless and full of excitement!" He lay one hand on his heart and threw the other wide.

"Let me draw your attention to our first act of the evening: Alastair the Lion Tamer and his mighty beasts!"

The lights came up, and a man stood caged, accompanied by a large male lion and a Siberian tiger. He raised his arms above his head, then flourished them in an elaborate bow.

Something tickled my nose, and I sneezed into my elbow. Around me Percy, Hades, and Lacey-Marie started sneezing as well. We looked at each other.

Magic.

Normally, I was the only one who smelled it. Lacey did occasionally, and Percy could sense it, but it had never made her sneeze before.

Were the big cats magicked? Or were we just getting tickled by cat hair?

Lacey gave me a questioning look, and I shrugged in reply. That was it, no more sneezing.

The enormous cats were jumping through hoops like poodles, appearing for all the world as if they were enjoying it.

The performer's tight cowboy jeans would have looked better on a man with an actual backside, and his long hair was in serious need of a trim. I pulled myself out of hairdresser mode and tried to watch his performance.

The lion and the tiger were twining themselves around each other like lovestruck teens. Even their tails curled around each other's bodies.

Alastair cracked his whip, and they sprang apart, swiping at each other and roaring at a deafening volume. He stood between their pedestals as they took non-lethal swipes at each other. The whip was cracked again, and the cats obediently sat beside their trainer, rubbing their massive heads against him.

The audience broke out in applause, in awe of the best show any of them had probably ever seen.

I clapped half-heartedly. I was pretty much convinced that he was the magic user, which seemed like cheating.

He exited the tent with a cat on either side of him, tails in the air and purring.

A girl and her horses were next. The mixture of horses weren't your garden variety white Lipizzans. It looked like she'd pied-pipered a horse auction. A very well groomed, good looking auction.

She had minis, drafts, and everything in between. After making their entrance, they circled the edge of the ring, trotting with their necks arched and their legs lifting in time with the music coming over the loudspeaker. The girl was standing in the center, a huge smile gracing her face. She didn't have a mic, but I could hear her calling commands and see her signaling with the fluorescent blue whip in her right hand.

The horses moved into a pattern somewhat resembling a Celtic knot.

Again, I suspected magic, though I wasn't sneezing, and this was a much more sophisticated display. I only smelled the pleasing aroma of horse and hay.

She called the horses to line up, then vaulted onto the center one. Other vaulters joined her, mounting every other horse. They worked as a drill team, each with a loose horse at their side.

I was enthralled. I'd never seen such magic in my life. I wondered how the humans couldn't sense something different. I watched closely and noticed a metallic bridle on the horse the girl was riding, and I understood.

She wasn't fae, the horse was. It appeared to be a black-as-night Friesian, but I knew better. The horse she was riding was a kelpie, a Scottish water fae. They lured humans onto their backs, then drowned them for fun. If, however, one could bridle them, the kelpie became the person's obedient servant, until the time the bridle was removed.

I wondered if the creature was forced to wear the bridle full time, or if it was caught fresh on a daily basis. There were other stories where kelpies appeared in human form. I distracted myself from the line of thinking to pay attention to the performance as the horses trotted out in a line.

The spotlight moved, and acrobats became the new highlight. I watched them fly back and forth without a hint of magic. There wasn't a net set out for them, which frightened me a bit.

I was sucked into the show. It had probably been 20 years since I'd last been to a circus, and I hadn't realized what I'd been missing.

When it was over, I joined the others in a standing ovation. The ringmaster took a bow at center ring, where he was joined by most of the other performers.

I clapped extra hard for the horse girl. You've gotta respect a girl that can trap a kelpie.

I hugged Mem and George goodbye, then filed out to the parking lot with the rest of the crowd and climbed into the back seat with Lacey-Marie.

"So, Hades," I said.

"So, Gretchen." He started the car.

"You said you were going to fill us in on why you left us earlier." I leaned towards the front seat instead of buckling in.

"Ah, you remembered. All right, ladies. I made some inquiries about the circus when I first suggested we go. It turns out, there's still a sort of side show. It's exclusive, and I'm guessing illegal. They hold a dinner for their more elite guests." He snail crawled the car through the traffic.

"How did you manage to get an invitation? There was no mention of it in the brochure," Lacey-Marie pointed out.

"I paid for it. They were very forthcoming with the invitation after I opened my wallet. Apparently the rich are perceived to be unscrupulous enough to keep the dinner a secret." he said with a wicked grin.

"Dinner?" Percy asked.

"It's a formal dinner, held in a tent behind the big top. We're going out in style tonight. I'll be calling a limo to bring us over."

"I don't do formal wear." I rolled my lip at the thought.

"I've got something that will fit you," Percy promised, with a smile that made me nervous.

"Ah, you're somewhat shorter in your human form," I pointed out.

"True, but I'm not always in my human form." Her smile grew, along with the gleam in her eyes.

"And you won't be tonight m'dear. No need to hide where there won't be clients." Hades sounded absolutely certain.

I wondered how he could be. Apparently, it had cost him quite a bit to get us in. Not that money meant anything to him. It's not like he'd ever run out.

"All right, but just this once. Don't think you'll ever get me in a dress again," I relented.

"Of course, dear," Percy said with a smug smile.

When we got back to the house, Percy hurried me right up to her room and into her dressing room. Ancient artifacts, possibly as old as she was, were displayed like knick-knacks on her dresser. I kept my mitts behind my back to keep from touching them.

She emerged from her clothing rack carrying a long, slinky red dress.

"Uh-uh, no way am I wearing that." I backed away with my hands up.

"You're wearing it if I have to strip you and force you into myself, and that's final." She thrust the dress into my unyielding hands.

"I can't wear a bra with this. I'm not wearing anything I can't wear a bra with. I need a bra." I tried to give the dress back.

She refused to take it and instead went digging in her dresser. She came up with a couple boxes of sticky bras marked single use.

"You've got to be kidding me." I took one of the boxes and opened it.

"You'll look great." She took the other box for herself.

I pulled out two separate cups, backed with peel away paper. All I had to do was position and presto, instant support.

I didn't trust it.

"Come on, time to change, and I don't want to see underwear lines, young lady." She shooed me out of her closet and closed the door in my face.

I took my armful to my room. I was on my own. No one was going to rescue me from this one. I selected my underwear carefully. Percy would make me change if I didn't.

Okay, I could do this. I peeled my clothes off and pulled on the fresh undies. The sticky bra proved to be difficult. I kept getting it crooked, but I managed not to kill it before getting it all into place. I climbed into the dress and fastened it at my shoulders.

It was definitely a Persephone dress. The fabric hung like liquid around my body, with a neckline that draped in a low cowl. The back was non-existent and shaped the same way just above my rear.

I went through my things and found some double-sided sticky tape that usually got reserved for performances, and applied it all around the edges. I was a little afraid it would fall off, but I wiggled a bit, and it stayed put. Good, hopefully that would be crisis averted. Now I just had to do my hair and makeup.

I'm quick at braids, so I cornrowed it all around the edges and pinned my wild curls at my crown. The makeup I kept simple, though I may have gotten carried away with the black eyeliner. I applied my stage makeup with a light hand. What can I say? I liked the gold.

When I made it downstairs, I found that Percy had

indeed become Persephone, in a light blue dress in a similar style to my own, only higher in the back.

No fair.

Her butt-length blonde hair defied gravity piled atop her head. Red lips were the dominant feature on her face, though they barely outshone her violet eyes.

Hades was in tails and combat boots. Full on god. Look out, circus freaks!

Lacey-Marie took her time joining us, dressed in a little black dress, sky high heels, and flat ironed hair.

Apparently I needed to stock up on formal wear so I wouldn't end up in something quite so... backless.

The limo pulled up, and we piled in and enjoyed some champagne.

Percy pulled lavender oil from her purse and made me douse myself in it.

Bah. Just once I'd like to smell natural.

We were directed to park out back. I carefully climbed out of the car, not wanting to pull the dress loose from any of the millions of stickies.

We were surrounded by cages, RVs, and tractor trailer trucks. I could make out their shapes in the dark, parked like a wagon train on the Oregon Trail.

The black dinner tent was big enough to have fit our barn in. The flaps over the entrance were drawn closed. The ticket man, who introduced himself as Richard, appeared and pulled back the curtains.

Long tables were arranged from end to end, surrounded by comfortable looking dining chairs with a dozen or so people mingling around.

The smell of magic rolled through, staggering me. Now this was a freak show in the traditional sense. There were two cages and a glass aquarium arranged across one wall of the tent, each containing a humanoid creature.

The first one we came to contained what looked like a girl, perhaps thirteen years old, glaring at her audience from the back of her cage. She attempted to use her misshapen black feathered wings to shield her body from view. Someone had dressed her in a white halter dress that managed to look innocent. She hissed, revealing a mouthful of sharp teeth, her too large eyes as alien as the rest of her. She scooted farther back, crossing her arms across her chest, a sullen expression on her face.

The next cage I walked up to was similar to my kennel, but with bulletproof glass in front of the bars. He, unlike the girl, didn't hold himself back from his admirers, throwing himself against the bars, spitting tongues of fire.

I stepped closer to inspect his green, scaled skin. His shorts had a hole in the back, showing off a stubby little tail. Poor kid. He gripped the bars in his hands and rattled them against the glass, showing off his clawed-tipped fingers much like my own. He wanted out, now, and he wasn't getting his way.

I didn't like it at all. They were fae, but I could smell human on them as well. I deduced they were crossbreeds gone wrong. They belonged nowhere, so the circus had taken them in.

The tank was my next stop. Its occupant swam right up and pressed his face to the glass. I put my hand up, and he did the same on his side. I smiled. He smiled. I counted two sets of gills lining his ribcage, and I guessed he wouldn't be able to breath out of water. His skin had a purple tone to it, and he had inquisitive black eyes. The face he pressed against the glass lacked a nose, which I found even odder than the rest of it because it looked right.

He swam away from me, using powerful strokes of

his webbed hands and feet. I got a good look at his legs, which were fused together. He turned and came speeding back towards me. A few bubbles popped out of his mouth like he was laughing. At least he was happy to be cooped up. I would hate it myself.

"He likes you," said a voice to my right.

I jumped, having not noticed the intruder approach. The young man was an albino dressed in black. He smiled, showing off teeth that had been filed to points. I could smell faint traces of coloring chemicals, revealing that black hair was not his natural color. If that didn't give it away, his white eyebrows would have.

"What's his name?" I asked, putting my hand up to the glass again.

"This is Caleb, The Simpleton Water-Boy. And I am Demothi the—"

"Vampire?" I supplied, knowing very well that he was just playing the part of one. He smelled very much alive, without a hint of magic or death on him.

"Let me show you around. I'll introduce you to the others." He placed a hand on the small of my bare back.

I stepped away.

"Sure, why not?" I said stiffly, not appreciating his flirtation. He seemed like a man who was very sure of himself with women.

He led me back to the winged girl. "This is our Angel, Tsarina. She's kept in a cage for your safety, of course."

I doubted very much that she could hurt me, but I just nodded and led the way back to the fire breathing lizard spaz.

"And this is Burn, the Demon Dragon Boy. The police were going to put him down before we intervened." He'd found my soft spot for the caged critters.

A low growl emanated from the other side of the tent.

"Ah, Doug wants his introduction. Don't worry, he's housebroken. Let me introduce you to our resident werewolf-man." He led me across the tent to where a hairy man-shaped creature was chained.

He leapt easily to his feet, straining against his bonds, as we approached.

I had to laugh.

"What does the lady find so humorous?" Demothi asked, his eyebrows scrunching in confusion.

"Well, I hate to break it to you, as you're so into this, but he's not a werewolf." I gained control as best I could, but a giggle or two escaped.

"What makes you think that?"

"Well, for one thing it's not full moon, and wolves don't stop halfway through the change. They become fully wolf. This poor guy just has hypertrichosis. Thanks for the introductions, but I can make my own now." I separated myself from the Vampire wannabe.

"Hi, I'm Gretchen. It's nice to meet you, Doug." I held out my hand in greeting.

Doug straightened up and took my hand without a word. He bowed over it, kissing my knuckles.

Puppy got manners.

His loose, pirate-style shirt slid up his arms, revealing forearms that were slightly less hairy than his head. He might have been imposing if he stood straighter.

"Ah, beauty and the beast," Demothi murmured, stepping back.

"Get lost, Demothi." Doug spoke with just a hint of a French accent.

Demothi scowled and left.

Doug let go of my fingers as a group approached, and went back to growling.

Hopefully they hadn't observed his gentlemanly behavior.

I wandered over to join my friends, who were deep in discussion with a pair of conjoined twins.

"Gretchen, come on over! Let me introduce you to Jerry and Rochelle," said Percy.

I shook hands with the unique conjoined twins. The left was male, Jerry, and the right a woman, Rochelle.

Each had their own set of arms, and a leg each, with a shared center leg. As far as I could tell with them fully clothed, Jerry had boy bits while Rochelle had girl bits. It made for an interesting outfit to say the least. They did have the faint odor of fae emanating from them.

"It's a pleasure," said Jerry squeezing my hand in a much too personal manner.

Rochelle took my hand in turn, and shook it without a word.

"Ladies and Gentlemen, if you would take your seats, it's time for dinner," Ulysses boomed as he entered the tent.

We excused ourselves from the twins and found seats.

Someone walked in behind us, and I whipped my head around. The woman, dressed as a gypsy, complete with bells on her ankles, dripping magic like she was holding the place up.

She greeted people as she approached them and took a seat by Demothi.

I spied him eating a salad and flirting with the woman on his other side, who was hanging on his every word.

Bimbo, I thought. For one thing: blood sucking is not sexy—it makes you dead. Another: he couldn't be more obviously not a vamp.

It made for good dinner conversation for those of us in the know.

Chapter 8:
Late Night Mission

When my eyes opened the next morning, they were immediately drawn to the crumpled mess of a dress I'd left in the corner.

Crud, I thought. It probably shouldn't be lying on my floor getting all wrinkled.

I poked my toes from under my blankets, then quickly pulled them back in. Nope! My blankets were far too warm and comfy to leave, so pulling my blankets to my nose, I snuggled back down.

The first hint of sun kissed the sky, and while it wouldn't stream across my room until late afternoon, it was still too bright for me to fall back to sleep, so I threw off my blankets and forced myself upright. The cold didn't bother me, but I still preferred a warm bed. I grabbed the mug of room temperature water from my bedside table and took a gulp, getting rid of that morning blah taste.

The dress was hopelessly wrinkled, and it said right on the tag that ironing was a no-no. I hung it on my bathroom door, hoping the steam would take the wrinkles out while I enjoyed a nice hot shower.

I started the water to warm up, then made the mistake of looking in the mirror. Scary. I'd neglected to wash off my makeup and brush out my hair.

After dousing my eyelids in makeup remover, I jumped in the shower so the hot steam would soften up the remainder of last night's mascara. I sighed and sank down to the floor of the shower to let the water pound away my stress. It was far too tempting to curl up and fall back asleep, so I stood and commenced shampooing.

A quick inspection of the dress showed an improvement in wrinkle quantity. Percy could deal with the rest. It was her fault I was forced to wear it, after all.

I'd had a good time, despite the artifice of some of the freaks we dined with. Something about the gypsy girl unsettled me. It wasn't just the magic she had been sweating. There was a look of fright on her face upon seeing Lacey-Marie, as if she'd guessed Lacey's true nature. Her glamour had been firmly in place, so there wasn't anything physically about her that should have made the woman nervous.

It wasn't just her. The wolf man bothered me as well. He'd been a perfect gentleman, but his eyes never left me. It wasn't what I would call a friendly or flirtatious gaze. It was a hard look.

I shivered as I dressed, my thoughts lingering on the previous evening. How on earth did I have a good time at dinner? It was downright creepy. I'd met fae before, but the 'freaks' were wrong in so many ways. I picked up and reread the program, everything from where the animals had been obtained through the history of the circus. It was all a lie. Wrong. Wrong. Wrong.

I needed to learn more about that circus. I wanted hard facts.

The library, and all its information, waited for me. I slid up the lid of the antique roll top desk and booted up the computer, my fingers tapping with impatience.

I typed "Treats & Freaks Circus" into the search engine and waited for the results to load. The first thing that popped up was their personal website. I skipped it in favor of a link promising their tour dates. I skimmed until I hit Maine. They'd made it to Portland just in time for Penny's murder. They'd be in the state for the remainder of the month.

This had to be it. I pulled my cell phone and called Lacey.

"Hello?" her groggy answer came through the receiver.

"Mornin', sunshine. Get your skinny ass down here. I wanna show you something." I stared at the screen in fascination.

"Down where." It was not a question. It was resignation.

"Library." I minimized the list of dates and scrolled through the other links, looking for something incriminating.

"I'll be there in a few minutes." Lacey hung up on me.

The next link led me to a small town newspaper article dealing with Bigfoot sightings and the possible relation to hypertrichosis, excessive hair growth, sometimes covering the patient's whole body, and hirsutism, which is when woman grow hair in a male pattern. A few more links featured more sightings around the state, all within the dates of the murders.

Lacey shuffled in clad in bathrobe and slippers.

"What." She pulled a chair up next to mine.

I reopened the tour dates and pointed. "That's when the murders started."

We dug up more information, coinciding the murders and the circus. Nothing pointed direct fingers.

The connections I was making weren't what the police would put together, unless they were fae. I'd yet to meet a fae cop.

Maybe I should sign up when I'm done with hairdressing.

"So, what do you think?" I asked, after printing the information.

Lacey pulled the pages from the printer and skimmed through them. "I think we need to get a closer look at the circus itself. You know, see what's going on after hours."

"After hours where?" Percy asked, joining us.

Lacey handed her the pages, while I shut the computer down.

"I had a thought this morning. The dinner last night didn't sit well. Mentally, I mean," I said, leaning forward in my chair, elbows on knees.

"Now don't go looking for trouble," said Percy as she read. "Huh."

"What?"

"Their first performance was on the night of the first murder. It could just be a coincidence—"

"Or one of the freaks could be a murderer. There's been sightings of weird creatures as well. See?" I interrupted and pulled out the pages about the freak sightings.

"You may have something here, but we need facts before actions."

"That's the plan. Lacey and I are going to go check them out. Tonight."

"Tonight?" Lacey's eyes narrowed.

"Yeah, tonight. The sooner we can get this whole thing settled, the less likely there will be another murder."

"Why are you so certain it's one of the freaks?"

asked Percy.

"Well, there was that gypsy chick. She was having a hard time holding it together. Then there was the wannabe werewolf." I ticked each off on a different finger.

"Yeah, he stared at her all through dinner, like he wanted to maul her, and not in a good way," Lacey added.

"So, do you think it's the man or the woman?" Percy asked.

"My money's on him. But she could very well be in on it, covering his scent or something. I don't know what her brand of magic is, but maybe it helped them break into the girls' houses and keep the noise down." My opinion was a spur-of-the-moment one.

"Agreed. What she said." Lacey spun in her chair, playing with the ends of her hair.

"What time do you plan on doing this?" Percy brought me back down to earth.

"Um, when did the dinner get over last night?" I asked.

"Around midnight."

"Does getting there around one sound good to you?" I turned to Lacey.

"Sure, but we're open Thursday, right?"

"That is correct." Percy nodded.

"We'll try to be quick. We don't want them to know we're there." I stood and paced.

"Sounds like a plan," Lacey said, "See you later. I'm going back to bed." She shuffled out, leaving the door open behind her.

"Do you really think this is wise? It's almost the new moon, and you've said yourself that Lacey's been a little wacky." Percy crossed her arms and raised her eyebrows in challenge.

"That's why I want to do this now. I'm well aware that I can't shift during the new moon. We'll be fine. I won't start anything without you there to back me up."

"You better not." She grabbed her book and left.

I should have followed Lacey's example and tried to get more sleep, but my mind was racing a million miles an hour. What if we got there and discovered that we were right? How long could we afford to delay before neutralizing the problem? I wanted to avoid another death, even the killer's. I would do it if I had to, but I wasn't making it my plan or anything.

My heart was speeding up with every minute, and if I wasn't so close to a new moon, I would have been at risk of wolfing. I was ready to go by sundown, despite another five or six hours until go time. I'd dressed in black, complete down to hat and gloves. I was prepared.

My digital camera took decent night pictures, as it was meant for wildlife photography. It also had bluetooth connection, to download directly to my laptop.

Lacey knocked on my door around ten.

"Come in!" I called while stuffing my hair up into a black beanie.

"Wow, you are way too excited." She was decked out in black, but her blonde hair was down around her shoulders, and she reeked of cigarettes.

I dug in my bedside table for a hair elastic and flung it at her. "Aw come on, you're excited too. You're all dressed up and everything!"

I looked down at her shoes. Pointed toes peeked out from her dark jeans. "You can't be stealthy in heels. Don't you have any boots or sneakers?"

"No. My boots have higher heels. Would ballet flats be satisfactory?"

"They'd be better than those." I pointed at her feet and rolled up my lip.

She made a face at me and pulled her hair up in a messy bun. "Better?"

"Yes. And I have a hat and gloves for you."

"I'm not wearing a hat."

"Yes, you are. Your hair is light enough to glow in the dark." I handed her the hat and gloves.

"I'm surprised you're not painting me up in camo," she muttered.

I tapped a finger on my chin. "That might not be a bad—"

"Forget I said that!" She threw her hands up in the air, palms out.

"Fine." I sat back down on my bed, and we stared at the clock. Tick, tick, tick.

"This is going to be a long night, isn't it?" Lacey asked, flopping down beside me on her belly, fiddling with a loose thread on my quilt.

"Uh-huh." I nodded.

She rolled back over and balanced back on her elbows. "Wanna watch a movie?"

"Sure."

We sneaked down the hall spy style, darting into doorways and signaling each other to go until we got to the right room, collapsing on her couch in a fit of giggles.

"God, will we ever grow up?" she asked after getting ahold of herself.

"I hope not." I pulled myself upright and wiped an arm across my eyes.

Lacey popped in a chick flick. Blech. For a dead girl, she sure melted right into those movies, and the only books I'd ever seen her read were romances.

"Why on earth does she find that sexy? He's an ass,

dump him! Get on with your life!" I fumed at the TV, waving my arms.

"It's a movie, relax. Besides, she'll find someone better." Lacey justified.

"I know, we've only watched this one, what, 50, 60 times?" I crossed my arms and leaned back. It killed time either way.

"Are we walking or driving?" Lacey asked as we made our way downstairs.

"Running. Oh wait, I need to get my laptop." I ran back up the stairs and picked up my backpack. "All right, you ready? I'm ready." I slung the pack over my shoulders, buckling the chest and waist stabilizing straps.

"I guess I'm ready. What's the computer for?"

"Pictures, in case we get caught and something happens to my camera. I'll set it up in the woods."

"Aren't you worried someone will see it glowing through the trees?" she asked, heading towards the door.

I followed her out. "Nope. Besides, I don't plan on getting caught."

"Me either."

"Good, let's get going." I double checked my straps, then took off with Lacey in hot pursuit. We stuck to snowmobile trails, instead of the roads. It would suck if we got hit by a car. For the car anyhow. It would hurt us, but we'd bounce back.

I tugged on my gloves as I ran, more for stealth than for warmth.

I smelled fae before we saw the lights in the dinner

tent. Good, dinner was still in progress.

I set my computer behind a tree and opened it up. Lacey snuck out to where the cars were parked, to tell me if she could see any light from my screen.

She returned quickly. "Nothing, you're good."

"Great. I want to take some pictures of the dinner."

"You're gonna get us caught," Lacey cautioned me.

"No, I won't. I'll take them from outside the tent. I can keep out of the light just as well as you."

"Fine, but I'm waiting here until you come back. And don't expect me to come rescue you when you get caught." She plopped herself down on the ground with her back against a tree.

"I'm not getting caught. You man the computer. I'll be back in a few minutes." I slung the camera strap around my neck so the camera rested against my stomach.

"Be careful," she whispered loudly.

"Shut up, and quit worrying," I whispered back.

Sticking to the shadows, I darted from tree to tree until I reached the open space the circus had settled in. I snuck down to the big top first but didn't sense anything suspicious and snapped a few photos just in case there was something there I wasn't seeing. Climbing into the big cat performance cage was easy, so I took pictures there as well. The smell of magic had dissipated, leaving me with the unpleasant stench of angry kitty.

I was just about to exit the main tent when I heard something jingle. The gypsy woman walked past, the bells jingling obnoxiously around her ankles serving as warning.

Maybe I should get a set for Lacey, I mused. As soon as the sound faded away, I came out of hiding and headed for the dinner tent.

I tried a couple of hiding spots before hunkering down and lifting my camera. I got the fish tank in my sites and zoomed in. It took a moment for the image to clear up, but I got a decent shot featuring my fish boyfriend plastered right up to the glass. I took a couple more as he swam around, then shifted to find another subject.

My sights settled next on the wolf man. He was looking in my direction. Could he see me? No, it was pitch black out, and the tent was brightly lit. He probably couldn't see any further than the tent flap, so I snapped pictures.

Dragon boy flamed nastily, giving me some spectacular photo options. The one they called Tsarina kept her back to me or would tilt her head forward so her scraggly blonde curls hung over her face. I wasn't satisfied with the shots I got, but there wasn't much I could do.

Jerry, flirting with the young woman in a nearly see-through white dress, and Rochelle, arms crossed over her chest, scowling at her brother with narrowed eyes, mingled near the opening, and I took advantage of the easy shots.

Demothi made it easy as well, what with the bimbo he'd chosen for the evening hanging all over him. His very demeanor begging me to reach in there and smack him.

I didn't get a single photograph of the gypsy. I berated myself for not taking the opportunity when she jingled by my hiding place. Oh, well, Woulda, shoulda, coulda, didn't.

I decided to get some shots of the ringmaster, the lion tamer, and the ticket man as they walked by, so close I could have reached out and touched them.

People were standing up from the table and shaking

hands. My cue to leave. I didn't want to get discovered in the mass exit. I booked it back to Lacey's hiding spot and flopped down by my computer.

"Well?" I asked, pulling the laptop towards me.

"These are awesome! Too bad we can't make these public." She grabbed it back and clicked through the pictures, her face illuminated by the screen, making her look even more sickly than before she started using the spray tan booth.

My subjects had made it easy. I'm not much of a photographer, but I'd managed to get some beautiful shots.

"Look at those teeth! I hadn't noticed those last night." Lacey pointed at Demothi's grinning mouth.

"I saw them up close and personal when he tried to make me his toy last night. I'm surprised he didn't try you." I was unimpressed.

She thrust her elbow into my ribs. "Hey, what's that supposed to mean?"

"Absolutely nothing." Luckily she didn't pick up on my lie.

"He is supposed to be a vampire, right?" She turned her attention back to the photographs.

"Yup. You're not convinced? It's working on her." I pointed at the girl glued to his lap. "I guarantee we'd find her in his RV."

"Oh, goody. You can find her. I wanna check out the tiger." She rubbed her hands together.

"We're looking for a murderer, not your next pet." I pushed her jokingly.

"I know that, but Alastair is a creeper. And a creeper with magic is definitely a potential suspect," she argued, pointing at the picture on my screen.

"Very true. So, now we just need to wait for the humans to go away." I settled back to wait.

It seemed like forever before the last of the tail lights faded away. I saved the pictures, then emailed them to myself. One can never have too many backups.

"Ready?" I stood and dusted dirt and pine needles off the seat of my pants.

"Yeah, but I think we should stick together." She did the same.

"Why?"

"We've only got one camera, and I don't want to waste time looking for you if something goes down."

"Good point. Put that hat on. We're going in." I posed Charlie's Angel-style, holding my imaginary gun.

Lacey snorted and tugged the hat down over her hair, taking a moment to tuck the wisps up inside.

We kept low and quiet as we approached the caravan. The first RV had a light on inside, but the window was too high to see in.

"Get on my shoulders, and take the camera," I whispered, kneeling down.

"Oh, come on. We'll fall over." She crossed her arms and shook her head.

"Get up there now. The quicker we do this, the less chance of us getting caught." I crouched down farther.

"Fine." She climbed so she was sitting on my shoulders, then took my camera.

I wrapped my arms around her legs, holding her steady as I stood.

"A little to the left. Oh, ew!" She snapped pictures, then thwacked me on the top of my head with an open palm.

I dropped to my knees. "Ouch! Not necessary!" I hissed.

"You can do the next one." She handed me the camera. "I can boost you."

She could, but her height wouldn't be much of an advantage.

It was Demothi's home we'd stumbled upon first, and he and the bimbo were getting down and dirty.

"Perv," I teased my reluctant partner.

"Hey, you wanted pictures, I took pictures," she grumbled, and headed for the next patch of light.

Dragon boy looked different now that he wasn't on display. I showed the pictures to Lacey without a word. The flames he now spit were barely a flicker, there and gone without much notice. His green skin had swollen patches dotted with scales. His eyes were sad instead of angry.

That's horrible, Lacey mouthed and I nodded my agreement.

I was climbing up onto Lacey's shoulder for another photo op, when I was yanked backward by the back of my sweatshirt. Our attacker, Lacey, and I all landed in a heap.

"What the hell do you think you're doing?" Gypsy girl wheezed from under me.

"Taking pictures of y'all de-glamoured. You make fascinating subjects. Tell me, have you murdered anyone lately?" I stayed put, resting my full weight on her.

Lacey army crawled out of the pile. "Ow, seriously?"

"What are you talking about?" the girl asked.

"Uh, someone's been murdering hairdressers. It started when you guys arrived in Portland." I rolled over and pinned her shoulders with my hands.

"You are so full of shit," she said. A tingling of magic hit my senses.

I glared at her.

"You're serious. You think I've been killing

people." She quit struggling, and the tingle dissipated.

"Not just you. Your wolf man caught my eye too."

"You're the girl from last night. Wow, you look a lot different without the skanky dress."

I growled and bored down harder on her back.

"Easy, psycho. Would you please let me up?"

I stood and offered her my hand.

"All right, first off my name is Sabrina, and I'm not a murderer. And neither is Doug. Come with me, and be civilized." She wagged a finger at me, then turned and walked so we followed.

I kinda believed her, which sucked because if no one from the circus was the killer, then I still had my work cut out for me.

"I'm Gretchen, and this is Lacey-Marie." I slapped the front of my friend's shoulder with the back of my hand.

"Where's the rest of your crew? They're not hiding in the bushes, are they?"

"Nah, they stayed home," I promised. Then added, "But they know where we are." I didn't want her thinking we were easy targets if she was lying. I was less than my best with the new moon right around the corner.

She led us around the perimeter of the RVs, opening the door to the one on the end. It was a cramped little place and probably contained all of Sabrina's worldly possessions. It was decorated in browns and greens, and hand-knit throws and cushions made her bed look cozy. The whole thing was one room, so the bed was one of the few places to sit down besides a little table and chairs attached to one wall. It smelled pleasantly of cinnamon, coffee, and magic.

"Coffee?" she offered, holding the carafe aloft.

"It's not a good idea to give me caffeine," I

declined, taking a seat at the table.

"And I'm guessing you don't drink a whole lot either, do you, vampire," Sabrina accused Lacey. "I can see through glamours, not just create them."

"No wonder you were seeping magic. You had a lot to uphold during dinner last night," I commented with respect of her talents.

"I was? I'm gonna have to work on that. I do juggle a lot, keeping prying eyes away from the side show and keeping up appearances."

"I'll have coffee," said Lacey, sliding in beside me.

"Oh, sorry. Do you want anything in it?" Sabrina filled a clean mug and handed it over.

"Milk and sugar, please."

She pulled a small container of milk out of her mini fridge.

"So, what are you?" I asked, leaning back in my seat.

"What are *you*? Doug says you must be something, else you wouldn't have questioned his being a werewolf."

"Uh-uh, you first." I wasn't giving up my identity until she did.

"I guess you could call me a petty sorceress. I've got faerie in me a few generations back. I can create glamours and mix a few potions. Your turn." She poured herself coffee and joined us at her little table.

I waited until she sat and put her mug down. "I'm a werewolf." I smiled wolfishly.

"Huh. Figures. We should have guessed that one." She sipped her coffee calmly.

Damn. I had hoped to shock her. "And we're hairdressers."

"So you're taking this killing thing seriously. Sorry to disappoint you, but it's not us. We like pretty people's money, not their still warm blood."

"Good to know," I said with a nod.

"Well, I might as well introduce you to the rest of the clan. Would you mind de-glamouring?" She addressed Lacey.

I hadn't seen Lacey fanged out in years, so it was a little weird to see the illusion fall away as she unclasped the magicked necklace from around her neck and put it in her pocket. She pulled out her contacts as well and tossed them in the garbage. The smell of death that always enveloped her intensified, making my eyes water slightly.

I thought she looked more silly than scary with her fangs pushing against the skin of her upper lip. She could close her mouth around them, but it looked like she had a wad of chew stuck up there. Her scarlet eyes were by far her scariest feature.

I tossed my contacts as well. Might as well join in.

"Pretty eyes," Sabrina said to me, then turned to Lacey, "Sorry, yours are just plain creepy."

"I think that's to a vampire's advantage," said Lacey, smiling toothily.

Sabrina wove her way around until we got to Tsarina's trailer. She was no longer caged, but she was locked in.

"I had to give her more feathers. Ulysses decided she was too creepy looking, and he wanted to bill her as an angel. All these guys are fae/human crosses that didn't work out so well."

"Is it all right if I take a picture?" I held up my camera, thinking I might as well finish up since I had all the before shots.

"I guess. So long as you promise not to publish them or anything."

"I promise." I lifted the camera and took a picture,

focusing on Tsarina's pouty expression rather than the wings that were as sad as her hair.

"How come you showcase them, if they're so clearly unhappy?" I asked, a wave of sympathy making me lower my camera.

"They agreed to it. It's mostly an act. Caleb's personality is genuine. He's… simple and very sweet. I saw no reason to change that." She referred to the fish boy.

"How about her?" I indicated the child I'd just photographed.

"She's a spoiled brat. She's locked in because she has a tendency to wander away and steal things." Sabrina moved on, and we followed.

She knocked on Demothi's door. He answered wearing only a sheet around his waist, reeking of memories I'd rather remained buried.

"Hey, babe, what's up?" he asked, then spotted us. "Who're your friends." He licked his lips.

"Drop the act, jackass. They know you're not a vampire," Sabrina ordered.

"Shh, not so loud. Yon lady still believes." He pointed his thumb inside.

Sabrina crossed her arms. "Strangely enough, I find myself not caring."

"So, how'd they figure it out?" he asked.

"Well, for one thing, you ate food last night," I pointed out.

"Ah, the one who got away. I recognize you now. Your eyes are all weird."

"Don't insult the nice werewolf," Sabrina said, a sardonic smile enveloping her lips.

Demothi backed up a step. "Werewolf?" The reek went away and was immediately replaced by fear.

"Yeah, and your teeth are all wrong." Lacey came

forward and smiled at him, flipping her lower lip underneath her fangs.

"Jesus!" he stumbled back with a bang as he hit the side of his trailer.

"Yeah, he's got nothing to do with this," I commented, menacing over him.

"Sorry, sorry!" He nearly fell over, backing up the steps of his RV, the lock sliding in place after him.

"That was fun!" I grabbed Lacey, tossed her up towards the window, catching her legs cheerleader style.

She plastered her face to his bedside window and hissed loudly, her mouth open wide, displaying her fangs to full effect.

Feminine shrieks followed, and she tumbled to the ground giggling.

"All right, where to next?" I asked, pulling Lacey-Marie back to her feet.

"Doug. Come on." Sabrina led us to yet another RV.

I wondered how she kept them all straight. All the RVs were the same style and brand.

Doug, the intensely hairy man, answered the door before we got a chance to knock.

"I heard screaming, what's going on?" he asked, crossing his arms over a bare chest defined with muscle, as were his arms under all that hair. I was curious what he actually looked like.

"Oh, it's you." He stepped back away from us.

"Nice to see you too." I extended my hand like I had the night before.

He didn't take it. "What are you doing here?" His voice was quiet.

"Taking pictures." I picked up my camera and captured the moment.

He turned, slamming the door in our faces.

"He's a bit shy," Sabrina stated with an apologetic tone.

"Thanks anyhow. I'm sure Gretch didn't help with her extra snappy camera." Lacey shrugged off any offense.

I checked my watch. "I think we'd better get going. We've got to work in the morning."

"Well, good luck. I hope you find your killer." Sabrina offered her hand.

"Sure. Sorry for uh—" Was it breaking and entering if we stayed outside? "Stalking."

"No problem." She smiled as she shook my hand.

"Night," said Lacey.

We headed for the woods, where I shut down my computer and packed up.

NEW MOON

Chapter 9:
Farm Prep

Percy and I took the morning off. Summer was fast approaching, and the farm aspect of the property needed to be settled before temperatures skyrocketed. I've always been an early riser, so I had no problem meeting up outside, in barn clothes, as soon as the sun made her appearance. By eight o'clock, we were good and grubby.

Percy thrust a pitchfork into my waiting hands and directed me to dig up and turn over a patch of soil. I loved getting my hands dirty in a non-lethal way. It was a great stress reliever. It was also satisfying to know that I'd contributed to something inherently good. I had so little of that in my life. Plus I loved the smell of fresh-turned soil. The pile of debris and rocks in my wheelbarrow grew as I worked through the tough clods that would become a new herb garden. A large pile of aged compost waited off to one side.

Percy was carefully lining up seedlings and consulting the planning chart she had designed for the upcoming season. She was a genius at placing every plant where it would thrive. I also suspected her compost had a little extra zing to it, contributed by some out-of-this-world additives.

Lacey-Marie was inside picking up our slack.

Besides having a major allergy to sunlight, she wasn't a fan of getting her hands dirty. If the girl got dirt under her fingernails, there was a minor freak-out involving a nail brush and a vat of soap. It wasn't as if she were capable of contracting any diseases. Being a vampire and, well, dead, she was kinda impervious.

It was shaping up to be a gorgeous day. The sun was blazing full force, which brought the thermometer to a dazzling 65 degrees, and it wasn't even noon. I shed my layers down to my dark tank top, soaking in the calming rays. I straightened up to stretch a bit, pulled my arms over my head, reaching back as far as I could, and got a satisfying snap. It was a good day to be human with no wolf in my head, even if I couldn't shift and I was weaker.

I got back to work, not wanting to fall behind. Percy was going like greased lightning, flitting here, there, and everywhere, making sure everything was just so.

Percy thrust her pitchfork into the soft, compost-filled earth to her right. "Are you ready for a break?"

"A change of scenery wouldn't hurt, but I can keep going if you want me to. Are your people taking care of the big gardens?"

Percy's people were all of fae origin. She'd given them all jobs, rather than forcing them to take disability from the state. They're physically capable of work, but it would quickly become obvious to humans that there was something off about them. The state would give them disability because they didn't want to employ super freaks. They're normal enough looking, or at least their glamours are when they're in place. I can usually smell magic, but I can't see through a glamour. All magic smells the same—well, except for tainted magics, like fae/human hybrids like vamps and weres.

They both have a distinct smell. Vamps smell like death and magic, while weres smell a bit like wet dog and magic. There were real hybrids around, of course, like the circus freaks.

Percy left her chart and her treasured seedlings in the hands of her most reliable worker bee, Christina, so we could move onto other things, like my kennel.

I tried to complete regular maintenance on my own, but we did a sweep twice a year together. I didn't usually cause too much trouble when I was fully wolf, but accidents happen, and I didn't want the accident to be me escaping and eating someone's cat. Or worse.

Sticking my pitchfork next to the other, I followed Percy out to the barn. The door creaked as I pushed it open. My changing room, which used to be a tack room when the barn actually housed horses, was a tidy little space with hooks for clothes and a boot rack for my shoes. I tended to rip things up when I was a wolf, so I needed a separate room from the actual kennel for my stuff. I also had a cot there for nights when I needed to be truly alone.

Everything looked in good enough condition, if a little worn. Percy hit the button on the space heater, and it chugged to life. I mostly used it to dry wet things during the colder months. She turned it off after a few seconds, satisfied that it was in working order.

There was a lock that only Percy and I had keys for, preventing anyone from walking in or letting me loose by accident. The lock worked from both sides so I could lock myself in and Percy could check in from time to time and make sure I was good on food and water. I unlocked the door with the key that I kept on a chain around my neck.

From the outside, my kennel appeared to be a boarded-up row of stalls, which masked the titanium bars lining the inside. They had worked well so far. I hadn't escaped since moving in. I used to escape all the time, hyped up on adrenaline, attacking and killing people, dogs, cats, and wildlife—really anything that ran. It's instinct, and without a pack to level me out, I was more susceptible to rage and changing. I was lucky I could function around humans at all. I hadn't always been able to.

"Everything looks good, but I think I'll leave the windows open a while longer," I commented, running my hands down the poles to feel for deformities and weakness.

"I don't know why you sound surprised. You inspect the kennel frequently." Percy kicked her toe through the thick layer of shavings that covered the ground.

"Yeah, I know. But I still have to worry about all the 'what ifs.' If I worry about them now, I won't have to regret them later."

"Very true. How are your Kongs holding up?" Percy was referring to my bouncy, snowman-shaped dog toys. Apparently I loved them while wolfy.

I checked the box of toys that sat in the far corner. "They look fine. Nothing too chewed up." I held one up to eye level for closer inspection. "Do you think we can stuff a few with peanut butter? That should keep me out of trouble for a while." Mmm, peanut butter. I like it in human form too.

"I don't see why not. Anything else you can think of?" She turned in slow circles, fists loosely balled on her hips.

"Maybe a blanket, something old and ratty, in case I chew it up." I inspected my L.L. Bean dog bed. I'd chewed on the corner, and there was some stuffing popping out. Leaving the kennel for a minute, I grabbed some old jeans from of the changing room and a sewing kit to patch the hole, then returned. I'd pull the rest of the stuffing out if I saw it, and the patch took only a few minutes. I hate sewing, but years of practice made me pretty good at it.

"You can have a good blanket. I'm not worried about it getting shredded. I'll make sure the food silo is full morning of, and I'll also get some wet food in to you at some point," said Percy, eying my handiwork with an approving nod.

"I can't believe you feed me that stuff. Wouldn't canned tuna be better? Or a steak?"

"You've never complained. In fact, you wolf it down in a matter of seconds."

"Ha ha." I stood from my crouched position beside the doggy bed. "I think we're good. The shavings are all fresh. The automatic waterer is working?"

"It is. All right, let's get back to work then." She dusted off her hands and headed out.

Back in the garden, I finished turning the soil. The smell of the compost was harsh even to my human nostrils, but I didn't complain. I'd be enjoying the fruits of our labor in the not-so-distant future. It felt good to really work, to feel how a pitchfork should feel in my hands if I were normal. It didn't take long to finish up. We were inside and showered by the time Lacey was closing up for lunch.

"Nice of you to join me. The phone has been ringing like crazy. There were some callers interested in interviewing for the stylist position. I wrote down the numbers on the sticky note by the phone." Lacey breezed into the kitchen, carefully avoiding the light streaming through the windows.

Percy pulled the blinds.

"Thanks." Lacey dug in the fridge and came up

with a blood bag. She'd have to start storing them in her room, if the new girls wanted to keep their lunches cold.

That gave me an idea.

"We should get a mini fridge for the storage room so the new girls won't be wandering around the house."

"That's a great idea! I've got my little fridge upstairs, but it's nice to keep stocked up."

"Yeah, don't want anyone finding those blood cubes in the freezer," I said before tossing back a chunk of deli turkey.

"I don't think anyone would know what they were. They're not exactly labeled." Lacey said, tearing open the packet with her teeth and pouring it into her Princess mug before sticking it in the microwave for a few seconds for perfect body temperature.

Ewwy. "Probably, but you know how stupidly curious people are."

"I know how bothersome you are," said Lacey, poking me in the arm with her mug, just barely avoiding splashing me with the contents.

"I love you too." I threw a piece of meat at her.

She threw it back. "Who wouldn't? You, however, need some work."

"What, I'm breathing, aren't I?" I checked the pulse on my neck with two fingers. "Yep, still alive. Isn't that your criteria?"

"You forgot male. Which you are definitely not." She pointed at my chest with a circular motion.

"You have a point. You love me anyways," I said with a shrug of acquiescence and chewed the turkey she'd thrown back at me.

"Of course she does. I love you too. How's your turkey?" Percy asked, taking a big bite of her salad.

"A little boring." I held up the packet at nose level

and wrinkled my nose.

"You could have bread and condiments with it. There's plenty of lettuce," she offered.

"Do I look like a rabbit to you?" I curled my lip in mock disgust. "I eat rabbits. Yummy."

"You're horrible." She placed a hand to her neck, clutching at her non-existent pearls.

"Thank you. I better get ready for work. See you ladies in a bit!"

"Yep. Oh, do you wanna watch a movie with me tonight?" Lacey gulped down the rest of her lunch.

"Nope, I'm practicing with my boys."

"Mm, your boys." Lacey licked her lips.

"Are off limits." I was protective of my boys, especially from the likes of Lacey-Marie. She's my best friend, but she's definitely not the type of woman my boys should be dating. They all deserve someone with a beating heart.

"I don't know why," the person in question grumbled, crossing her arms with a dramatic flair.

"I like them alive. And besides, they'd be less likely to hang out with me if you broke their hearts." I left the conversation at that.

I was really looking forward to band practice. It was my chance to be truly human. I love my job and my girlfriends, but it's really nice to be normal, or at least sort of normal, every once in a while.

It was a good afternoon, with no screaming kids, which is always a plus, let me tell you. Screamers give you headaches. Screamers make you chop up your knuckles. Screamers make you want to cuss out them and their parents. Of course, you can't because the client is always right, even when that client is three.

My adults behaved themselves as well, which was an added bonus. When closing rolled around, I shot up the stairs, leaving Percy to finish close out.

Now, what to wear? It would probably be hotter than the hinges of hell at Austin's house. We almost always practice at his place for two very good reasons: He is the drummer, so it's easier for us to drag our gear to his house than it is for him to pack up his drums and haul them somewhere else. The second reason being: He actually owns a house.

The other two guys rent apartments, and I, of course, live at Percy's. I rarely invited them over. Too many questions to be raised. I even did their haircuts at Austin's house most of the time.

Given the hot factor, I went for another dark-colored tank, tight jeans, and my buckle-infested biker boots. To keep it off my neck, my hair went up into a messy bun. When we performed, I punked it out, but for practices, practical was key. I threw on a black sweatshirt for good measure, then packed up my things.

My laptop, music, and tuner went into a backpack. Then I checked and rechecked the clasps on Lola's case before adding her to my stack. My big amp stayed at Austin's house; I used a little one at home since I was only playing for myself, not highly distorted guitars and testosterone-crazed men.

It was too bad I had so much to carry. It would have been a good night to take out my motorcycle. My pack was safer on the front seat of my beat-up black Ford F150 anyhow.

Austin lived in Bangor, which wasn't too far of a drive, thank goodness—less road for me to get caught speeding on. I happen to like driving. I like to drive fast. If I could find trails to off-road it to his house, I would. I hand cranked both windows down and let the cool air burst in around me. WTOS roared out of my stereo as I drove. My preferred station usually played good driving music, definitely not family-friendly, so we don't play it in the salon, but good for driving and kickboxing. It also covered up my roars as I change once a month, or whenever I felt like letting my beast out.

I parked on the road and lugged my things in through the front door without knocking. It was band night, no need for niceties.

I was the first one there, besides Austin of course. He was really into his warm-up, his eyes closed and his sticks blurs. He had no idea anyone else was there.

I held on to a bit of satisfaction as he jumped, sending one of his drumsticks flying.

"Not cool, Gretch. You shouldn't sneak up on people." He retrieved his wayward stick and resumed his seat.

"I didn't sneak. I even slammed the front door. You're just oblivious." I set my things on my amp.

Austin's living room doesn't have any actual living room furniture. All that is downstairs in his rec/ TV room, where we sometimes hang out after practice.

Flicking the latches of my case open, I retrieved Lola and plugged my tuner into her.

"How was work?" Austin asked, rubbing his hand over his short, dark buzz cut.

"Great. I only worked half a day since I helped Percy with her gardens this morning."

"Cool."

"How about with you?"

"Fine. I kept busy." Austin never talked about work, unlike me, who whined on a regular basis.

I finished tuning, plugged into my amp, and set Lola on top of the pile.

It took me a minute or two, but I managed to

untangle all my cords, including my nifty foot pedals that change my sound with the touch of a toe. I could add distortion or make myself sound like a flute. There were hundreds of options, making the pedal one of my favorite toys.

I worked on some finger limbering exercises at a low volume, and by the time I was finished, the rest of the guys were present and completing their own warmups. I did my best to stay quiet while they tuned. Tuning makes them cranky, for some reason.

As soon as I finished, I cranked up the volume and tapped out a sequence on my pedal. I set my bow to my string and became an orchestra.

"Knock it off, Gretch!" Mark shouted over my din.

"Aw, you're no fun!" I shouted back as I continued to play a bit longer, then tapped my magic stomp box and became a slightly distorted violin.

"That's better!" He plugged in his mic and fiddled with the knobs and slides on the soundboard.

My sound came out of the monitors, and I was soon joined by bass and guitar with little pauses in between as Mark adjusted to his heart's content. He was a bit of a perfectionist when it came to sound, which is fine because he was good at it. Luckily for us, he could also sing and play guitar.

"Great, let's get started. We've only got a couple of gigs this month, so let's make them count. Any ideas for the sets?"

"Nope!" I called out, not caring what we played.

Scott made a few requests, and Mark wrote them down, tweaking and adding to the lists he already had.

"All right, guys, I've got a tentative set here. All stuff we know and love." He handed us each a copy.

He's so very organized.

"Gretchen, have I told you what a beautiful woman

you are?" Scott called out.

"At least once every time you see me." The compliments would get him nowhere. I knew better than to date humans. It never ended well. Besides, despite it only having been a couple of dates, he had been going out with Penny.

"Oh, chilly," he laughed.

"Quit flirting and practice, lady and gentlemen. One! Two! Three!" Mark counted us into the first song. Mark had written the intro to the rock ballad as a waltz, and it worked surprisingly well.

I love music. Absolutely love it. We all got lost in the rhythm of practicing, stopping each other periodically to work over rough patches. All in all, we had those songs down pat. We ended the practice with a jam session, all facing in toward each other, making it easier to improvise and follow along as we watched each others' fingers, tapping feet, and nodding heads.

I got a little carried away, then brought myself back down to someone who didn't have a hundred years worth of practice. I hadn't thought anyone noticed.

As I was packing up, Mark wandered over.

"That was killer. Do you think you can work that in somewhere?"

Crap, someone did notice. "I don't know if I can do that again," I confessed untruthfully.

"I bet you can. Come on, Gretchen. You're really good. I don't know why you dumb down your playing like you do."

Because I can't afford to be noticed. "It was a fluke, but I'll do the best I can."

"Are you going out with us tonight?" Scott asked, hugging me from the side, his shaggy hair tickling my cheek.

"Yeah, sure. Now get off me." I shoved him away.

His flirting might seem harmless, but I'd smelled his interest before. Drinks could make that worse, but we could still have some fun.

"Great. Leave your stuff here. You can ride with me."

"Only if you let me drive back."

"Sure, but only if you can get the keys out of my pocket."

He was teasing. He'd better have been teasing. I rolled my eyes and chose not to respond.

"I'll see you guys over there. Don't forget to lock up," Austin called on his way out the door.

We finished packing up, and I followed Scott out to his gorgeous Mustang.

"Can I drive there?" I batted my eyelashes at him.

"No."

"Please?" I snaked my bare arm around his waist.

"Okay."

"Yay!" I took the keys from his hand, ran around to the driver's side, and slid onto the leather seat. I breathed deep of man and leather. There isn't a better combination.

I turned the key in the ignition, and she roared to life. Ah, bliss.

Scott slid into the passenger seat, and we tore out of the driveway. I had some fun hugging the corners and gunning it down hills until we got into town, where I behaved myself. It was a short drive, about seven minutes total. I pulled into the parking lot and turned her off, waiting until Scott got out before locking the doors and shoving the keys in my pocket.

Scott slung his arm around my shoulders, and we walked in. Then I shrugged away from him to grab a chair.

I ordered a rum and coke. The boys all got beers.

"We got a new girl," I announced.

"Yeah? Is she hot?" asked Mark.

"Is she single?" asked Scott.

"Yes-ish, and no, she's married with two kids. Sorry, guys. She's been a lot of fun to work with. You should have seen the other girl we interviewed. She was nice at first, then Toni walked in—"

"Toni?" asked Scott.

"The new girl," I clarified.

"Good name," Mark commented.

"Yeah. I'll try to drag her out sometime. Anyway, the other girl tried to start stuff, and Toni just ignored it."

"That's good. She's gonna have a lot to put up with, with you girls."

"Gee, thanks, Austin."

"You're welcome."

"Anything new with you guys?" I asked.

"Nope," said Mark.

"Nada," said Austin

"Not a thing. Come dance with me." Scott grabbed at my hand.

"Help?" I pleaded to the others.

Mark and Austin shook their heads and raised their hands.

Troublemakers. I think they'd have liked it if Scott and I got together. Of course, there's the fact he's a lot younger than me, and the fact that I turned into wolf while, um, amorous.

I let him drag me to the dance floor and danced until a slow song came on, when I attempted to beat a hasty exit.

"Relax, Gretch. I'm not going to bite," he muttered at me.

"Yeah, but I might."

"I'm not afraid of you."

You should be, I thought.

I danced with him until the song was over. Then I extracted myself from his arms. "I want another drink."

It was as good an excuse as any.

"Yeah, me too." He followed me off the dance floor.

I ordered myself a draft beer. It was more than I usually drank when I was out with them, but I had the next day off. I wasn't going to get drunk, and I was going hunting with the wolves the next night.

"Shots on me!" I called out to my group.

I got a few extra moochers, but I didn't really care. I had a pocket full of tips.

When we finally got out to the car, Scott was starting to slur.

"You're gonna stay on Austin's couch. How much did you drink?" I asked.

"Dunno, a few."

"A few too many."

"How come you're not drunk?"

"I pace myself. Come on, get in." I also hadn't taken any of the shots I'd bought.

"Yeah." He flopped into his seat, and I closed the door behind him.

The drive back to Austin's house was a quiet one. I drove nice, knowing the cops would be out looking for troublemakers. I walked Scott into the house and let him make it down to the basement on his own. I packed my stuff, and turning to leave, walked smack into Scott.

"Gretchen?"

"What, Scott."

"Go out with me sometime?" he asked.

"No. Go to bed."

"Why?"

"Because I can't."

"I'll ask again."

I sighed and walked him back to the top of the stairs. "I know."

"Night." He leaned over and kissed my cheek.

I watched to make sure he made it down the stairs all right. Mark was watching me.

"What?" I asked.

"Nothing." He got his stuff and walked outside with me.

"See ya later?" I climbed in my truck.

"Yup. Night, Gretch."

"Night."

I sat in my truck for a few minutes, listening to the distant sound of spring peepers. The quiet calm was nice. Being alone wasn't so bad. Scott would never be an option, no matter how much he tried to be.

Chapter 10:
An Invitation

The vaguest hint of sunshine woke me, and I rolled to grab my phone from the nightstand. *5:01* a.m. glowed brightly back at me. I groaned and threw an arm over my eyes. I'd slept like crap. With several deep breaths, I tried to will myself back to sleep, squeezing my eyes shut and burrowing my face into my pillow. Just as I felt my body relax, my eyes popped open. If only my brain would just shut off. If I were one to journal, getting my thoughts out would help. But I'm not. Been there, tried that.

Releasing a sigh of exasperation, I threw the blankets off and heaved myself out of bed. I wasn't going to sleep, so I decided to do something semi-productive. I snuck down the stairs, keeping close to the railing where it was less likely to squeak and creak, and padded barefoot around the salon as I debated washing the floors.

Later, I thought.

In the kitchen, I rummaged in the fridge for milk, mourning the fact that I couldn't have hot chocolate. I loved chocolate, but with the whole doggy thing, it's a definite no-no. I allowed myself a piece of really dark chocolate perhaps once a month while the moon was still in the sky. I haven't gotten sick yet.

The chocolate syrup was sitting next to the milk, tempting me with its sweet goodness.

No, no chocolate.

My willpower failed, and I measured out a teaspoon of the goopy stuff into my glass. It wouldn't be strong chocolate milk but it was better than none.

I deserve it, I told myself, as I inhaled the rich scent.

Sitting on the counter, I crossed my ankles and sipped. Come on, tryptophan. No go. The sugar was strong in my system.

I set a frying pan out and tossed on several slices of maple bacon. I could eat it raw, but I wanted to feel as human as possible.

The sizzling hot meat got transferred to a paper towel to soak off some of the grease. The grease in the frying pan got dumped into a plastic coffee can we kept in the fridge door which Percy made dog cookies with, as all her treats, for people and animals, were made from scratch. I've never even seen her buy a doughnut.

An egg went into the pan next, and some bread into the toaster. My yummy breakfast disappeared with a few big bites, burning my tongue in the process.

I hand-washed the remaining dishes from the night before, swept and mopped the floor, and organized the fridge. Not stopping there, I scrubbed down the salon floors, mirrors, counters, and cleaned everybody's combs.

Needing to burn off more energy, I wandered to the gym. Most of the equipment belonged to Percy and me, except for one treadmill that belonged to Lacey. There were three, all in a row in front of a big mirror. Why Percy believed mirrors were good for workouts, I'll never know. We liked to run outside whenever possible, but in the winter, when the woods have three feet of snow, it's more convenient to use treadmills. We can't go to a public gym or run on the roads because, you know, we're just a wee bit fast. All right, that's a massive understatement. Lacey could run from border to border of the state in just a couple hours. It takes several hours to do it by car. I can run it in about a day on two legs. In wolf form, it's half. Not a bad deal.

I completed some warm-up exercises with the previous night's band practice turned up on my iPod. Jumping rope brought my heart rate up before going to town on the rowing machine. Sweat beaded on my forehead, and I yanked off my sweatshirt. My tank top smelled from the bar, and my fuzzy pj bottoms were a sight to see, but I had no one I cared to impress.

I pushed my way through a rather intense workout, and it felt wonderful. I was cooling off when Lacey-Marie entered, sporting blinding pink Lycra shorts and a black sports bra.

"How long have you been up?" she asked, beginning her own routine.

"A while." I took myself down to the mat to stretch back out as my muscles cooled.

"You're crazy. You know that, right?"

"Takes one to know one." I smirked up at her.

"True, but you take the cake. What time is the pack making their appearance?" She worked her way through a sun salutation.

"The alpha didn't say, but I think it will just be one wolf, not the whole pack." I wiped my face and neck with a towel and threw it down the laundry shoot. I can honestly say, I've never seen the laundry room. It was one of the many perks of residing in a living house. Clean laundry usually appeared in a pile in the middle of my room around the middle of the day. If only it did the folding.

"Huh." She moved into cobra pose with a fluid grace. "I wonder why now? They neglect you then, 'Oh, we love you. Move back with us?' It's such a weird situation."

"You'll get no argument from me. I'm gonna go take a shower. See you later!" I took my hair down from the messy bun it'd spent all morning in and shook it loose.

"Oh, god, that's just scary," Lacey commented just as I got to the door.

I turned and stuck out my tongue. "At least I'm naturally hot. You have to try. Let me emphasize: *try*."

"Bitch." She smiled up at me from downward dog.

"Psycho."

"Don't let the door hit you in that Texas-sized ass on the way out!"

I didn't. And my rear is not Texas-sized. It's just in existence, unlike Lacey's. I didn't bother with a comeback. I wanted that shower sooner, rather than later.

The scalding hot water, sluicing sweat and the bar smell from my skin, felt even more wonderful than the workout. I think getting good and yucky makes me appreciate bathing all the more. Nothing makes me enjoy a good, long bath like shifting, though.

I dried off and got dressed with regrets. I could have spent all day in that shower.

Percy's name flashed across my cell's screen.

To answer or not... I answered. "Yeah?"

"Hey, Gretch. You've got a visitor downstairs."

"Wolf?" Who else would it be? My heart rate picked up slightly as my inner wolf woke up.

"Scott."

Crap. "I'll be right down."

Scott could not be there when the wolf showed up.

I threw my hair up and yanked an elastic around it as I booked it down the stairs.

"Morning, beautiful." Scott smiled crookedly at me from his spot on the couch in the waiting area.

"Morning. What are you doing here?" I asked, twirling the elastic around one more time.

"It's nice to see you too." He sat forward and lost the smile.

"Yeah, yeah. What do you want?"

"You've got my car keys. Austin drove me here."

I glanced down at his clothes. Yep, the same tee and jeans combo as the night before, accompanied by the smell of beer and sweat.

"Oops. Follow me upstairs. I think they're still in my pocket." It may have been a mistake to take him up to my room, but I didn't want to leave him waiting around in the empty salon either.

He ran up the stairs behind me and caught up to my side as we reached the hallway.

"So this is the Lady's Secret Sanctum," He joked.

"Not even close. You're not allowed there."

"Never?" He stuck out his lower lip absurdly.

"Never." Thing is, we actually have one in the attic. All the fae junk, spell books, herbs hanging from the ceiling, were all reasons not to invite outsiders up.

"I'll have to settle for your bedroom then." He dashed in front of me so he was walking backward down the hall.

"The doorway of my bedroom. You're not getting any further than that." I shoved my door open, wishing I'd cleaned. There were clothes all over the place, and my bed was unmade. My bathroom and dressing room doors were open and viewable from the doorway.

"Wow, Gretch."

I turned and glared at him.

"This place is enormous."

He'd been kept in the downstairs up until then. Maybe I should have kept it that way. Too late now.

"You have no idea. Percy's kinda well off."

"You guys can't be making money like this off the salon." He eyed my heavy four-post bed.

"Percy's husband is loaded, and I'm good at investing." It was a half truth at best.

"I should have you invest for me." He paused as my words sank in. "Wait a sec, Percy's married? How come I've never met her husband?"

"He doesn't exactly live around here." Nowhere near.

"Where does he live?"

I tried to throw him off. "What is this? 20 questions?" It didn't work.

"Sorry. But where does he live?"

"Greece."

"What the hell is Percy doing in Maine?" Scott's jaw dropped.

"She lives with him over the winter."

"I thought she went to Florida."

"It's a long story that I will never tell you."

"Never?"

"Absolutely never. Not a chance." I dug through my clothes and came up with the jeans I had worn to practice. "Tada!" I triumphantly produced the keys from my back pocket. Now he could go away.

"Thanks." He took them from me. Then he took my hand.

I pulled away. "No."

"I didn't ask you anything," Scott protested, managing to look hurt.

"Yeah, you were going to, and 'no' is an appropriate answer to just about any question you might ask." I pushed him out of my room and back down the hall with an outstretched hand. Thankfully, the house had behaved, and everything remained as we left it.

"You're a cruel woman. I'm not giving up." He followed me down the stairs.

I felt a change of subject was in order. "How are you feeling?"

"Fine. Who's that guy?"

Double crap. Quinty, or whatever the heck that guy's name was, was sitting in the waiting area.

"Do you want some breakfast or anything? I'm sure Percy can hook you up. Or are you in a hurry to leave?" I brainstormed ways to get Scott out of the same room as the other werewolf.

"I'm fine. No hurry. I don't have to work today. I was sorta hoping we could hang out."

Wolf boy stood up from the couch when he noticed me. "Gretchen, I'm here to formally invite you to the pack hunt tonight. We'll be picking you up at seven p.m. The quarry will be moose."

"And you are?" Scott bristled at the other man, his testosterone scenting the air.

Not good.

"Quintavious. I'm Gretchen's brother." His posture was tense, his hands tucked behind his back, elbows bent, making him look larger than he was.

Scott looked to me for confirmation.

"I was... adopted." I was a terrible liar. Hopefully he didn't notice.

"Scott." He held out his hand.

"He's the bassist for the band I play in," I filled in quickly.

"Pleasure," Quintavious accepted the gesture, shaking his hand firmly.

Scott quickly took his hand back and shoved it in his pocket. "Is all mine."

"Tonight, then?" Quintavious asked me, without turning from Scott.

"Yeah, fine. I'll be here." Get out, please. Just leave.

He fulfilled my silent pleas and walked briskly out the front door.

"You're moose hunting? At night?"

"Yeah. Family bonding and all that." I watched Quintavious climb into his car and drive away, then turned back to face Scott.

"I didn't know you hunted. Isn't it illegal to hunt after dark? You know it's not moose season right?"

And for another lie. "It's on private property, and we'll only track it." It would be in unpopulated woods in northern Maine.

"Huh. So what are you doing today?"

"Shopping with Percy." I bluffed and bluffed some more.

Lucky for me, Percy came through the door just then.

"Gretchen, I want to get going soon so we can beat the crowds. We need to re-stock some things before the shipment comes in." She sashayed up to us, becoming my hero. We got shipments direct from warehouses, but sometimes we went through stuff faster than we could get it in.

"Sure." I breathed an internal sigh of relief at her timing.

Scott slumped with what I could only imagine was disappointment.

"Some other time?" I suggested weakly.

"Yeah, sure. Whatever." He squared his shoulders. "Later."

"Yeah, bye."

I watched as he stalked towards Austin's car. I felt terrible lying to his face, but he could never know. None of my boys could ever know.

I turned to Percy. "Are we actually going to go shopping?"

"Sure, why not? I think you need some girl time."

If only to cancel out my lies. "I do, thanks. Let me throw on some shoes, and I'll be right down. Is Lacey coming?"

"Am I coming where?" Lacey asked, appearing from out back with a towel draped across her shoulders, despite lacking the ability to sweat.

"Shopping," I supplied.

"Are you leaving right now?" she asked, running her fingers through her loose hair.

"Pretty much," Percy answered.

"Then no. Besides, it's a nice sunny day, and I'm not up to dodging through the shadows."

I trailed her up the stairs, then parted ways at her door.

The drive to Brewer was a quiet one. I needed to think before talking, and Percy respected that fact.

We got to Salon Centric, our preferred supply store, quicker than usual. The traffic was pretty non-existent for a Sunday morning. We split up and loaded up hand baskets with the supplies we were lacking. I lingered in front of a display of new colors and splayed some swatches against my skin. Percy joined me.

"What do you think? Am I a redhead underneath it

all?" I fanned the swatch up by my eyes.

"Shit, Gretch!" Percy's pitch edged on shriek.

"What, is it really that terrible?" I knew it had to be bad if perfect Percy was swearing.

"It's terrible, but that's not what I mean. You forgot your contacts. Hold still just a tic." Percy placed a hand over my eyes and squeezed shut her own.

The scent of her magic headed straight up my sinuses, like fizz from a soda. Percy was glamouring me. Too bad it hadn't happened before Scott had shown up. The fact he hadn't mentioned them meant absolutely nothing. He might think of it later.

I opened my eyes and blinked a few times to get used to the illusion. A little bit of glare flitted around the edges, like seeing through useless dollar store glasses.

"Thanks," I said, still blinking.

"No problem. Shall we check out?" Percy lifted her filled basket.

"But what about the red?" I was feeling up for something crazy.

"Maybe some chunky streaks. We'll discuss it with Lacey when we get home."

"She'll try to talk me into pink instead." I wrinkled my nose at the thought.

"Probably."

We headed for the front counter, paying for everything with the debit card attached to our business account.

We each lugged armfuls of bags out to the car and continued on towards the mall in Bangor. The mall, unlike the roads, was packed. And I had to pee.

"I'll meet you in front of Bath and Body. I've gotta hunt down a restroom." I took off, my purse bouncing against my back.

The good thing, and perhaps bad thing, about having a good doggy nose is I can sniff out a bathroom in a matter of seconds and determine whether there's a line or not. There are so few perks, I was going to go with this as one of them. My second attempt turned out to be the golden ticket.

Percy was sampling body sprays when I located her again. I'm not a huge fan of spray scents. They really clouded up my olfactory receptors.

"Smell. Lavender!" She thrust her wrist at my unhappy nose.

"Great. You can make me some." I backed away and breathed deep with my nose in the crook of my arm to clear my sinuses.

"I can, but this is already made. This is a very busy time of year, getting ready for farmers markets."

"I'd rather have more lavender and less alcohol." I maintained my distance.

"Good point."

Of course it was a good point. Anything that Percy made was better than anything you could find in the store. She was really good with plants, and a chemistry wiz to boot. A useful gal to have around. You might even call her magical.

"Clothes next?" Percy asked.

"Clothes it is. I need to stop at Hot Topic."

It was Percy's turn to wrinkle her nose.

"I'll go by myself. Meet you in an hour?" I knew Percy's aversion to everything goth.

"That sounds better. Do you have a watch?"

"I have my cell phone. See ya."

"Think happy thoughts, and don't eat any shoppers, no matter how obnoxious they are," she said, waving her fingers at me over her shoulder.

"Yes, Mommy," I said as I walked away.

I checked out some baggy black jeans, all chained and zippered up to wazoo. Thinking they'd be perfect for performances, I shuffled through the rack until I came up with a pair in my size. There was also a red and black corset-style halter top that got added to my pile. It wasn't something I would wear outside of performances. Or a brothel.

I tried them on together. Both pieces were eye-catching, but together they were a hot mess. I hemmed and hawed and put the pants back. I had plenty of black pants. The top would go well with my leather pants. And no, I don't care how sleazy that made me sound. Performance. It was all for the sake of performance.

I settled up and went wandering. It was the only thing I bought in the entire mall that day. I'm not much of a shopper.

Percy was, though, so I helped her carry her bags to the car.

"So, we haven't talked." Percy started the engine of her BMW.

"Nope, we haven't. I'm nervous, and I don't know what to do."

"About Scott or the wolves?" She tilted her head to one side in thought.

"Yes."

"It's quite the muddle you've found yourself in, but are you sure you're not encouraging Scott's attentions?" she asked.

"Maybe?"

"Gretchen." She gave me her stern mommy look, all furrowed brow and pursed lips.

"It's nothing I'm doing intentionally. The dude should be in mourning, so I've been trying to be a good friend. He perceives everything at a whole level I don't want to be on. I'm well aware that nothing could be allowed to happen between us." I'd never admit it out loud, but there was a time I'd been attracted to him when we first met. He's sweet, if a little pushy. My better sense, also known as my human side, squashed those thoughts flat. Too many deaths after attempted relationships littered my past.

"Good girl. But maybe you should back off a bit more. You don't want to put yourself in a compromising situation that will inevitably bring out the beast. You'll either get annoyed or you'll open yourself up. I know you're lonely."

"As always, you're right. This sucks." I slouched in my seat and crossed my arms.

"I know, honey. I'm sorry. And play the wolf thing one day at a time. You're smart. You're also extremely dominant, more so than any alpha I've ever met, be careful with your decision. You won't be able to change it."

We got back to the house and went about the rest of our day. I spent the afternoon pacing around outside, dreading the night. Too bad it wasn't as simple as saying no and walking away from the pack. I wanted a family and, yes, I was lonely. I didn't know them or what the whole pack thing was all about. I should have considered that when I consented to the change.

A long, shiny black limo showed up at seven on the dot. I took a couple of deep breaths and looked down at the jeans and tee outfit I'd been wearing all day. I was woefully underdressed for a limo. The driver got out and opened the back door for me, revealing the empty interior, which meant I was free to relax, or at least try, for the next hour.

That hour sped by at lightning pace.

The other wolves were waiting for me, all still in

their human forms.

"Welcome, Gretchen. I'm glad you could make it." Kaine greeted me with a nod.

As if I had any real choice. I nodded back but didn't say anything. The sooner I could be wolfy, the better.

"Let's change. We'll be heading north as a group. I'm the anchor hound. The first one to send out a howl gets to lead the rest of the hunt." Kaine pulled off his white t-shirt as he spoke and then went to work on the rest of his clothing.

All around me, people were discarding clothing in haphazard piles without a glance at any of their companions. I'm not used to changing in company. I turned my back on the rest of them and began peeling off my clothes, leaving them in a neat pile on top of my sneakers, hoping I wouldn't come back to a tick infestation.

Deep breaths, relax, change. It came slowly at first. My joints creaking then snapping. I sucked in air against the intense pain that accompanied a change so soon after a new moon. I've been told the change is less painful for non-dominant wolves. Must be nice. My body was on fire like I'd been smashed between two colliding semi trucks. Adrenaline poured through me as the change rapidly sped up, dulling the pain ever so slightly.

I dropped to all fours and resisted the urge to scratch myself as fur spurted from every pore on my body. Where does the extra mass come from? My best guess is magic. I packed on bulging muscle until I hit the grand total of 400 pounds. I'm a big puppy.

I was bigger than Kaine, I was satisfied to note, and he was huge. If he had any doubts about me being a dominant before, he couldn't deny it now. We both came from a time and place where women were used and not heard. I could understand his unwillingness to adjust, but some things you just have to accept.

As soon as it was over, I took off, tearing up the ground as I raced forward. I love running like that. I love being like that, when I'm in control.

The others were already ahead of me, so I surged forward to join the group.

It didn't take us long to scent a trail. Moose leave an obvious trail for anyone to follow. Dirk sent up the howl, and we followed him through a stream and up a steep hill, following a trail that was about two hours old, and tangled.

There were plenty of rabbit trails to follow, but our course was set. We bunched in a tight group until the scent grew strong. Wolves work well in pack form, and that's true even if the wolves are of the were variety. We fanned out, surrounding our prey. It didn't even smell us coming. The air was stifled by the dense woods, but we kept downwind anyhow, slowing to a crawl.

I slithered along on my belly, ears flat to my skull and my tail resisting the urge to wave. It wasn't like the moose would be able to pick ears out of the darkness, but still.

Kisa, Quintavious, and I sprang and chased the moose towards Kaine, Jacque, and Dirk who waited in a semi circle. That moose didn't stand a chance. We all leapt at it at once, Dirk going in for the kill.

Moose are hard critters to take down. They fight to the very end, and they can be lethal. This was a bull moose, and he bellowed for all he was worth, twisting and turning this way and that, frantically trying to escape. He sent Quinty flying through the air and into a tree, knocking him breathless.

I thrust against the hard packed ground and propelled myself up onto his back, sinking my fangs into the tough hide of his neck, snapping his spine. He went down hard, and we didn't waste any time getting at all the best pieces.

It's disgusting to think about killing anything. Especially when you're standing under a hot spray of water, washing dried blood out of your hair and scrubbing it out from under your fingernails.

The hot taste of blood and raw meat flavored my breath, and I brushed and flossed several times, even going so far as to gargle a couple capfuls of hated mouthwash. All the raw flesh that's so great when you're a wolf is not so awesome when you change back.

Scrub, scrub, scrub. Lavender body wash works wonders. And candles and scented oil. And boy was I tired.

I dragged my heavy limbs into my most comfortable worn-out pajamas, not bothering to tie the bottoms, then spritzed some leave-in conditioner on my damp hair before I flopped down on my bed and pulled an afghan over me. I was too tired to crawl under the covers, even if they were already pulled down.

I should start making my bed, I decided as I started drifting off towards sleep. And I need to make my own tea, and Zzzzz, a bit of drool, dead to the world.

Chapter II:
Freak Out

My client was a cute little girl who was badly in need of a trim and a good conditioner.

"But conditioner makes her hair tangly," her mother argued.

Tangly? Really? "A thick moisturizing one will help these tangles slide right out," I promised, fingering my way through a particularly tough snarl.

"The heavy ones make her hair greasy." Her mother's brows furrowed.

"Use about a nickel-sized dollop, and emulsify it in your hands first," I demonstrated by rubbing my hands together. "Then apply at the very ends. That's where it's going to do the most good. Then work it up to about mid-shaft." I pointed. "Any further than that, it may very well make her hair seem greasy."

"Really? I never knew that!" Her face brightened, and she reached out to stroke her daughter's long, deep brown strands.

I hazarded a guess that she was applying it right to her scalp, like shampoo, globing it around before rinsing.

"Let me get you set up with a good one. Do you have a leave-in detangler at home?" I asked.

"I do."

"Good. Spray her down with that as soon as she

2

gets out of the tub. Then comb it out with a wide-toothed comb, starting at the ends. I bet you'll see an improvement."

I dried the little girl's hair, then led them over to the display of products right next to my station. They settled up and left. Hopefully they'd follow my instructions and weren't just doing the smile and nod routine. Sometimes I wonder.

I called on Greg next, a man I'd never seen before, in his early forties, balding, slightly overweight, and reeking of fast food. I wasn't going to judge his diet choices, but the smell does linger.

Toni emerged from her hidey-hole to wait for her next client. She was already getting steady business, but she often played desk jockey for the fun of it. Which was fine by me. It meant she could answer the ever-ringing phone.

Greg lumbered over to me with a scowl on his face.

Great, someone who I wasn't going to be able to make happy no matter how spectacular his cut turned out.

"You're cutting my hair?" he questioned with a sneer.

Wow, mister, let it all hang out. "Yes, sir, I am." I pasted a smile on my face and a happy note in my voice, trying to ignore the inner one that was muttering: kill it, kill it, kill it.

"I want someone else." He was studying me from head to toe, his lip curling at the sight of me.

"All right, sir," I backed away a step and turned to the side, trying to look less intimidating. "But it's going to be an hour or so before either one of the other girls has an opening."

"What about the one behind the counter?"

"That's our manicurist. She only does nails." I

narrowed my eyes and tried to avoid clenching my fists.

"I know what a manicurist is. Don't talk to me like I'm the stupid one. Well, I need a cut, so I guess you'll have to do."

What a jerk. I forced my curled hands to relax.

"Right this way." I led him to my station

He stepped on the footrest, flipping the chair up, which caused him to lose his balance. I heard him mutter something that sounded distinctly inappropriate for our family-friendly salon as I pushed the back of the chair down, setting it back onto the floor. He sat down with a thump.

"Just clean it up. I don't want to have to get this fixed," he said.

"Excuse me?" I tried to keep the bite out of my voice.

"I guess it doesn't take much to do hair. Would they not let you into a real school?"

My fists tightened, and I felt the hairs on the back of my neck hackle.

"It's gotta be hard for a black woman to get into an actual college."

My breath quickened, and my pulse raced. I grabbed the back of the styling chair, sinking my claws into the dense material with a pop.

"Of course, what else is someone like you gonna do in Maine?"

"Someone. Like. Me." I spat the words out slowly, a bit muffled as my teeth started to grow. My contacts split, revealing bits of brilliant amber between brown tatters.

He watched me in the mirror, his eyes growing wide. His brain wouldn't acknowledge what he was witnessing, but the smell of his fear fueled the beast I was trying to keep leashed.

"Get out of my chair. Don't ever come back." I growled low and stepped away from the chair.

My bones snapped loudly enough for Toni's head to whip in my direction. I took a deep breath and grabbed my mug as my client stood.

"I'll be right back, ladies. Make sure that man makes it out of here." Safely, just in case.

"Of course," Percy said as I passed by her, her posture more relaxed than she smelled.

I fled up to my room, slamming and locking the door. I stalked to my closet and hid inside without turning on the light. I curled up into the littlest ball I could manage and focused on being a person, willing myself to breath slow.

I'd almost changed in front of Toni. She heard my bones snap. Hopefully Percy could give her a good enough explanation, and I wouldn't have to say anything. I didn't think the regular 'seizure' excuse would cut it this time.

I rocked back and forth as my bones snapped down to normal size, my pulse steadying. My mouth began to water profusely, and I dashed for the bathroom, making it just in time to reverently worship the porcelain goddess. It wasn't out of the norm for me to be sick after a sudden change. I brushed my teeth, popped a mint from the ancient tin on my bed stand, and grabbed my mug and sipped, slowly dissolving the mint and checking the clock to see how long I could pansy around before my next appointment.

15 minutes. I'd scheduled Greg a half-hour block, not having worked with him before and therefore not knowing how picky he would be.

If things escalated any more, I might just lose it and eat someone right in the salon. That would suck.

I'd have to leave and change my identity. Again.

Or I could join the pack, the more appealing choice. The whole pack thing was sounding better and better, except for the whole ownership thing. They'd watch my every move, schedule my days, and tell me who I could or could not be friends with. Never mind, the pack is a bad idea. Losing it is a bad idea.

Curling up on top of the covers, I melted. I'd actually made good on the promise to myself and made my bed for once.

I successfully kept track of time, making it down the stairs and proceeding through my next cut without a hitch. In fact, Toni never said a word to me. I don't know if that was a good thing or a bad thing. I'd have to wait and see.

Percy looked me over periodically. If she was checking for fur, she would be satisfied that I was staying fuzz free.

During a small lull an hour later, Lacey pulled me outside while she took her smoke break next to the kitchen garden.

"So what happened?" she asked as she lit up.

I watched as her cheeks sucked in with her first pull. She held her breath in for a minute, then expelled two streams of smoke from her nostrils.

I stepped away from her cloud. "Are you aware that, first off, I'm black and therefore a complete moron? I'm too incompetent to do anything but hair? And I have no right to live in Maine?"

"What an idiot," Lacey said, raising a blond eyebrow.

"True words. Besides, how is that my defining characteristic?" I looked down at myself. My coloring and build didn't point a finger at any one point of my heritage.

"I heard the snapping." She blew out another stream of smoke.

"Yeah, so did Toni." I waved a hand through the smoke. I hated how smoke clouded everything, but I put up with it to be outside for a few precious moments.

"Huh. She hasn't said anything." She flicked some ashes, sending them scattering in the slight breeze.

"Percy hasn't talked to her?" I asked, wondering what she possibly could have said.

"Not that I've noticed."

"Huh."

She took a few more drags from her cigarette, then let it dangle from her fingers for a bit. "Well, at least you didn't go furry."

"No fur, but there were fangs and eyes."

"Really? I didn't catch a scent off you." She sniffed at me, like she was going to find it.

"Yeah. And the guy saw it all in the mirror. Hopefully it just scared the crap out of him, and he won't tell anyone."

"Who'd believe him. We're the stuff of myth and legend, remember?" She struck a pose with her arms outstretched and one foot pointed.

"Let's hope we stay that way."

"It would be so much easier if we didn't have to." Lacey pulled her arm away from a sunny spot as the tip of her elbow glowed cherry red. As soon as it was back in the shade once more, the intense burn faded and returned to its normal pallor, glazed over with spray tan.

We stood in the shadow cast by the house, but the sun was traveling in our direction. I switched spots with her, holding my breath as I made my way through her smoke.

"They were my third pair of contacts this month."

"I think you can afford it." Lacey's tone changed from sympathetic to admonishing.

I could. I didn't like to talk about money with Lacey, or really anyone besides Percy.

I wondered how the pack made their money. If it was just old investment money or if any of them actually worked. I think I'd go crazy without some sort of job.

Lacey took one last hit off her cancer stick, then crushed it beneath the toe of one of her purple suede pumps.

"Are those new?" I hadn't seen them before, and I didn't think she'd been shopping recently.

"Yeah, you like?" Lacey modeled them with a twist of her leg.

"They're very purple."

"You don't like." She pouted.

"Not really. Not my style, I guess."

She shrugged and headed for the door.

Back to work then. Despite the unpleasant aroma of cigarettes permeating the area, I was reluctant to go in.

Toni was back in her booth, so I stopped in to say hello and test the waters.

"How's it going?"

She was in between clients and cleaning her tools. "Great! I think I'll have some repeats." I thought she was a little louder than usual.

"Been handing out business cards?" I asked, leaning against the doorway.

"Yeah, and promising free manicures when I get three new clients who mention their name. I've been writing them all down so I could keep track." She pulled out a spiral bound notebook and turned open the cover. There were neat columns of names, some with check marks already beside them.

"Good idea. People can't resist a freebie."

"Neither can I. This is so much fun! I'm getting to be so much more creative than I was at the last place I worked." She smiled and put the notebook away.

"Good." I stood there for a moment, feeling a bit silly. "So, ah, I'll see you later?"

"Yup!"

Well, she was either clueless, had a very selective memory, or she was really good at hiding what she felt. I hoped it was the first option, which would be the safest for me.

Percy met me at the door with an odd look on her face. "Gretch, you've got a walk-in requesting you." She didn't elaborate, just went back to work.

I walked out to the waiting area and was surprised to see Doug sitting on the couch, flipping through a magazine. He was dressed like a normal guy in track pants, t-shirt, and sneakers, a far cry from the barbarian monster he had portrayed during the dinner. Before our formal introduction anyhow. He stood when he saw me, and I noted we were about the same height.

"Ah, come on over, Doug." I pointed over at my station, then headed there myself.

He set his magazine down and strode over with steady, even steps.

I got out a cape and clasped it around his neck.

"So, what did you have in mind?" I asked, wondering where to start. Did he cut his facial hair? Or was I supposed to trim that up too? It was kind of awkward. Was there a politically correct way to ask?

"Just a trim. Ulysses wants me to keep it shaggy looking for the show."

Wow, a full sentence. "All right" I combed through

162

the hair that was within the normal boundaries and studied the ends. "How does an inch sound?"

"Fine." He watched my every move in the mirror. He seemed . . . curious.

I spritzed him down with a spray bottle. I wouldn't touch the face fluff unless he asked me to. It looked like he had it pretty well taken care of. This was my first close and personal look at him. I hadn't ever met someone with hypertrichosis before, and I found it fascinating.

"So how's the show doing?" I asked in a desperate attempt to make conversation.

"Fine."

Conversation crashed and burned.

"How long have you been with them?" I tried again as I completed the back guide and started trimming his layers in relation to what I'd taken off the bottom.

"A few years."

Apparently, I wasn't going to get much out of him. "Do you like it?"

"It's all right." He sat perfectly still as I worked.

Really now. He hadn't looked too thrilled to be there.

"I can't really do anything else," he added.

Ah, volunteered information. I couldn't think of anything to say in response to that.

"So," I scrambled for another question, "What do you do for fun?"

"I get my hair cut," he replied immediately.

Low and behold, the man could make jokes. I smiled at him in the mirror.

"Uh, I like learning new things. School and me weren't friends when I was the appropriate age, but now I'll pick up at-home courses, or take online classes. How about you?" he asked.

"Well, I love running. I used to do kickboxing, and I'm in a band." I picked the first things that came to mind.

"Use to do kickboxing? Why did you stop?" he was watching me carefully in the mirror, as I moved to the sides of his head.

"Well, it's considered bad manners to knock the wind out of your instructor with a punching bag. I spar with friends occasionally, but I don't play well with others, so a class setting really isn't for me."

"What do you play?"

My, my, what a curious boy."Violin."

"Oh."

I didn't know what he had expected, but it wasn't that. He didn't ask any more questions about the music. I'm pretty sure he assumed I played classical, which I do. It's classical with distortion.

He didn't ask any more questions. I finished up the cut in silence, combing it this way and that looking for imperfections. When I was satisfied, I took my hands off him and stood back.

"Check that out, and tell me what you think."

He turned his head a little to the left, then to the right. "Looks good to me."

"Great." I took his cape off and blew the loose hair off with my blow dryer. "I'm just going to clean up, and I'll meet you up front."

He nodded.

I swept up my mess, then cashed him out, expecting him to leave.

But he didn't. Instead, he wandered around our little museum, reading every tag, every plaque, and inspecting every detail.

I kept an eye on him as I worked. Why wasn't he leaving?

When I finally got a moment, I made my way out back, closing the door between the salon and the rest of the house firmly, then heading for the library.

I heard the door open and shut behind me, and I whirled around, snarling, about scaring the pee out of Doug.

"Whoa, I just wanted to ask you some questions." He held up his hands palm out, keeping me at bay.

"Sorry, I don't have time." I turned again, continuing my trek to the library.

The sound of his footsteps following me set me further on edge. "Seriously, Doug, I'm busy. I've got a lot going on right now, and I just don't have time to be a curiosity."

"Sorry," he said quietly, standing his ground.

"Leave before I make you leave." I took a step towards him, trying to scare him again. I drew my wolf on around me and wore her like a mantle.

"I need your help," he confessed, his hands still held steady up in front of him.

"Gretchen is closed for business. Is there anything I can help you with?" Hades emerged from the library, bearing a tray of empty tea things.

"I doubt it," said Doug. "Unless you're the same as her."

"We have certain... similarities."

"But you're not a werewolf," Doug persisted, letting his hands fall back to his sides.

"No, I'm not. I'm Hades. Nice to meet you." He held out a hand, demanding return.

Doug shook it.

"He's clean. Not a drop of blood on him." Hades turned to me and nodded his approval.

"Huh?" He'd lost me, I didn't have a clue what he was talking about.

"He's not your killer. He's very human and has definitely never taken a life," Hades clarified.

"How can you tell that?" asked Doug.

"He's the god of the dead. I think he can sense stuff like that," I said, trying to hold back a smirk.

"Like from the Greek myths?" He finally caught on.

"Exactly from the myths. He's the one and only Hades. Hades, this is Doug the circus freak." I made the introductions and left them discussing in the hall, giving me the opportunity to slip past them and get back to work.

The remainder of the day was going to be tense, knowing that Doug was still in the house, still waiting to ask questions that I definitely did not want to answer. I might have butted my way into his life, but did he really have to retaliate? I was under the impression that he'd had enough of me when he slammed his door in my face. Hey, what do I know?

When I got back into the salon, everyone was gathered around the woman in Lacey's chair. She hadn't even started the cut yet, and their faces were all serious.

Hopefully Lacey hadn't gotten a jerk too. She wouldn't sprout fur or anything, but she could easily break her neck.

"What's going on?" I asked, joining them.

"More bad news, that's what," said Lacey, with a scowl on her face and her arms crossed tightly over her chest.

Was this something I really wanted to know? Curiosity got the better of me. "What?" I stood with my own arms crossed and studied the petite brunette in the hot seat.

"My best friend's sister was murdered last night."

Was it someone I was supposed to know?

"She was a hairdresser," Percy filled me in quietly.

I looked from Percy to the client. I wanted details.

"It sounds like something from a horror movie." The client spoke in a hushed, frightened voice.

I waited as patiently as I could force myself to be, shifting my weight from leg to leg.

"Her fiancé found her. He'd only taken a 10 minute shower, but when he got back she was in bed, dead."

"How?" I asked.

"Gretch, don't be morbid." Percy placed and an admonishing hand on my arm.

"No, it's all right. I didn't really know her. Her jugular was cut on one side. The killer managed to drain all her blood and not spill a drop. My friend said the cops don't have a clue how it could have happened so fast. There was no mess, no sign of a struggle. Her fiancé said he never heard a thing."

Either he was lying, or we could all be in trouble.

"That sounds bad." I didn't know what else to say. We hadn't heard anything the morning Penny's body showed up in the salon either.

We appeared to have a serial killer on our hands. We'd be okay, being a bit better with defensive techniques than your average cosmetologist. We knew a lot of girls in the area through classes and such. They were competition, but we didn't wish harm on them, by any means.

"Percy, do you think it would be acceptable for me to make some phone calls?" I would make one or two calls anyway, but I'd limit it to just that if she wanted me to.

"Yes, I think you should. Whether or not the cops wanted this public, girls have a right to know and to protect themselves. Do it."

I didn't have to be told twice. "What's her name, and where did she work?"

"Her name was Heather McKay," said Lacey's client.

"She's local. Bangor, right?" I'd heard her name mentioned by some clients before. In fact, the people who didn't go to us generally went to her. She was real competition.

I booked my patootie over to the front desk and plopped it down on the stool by the phone. We have an address book specifically for the numbers of other salons. I pulled it out and looked up Amanda's number first.

"Good afternoon, Babe's Salon, Amanda speaking." Her voice crackled over the line.

"Hey, it's Gretchen."

"What's up?"

"What's down," I joked weakly. " Another dead hairdresser. Heather McKay from Bangor."

"The name sounds familiar. Was it on the news?" Amanda asked.

"Not yet. We got a woman who's best friend was McKay's sister."

"Really? Did you get the details?"

"Oh, yeah." I filled her in on everything we'd just been told.

"Shit."

"Yeah."

"This is scary stuff. Does anyone else know?"

"I have no idea, but you've got a directory, right?" I flipped mine to the middle.

"Yeah."

"If you take the second half, I'll take the first. We've got to start being careful, locking doors and all that."

"No kidding. Hey, I've gotta get going. Work to do. Call me later?"

"Absolutely. Be careful," I warned her.

"I will, you too."

"Yeah, bye."

"Bye." She settled the phone down, leaving me with a dial tone.

I flipped my directory to the beginning and worked my way down the page. Some places had already heard. Others hadn't and were obviously frightened to hear. There was no proof that it was by the same person. But four hairdressers in less than a month? Most disgruntled clients just never return and tell all their friends about it, not kill their stylist.

I paused to do a haircut, then got back to the important work. We didn't talk about it with our clients unless they'd already heard about it. Dead hairdressers, especially locally, is bad for business. It creeps people out, and it should.

I reached the end of my half around dinner time.

Percy had a big, very rare steak waiting for me. Absolute heaven in the first bite.

"Persephone, you are the best goddess," I muttered around the juicy mouthful.

"You're not so bad yourself." She smiled over at me from her place by the stove.

"Yeah, but I can't cook." I cut another bite and savored it.

She piled stuffing on my plate.

"I love you."

Percy laughed at that. "Well that's good."

Lacey rolled her eyes from her perch on the counter. "You two are so human."

"And that's bad because…?" I trailed off, waiting for her to fill in the blank.

"It's not bad. You're just weird."

"Well, thanks."

"You're welcome."

She was just cranky because all she could eat or drink was blood. I could smell cayenne pepper and cumin. Apparently it was fiesta night in her mug.

"Bloody good fun," I muttered.

"You're a brat," Lacey spat at me.

"Yeah, I'm okay with that." I finished my steak and got up to help Percy with the dishes, drying them and putting the dinnerware in the rack away as we had yet to invest in a dishwasher.

I settled into bed that night with a lot to mull over. All in all, things had added up to a horrible day. Could it get worse? I had no doubt. This was only starting, the killings. My wolf was raring to go.

Chapter 12:
The Replacement

Tuesday brought about another interview day. After the manicurist interviews, I wasn't looking forward to it. We were going to choose a stylist to take Penny's old booth.

We'd repainted the vanity and mirror frame to help cut back on the feel that it belonged to Penny. I became the one responsible for putting it back together. The mirror was large and unwieldy, but I managed to hang it straight on the first try. Lacey muscled the vanity into place when she first came out. I just had to put the drawers back. Percy had lined the three drawers with flowery contact paper, which replaced the white-and-black polka dots from before.

On a whim, I decided to clean out my own station. My drawers were getting hairy, and my brushes were in need of cleaning, so I sat on the floor to do just that. I retrieved a comb and scrubbed it back and forth over the brush bristles, loosening the hair and bringing it up to the tips and edges. I grabbed off the loose bits, then used a razor to cut through the rest of the tangled mess, repeating the process for every brush.

All my brushes, combs, and clips were red because

having signature colors is the easiest way to tell our stuff apart. Lacey-Marie, of course, had pink tools, while Percy had purple, to match her eyes, I'd guess. I'd gone so far as to get all my hot tools, blow dryer, and clippers in red. Lacey-Marie's were pink, but Percy had a mishmash of colors.

I filled a Tupperware container with hot water and some concentrated barbicide solution to soak my clips. After a moment's thought, I dumped in my clipper guards and all my combs in with them, glancing at the clock to note the time. I had to keep careful track because if I didn't, the solution would eventually start eating away at the plastic.

My barbicide container was a bit crusty, so into the sink it went with the hottest water the tap could spew out. It would still need elbow grease to scrub, as loose flakes settled and stuck to the bottom instead of being soaked up by the water. Little bits of hair came with it as I scrubbed. After refilling it with powdered barbicide and more water, I set it back on my vanity along with my shears and razor to occupy their usual space at the center. Those, I meticulously cleaned every day.

Our first interview was due as soon as the doors opened. The plan was to get them all done by lunch, debate about which one to choose during our break, then call the winner to start on a trial basis for the afternoon. We only had two applicants, which we made sure to receive resumes and portfolios from ahead of time.

Apparently, the whole serial killer theory had made it around, even through the schools. These would be the women who really needed a job, who really wanted the job. The economy being what it was, a good job was hard to find. Working for us would be a very good job. Not only would they be doing hair, but they would be performing receptionist duties as well. We all did a little bit, but we were simply too busy to keep leaving our clients to answer phones. Hiring another girl would mean we would get to expand into being an actual day spa, which would mean more business and broader clientele. I was kind of excited.

My last-ditch cleaning effort was for my chair. Hair really does get everywhere. I sprayed it thoroughly with cleaner, wiped it down, pulled up the cushion, and wiped that down as well.

The whole salon was starting to gleam, and the three of us stood back to admire the effect.

"We should have done this whole cleaning thing a long time ago," Lacey admitted.

Normally, we were all talkative when we occupied the same room, but it was first thing in the morning, and moving furniture was serious work.

"I agree," said Percy. "Also, it will be nice to get some fresh blood in here."

"I'll third ya, Lace, and second Percy. I wish these interviews were over. I think I hate interviewing." I said.

"You're not kidding." Lacey wandered away to study the waiting area. "I want to redo this." She waved her hand at the whole set-up.

"Actually, that's a good idea. We should. I'm thinking new furniture, and repaint the coffee table," said Percy.

"Oh, yeah." I wandered over to the couch. "We should move the furniture so it's facing the museum instead of the front desk or us." I turned to face our little museum.

"We could put the TV here," I indicated the area closest to the museum, "and put everything else in a semicircle around it, and maybe we should close up the front desk so it's more of a booth than a table. You know, have a half door to get in and out by. Then we won't get kids sneaking over and messing with things quite so much."

"Yeah! I like that. Could we hire a receptionist?" Lacey bounced on her toes.

"Hold your horses on that one. I don't think we need to hire one full time. We're taking on this girl part time at first anyhow. If we notice that she is in dire need of an extra paycheck, we'll offer her reception work to bring up her time." Percy was one smart cookie. The idea at the moment was we all took blocks of time to answer the phone. Having the new girl doing it officially would be even better.

"That's a really good idea, Perce. But let's not offer it right up front. We want to make sure we hire someone who really really wants to be a cosmetologist and will only do receptionist stuff as a last resort. We don't want to give money to someone who only pretends to need it if there's someone else who really does," I pointed out.

Lacey-Marie nodded in agreement. "It's opening time, and I think our first interview is here."

"Go open the door then," I said, running back to rinse off my stuff, then dumped it all in no certain order in my drawers.

I jogged back to the waiting area and grabbed the résumés off the coffee table.

"Who's first?" I asked.

"Meredith Winders," Percy muttered to me as the aforementioned person walked through our front doors.

I glanced quickly over her credentials, then flipped through her stapled portfolio. I was ready.

She was young and had only been out of school for

a year. She was out of work at the moment, which meant she badly needed the job. She looked cute in knee high, low heeled boots, jeans, and peasant top. It wasn't exactly an interview outfit, but I suspected she hadn't had the money to go out and buy one.

"Why do you think we should give you this job?" Percy asked as the phone rang.

"I'll get it." I reluctantly left the interview in lieu of secretarial duties. We really did need a receptionist.

"Good morning, Olympian's Salon and Day Spa," I spoke into the receiver. "Gretchen speaking."

"Hi, I was wondering if you had any openings for next Thursday afternoon?"

"Do you have a preferred stylist?" I asked, with all our schedules spread out in front of me.

"No, I've never been there before."

"Okay, give me just a moment, and I'll see who's free."

I flipped through my own appointment book. It was full, just as I suspected. I grabbed the blank book that we'd purchased for the new girl.

"I'm putting you down for one o'clock, is that all right?"

"Two would be better."

"Two's fine as well. What's your name?" I waited, pen poised.

"Portia Hollidat."

I wrote the name down on the two o'clock spot. "And what are you looking to have done?"

"A cut and a wax."

"Perfect. Next Thursday at two." I noted down the service, balancing the phone between my ear and shoulder.

"Thank you."

"No problem."

"Bye," said Portia.

"Have a nice day." I hung the phone up and put the appointment books away and made it back for the end of the interview.

"Okay. We've got a little scenario for you," said Percy, pointing her pencil at me.

I stood up. I'd teased my curls, making them frizzy and puffy.

"Gretchen is a client. She wants to tame down her hair. She likes curls, but she's got more than she can manage. What do you recommend?" Percy set up the scenario, and I sat down. I was merely a visual aid, and I would be the model for both the interviews. Curly-haired people tended to be the ones stylists wanted to change the most and had the poorest suggestions for.

Meredith paused for a minute, studying me. "A perm on big rods and a deep conditioning treatment. I'd probably try to send her home with some moisturizing shampoo and conditioner, and a bottle of Biosilk."

Percy doodled and took notes. We wouldn't be critiquing their answers in front of them—we wanted to know what they would possibly do if we weren't around.

A client came in, and Lacey left to do a cut.

We formed our opinions almost right off, the questions being more of a formality, and Percy was taking down important observations for us to go over later so we wouldn't really miss anything.

We all took clients before the next interview. I'd loved to have seen them back-to-back for better comparison purposes. I wasn't super excited about Meredith as a stylist, but she seemed sweet, if a little too quiet.

Nicole, the second interview, read straight-up

attention seeker on first appearance. Spiked heels, clothes suctioned tight to her curves, low-cut shirt revealing cleavage popping nearly up to her chin. She would not have been out of place in the brothel I grew up in.

We went through several questions before Percy asked, "Why do you think you're right for the job?"

"I'm a hard worker. I can do any hours. I'm out of debt because I worked my way through school and paid for my car up front. I'm willing to learn whatever you need me to." Nicole ticked off each item on a manicured fingertip.

"Why this salon, in particular?"

"Well, you're hiring," Nicole's joke fell flat. At least, I think she was joking. "I think I'd get a lot of opportunities working with you. I think I could learn a lot from you. This salon has a reputation for holding on to its employees."

Yeah, and that might be because we all own the business.

"Uh huh, all right." Percy doodled.

She signaled me, and I played my part again.

"Gretchen wants a wash and wear look. She likes her curls, but she's finding them hard to manage. What would you recommend?"

Nicole studied my hair, tapping her tooth with an acrylic nail. "I think she should shorten it and lighten it up. The color's too dark. It makes her look too black— not that that's a bad thing," she stumbled, "but I think she'd look more exotic with light hair."

I snarled silently when Nicole looked to Percy for her approval. Percy scribbled around on her notepad, then glanced over at me. I lowered my lip.

Nicole turned to me. "No offense."

I hate when people say 'no offense.' It means that

whatever they were saying, they knew it was offensive. If you know what you're saying is offensive, find a diplomatic way to say it, don't say it, or don't preface it with 'no offense, but.' I was offended, and she couldn't afford to offend the people in charge of hiring.

Apparently, she didn't get the fact that she was being interviewed by all three of us, not just Percy. We weren't asking the questions, but our opinions each counted for a third of the vote.

I was unusually happy to take my next client, whom I was able to talk into scheduling an appointment for highlights. It was that time of year. I personally liked to lighten up for spring and summer, and darken up with warm tones for fall/winter.

As soon as we finished off that bout of clients, I flipped the open sign over and hurried to join the others in the kitchen.

"So," said Percy.

"That was... interesting." I hopped up onto the counter and leaned over to open the fridge.

"That's a word for it. And we only have to do it one more time." Lacey referred to the interviews for a possible masseuse and joined me on the counter.

"Thoughts, feelings?" Percy took a more adult position on a kitchen chair facing us.

"If we hire the second girl, I'll maul her." I wouldn't be able to help it. Any time spent with that girl would be hazardous for her health.

"Lacey?"

"I can't say I'm a fan," said Lacey.

How diplomatic of her.

"All right then, do we wait around for more applications, or do you think Meredith will fit?" Percy balled up Nicole's application, shot it at the trash, and missed.

"Well, as I have no magical superpower patience, I'm gonna go with Meredith just to spare us from another potential Nicole."

"I don't have anything special as far as patience goes," said Percy, scrunching her eyebrows together.

"Yeah, but you've had centuries to hone them," I pointed out.

"True."

I suddenly felt young, a rare occurrence.

"Now about Meredith, I'm all for giving her a shot," said Percy.

"I already said yes. And started the bunny trail." I popped a hot dog into my mouth and swallowed after a couple of chews. Bad doggy, I know.

"I guess I'm all right with her," Lacey relented.

"Good. I'll give her a call and also offer her the receptionist position. And Gretchen, eat some real food," Percy reprimanded.

"Yes, Mommy." I slid off the counter and perused the fridge face-on.

Bread, peanut butter, jelly. If no one else had been in the room, I would have just dipped the bread into the jars. Since I was not alone, I toasted my bread and spread everything neatly, like a civilized human being. Sticky and yummy. It's a good combination, almost like dessert. I shoved it down and cleaned up before returning to the salon.

Meredith was able to make it back a few minutes after we reopened for the afternoon.

The first client to come through the big double doors was Byron Ulm, one of Percy's regulars. He came in like clockwork every month. He was one of the good reasons to be a hairdresser. Lacey-Marie and I smelled him coming. Delicious. There was another smell with him. A woman. We'd thought Byron was a perpetual bachelor. We both rolled a lip, then gained control.

"I could eat him with a spoon," Lacey-Marie muttered so only us girls could hear. She'd made him a subtle offer before, which he'd graciously turned down.

"Well, I could bury her with a shovel," I muttered in response.

The woman with him was dressed for success in slacks, button up, and a blazer.

"Ladies, this is my sister, Marcy. She wanted to check you guys out. Do you have time for a walk in?"

"As a matter of fact, we do," said Percy. "Meredith, do you have an opening?"

Meredith took her cue that we weren't letting on that she was new.

"Absolutely! It's nice to meet you, Marcy, I'm Meredith." She greeted her potential client with a firm handshake.

"Nice to meet you too."

"What can I do for you today?" Meredith asked.

"Just a trim, please." She ran her fingers through her hair.

"Great. Let's get you a shampoo first, and we'll go from there." Meredith lead her to the shampoo area, conducting a short consultation as she went.

Byron followed Percy to the last station, leaving Lacey and me to watch him go until the door opened. It was Lacey's lucky day, in a sarcastic sense. Walter Hedigar was a fiftysomething truck driver with a thing for Lacey.

I smirked and left her to it. My smirk vanished as Scott walked through the front door.

"Got time?" he asked, leaning over the front counter.

Normally, I cut his hair at Austin's house with the

other guys.

"Sure, come on over." I led him to my station and motioned for him to take a seat.

"New girl?" He indicated Meredith with a toss of his shaggy head.

"Yeah, shh. We also have a new client, and right now she doesn't know it's Meredith's first day," I whispered at him.

"Ah. Right."

"What do you want? I didn't cut your hair that long ago."

"I'm thinking about going short," he ran his fingers through his shaggy hair. He was lying. I could smell testosterone with a hint of fear on him. He was scared of me? Nope, this wasn't a business call.

"No, you're not. You're looking for an excuse to come here." I figured him out.

"Caught me."

"I'm gonna cut your hair anyway because I'm working right now." I pulled out the clippers. He wanted to play at this, and I needed him to back off. Maybe if I pissed him off enough he'd lay off the flirting.

"Uh, okay." He settled back in my chair.

I clipped him right down to the skin before he could protest, starting right down the middle so he had to let me finish.

He scowled at me in the mirror. Score one for Gretchen! The ball was in his court now.

"Thanks," he said when I finished, not leaving my chair.

Crap, there goes my point. "What else can I do for you?" I put on my professional voice. My professional hairdresser, not my professional prostitute. Those are very different voices.

"You know what you can do for me, Gretch."

"Besides go out with you. That's not an option." I took off his cape and tossed it into the laundry basket, crossing my arms and maintaining my distance. This wasn't good. I wanted to stay friends with him. The whole band thing would work better that way.

"Are you sure?" he asked.

"Positive. If you need a date, ask Lacey-Marie."

Scott's shoulders slumped as he stood from my chair and walked out. I didn't charge my boys for their haircuts. It was all for the band.

"Who was that?" asked Meredith, putting the finishing touches on a smiling Marcy's style.

"That was Scott. We're in a band together." I watched out the window as he drove away. "I'll introduce you sometime."

"Cool." She gave Marcy a light coat of hairspray. "What do you think?"

"I love it. You did a great job. Can I have your card?" Marcy stood up and tossed her hair. The smile stayed in place.

Toni wandered out of the back room and slipped Meredith a blank card that she'd already doodled on the front of.

"Absolutely. Come on up front, and we'll get settled up," said Meredith, leading the way. She wrote her information on the card and handed it to Marcy.

"Would you like to schedule your next appointment now?" she asked.

"Sure! Any Tuesday next month?" Marcy asked, pulling out her planner.

"How about the second Tuesday at ten a.m.?"

"Perfect!"

Meredith wrote it down in her new appointment book. Her very first client would be a steady customer.

It was a good jumping off point.

Chapter 13: Vampires

Percy had been out all morning commissioning a new sign and logo for us. We 'd be ordering new business cards, which meant the ones I just received were useless. I could technically hand them out still—the actual information was the same—but if they got passed on to potential clients, I wanted them to say: "Olympian's Salon and Day Spa."

Meredith was settling in nicely. One day of working here was hardly anything to judge by, but still, so far, so good. We'd shown our color-coded tool system to her while letting her know it was perfectly fine not to follow it, and all the walk-ins would be hers for the time being.

I studied the calendar, feeling as if the pack were collectively breathing down my neck. They hadn't given me a deadline, but I wanted my mind made up before the next new moon when I'd be at my most vulnerable. I could only hope they'd respect my decision.

"Percy?" I stood relaxed, propped against her station during a lull.

"Yes, hun?"

"I need a vacation." What I wouldn't give to be able to run away from the building storm. I knew very well that I couldn't. Like it or not, I knew deep down that it was my duty to deal with the sickness invading my home.

"Don't we all?" she said with a rare flare of sarcasm as she patted my arm.

"You're getting one soon."

"Living in Winterland with my husband for three months is not a vacation. It's work."

We rarely talked about her marriage. She never brought it up, but I was feeling curious in my frazzled state, especially with the man in question staying with us.

"Is it really so bad, living with a dark fae? I mean, you've been married for eons. Do you hate him?" I drew myself upright and took her hand.

Percy was quiet as she patted my hand and deliberated. The other girls were busy finishing their cuts for the day, or at least the new girl was. Lacey would be working with us until seven, but the new girl, being part time, only worked until three.

"No, I don't hate Hades. I've learned how to love him over time, despite our radically different outlooks on life. It's the Winterland that I hate. It's not an eternal land of snow and ice, but it might as well be, as sick and twisted as it is."

"So what is Hades in charge of, really? He's cast as the god of the dead, but he's not really, is he?"

She took her hand back and hugged her arms around her middle. "He is, in a way. He rules over the creatures that love the night and the Necromancers who create zombies. All technically dead. Well no, that's not right. The vamps like Lacey are technically dead, but the pureblood fae that are in charge of changing them are alive. The necromancers are alive as well. Just the zombies are dead. There are some weres under his rule, but most of them live elsewhere."

I shivered. I'd never met an alpha vamp changer, but Lacey had described the one who made her. They sounded dead enough to me. Her metamorphosis was what would be termed a rape. There was no communication, but instead violent communion. She'd woken up in the closet of her college dorm room and killed her roommate without a moment's consideration.

The alpha werewolf changer responsible for me was scary, yes, but I assumed he gave most of his victims the choice he gave me, and I didn't feel even a little bit like a victim. He saved me and ruined me all in one go. I'd annihilated an entire brothel full of family, friends, and captures, then burned the place to the ground when I came to. I'm not aware of my actions during full moons when the wolf is completely in charge. The rest of the month, my humanity is mostly in charge.

My conversation with Percy was interrupted when Meredith approached us to say goodbye.

"Have a nice night," I said in response to her farewell.

"I will!" she said, flipping her straight hair over her shoulders and hiking up her purse.

"Bye," said Percy, giving her a little finger wiggle wave.

"See ya." She shifted her bag again and walked out the door.

I turned back to Percy. "So is the place where you live crawling with dead people?"

She shook her head. "Not usually. The part of the castle we live in is kept separate from where Hades keeps his council."

"Castle?" I latched onto that idea right away, giving her a toothy smile.

"Fortress, castle, whatever you'd like to call it."

She rotated each hand palm up with each option as if weighing them for the most correct description.

"Do you want to split a pomegranate?" I asked, cocking my head to the side and keeping my grin.

"You're a regular comedian today, aren't you? Absolutely not."

"Aw, you're no fun." I bumped her shoulder with my own.

"You don't even like fruit, Gretch."

"I do so! I like blackberries, apples, and bananas."

"And I've given up pomegranates. They take me places I don't wish to go."

Like an arranged marriage and Winterland. I was still a little unclear on that story, but I had a feeling it was time to drop that line of questioning, which was fine because there were people. I was flipping over the sign for the evening when a tall, thin, bland looking man pushed the door open, leading two others.

The bell tinkled merrily, and I scowled. "I'm sorry, we're closed. We open at nine a.m. tomorrow. Would you like to make an appointment?" I asked, blocking his path. Old death and magic rolled off him in potent waves.

"No, thank you. I'm looking for Lacey-Marie." The low tenor of his voice chilled me to the bone, making me feel dirty and unnerved.

"We're closed," I said again, trying not to show my fear.

"I'm not here for a haircut, so the fact that you're closed means little to me, wolf."

I growled low and quiet. He turned his gaze away from the back of the salon and fixed his red eyes on me. Vamp. Crap. His scent was so intense that I hadn't equated it with my friend's smell.

"What name should I give Lacey-Marie? I'll let her

know you'd like to speak with her." I fought to hold my ground and not piddle on the floor in terror.

"Just get her." His stony continence gave me no room to argue. He hadn't moved, but it was clear that he was far more dominant than I.

"I'll be right back." I spun on my toes and stalked towards the back. If I'd gone furry, my hackles would have stood on end. As it was, the little hairs on the back of my neck were doing their best.

Lacey was seated on the counter with a mug of blood in the kitchen when I found her.

"There's someone here to see you, a vamp," I growled at her, still fighting my own animal instinct to run.

"There's a guy out front," said Toni, poking her head into the kitchen. "He's giving me the heebie-jeebies."

"He's for Lacey. I'll walk you out to your car. I've still got to finish close out," I said to Toni, motioning her back out.

"Thanks, I'd sure appreciate it."

"No problem." I don't know if she suspected them of being anything but creeps. I hoped not.

Lacey set her mug on the counter and scooted around us and out of the kitchen.

Toni and I followed at a more leisurely pace, trying to stay as far back as possible.

"Kern!" Lacey's whole being lit up like Fourth of July fireworks as she fairly danced towards him.

It was the big man, the patriarch of the New York family.

Something was apparently looking to go down in the fae world. If the wolves were trying to pull me back into the fold, I could only guess the vamps were looking for a renewal of membership from Lacey.

"Hello, Lacey-Marie. You remember Helvia, don't you? And this is Motega." Kern gestured first to the professional-looking woman who appeared to be in her late thirties but was really somewhere around 280. The other one was someone I hadn't heard Lacey mention before, making me think he was a new convert.

I hurried Toni out the door and into her car with locked doors. I watched as she tore down the driveway, then darted back inside. I continued closing out, but my focus was Kern.

He turned his gaze on me, and I did my best to look busy.

"Let's go somewhere else to talk," said Kern.

"Lacey—" I started.

"It's all right, I'm fine. Tell Percy not to wait up for me."

"I'll have her back before daybreak. Little Lacey-Marie is safe with me." Kern held a hand out to my friend. She took it.

Safe. Right.

"I'll be fine," she repeated and walked out the door with the scariest creature I'd ever met.

I hurried through the rest of close out not caring how accurate I was being. I separated everyone's money into individual envelopes, then carried it all out to the library where I set the envelopes on an end table before pushing against the right side of the moose painting that hid our antique safe. It swung out on silent hinges that kept it flush against the wall. I fit the key into the lock, jimmying it a little before it turned. The safe was pretty, but a pain in the rear. I would be more than happy to pass the key over to Percy in a couple of minutes.

I placed the envelopes on top of the stack already sitting there. Percy would go through them the next day, then make a deposit. We got paid once a week after everything was counted and logged. I closed and locked the safe, swinging the picture shut again, and pressed against the frame until the latch caught.

Curling up in a comfy armchair, I picked up the Jane Austen novel I'd left on the table. The people contained in those pages lived lives much different from my own. It would have been nice only to have to worry about who was marrying whom and living under my father's roof until then.

I'd never met my father, that I know of. I really hope I hadn't. He wouldn't have known I was his child either, as men weren't exactly notified if they'd gotten a good-time daisy pregnant.

There was a gentle knock on the door as Percy peeked in. "You have a visitor."

She entered, followed by Doug.

Great.

Percy took a seat with a book she'd already started. I think she had a book going in almost every room of the house, if you counted cookbooks in the kitchen.

I closed my novel with a snap. It wasn't an original, but Percy certainly owned an original Austen or two, published in volumes and everything. They were all locked up behind glass with its own temperature and dehumidifier gage. If she were ever to go broke for some strange reason, she could always sell some originals and be set.

I supposed it was kind of impossible to go broke when you're married to Hades. The man had connections, in and out of the fae world. Which was amazing, given that he rarely stepped out of Winterland.

Doug took a seat and clasped his hands in his lap.

"I invited him to stay for dinner," said Percy,

glancing up from her book. "Stop chewing your claws."

"I came to see Hades," said Doug, looking around the library.

I pulled my hand away from my mouth. "Sorry." I hadn't even realized that I'd been doing it.

"You're worried." Percy set her book aside, marking the page with a faded pink ribbon.

"I am. She's not back yet, and I don't trust those vamps."

"Well, vamps, as a rule, are untrustworthy," Percy pointed out.

"And yet you hired one."

"I hired a werewolf as well. Call me mad, but I like you people."

"You're right, you're insane." I couldn't help but jump on that one with an enthusiastic nod.

"Very witty."

"I try." And fail most of the time, but that's beside the point.

Doug watched our exchange with a confused look on his face. "Why are they untrustworthy?"

Oh, sheltered boy. He'd never had any real exposure to the fae. The half-breeds in the side show didn't count.

"Well for a long time now, vamps have wanted to come into the open. They think they're pretty high up on the food chain, so to speak, so they think it could only help them to go public," I explained, inspecting one gnawed black claw. I specifically kept my claws on the short side to make them less noticeable. Most people assumed I preferred an odd nail shape and black polish.

"And werewolves?" He leaned towards me with interest.

"We have bad tempers."

He nodded, deep in thought.

I shot Percy a glance. She shrugged her shoulders, then glanced up at the wall clock above the door.

"You're worried too," I said.

"I'm worried about both of you. I'm worried about the new girl. I'm worried about what will happen when I leave for the winter."

That's a whole lot of worry, I thought.

"I worry that you and Lacey-Marie will leave me. I'm worried about someone killing Meredith," Percy expanded.

"It might be better if we left," I said quietly, avoiding her eyes.

"No, it wouldn't." Percy came and knelt in front of me, making me look at her. "I need you girls. You have no idea how wonderful it is to be able to be myself with someone."

"You have Robert and them." I referred to the handful of fae and part fae who worked the farm.

"Not really. Most of them don't know what I am. I mean, they know I'm fae, but they don't know I'm Persephone, daughter of Demeter and Zeus."

I hadn't considered that. For some reason, the fact that Demeter was her mother hadn't phased me one bit, but I hadn't really realized that Zeus, god of gods, was her father. I honestly didn't know much about Percy at all. I also didn't know much about the myths she featured in.

"Are all the major gods and goddesses really siblings?" That would be gross.

Doug scooted forward in his chair, giving us his attention again.

"No, dear, not all of us. I'm sure there's inbreeding —that was excusable in the ancient world—but no,

Hades isn't my uncle."

"Good to know." I leaned back again, nodding.

Doug chuckled.

"Yes, it is," said Percy.

"I don't want to leave, you know."

"I know. And you'll do whatever you have to, and I'll accept it, but still." She didn't want to accept it. Neither did I, really, but I also knew that at some point I needed a pack of my own, and I would do whatever it took to achieve that.

"That vampire didn't look all that horrible," she said.

"Looks can be deceiving. You know that. Were you watching from the door?"

"I was," she admitted sheepishly. "Who was he?"

"Kern, the patriarch of the New York family. The family Lacey joined after she died. He's about 800 years old."

"He's just a youngin'." Percy smiled.

"He was 17 when he was turned, and thanks to modern medicine, he's had plastic surgery to age him enough to make him a viable persona in the business world."

"How do you know about him?" she asked.

"Lacey told me about him when we lived in New York." Who knows, I may even have met him. Lacey hung out with a lot of vamps back then. She was a bit of a wild child in the eighties, less than 10 years after she'd been made.

"Why did she move away from the city?" Doug asked. "She doesn't seem like much of a country girl."

"She was looking for a change of pace, with less temptations. She got it. Plus Percy's been a huge help to both of us."

I glanced at the wall clock. Time was crawling

along with my skin. What could they possibly be talking about for so long? I felt somewhat like a parent waiting for her daughter to come home from a first date. What can I say? I'm protective of my friends. They're the closest thing I've got to family. I knew Percy felt the same way, though I wasn't sure about how Lacey felt.

I called her my best friend, yes, but I never really knew what was going on in that blonde head of hers. In a normal world, we never would have been friends, but similar circumstances and cosmetology school had made us that. What had started us off as a grudging alliance turned into calling each other every night and going dancing. Funny how relationships evolve.

I'd known Percy for less than half the time I've known Lacey-Marie, but I've grown to respect and love her during that time.

"Tea?" Percy asked, getting up from her chair.

"Please. Would you throw some green tea in with my usual mix?"

"I do believe I could. Doug?" She placed a hand on the back of his chair.

He twisted to look up at her. "Coffee?"

Percy nodded. "I'll be back." She left the door open in her wake.

I picked my book back up but was unable to keep my attention on the words. I'm not much of a reader. I owned very few books of my own and only borrowed from Percy's vast collection on nights like the one I was experiencing, nights where I knew I wasn't going to sleep.

Not sleeping would make me cranky, especially with more interviews coming up the next day, but I didn't care. I can go without sleep for several days. It just isn't advisable.

Percy returned carrying a tray. I made a spot for it on the table I'd set the money on earlier. She pulled the cozy off the pot she had brewed and poured it into the delicate antique tea cups that only came out for special occasions. I was a little worried that I would break one, but Percy didn't share my fears. There was a thermos of coffee for Doug on the tray as well.

She placed a couple gingersnap cookies on each saucer and passed us each a cup. I settled mine on the table next to the lamp I was using and snagged a cookie. The tea was too hot to drink for the time being, but perfect for dipping. I soaked the little round bit of goodness for a couple seconds, then popped it whole into my mouth and savored it. Gingersnaps are yummy and absolutely necessary for social tea consumption.

Percy dunked hers in a more ladylike manner: one edge into her tea, nibble, dunk, take a sip of tea, dunk, nibble. It was quite the little ritual for a snack.

It was nice, sitting quietly and eating. "We should do this more often, you know, when we're not stressing over stuff." I popped in another cookie, then grabbed some more from the bowl.

"Agreed. I'm always so surprised how much I like lavender in my tea. I grow it myself. I shouldn't be surprised. Of course I'm more accustomed to utilizing it for aromatherapy these days."

The aromatherapy was also for my benefit.

"Do you think she'll go back to New York?" She returned to the Lacey/vamp topic.

"I don't really know. I hope not. They don't exactly share our lifestyle. It's not like anyone polices them, beyond their own people."

Lacey and I had adopted Percy's more conservative lifestyle when we moved in. I liked it. I felt better knowing that I was jailed once a month away from people. I'm old, but I'm still human. In fact, my morals have improved rather than declined.

Lacey was my opposite. She'd gone from good little straight-A cheerleader to wild child. She became addicted to the lifestyle, so moving in with Percy probably had been a shock to her system, especially the no hunting policy. Blood donor bags just aren't the same as fresh, warm, pumping blood. She'd conformed out of respect for Percy and to keep her house clean.

Killing people is messy business. I should know. The brothel wasn't my only kill. I tried to lock myself up over the years, but people were wild cards, and sometimes accidents happened. I didn't just attack at random. I have to be provoked unless I was already hunting. Wolves tend to avoid humans, but sometimes we'd end up in the same territory. Here's a hint: don't pet strange dogs, especially if they're actually giant wolves. Wild animals should be left alone. Hunting me wasn't a good option either. That kinda ticks any animal off, and 400 pounds of pissed off is going to fight back.

Percy was good with my wolf. She made herself non-threatening, not trying to pat me or get too close. She brought me food, then left, making sure I was on the other side of my cage before she opened the door. Even if I were to go spastic on her, she's kind of powerful. She could definitely protect herself from me.

We ate and talked until I heard a car pull up in the driveway. The sky was lightening up— not quite sunrise, but it would be within the hour.

Percy and I set aside our tea things with clatters and rattles. We'd filled up several times, and we still manage to slosh the last dregs on the coffee table. Not that we cared. Doug, who was passed out on the couch, didn't stir, so we left him.

Lacey was already making her way up the stairs, then turned when she heard us coming. I was a bit startled to see she had removed her contacts. Her brilliant red eyes were truly terrifying.

"I thought I told you guys not to stay up," she said, crossing her arms.

"Yeah, well, I don't like doing what I'm told." My own arms crossed in response to her body language.

She was guarded, not even breathing as she stared at us.

Percy didn't say anything.

"So, what did the dead guy want?" I ascended the steps until I shared one with my petite friend.

"CPR," said Lacey, narrowing her eyes.

"No, really, what did Kern want?" I asked again, gripping her arms.

"He wants me to move back to New York to be a part of the family again."

"And?" I pressed, trying not to shake her.

"I said no. I like living in Isenburge, Maine just fine, thank you."

"Really? That little conversation took you all night?" I let go, giving her some space and following her the rest of the way up the stairs.

"Yes. We had a lot of catching up to do. It's been a long time." She stopped at her door, her hand resting on the antique brass knob.

Not that long and he could have checked up on Lacey without showing up in Maine. In fact, he could have asked her to move back over the phone. No need to cross three state lines into my territory.

"Listen, get some sleep. He's leaving tonight, so quit worrying." She let herself into her room

"Are you sure?" Percy asked, coming up behind us.

"Everything is fine, I promise." Lacey closed the

door in our faces with a little more force than necessary.

I took her word for it. She didn't sound remotely worried, and I could usually read her pretty well.

I admit, I was jealous. She talked to the vamps, and they were going home, no muss no fuss. I hung out with the wolves, and I didn't know what to do. I was almost certain I didn't want in on Kaine's pack but at the same time, I did want a pack of my own.

FIRST QUARTER

Chapter 14:
Family Dinner

I stumbled down to the salon with two hours of sleep under my belt. Wild, frizzy, disheveled hair greeted me in the mirror, so I flicked the switch of my one-inch curling iron with my thumb in preparation to tame down my curls to a manageable volume.

Toni was the first one in, and she was wide awake. "Morning!" she called over to me as she set her coffee mug down on the front desk.

"Ugh," I grumbled in reply, and yanked a wide toothed comb through the mess on my head.

She ignored me and grabbed a sip of her drink.

Percy joined us, saving me from having to make coherent conversation on my own. I don't know that she actually needed to sleep.

"Here." Percy handed me a mug of tea.

I could smell the extra green tea in the mix. Domestic goddess, that's what she was. Plants, food, wolf care, whatever life threw at her.

I sipped and tested my iron with a quick tap of my fingers. The wonderful thing about professional tools is they heat up fast. I checked the dial for heavy, hot, and hell of a lot, the hairdresser standby—not recommended for everyday use, but we all did it—then ran my fingers through my curls, testing for tangles.

"What's happening?" Lacey asked, sipping from a covered travel mug.

Was everyone bright-eyed and bushy-tailed? It wasn't natural.

"Where's Meredith?" asked Toni, looking around for our newest recruit.

"Here, here! Running late! Sorry!" Meredith burst in right on cue. She had bags under eyes to rival the ones I probably sported.

"No problem, it happens," said Percy.

Meredith dashed around flipping switches and setting out her blades.

I spritzed my hair with a working spray and set about making it pretty. By the time my first client sat in my chair, I looked less crazed. Looks can be deceiving.

"Can I use your microwave?" Meredith asked, pulling a packet of oatmeal from her purse. "I didn't get a chance to eat before I left."

"Of course. And that's not a full breakfast. I've got some fresh strawberries from my greenhouse if you want to add them," Percy offered.

Mmmm, strawberries. See, I like fruit.

"Really? Thanks!" said Meredith.

"Follow me, and I'll get you set."

I consulted with my client while this went on, then proceeded to the back room to formulate for an all over color and highlight.

Gotta love drastic changes. They made me money. Of course, I checked and rechecked all my formulations before applying anything when I was overtired. Thankfully, it was a virgin application, so I could do everything at once with color. I love it when that happens. It would never happen again with her, so I savored the moment.

While she processed, I planned to drop in on the

masseuse interviews.

Paint, fold, seal. Paint, fold, seal. It was an easy rhythm as I half focused on my client's words. Thankfully, she just talked about herself and didn't ask any questions, so I smiled and nodded my way through, then left her with a magazine to keep her company and made my escape from the fumes that clogged my senses.

Percy was already seated with the potential new girl and asking questions. I casually picked up her résumé from where it lay to Percy's right, sat down in its place, and perused.

I liked Fern right away. Maybe it was her name, Fern Mayberry. Whatever it was, we clicked. She'd been in and out of work since she graduated three years ago. She probably still had a lot to learn, but she seemed eager to work.

"Hi, I'm Fern." Her handshake was firm and her composure relaxed. I smelled no trace of fear, revealing her confidence and ease with meeting new people, which was essential, especially since most people she would meet would be half naked. She couldn't afford to be shy, and she needed to put her clients at ease.

"Tell us about yourself, Fern." Percy sat poised with her pen and paper.

"Well, I'm 25. I'm renting an apartment in Bangor, and I own my vehicle. Um, I'm willing to work whatever hours you can give me. I left my last massage job because I moved. I've been working at Mickey D's and I feel like I'm wasting a perfectly good education. I'm Irish." She circled the air around her face with her right index finger, indicating her red hair, green eyes, and freckles.

Fern stood at the end of the interview and shook all

our hands again. I towered over her. Tiny little spitfire.

"It was nice meeting everyone!" She gave us a smile as she paused by the front doors.

"We enjoyed meeting you as well. You'll hear from us after lunch either way," Percy promised.

"Sounds great!" She made sure the door latched behind her before waltzing out to her truck.

I turned to Percy. "I like her."

"So I noticed. I've never seen you cotton to someone like that before."

I shrugged my shoulders. Her temperament was soothing, and she seemed like fun.

"All right, I'll leave a message on her home phone." Percy headed for the front desk, answering the phone after it rang for the millionth time.

In the middle of our lunch break, Percy called everyone together.

"All right we're now fully staffed. Fern Mayberry will be our new masseuse."

I pumped my fist in the air and let a grin take over my face. "Hooray!"

"It's all settled. What does everyone think?" Percy opened the floor for discussion.

"Do we have to pay for the massages?" Meredith asked.

"Nope. Consider it a bonus, but only one a week." Percy shook her head and smiled. "I'll kick in to pay for her time, but remember to return the favor with hair and nails.

"You're a goddess," said Toni, her hand fluttering to her heart, her head tilting back slightly and her eyes closing for a moment, wearing a blissful smile on her lips.

"I am." Percy laughed, ducking her head in false modesty.

"I'm absolutely fine with it," I said.

"Sounds good to me," Lacey assented with a nod. She had no problem at all with people touching her dead skin. In fact, the more attention she got, the better.

"Great! I have one other thing before I let you all go back to your lunches. Would you all like to come for supper tonight around eight?"

That nearly stopped my heart. Supper? Here? With us? Was Percy nuts? How were we going to explain Lacey's liquid diet and my meat obsession?

"I'd love to, but—" Meredith started.

"No buts! My farm staff will be joining us as well, as will some of their families," Percy interrupted.

Oh, this was going to be a blast.

"I'm in, then! Any day I don't have to cook and do dishes is a vacation."

"Wonderful. How about the rest of you?"

Everyone agreed to join us.

As soon as we separated, I cornered Percy with my fists balled up on my hips. "Are you completely friggin' nuts?" I whispered loudly.

"I think you already know the answer to that. Don't worry, it's going to be fine. I have a scrumptious selection planned, including a mooing cow on a plate for you. Lacey knows how to hide food in her napkin, and we'll pass off her blood as tomato soup," said Percy, waving me off with a flick of her fingers.

"Blood does not look like tomato soup," I grumbled.

"Glamour, dear. You've forgotten about glamour."

"You can glamour food?" I perked up with interest. I didn't know much about glamours and their many applications.

"Of course I can." Her smile was smug as she raised her eyebrows at me and crossed her arms under her chest.

I left work a couple of minutes early to go for a run.

"Hey, wait up!" Lacey called from behind.

"Who's the faster of the two of us?" I asked, faking innocent.

"Me," she said, breezing up to me before slowing to match my pace.

"I rest my case." I concentrated on maintaining my pace over the uneven terrain.

"So, what do you think of this dinner thing of Percy's?" asked Lacey, running as gracefully as a deer.

"I believe I told her she was completely friggin' nuts." I leapt to tap a branch with my fingertips, landing easily on my toes and continuing without missing a beat.

"That sounds like a fair assessment to me. Is she getting everything ready all by herself?"

"Nope, her worker bees are helping her out." I puffed and sped up the pace.

"Last I checked, our co-workers don't know what we are. Aren't they gonna play connect the dots and figure us out?" She sped up with me.

"You'll be eating tomato glamour soup."

"Sounds tasty," she said glumly, brushing a pine branch out of her way as she ducked her head to the side.

"We probably shouldn't go far. I wanna get back in time to at least rinse off and change." I glanced down at my watch.

"I'm gonna need a rinse too, and a fresh coat of

paint." She indicated her carefully applied makeup. "Oh, I know!" Lacey skittered to a halt, sending up a hail of pine needles and decayed leaves.

"What? What?" I said, breaking with much less grace.

"You should invite the band!" She grabbed my hands in her cold ones and swung me around.

"Uh, yeah, 'cause Scott really needs more encouragement." I rolled my eyes at her and pulled out of her grasp.

"Have Mark call 'em," she persisted.

"Fine. I'll invite the band."

"Great! Race ya home?" Lacey stretched into a starting pose with one leg stretched back, balancing with one foot forward up on her toes and her fingertips, her rear poking comically in the air.

"You're on." I slapped her butt and tore off, knowing cheating was the only way I'd beat her.

She beat me by several minutes, waiting patiently perched on a large rock at the edge of the woods.

"Don't forget to call your boys!" she reminded me as we approached her door.

"Yeah, yeah." I left her laughing and grabbed my cell off my bedside table in my own room.

"What's up, Gretch?"

"Hey, Mark. Listen, Percy's decided to make a huge dinner and invite lots of people. Want to join the awkwardness? You and the rest of the guys, I mean."

"Yeah, okay. Food there is always good. Should I bring Rachel?" He'd only eaten Percy's cooking on a couple of occasions, and he'd been liberal with the compliments both times.

"Of course. The more the merrier. We're sitting down at eight."

"I'll call the guys. We'll be there," Mark promised.

"'Kay. See ya."

"Bye."

I hung up and stared down at my home screen. The dank woods that were my background tempted my madness. Without another moment's thought, I scrolled through my contact list, until I came upon the newest one and hit the little green phone symbol.

The line rang twice, then a voice that was quickly becoming familiar answered.

"Gretchen." Doug's French accent was light and pleasant in my ear, making me feel warm and chilled all at once. It was a beautiful, musical voice.

I paused, feeling awkward. "So, um, do you want to come to dinner? I mean, Percy is having a big dinner tonight. Will you come?"

"It would be my pleasure, *colombe*. What time should I be there?"

Colombe. I was unfamiliar with the term, and I figured it must be French.

"Eight. And a lot of people there will be, um, normal."

"I can keep to polite conversation," he said, chuckling softly, which made my heart speed up.

"Ha, that's not quite what I meant. I just mean that they don't have a clue about us." I took several deep breaths trying to sooth my curious wolf back into slumber.

"Like I said, I can keep the conversation polite. Don't worry, *colombe*, I won't reveal you."

"Right. Okay then, see you at eight." I hung up before I could think of something stupid to say, my wolf becoming dormant once more.

I slapped my palm against my forehead, having almost forgotten an important couple that should be invited. I typed a quick text to Mem with a short invitation and the time.

She answered back immediately: *We wouldn't miss it! See you soon!*

I showered quickly, getting rid of sweat, debris from the woods, and clipper hairs.

Dinner with the whole family. Oh, joy.

I got ready in record time, then thundered down the stairs to help Percy set up. I was a terrible cook, but I thought I could manage stirring and carrying. She put me right to work mashing potatoes. I'm a good potato masher. Those buggers were creamy when I was done.

Lacey helped us set the tables in the formal dining room we'd only eaten in a handful of times since I'd moved in.

The first person to show up was Robert. Big, softspoken, non-human Robert.

"Hey," I said, as I carried a stack of extra chairs in.

"Hello," he replied. He was a real talkative fella.

Jane, his wife, followed and gave me a hug hello, then went to join her husband.

Dante, Christina, and CJ rounded out the group of the farm staff, all of them part or full fae, plus their gaggle of children. Christina was quite possibly one of Percy's handmaidens from way back when.

The farm staff and I aren't really good buddies, though they tolerate me despite werewolves and vampires being the perceived bad guys.

Mem showed up on her husband's arm, bearing two bottles of red wine. After handing the bottles off, they surrounded me with their arms and a kiss on either cheek.

"Glad you could make it!" I said, giving them an extra squeeze. I really did love them both, though Mem held a special place in my heart.

Mem laughed and patted my cheek. "Of course, my

dear!"

Meredith showed up alone bearing a green bean casserole.

Toni brought her husband and children, who immediately gravitated towards the staff, noting common ground.

Doug looked around, shifting awkwardly from leg to leg, until he spotted me.

"Welcome," I said, handing him a platter of carved turkey.

"Putting me to work, then?" He accepted the tray, his smile a sharp contrast to the face hidden beneath all the hair.

"You've been lurking around quite a bit, young man," said Percy. "You've earned family duties."

We all sat together after the four of us brought in all the food and settled it down along the middle of the table. There was a lot of clanking and chatter as bowls and platters were passed up and down. I sat between my boys and Doug, not knowing how they would react to him.

"So, Doug, how's work?" I asked, cutting into my barely seared steak. Mm, juicy. I repressed the urge to close my eyes in bliss as all the smells and tastes congregated in my head.

"It's been good. I'm grateful to have a job where I can travel."

"Good, good. Hey, have I introduced you to my boys? This is Mark, our lead singer and guitarist. Austin, our drummer. Oh, and Scott, our bassist. You've met him, right?" I made my introductions, ending with the important one. "Gentlemen, this is Doug, my new friend."

"Nice to meet you," they each took a turn saying.

"So, how did you do it, Gretch?" asked Mark with

a glint in his eye.

"Do it? Do what? I didn't do anything," I spluttered out guiltily. I had way too much going on.

"Wow, guilty much? I'm referring to Scott's lack of hair. We'd been trying to get him to get rid of it for months. How'd you do it?" Mark crossed his arms and waited, tipping his chair back on two legs.

"Must be my wily female charms." I put my fork down and crossed my arms in response.

"Yeah, we'll have to talk about those and their effect on," he tossed his head in Scott's direction, "but not now."

"That and I think he gave me permission to do whatever I wanted. So I took out the clippers and mowed." I was hoping it would make Scott back off.

"Huh?" said Scott.

"Nothing, just talking about work," I said, taking another enormous bite of steak.

"'Kay," he went back to his conversation with Austin.

"Well, whatever. The hair needed to go. You are a goddess," said Mark.

That was going around. "Nah, Percy's the only goddess around here," I argued.

"Yeah, okay. Gotta love a girl who can cook." He winked at his girlfriend, who was listening in.

"I suppose, but I did the potatoes." I pointed at the mound on my plate with my fork.

"The potatoes are good," said Rachel, giving me a smile. I liked her. She and Mark were good together.

I took another big bite, ending the conversation. Mark and I tend to have those pointless conversations that disguise themselves as small talk.

Someone had flipped on the TV, and my attention was caught.

"Hey, turn that up!" I called, scooting my chair back so I could get a better view.

"25-year-old Joslin Webber was found dead in her apartment at the foot of Sugarloaf Mountain. Webber was a popular hairstylist with the mountain crowd and appears to be the latest in a series of murders over the last few weeks. These women were all successful with no apparent connection to each other, beyond their choice in profession. Police are urging stylists all over the state to use the buddy system when leaving work and to check up on each other once they've gotten home. No evidence has been brought forward to indicate who the murderer might be. If you have any information, please call your local authorities or this hotline. Stay safe."

A 1-800 number flashed across the screen. Apparently it wasn't just us who thought we were being targeted. Problem was, these girls were being killed in their own homes, not anywhere near the salons where they worked.

I growled quietly, and Mem shot me a worried look.

The room was silent as Percy stood and turned off the television.

I caught her eye and jerked my head in the direction of the library. Percy nodded, and I stood.

"Ladies and gentlemen, I'm going to steal the hairdressers from your midst to go have a little powwow. Manicurists and masseuses are welcome as well. We're heading over to the library, so if you'll just follow us."

I pushed my chair farther away from the table and led our ragtag little troop to the door and shoved it open. It felt as if I were leading a charge. We hurried to the library and arranged ourselves around the room on various favorite pieces of furniture. I grabbed my normal comfy chair and stared at the door, avoiding the gazes of the other stylists in my presence.

Percy joined us within minutes. "All right. We all heard that. We all know that this is real, not a figment of our overactive imaginations. What we need to do is figure out how to protect ourselves. We have some information the media is not giving out." Percy perched herself on the edge of the study table.

"The girls were murdered in their own homes when there were other people up and about. Nobody heard a noise, no signs of a struggle. We don't know if that means the murderer is someone they all knew, or if they are just this good. Each girl was drained of all her blood through slices made through each jugular. There was no mess, no blood splatter found. There is absolutely no evidence of the guilty party, besides the bodies.

"Now, protecting ourselves from someone like this is going to be difficult. They are only targeting one girl at a time, and there are a lot of successful hairdressers in the state. It happened when the other person left the room. I'm not saying we should always have someone with us at all times, but I am saying it wouldn't be a bad time to take on a roommate, maybe even several. The more people you're in contact with, the less likely you are to be a target. Just be careful. Don't give out any personal information to clients, especially you new girls.

"Ah, I gave Scott my phone number. Is that bad?" asked Meredith.

He was relentless. "No," I answered with a sigh. "Scott's a decent guy, and I can guarantee he's not the murderer. A hopeless flirt at times, but he's not psychotic. Trust me. I can usually smell a psycho."

"And what does a psycho smell like?" asked Lacey-Marie. "I'm curious."

"You should know. She smells a little funny, likes to wear lots of pink."

"Haha." She rolled her eyes at me and sank back in her seat.

"But seriously. They're usually the 'normal ones,' but they tend to be shy, reclusive. They aren't the type to invite a big group over for dinner for instance."

"Oh, good, I was a little worried I was the psychotic in the room," said Percy, wiping her brow, adding a little drama to her sarcasm. "Let's get back on topic and brainstorm. What else can we do to make sure we all stay safe?"

"We should set up a call system. I'll call one girl, she'll call someone else, and so on. If someone doesn't receive a call by a certain time, or no one answers, give us a call here, and we'll check it out. That way we can at least keep ourselves connected. People are less likely to be targeted if their bodies can be found right away," I said.

"Wow, that's morbid," said Lacey.

"Yeah, well, if it works, morbidity is gonna have to be the way of it." I settled back in my chair and tapped the cover of my Austen novel.

"We could walk each other to our cars, like they say. And inspect the cars before getting in. Maybe the killer is hitchhiking, like he's breaking into their cars and riding home in their trunks or back seats," Meredith suggested.

"That's a very good point," said Percy.

We hadn't thought of that. The killer obviously had personal information on his victims. Why not hitch a ride while he was at it?

"Well, I suggest everyone go home and get a good

night's sleep. Sorry to cut the party short." Percy stood and led the way back to the dining room.

I lagged behind so I could talk to Meredith. "So, Scott?" I asked quietly.

"Yeah."

I shrugged my shoulders and let her go. I wasn't really all that sad the evening was over. I was definitely feeling the bone weariness of not having slept the night before. Add in another kill, and I was wiped.

"Are you okay?" Mem's eyes were still full of worry when I found her.

"Yeah, I'm fine. Have a good night, Mem. Thanks again for coming." I gave her one more hug.

"If you need anything, never hesitate to ask, no matter the time or what it is."

"I will."

I walked her to the door and turned to find one more guest to send off.

"Thank you for inviting me." Doug had lost the tension from earlier in the evening, his arms loose at his sides, and he'd quit the dancing motion.

"Of course. I'd asked you to stay longer, but—"

"You are exhausted. I see it." He touched the skin at the corner of my eye. "Rest well."

I expected to feel offended by the uninvited touch, but instead I found it soothing. "I think I will."

Chapter 15:
Club North

We were all subdued at work, engaging in little small talk with our clients. The news from the previous night hit us hard. It was official. Real. Hairdressers were being murdered, and there was no telling who could be next. We'd made a pact not bring up the subject with our customers, but it was all we could think about.

Percy's client, Jenni, noticed her stylist's conspicuous silence and left her alone. At first. She made as far as the chair before she dared broach the subject.

"You're quiet today," Jenni commented, heaving herself into the chair.

"Am I? Sorry, I must not have had enough caffeine. How are you and baby doing?" Percy began combing Jenni's bra-length red hair with a helpful dollop of leave-in conditioner.

"We're doing great! Our last check up was on Monday, and the doctor says we're healthy and right on track." Jenni rubbed her belly over the cape, smiling down at it as if she were cradling the actual child.

"Wonderful! How far along are you now?" I could hear the forced enthusiasm in Percy's voice as she

pulled apart a particularly stubborn tangle with her
fingers.

"About eight months."

"Wow, that's coming up fast, isn't it?" She
continued with her comb, avoiding looking in the
mirror in front of them.

"Yup! I'm so excited. I'm having my baby shower
at the end of the month, and it's my first. I can't wait to
play with all the stuff!"

"I bet!" Percy's voice warmed and her face
brightened as she settled into the work and the
conversation, probably happy to talk about something
other than her husband or the recent tragedies. "How's
your husband holding up?"

"Good. He's nervous, I think. We chose not to find
out if we're having a boy or girl. I think he's nervous
about having a girl. He doesn't have any sisters to ease
him into it. Just me. We'll see." Jenni's words dropped
off, and she bent her head forward as Percy cut her
guides.

I stopped listening to their conversation and took a
deep breath because my next client had arrived.
Monique could be difficult, to say the least

"Are you ready for your cut?" I asked, approaching
her.

She glanced down at the magazine in her hand and
shook her head. "I think I need to look a bit more
before I decide."

"All right. I'll be waiting behind the front desk.
Come get me when you're ready." I walked away and
let her look.

She always asked for the same thing. I really don't
know why she felt the need to look at different
magazines and books every single time. Her haircut is
what I called a modified wedge. It had the same

general shape, just not as defined and with longer sides. She had yet to vary from that cut, and I'd been doing it for a couple of years at that point. It's something she had to get trimmed every month in order to keep the shape intact.

I leaned against the front counter, arms folded under my chest.

Meredith was scheduled to arrive in about half an hour, so I had a moment to myself. The phone didn't even ring.

If the crazy bat didn't make a decision soon, it was going to be time for my next client.

She approached the desk holding the same book as always. She held a spot with her finger and opened to it as she flopped it on the counter.

"I want something like this," she pointed at the picture of the same old wedge. "Only less full and a bit longer on the sides."

"Maybe take the sides to about here?" I indicted a line just about chin length, with the side of my hand on the picture of the model.

"Yes. Maybe just a smidgen shorter, but yes. Do you need the picture?" she asked, holding the book out to me.

"Nope, I think I've got the idea." I knew my part of the script well. "I'll put that back and meet you at the shampoo bowl."

"Oh, I don't need a shampoo today, I already did it." She patted her dry hair with one meticulously manicured hand.

"At least let me wet it down there. It's quicker than the squirt bottle." I was running short on time, and Monique had massive amounts of hair.

"All right." She marched herself over to the shampoo bowls to wait for me.

I set the book back on the coffee table and took my time following her, mentally preparing myself to deal with her.

The water temperature I used may have been a little cool for her taste, but I really didn't care.

She moved to my chair, and I started combing her out.

"Can you go a little gentler? My scalp is a bit tender today." She stopped me with a scowl aimed at me in the mirror.

There was nothing tender about that woman, skinny broad that she was. If she didn't tip so well, I'd become suddenly unavailable.

"Sorry about that. Let me know if I start pulling again." I slowed my combing, still managing to finish in record time.

I had her tip her chin down and began cutting my base-line. I had to repeatedly push her head down as I started angling the back of her hair out at 45-degrees and then rocking up as I reached the hair at the top of her occipital bone. That's where the wedge was modified—a true wedge is kept at 45 degrees all the way up.

I straightened her head and trimmed her side angles. When I finished, I offered her a hand mirror and spun her around so she could inspect the back.

Monique turned her head this way and that, examining my work, a frown creasing her features.

"I think the sides are too pointy, don't you think?" she fingered the tips of her hair.

"They're not any pointier than usual but I can round them if you want me to." I put on my professional I'm-hiding-my-need-to-throttle-you voice.

"Yes, please do that." She returned the mirror and folded her hands back in her lap as she continued studying my every move in the mirror.

I spun her to the side, preventing her from watching me work. She drove me nuts, with her watching and critiquing, usually when I hadn't even touched the sections she was whining about.

I rounded up the points, checked them for balance, then spun her back towards the mirror.

"How's that?" I asked.

"Well, the sides are a little shorter than I wanted, but I guess it will do." She ran long, almond-shaped nail through the cut.

"Great, how about a blow-dry?" I reached for a medium-sized round brush and my drier.

"I think you'd better. It's chilly out."

I filled my hand with a mound of mousse, emulsified it, and ran my hands through her hair, then dried it with extra care to keep the shape in the back from getting too bubbly. Using a soft-bristled brush, I smoothed everything, then gave it a coat of hairspray before letting her examine it again.

"What do you think?" I asked, standing back with my hands on my hips, trying to inconspicuously clear the hairspray residue from my nose by wiping it on my shoulder.

"Good. I should be set for another month."

Thank the Lord. "Great, I'll meet you at the front desk in a moment. I'm just going to clean up real quick." I swept up, pulled hair from brushes, and stuck my comb in the barbicide container on my dark wood vanity top.

I cashed her out and scheduled another appointment in exactly one month, getting three seconds of breathing room before my next client.

Wash, cut, blow-dry, repeat.

When we all got a moment, I called for everyone's

attention.

"Hey, ladies, my band is playing at Club West tonight at nine. I'd love it if you'd all stop by." I smiled at Meredith. It was kind of guaranteed that Scott would be there, so I was betting she'd show up.

"What's the name of it?" she asked, tucking her hair behind her ear, then running her fingers through the length.

"Club West," I repeated.

"No, your band."

"Oh, Chaos Theory. Austin came up with the name right before I joined up."

"Do you do covers or originals?" Toni asked.

"Both, but mostly originals. We'll probably do a few covers tonight so people can actually dance a bit." I took a seat and propped my tired feet on my station.

"Cool, I'll do my best to escape and come check you out." Toni left us to do a pedicure.

They all promised to make an appearance, and I wondered who would actually show up.

I went back to work, inviting clients I thought would appreciate our heavy sound. With any luck, we'd draw a bit of a crowd from Orono since we played on campus often and had a pretty loyal following in the area. It's nice to be adored.

I started getting ready as soon as we closed, grabbing my already prepared ensemble from the closet.

Plugging my iPod into its surprisingly amped-up speaker system, I cranked up the volume, letting the music get me energized and into performance mode. I scrubbed the hairspray and styling products out of my hair in the shower and shaved the hair in my armpits that grew a little faster than is normal, as I was planning on wearing a tank top. I threw my hair up in a towel before pulling on a clean black bra and underwear.

Standing in front of the mirror, I pumped a few squirts of straightening cream into my palm, emulsifying it and applying from ends to roots, distributing it further with a comb. I blow-dried with a huge round brush and ran a straightener over it. It's a pain in the butt to squirt down your hair with protective spray, but it keeps it from frying. It all went up into a sleek updo away from my face with a billion bobby pins and shellacking hairspray to keep it all in place. There is nothing worse than hair sticking to your sweaty face and neck when you're on stage.

Heavy black liner, gold shadow, and dark red lips were my signature stage makeup, so I had plenty of practice getting it done quickly.

Now for the hard part: getting the tank top over the hair and makeup. I should have dressed before putting it up, but hindsight is 20/20, or so I've heard. I managed by stretching the neck and body wide, then slowly lowering it over my head. Wriggling into tight black skinny jeans was only slightly less difficult. My new red corset went on top of the tank, and I pulled on my multi-buckle biker boots over the jeans. I kept my jewelry minimal as it was too easy to catch things with my bow.

I shamelessly tucked my money and ID into my bra, which was accessible through my neckline. I just had to remember to remove them before I got to the bar. I wouldn't have to worry about keys because they would be locked safely in Austin's house. We'd be taking the van, and if I wanted to leave early, I could always hitch a ride from Percy or Lacey-Marie. Or run home. I'd done that before as well.

When I reached the bottom of the stairs, strains of

music caught my ear from my bedroom.

"Oops," I muttered, dashing back up to turn it off. I had a one-track mind, and it was focused on leaving. It stopped just as I reached the top of the stairs. Thank you, house.

With my bag of violin junk under one arm and my performance amp under the other, I struggled to my truck.

Hades beat me to the door and grabbed my amp before opening the door for me.

"Thanks," I said. I didn't find it heavy, just unwieldy.

"See, I'm not really as bad as you believe," he said, leading the way.

"You're working on changing my mind, but you still have a ways to go. I have a lot of preconceived notions." I opened my door and slid my bag across the worn seat.

Hades lifted my amp into the bed of the truck, then turned to face me. "Why don't you just leave those notions behind?"

"Sorry, can't. You're just going to have to deal with being guilty until proven innocent." I leaned against the truck bed, studying the hulking fae man before me.

"Fine. Would it be all right if I escorted Percy to your performance tonight?" He closed my tailgate with a bang, causing the whole truck to shudder under my arm.

"Yeah, sure. As so long as you behave yourself." I opened the door and climbed into the driver's seat.

"I think I can manage that. See you in a bit." He strode back to the house.

He was rapidly racking up points for himself in the I'm-going-to-have-to-like-him column. I hate it when I'm forced to like someone. It takes away any sense of independent thinking. I could live with it for Percy, despite the uneasy feeling he still gave me. I could smell the power rolling off of him whenever we were in a room together, and my every instinct told me to run from the bigger, badder predator.

The guys were already loading up the van when I arrived, so I scrambled out and jumped into the bed of my truck to slide my amp towards the tailgate. Austin pulled the tailgate open and balanced the amp while I jumped down to heft it to the van. Luckily, the thing had wheels, so I didn't have to pretend to be weaker than I was while shoving it forward. I parked it right outside so it could get loaded in whatever neurotic order the boys chose.

People always looked at me funny when I called them my boys. I guess it's because, for all appearances, I'm the youngest of the bunch. No need to burst their bubbles and let them in on the secret that I was alive and terrorizing the world long before they were even a twinkle in mommy and daddy's eyes.

I watched as they puzzled in amps, tubs of equipment, and Austin's drums. If it didn't fit just so, I knew there was a very good chance it would all come out, and they'd start again.

My bag of equipment and Lola would stay with me. No way were they packing those out of my sight.

Scott's bass got pieced in next, wedged between two amps and the tom. I started to wonder if there was going to be space for actual people. There were only two seats: the driver and one passenger. Two would ride up front, all buckled in and legal, while the other two sat jammed in with the equipment. There were blankets to hide under if we got pulled over. It had yet to happen, but one can never be too careful about these things, though evidently not careful enough to take a second vehicle to gigs.

The boys always tried to force me to ride up front. Maybe it made them feel macho to take care of the lone woman, but I never gave in to them. I can outstubborn just about anyone, and I'm the one least likely to get hurt if we got in an accident. They didn't get to know that tidbit, else it would have been a handy excuse.

"You look hot, by the way," Scott said as he came up beside me and slid an arm around my waist.

"Thanks. Meredith might be coming tonight." I said, sidestepping his advances

"Really?" He pulled away, looking mildly interested.

"Yep. I invited all the girls."

"Oh." His bravado deflated slightly.

"And Doug. Meredith seemed especially excited to come."

He scowled and slouched off to finish packing.

We would be getting to the club an hour or so early to set up and do sound check. It was a good thing it wasn't busy early on. If you came expecting to see a band and saw the opening act of tuning instead, it's a bit of a letdown.

We had our customary where-does-Gretchen-sit argument, which I won. They've physically placed me in the front seat before when I just didn't have the heart to kick their asses.

I scrunched myself between my amp and a wall. As long as Austin didn't take the corners at his normal NASCAR pace, I'd avoid any bone crushing injuries.

Mark must have drawn the short straw because he ended up back there with me, hidden behind half a drum kit.

"Work go good?" Mark asked me over the blaring

stereo.

"Yeah, same old, same old. You?"

"Yup."

We didn't carry on much of a conversation beyond that. It was hard to stay coherent. Apparently, Austin was bent on making us all deaf before we even got to our destination.

I normally wear earplugs while performing. Wolves have sensitive hearing, and that carries over into my human form as well, so I have to be careful even if any harm I could come by would be temporary. Temporarily could end up being too long, especially with the pack around.

The parking lot at Club West was still relatively empty, which was good for us. No one would be jonesing for dance music while we were getting our levels adjusted.

When Scott opened the sliding door, I jumped out, somewhat stiffly, clutching my violin. I slung my bag over my shoulders so that it hung diagonally across my chest.

Unloading was something I could participate in without messing up the order of things too much. When my amp came down, I went ahead and wheeled it towards the entrance. I didn't get 10 feet away before Mark caught up and plopped a duffel of equipment on top. I smiled venomously at him and continued pushing. I would have to come back for more stuff after I got my things settled.

It had been a long time since I'd been inside Club West. They had built a new stage with steep stairs that someone had thoughtfully placed a ramp over. I left my equipment for a second to check it out. I placed a foot on the plywood, checking for wobble, then walked halfway up and bounced forcefully. It was a little creaky, but it seemed safe enough.

The place smelled like old sweat, alcohol, and a slight tinge of cleaning products. I loved it.

Backing my amp up in line with the ramp, I got a running start. It seemed like the easiest way to get it on stage without mishap.

My plan worked out in my favor. I was soon joined by Austin, so I felt comfortable enough to leave my stuff. I wouldn't have if one of the guys wouldn't always be on stage. I don't trust people not to touch what isn't theirs.

On my next trip, I toted mic stands and a kick pedal. Not exactly heavy lifting, but I got to feel useful. With all of us coming and going, we got unpacked in 10 minutes, about the quarter of the time it took us to pack up.

See what happens when you let me help? I'm efficient, I tell you!

Once we got all our junk on stage, we set things up to our liking, plugging in this, tuning that.

I set my laptop up on a music stand and turned it on. There were some rifts I prerecorded to play harmonies live with. You got my electric harmonizing with my acoustic, and it was shivers-down-your-spine magic as long as I kept it toned down to human and avoided sounding something 'other.' It's a slightly different sound.

The club's sound guy got us plugged into his system, and we told him what we liked, then left him to do his work. He was new as well. Some sound guys can make you sound like professionals. Others would make sure you never got a following. I was crossing my fingers, hoping he was the former.

I finished tuning and turned on my sound. I plucked a little for sound quality, then picked up my bow and started jamming. I cranked the volume on my amp and half sat on it, one foot planted on the ground. I like feeling the sound as much as hearing it. Austin picked up his sticks and started a rhythm. We fell in together beautifully, which was promising for the rest of the night. I liked playing with the guys because we read each other so well, musically speaking.

I wasn't always part of the band. Mark had picked me up at a music store where I was playing around with different model electrics. He introduced me to the rest of the guys, we jammed for a few weeks, then I started playing with them at gigs. Not much more to it than that.

Mark and Scott joined in quickly, and we jammed on stage while the sound guy played with his slides and tried to make us sound good out on the dance floor. He'd have to readjust as the night wore on and the sound changed as the place filled up.

Mark brought us around to our opening song so the microphones could be added into the mix. There were a few minutes of 'thumbs up,' 'thumbs down,' 'okay' sign language with the sound booth, but we eventually got pretty close to what we wanted to hear, at least up on stage.

"We good?" I asked, setting my violin atop my amp.

"I think so," said Mark

"Great! I need a bottle of water. See you guys at nine!"

I skipped the whole stairs and ramp routine, and jumped from the stage to the floor.

I'm sure the bartender would have been happier to serve me an actual drink, but I craved hydration. I'm always hot. Compound that with spotlights, and I was roasting.

I beat a mad dash to the ladies room to check my makeup—no globs of streaming eyeliner yet, but the night was young. This would be my last chance to use the bathroom for a while, so I took advantage. There was nothing worse than the urge to pee in the middle of a set. Been there, wanted to avoid that.

The place was starting to fill up. Good. Hopefully we'd get a good crowd of people who'd never seen us before, along with our regular fans. Most of our normal crowd I could at least pick out on sight, even if I didn't know most of their names.

The lights dimmed, and I booked it up to the stage, jumping up in the same manner I got down, maybe with a little too much spring—though I did use my hands to look like I was propelling myself—but no one really noticed in the darkened room.

I picked up my violin and waited, motionless with my bow poised in the air.

"Ladies and gentlemen, thank you so much for coming out this evening. We've got a great night ahead of us. A lot of you know and love tonight's band, so I'll turn things over to them. Please welcome Chaos Theory!" Our host leapt to the side as the spotlights turned red over us.

I placed my bow to string and slowly drew it across the lowest note. The opening to our first song drew attention better than our introduction. Music is always better than words for that. The rest of the band jumped in, and we were off. We played hard, fast, and loud, loving every minute of it.

We completed the first set to thunderous applause and promised to be back in 15 minutes.

A DJ took over, and we took advantage of the dance floor. We dance, mingled, and talked our way across the room and back. I got the barest moment to say hi to Doug, who was lurking around the edge of the room.

I was somewhere near the middle of the floor when I felt a large hand grab my backside. Before I could stop myself, I swung, fur bristling and a deep snarl ripping out of my throat. The look on the guy's face was priceless as he beheld me partly changed. It was even worse than in the hair salon the other day. The bristling I felt was actual fur sprouting from my pores. Thank goodness it was dark and loud so no one besides my groper noticed.

You can always depend on people to act oblivious of things that frighten and confuse them. Their brains disengage, which in that particular case is a good thing.

I shoved my way off the dance floor and out the back door. It was relatively empty where I exited, so I chose a corner to take deep breaths of cool night air and bring myself back to humanity. My contacts were wrecked but I wasn't really worried about that. While I was on stage, people would accept amber eyes as part of my look.

Austin noticed right away when we got back on stage.

"Did you just put in contacts?" he asked, staring at my eyes in fascination.

"Yeah, what do you think?" I batted my lashes at him, improvising on the fly.

"They're awesome! You should wear them all the time."

"I was going to put them in earlier, but I forgot," I lied. Maybe I would start performing without contacts. I could certainly see better without them.

I could spot the girls now and then through the spotlights, and I wondered if Meredith had actually made it and if Scott had found her.

I didn't see Hades, so that must have meant he'd actually kept himself down to manpower. He'd have stuck out like a beacon if he hadn't covered himself in a glamour.

If you didn't count my almost change on the dance floor, it was a very good night.

Chapter 16:
Mourning

Monday morning was one of the busiest in a while, and that was saying something. Things escalated when Mem Franz walked in, looking how I felt. She wasn't wearing makeup and her hair was thrown into a crooked ponytail. And she was alone. Mem never came alone. Her husband always drove her.

She waited until I had my current haircut complete, then she pulled me aside.

"My George died this morning," she sobbed into my shoulder.

I wrapped my arms around her. "Oh, Mem, I'm so sorry." I didn't want to ask what happened. It seemed disrespectful somehow.

She pulled away just enough to speak. "He had a heart attack. He was out for a walk with his dog. When Cecil came home without George, I knew something was wrong, and then my neighbors called. They found him and called an ambulance." Her shoulders shook with her sobs. "He died before they got there."

I gently towed her into the kitchen and sat her in one of the worn chairs. My next appointment would just have to wait. I started a kettle for tea and got out two mugs. She was about to be treated to my anti-wolf tea. I figured she could use something soothing.

I let her babble as I poured, but eventually, I had to interrupt her. "Mem, I'm so sorry, I've gotta go do a haircut. Will you be all right here for a little bit?"

"Yes," she sniffled into a handkerchief that she'd probably embroidered herself with teal paisley edges.

I didn't believe her, but I got up anyway and kissed her on the forehead before heading back out to work.

My next client was a little perturbed at being made to wait, but that was just too bad. Mem had been a client and friend for a long time. I was extra nice, or at least as close as I could get to extra nice at the time. They tipped and left without any more complaint.

When I had a lull, I went back to Mem, who was still clutching her now cold mug of tea. Without a word, I took it from her hands, reheated it in the microwave, and handed it back.

I took up my insulated tumbler and sipped. She copied me.

She'd stopped crying, but I could tell the tears were still close to the surface. I'd known she'd come to me for a reason, so I waited silently. If she wanted to talk, then I'd let her talk. If she just wanted companionship, then I'd be there for her.

She took my hand. "Thank you."

"I wish I could tell you everything was going to be all right. I wish I knew that was the truth. I've lost before, and it near killed me. Whatever you want from me, I'm here for you." I squeezed her hand with both of mine.

"You've seen a lot, haven't you?" She was watching my face as she spoke, her eyes tired.

I nodded in response, looking down at our clasped fingers.

"You're something different, aren't you. What have

you seen, Gretchen? What's your story?"

My breath hitched at her proclamation. "How could you possibly know?" I hadn't meant to say it out loud.

"Oh, little things. You've forgotten your contacts before, and you have claws. Also, I'm positive I've heard you growl. Like a dog."

I would have thought she was just out of it, but I could distinctly remember the moments she mentioned.

I took a deep breath and let it out. I'd known Mem for a long time. Probably long enough that she'd notice I wasn't aging and that I didn't work certain days. I decided to give her the truth. "Are you sure you want to know my story? There's a very good chance that you won't believe me. There's also a chance you'll be afraid of me."

"Tell me." She insisted, clutching my smooth-skinned hands in her papery ones.

"All right. I was born in 1829 in a brothel in Texas. My mother was probably some mix of Mexican and African, a rarity. My father was white, and he didn't know about me. The girls there named me Maude, and I worked as a maid until I was 14 and they started training me.

"One night, I was called out to serve a client at the local hotel. This client offered me the chance of a lifetime. I could become as he would make me, live forever, and be free from what they made me. Knowing fully what he was, I accepted, and he changed me. I woke up a few days later and went back to work until the full moon when I changed for the very first time. For three days, there was nothing left of my humanity. When I became myself again, I discovered that there wasn't a living soul left inside the building. I set the place on fire and fled. I kept on the move until Percy found me and offered me a job and a safe place to stay."

"You're a werewolf." Mem's tone didn't contain the doubt or even the fear that I had expected, just acceptance.

"I am."

I waited, but Mem didn't say anything further. She just patted my hands, then let go to sip her tea.

My being a werewolf was easier to accept than her husband's death.

"You're not afraid of me?" I asked, feeling the need to broach the subject.

"No, why would I be?" she asked in return, her eyebrows furrowed and her head cocked to one side.

"I'm a monster. Anyone in their right mind would be afraid of me." I drew my arms wide like I could expose everything inside.

"I'm not in my right mind, dear, and even if I was, what would the point be? You've been cutting my hair for years, and you've yet to take a bite out of me."

I laughed softly, then leaned over to top off her tea with the pot sitting over the warmer on the middle of the table.

"This is good. I can't quite place the flavor. What is it?" She sniffed the steaming liquid.

"It's lavender, chamomile, spearmint, and lemon. It helps keep me calm so I don't wolf out on my clients."

"Hm, well it's *magnifique*. Just the right thing. And I thank you for telling me your story. I needed the distraction. Will you help me?" She paused to pull herself together again, sucking a deep, shaky breath in through her nose. "Will you help me make the arrangements for George?"

"Of course. Just tell me what needs doing."

"Would you mind if I stayed here for a while? I know you have to work, but I just can't go home right now."

I nodded. "Would you be more comfortable in the library for now? Percy's got a hundred books, and I could set you up with some more tea if you'd like."

"Please."

I went about making another pot of tea for her, spooning into a clean steeper basket, setting it in another pot, and pouring boiling water over it. I grabbed the box of ginger snaps and dumped them in a shallow handmade blue bowl. "All right, come with me." I held a hand out to her and picked up the tray of goodies with the other.

She took my elbow instead, freeing up my hand to balance the tray.

Hades met us halfway down the hall and silently took the tray from me.

"Hades, this is Mem, an old friend of mine. Mem, this is Percy's husband, Hades."

Hades bowed over Mem's hand and kissed her knuckles. The man had some impressive manners. "It's a pleasure to make your acquaintance, *madame*."

"Pleasure is all mine," she murmured back, her voice sounding empty after so much crying.

"Mem's going to hang out in the library for the rest of the day. Would you check on her from time to time and see if she needs anything?" I requested like he was a servant instead of a god.

"Of course. It would be a pleasure." He walked into the library with us and set the tray on the coffee table.

"Hades is a gentleman of leisure at the moment. Feel free to ask him for anything," I said.

"Thank you so much." Mem settled herself in one of the big overstuffed armchairs while I located an afghan for her.

"Not a problem. I'll be back in a while. If you need anything—"

"I'll be fine." Mem interrupted me and sent me on my way.

Hades followed me out.

"Her husband just died," I whispered. "And I just told her about me."

"Was that wise?" he asked, his smile making it seem as if he wasn't at all perturbed at the idea.

"Apparently she already knew something was up with me. We'll see how she is when it sinks in. I didn't say anything about the rest of you, so don't worry."

"I don't really care what she knows, either way, but Percy and Lacey-Marie may." He followed me down the hall to the kitchen.

Doug was helping himself to a cup of coffee. Nice that he suddenly felt so comfortable in this crazy house. I smirked when I saw the pink unicorn mug he was frowning at.

"You didn't pick that out, did you?" I asked.

"No."

"It's the house. It's magic."

He might have been giving me 'a look,' but it was obscured by all the hair.

"No, really. The house is alive. Just use it. It's impossible to argue."

He sighed and poured the coffee, leaving it black.

"Since you're here, will you do me a favor?"

He stood holding his steaming coffee, waiting.

"A good friend of mine is sitting in the library because her husband just died. Will you go sit in the room with her? You don't have to talk. Just sit and read or play on the computer or whatever. I just don't want her to be alone. Hades will look in from time to time, but since you're here mooching coffee..."

"Yes. I could do that." He nodded. "I won't make her uncomfortable?"

"I just told her I was a werewolf."

"Oh, I see." He sipped his coffee, nodding his head as he swallowed.

"Yeah. Come on, I'll get you settled. Welcome to the house. Oh, and Mem teaches French, so I'd bet she'll love talking with you."

"I want to speak with you later."

"Fine." I led him down the hall and got him settled in front of the computer, then excused myself back to my job.

Focusing on my work was difficult, but I didn't receive any complaints. After shutting down the salon for the evening, I got to discover that Hades had invited Doug to stay over for dinner.

We didn't have anything fancy planned, so Percy dropped her glamour, Lacey-Marie poured her donor blood into a glass and sipped it with a twisty straw, and I tore apart a half mooing cow. It was us in all our disgusting glory. Appetizing.

Doug didn't utter a word during dinner. Neither did Mem, who was in too much shock to notice anything strange.

I was more worried about Mem than Doug. He couldn't have picked a worse time to come check out how the real freaks lived.

I watched her lift a couple of forkfuls of shepherd's pie to her lips, but she barely took a nibble. She did drink her water, so at least we didn't have to worry about her becoming dehydrated. She looked tired and as if she was barely holding it together. In this case, I was sure the truth was on display.

I led her up the stairs to my room after dinner. "I'm going to send one of the girls after your stuff. Do you have a key with you?" I rushed around the room, trying to tidy up.

"You don't need to do that for me," she said, standing with her arms tightly hugging her rib cage like she was trying to hold herself together.

"You need your things." I paused to rub her shoulder. I wasn't really sure how to do the whole comforting thing.

"No, I mean clean. I'm not really worried about that right now."

"Oh." I kept tidying anyhow while Mem dug keys out of her purse, which I brought downstairs to Lacey.

"Can you pack her some things?"

"Of course." She took the key from me and headed for the door.

"Don't forget to lock up after you're finished!"

"I won't!" And she was gone.

Doug was still sitting in the kitchen. Alone.

"All right, what do you want?" I crossed my arms and settled my weight onto my right leg with my left extended slightly to the side.

"What's it like? Being a werewolf, I mean." He got up and walked across the room to stand by me.

That was his question? Did he want me to help improve his show?

"Sometimes it's great, and sometimes it really sucks," I answered

"Example?"

"The change is incredibly painful, but once it's over, and you let the wolf out of its cage, it feels like nothing can stop you." Why was I telling him this?

"If you bit me right now, would I become one?"

Oh, God. He was serious. "No. I'm not an alpha changer." And I was beyond thrilled that I couldn't change anyone. It wasn't a responsibility that I wanted.

"What's an alpha changer?" He looked up from his mug, his eyes shining with interest.

"He's a pure fae, not actually a werewolf. He doesn't change, but his bite alters human DNA. I'm still human. I've just got fae magic in my blood."

"Did it hurt?" He turned his gaze down to his feet as he shuffled his sneakers.

"Probably. I wasn't really conscious after the bite."

"Do you think, if I could get an alpha changer to bite me, I could be normal?" His eyes looked like a lost child's, peeking out from his hairy face.

He thought being a wolf was more normal than having hypertrichosis?

"I honestly don't know, but I wouldn't think so." I had to be honest. He was so hopeful. I rested my hand on his forearm, wishing I could soften my words to make him feel better.

"But it's worth a shot." Doug pushed himself away from the wall he was leaning against and left me feeling a troubling sense that I was responsible for whatever he tried to do.

Chapter 17:
Journalism

I could hear Mem alternately tossing and crying throughout the night. I'd let her have the bed while I sacked out on the floor in a sleeping bag. I didn't mind. It felt right having her there instead of sending her home alone.

We hadn't discussed how long she would stay, but I'd tried to make it clear that she was welcome to stay for as long as she needed.

I stopped by the funeral home early in the morning with her list of wants for George's funeral. She'd requested that I comb his hair. He didn't have much, and the undertaker could have done it, but it meant so much to Mem for me to do it. It isn't uncommon for someone to request their stylist to care for a deceased loved one's hair, or for theirs. A time or two during my career, I'd had older woman request that I style their hair when they died. I agree every time. It's not something they need to be worrying about, and I'm not uncomfortable with dead bodies. I got over that a long time ago.

However, spending my morning in a funeral home did not prepare me for what was coming that day.

Stress, stress, and more stress. There's only so much a werewolf can take.

I checked on Mem as soon as I got back, but she was still asleep. Not wanting to disturb her, I got ready in my bathroom, trying to avoid the clatters and slams that accompany such activities.

A yawn cracked my jaw as I worked through my clients. I thought I had some pretty good excuses for being distracted. Now I just needed to get back on track.

It was a kid morning. We got Matty, Thos, and Dale right off. And then I got Evelyn Gagner. She was a new client for me, but I swore I knew her name from somewhere. I studied her as she made her way over to the shampoo bowl. Forties, solid build, trendy professional. Nope, I wasn't placing her.

I vigorously scrubbed shampoo into her hair, rinsed it, then let her conditioner set for a moment.

I asked her about the weather. It was apparently a beautiful day.

I checked the water temperature one more time with my fingers before rinsing her hair out, wrapped her up in a towel turban, and led her to my chair.

"So what did you have in mind for today?" I utilized my customary opening line to break the ice.

"Just a trim. Maybe like this much?" She held up a clump of hair pinched about an inch up from her ends.

"Sure, that should clean it up nicely. Do you want me to take the same amount off the layers?" I combed and sectioned her hair with clips.

"Please. So how long did Penny work with you?" she asked, as if we were still talking about the weather.

"Uh, a year or so." I didn't think anything of it and began cutting.

"What was she like?"

"Outgoing, eager, fun." I continued on with my work.

"Uh huh, and did she ever say she felt like someone was ever, uh, watching her?"

Why was she asking so many questions about Penny? "No."

"Are you worried you're going to be next?" Evelyn asked.

"Are you a reporter?" I dropped my comb on the floor and kicked it under my station.

"Yes."

Well, a cookie for telling the truth. "Don't ask any more questions."

I grabbed another comb from my drawer and pressed my lips shut.

She turned herself in my chair so she could view the rest of the salon and whipped a little notebook out of the purse she insisted on holding in her lap.

I breathed deeply, willing my self-control to remain intact, and hurried with the cut. As she continued taking notes, I turned her to face the empty fireplace. Let her take notes on that.

I blow-dried her hair and charged her extra for the style. I'm a firm believer in pain-in-the-ass tax.

Thankfully, I got her out the door before she could con someone else into answering her questions. I really hoped she wouldn't use my name in the article. I hadn't thought of protesting that.

I decided I didn't like reporters.

As soon as I got a chance, I pulled Percy aside and told her what had just occurred.

"I have a feeling she won't be the only one. Is there any way we can keep them out?" I asked.

"Not if they're paying. Just do the best you job you can, and steer the discussion back to small talk. I know it's not right to use them as an advertising opportunity, but we might as well while they're breaking down our doors."

Percy was probably right, but I didn't like it.

Mem shuffled down the stairs partway through the day, then on into the kitchen. Her eyes were swollen and bloodshot from crying, with bags underneath large enough to carry small dogs. She seemed to like Hades, nice young man and all that, so I hoped he'd be back there to keep her entertained and not thinking about her circumstances.

It was definitely a kid day. Big people ones and little people ones. There is no need to differentiate if the mentality is the same. Of course, 'adults' paid more, so I guess I would have to acknowledge the age portrayed on the Big People kids' IDs.

I'd just finished blow-drying one such 'adult' when a van pulled up outside the salon.

Then another.

And another.

A guy climbed out of the back of the first van carrying an expensive looking camera and jumped to the ground without a wobble.

Not one, but three separate news crews were setting up outside the salon. I didn't even know we had three local stations.

Out of each van emerged the pretty people. News journalists in their suits and perfectly done hair. Oh, and really bad makeup. I could see the foundation lines from inside the salon. Of course, I have better eyesight than most.

There was a small commotion from their makeup teams as they completed a bit of primping and retouching.

Horrible, horrible work. How do people like that get hired?

Big, fake, too-white thousand-watt smiles took over

their overly made up faces. I couldn't hear a word, but I wasn't liking it.

Percy finished up a haircut, sending the woman back to her busy day. As soon as she made it out the door, she was mobbed by scary teeth and cameras.

She was a deer caught in headlights. Her eyes grew wide as she froze, glued to the spot. When the mics were shoved in her face, I could see the color drain out of her cheeks.

"Hades!" I shouted with more growl in my voice than I intended to let loose. I knew if I went out to direct traffic, I might rip some throats out.

"What?" Hades poked his head through the back door of the salon.

"Have a look outside, then go intimidate." I tossed my head in the direction of the window.

I watched as Hades threw off his glamour, little flimsy thing that it was, and became a god. On second thought, maybe I was the better choice. He opened the door with such force that I thought he'd take the door off its hinges.

Just because you can, doesn't mean you should, Hades.

He slammed the door behind him, shaking the whole house. I was shocked that he didn't crack the door frame. He towered over the news people, effectively blocking Percy's client from the media's view.

Another person pulled in, one of our regulars, scheduled for a haircut with Lacey-Marie. Hades had to escort him from the car to the salon. It looked like he had a job for the day.

The parking lot was getting backed up with four or five people coming and going at any given time and only one Hades.

Even with Hades escorting clients back and forth, the news crews still managed to mob a good half of our clientele. I could tell he was getting fed up with his new position, but he kept at it.

From time to time, Percy and I would go out and help clear paths, all the while trying to avoid being filmed ourselves.

Things escalated when a beat-up old car pulled in, and the door opened. Could Doug have picked a worse time to come play 20 questions with the werewolf? Not to mention that 20 questions with a werewolf really isn't a smart idea in the first place.

I could see his door, partway open, his furry head peeking up over the top, trying to detect the perfect moment to run for it.

Hades saw him and decided to come to his rescue. It looked like he was going to run one news anchor over in his pursuit of a clear path. Together, the two men booked it to the door. The resounding slam that accompanied them shook the room.

"That's it, we've got to do something about this. They've got to go." Hades set the lock on the door, keeping the media out.

"Honey, you can't lock the door. We're still open." Percy stood with her hands on her hips, tapping her foot.

"Yes, well, I'm done for the day. You want someone to make the news cracks play nice, you do it." Hades stomped across the room, not caring that we still had a salon full of clients.

"Can the police do anything?" I asked.

"I don't know. They haven't come inside yet," Percy answered, shaking her head.

"They're harassing everyone who comes and goes, but I doubt the cops can do anything about that.

They'll just wait off property and film there." Hades seated himself on one of the waiting area couches.

The woman waiting across from him looked frightened.

"Maybe we should shut down until this all blows over," I suggested, earning a pout from my client.

"You've got my vote. No one's gonna wanna go through that anyhow. Let's finish up everyone here. Then we'll post a sign at the bottom of the driveway," Lacey-Marie suggested, wiping her razor on her dark pink skirt, then following her customer to the front counter.

"I second that. We should've stayed closed in the first place." I fluffed my client's hair and asked, "How's that feel?"

"Perfect. Does this mean he's not going to walk me to my car?" she asked while running her fingers through her new hair.

"I'll walk you out. Don't worry." And then I'd march right down the driveway and plant a sign to tell people to go away.

"Just give me a moment. I'm making a sign. Sorry, Perce, you've been outvoted. We're closing. Can you go get me some wrapping paper?" I figured wrapping paper would be my best thing to wrap around our sign and secure with duct tape.

"I'll get it," Lacey volunteered. She'd finished cashing her client out.

"I'll go with you," Doug said, appearing at my elbow.

Sneaky little fuzz ball. "I can take care of myself, thanks. I don't think you need to get filmed again." Besides, I'd have to worry about him while we were out there.

Lacey danced up to me, carrying an enormous roll

of green paper printed with orange wrapped presents.

"This is god-awful," I said, taking it from her.

"I figured no one would miss it." Lacey curled her lip at the paper in mock disgust.

I located one of those jumbo permanent markers that make you lightheaded as soon as you pull off the cap, and wrote: 'Sorry, closed until further notice" in giant letters. A quick dig through the desk drawers got me a roll of packing tape.

"All right, ladies." I picked up the wrapping paper, stuck it under my arm, and wore the packing tape like a bracelet on my left wrist. "Are you ready?"

"Ready!" they called in unison.

"Wait for me!" Percy's client clip-clopped her way over in sky high heels.

"All right, stick close." I prepared myself with some deep, fortifying yet calming breaths.

Doug, ignoring my refusal, took up the rear.

Hades got the door for us. He was adamant about not going back outside. The door sounded very final behind our backs, like we were going to battle.

If we were a movie, we would have been filmed in slow motion. Me in front, set face, battle ready. Three frightened women keeping close behind. My faithful Neanderthal guarding our backs. The media crew was the attacking horde, brandishing their lethal . . . cameras.

All right, so maybe the fantasy film analogy didn't work. I wasn't allowed to cut anyone anyhow.

I delivered the first woman to her car without a hitch. The other two were a challenge because one of the cameramen figured out what we were up to. They were like sheep following a bucket of grain.

Doug ran interference, which was pretty effective —you don't see too many people covered in that much hair in Maine. Wait, I take that back, Maine was full of people just like him, with just their eyeballs peeking out from under bushy brows and above wizard-like beards. They came out once a year for their annual sheering in the spring.

Woman number two I shoved into her car. She helped us by gunning her engine, then driving at the camera crews while she had their attention. They scattered, and I got woman number three into her car.

The three vehicles acted as my escort to the end of the driveway and then took off.

I'd never moved so fast in my life, wrapping up that sign, and taping it in place. I grabbed Doug's hand and hauled ass back to the salon. I'm surprised he kept up with me. I wasn't even trying to be human at that point.

The door open, via Hades, and I grabbed the handle from him, producing my own satisfactory slam. I leaned against the solid wood of the door, sliding to the floor.

"Well, that was intense." I tucked my knees up to my chin and reached up to twist the lock, breathing hard.

The others were all busy going through our books, canceling the rest of the day. It was too bad we couldn't know how the next week would go, so we could stay ahead of the game.

Doug flopped next to the front desk, fighting to catch his breath. "I thought I was in good shape, but you, damn," he gasped out.

"You are in good shape. I'm just—" I stopped that line when I remembered I wasn't 'out' to the girls. "I work out a lot."

Doug nodded, catching on to what I actually meant. It didn't matter how in-shape he was. I had wolf magic coursing through my veins. It was an unfair advantage that I was okay with.

Mem wandered back into the salon.

"What on earth is going on out here." She caught a glimpse of the circus going on outside our front door. "Oh."

"I'll catch you up later," I promised.

She nodded and shuffled back out. She shuffled a lot, like her husband had been the only thing keeping her limbs working.

"Come on, man, let's go for a hike. I think the girls need to talk." Hades gave Doug the man nod towards the back door.

Doug pushed himself up off the floor and followed him out.

I shifted my carcass from my spot and headed to the waiting area where the others were gathered.

"So now what?" asked Toni. Not being a stylist, she wasn't feeling threatened by the current crisis.

"Good question. How about it, ladies, what do you want to do? We can't keep shutting down the salon. We're going to lose business." Percy started the impromptu meeting.

"I think we can probably get a restraining order to keep the media off the lawn," Meredith suggested.

I hadn't expected her to speak up. Meredith seemed to be the quiet, reserved type.

"Perhaps. I'll call the police. What about the rest of it? I know this is a hard time for all of us. How are you all doing?" Percy took notes. Real notes this time, not doodle notes.

Toni just shrugged. "I'm not particularly worried about me. I don't do hair, but I am worried about you girls out front."

"Me too," Fern seconded her.

"How about you, Meredith?" Percy asked the only new hairdresser.

She didn't answer right away, though I could tell by the look on her face that she was worried.

"I don't know. I'm kind of scared. It sounds like there's absolutely nothing we can do to protect ourselves. The killer is doing his thing with other people in the house, and no one's heard him, as far as we know." Meredith looked down at her hands as she spoke. "I need this job. I can't afford to quit just because I'm afraid."

"Meredith, if you need anything, we'll help you out, but you'll have to let us know." Percy placed a comforting hand on her shoulder.

"Thank you," said Meredith with a nod, her eyes downcast.

I had my doubts if she'd ever come to us. I was amazed that she'd said anything about her circumstances at all.

The back door creaked, signaling the return of the manly types. I left my spot. It was time to find out what the heck Doug wanted this time.

I hated to admit it, but he had been helpful in getting our clients out. I was also impressed by how all those women worked together.

Percy watched me go, then continued the meeting.

Doug was waiting in the kitchen, and Hades nowhere in sight.

"So, what do you want this time?" I slumped into a chair.

He shrugged his shoulders. "I don't have to work until tonight. I was hoping I could find more out about being a wolf."

"Such as?" Apparently I'd resigned myself to answering his questions.

"Well, what does it look like?" he asked.

"The change or the wolf?"

"The wolf." He took a seat next to me, propping his elbows on the table and leaning forward.

"It looks like a wolf," I answered truthfully.

"How big?"

"Depends." I crossed my arms, leaning back with my eyes closed.

"On what?" he persisted.

"The size of the person. Dominance."

"Dominance? I've seen some pretty aggressive little dogs."

I smirked and opened my eyes to look at him. "That's dogs, not werewolves. The magic translates dominance into size. I guess it helps the alpha wolf's intimidation factor.

He nodded. "Can I see it?"

"No," I replied quickly. My eyes widened, my breathing sharp. Like I'm gonna get naked and change in front of him. Ha!

He looked disappointed. His smell didn't betray desire. He was genuinely disappointed not to see my wolf. The guy was obsessed.

"It's too close to full moon. If I change now, I might lose it enough to hurt someone." I paused. "I've been slipping lately."

Mem wandered in, saving me from further explanation.

"When is full moon?" he asked casually.

"In a couple days," Mem answered him, surprising me.

Was she keeping track? Only a couple of days until I wolfed out completely. Things could get very interesting.

FULL MOON

Chapter 18:
Wolf in Charge

Two days before the full moon is my time to prepare. I inspected my kennel for weaknesses in the structure. Yes, I'd already done it with Percy, but my personal methods were a little different.

Dressed in exercise clothes, so I wouldn't damage anything I wanted to wear in public, I locked myself inside my cage. Starting at the door, I ran full tilt across my enclosure and threw myself against the bars at the other end, which didn't so much as rattle, I continued the process all the way around the enclosure. If I'd heard a creak, or felt a bar turn in its socket, I'd have to get out more materials and reinforce the weak spot.

I was more adamant than ever that my structure be secure. I couldn't afford to be another monster loose among the populace. Not to mention a well aimed bullet could drop me just as well as it could a moose. Of course, I heal quickly, so unless I was shot in the head, I'd just get ticked off.

I'd been shot before, waking up after the full moon in my den with half a hunter's carcass next to me. I did everything I could not let that happen again, but accidents happened. It wasn't until I came to live with

Percy that I'd ever been fully secure.

I gathered as much force as possible and slammed my body against the door again and again. It didn't budge, so I moved on to the creature comforts, pulling the bowl out of the automatic waterer and scrubbing it, releasing all my pent up anger and anxiety on imaginary grime. I wouldn't be fully satisfied with its cleanliness until it had a chance to soak for a good 15 minutes.

Every blanket and dog bed was inspected for loose bits that would be tempting for an oversized puppy to chew.

The shavings were fresh and clean but had settled flat, so I took a gardening pitchfork, digging it in deep and fluffing it.

There were smudges on the windows, interrupting the light, so I jumped up there, clinging to the bars with one hand, and washed the windows with Windex and newspaper with the other. Hey, a wolf appreciates a nap in a warm, sunny spot just as much as anyone. I let go, falling down and landing lightly on my feet like a cat.

That night I slept in the tack room, just in case. Mem remained in my suite, and I didn't want to risk changing in front of her. It also gave me the opportunity to catch up on the Austen novel I was reading. I don't normally have that much time, and I was kind of enjoying it.

Lacey-Marie came out to visit for a bit, but she got bored easily with no TV or music. I could have brought my laptop down, but I didn't want to demolish it on accident.

My sleep was unsettled, wavering between chasing things and nightmares. The night before is always like that. That's where a pack or a mate comes in handy, offering comfort. I had neither, so I dreamed alone.

Warmth and brilliant morning rays cast themselves over my eyelids, waking me early the next day. Too bad I couldn't get out and enjoy it.

I reluctantly left my book in the tack room and locked all the doors, hanging the key on the hook next to the door in my changing room. The key to the kennel went on a similar hook on the kennel side. I'd knocked it off once and had to spend over an hour looking for it in the shavings after I came to.

Now all I had to do was wait. I didn't always change the day before, but it was rare that I didn't. Once changed, I'd stay that way through the full moon and the day after. I never remembered anything. I was anxious, so there was little chance that I wouldn't change immediately. I stripped down to nothing, tossing my clothes out the door before jailing myself completely.

Despite my years as a soiled dove, and my years of changing after that, I'd developed some modesty. I avoided being completely naked, as best I could, even in front of Lacey and Percy.

Percy would come and check on me around noon. With a whole lot of nothing to do, she very well might check on me early.

I didn't need to worry anymore. Worrying made things happen. Worrying brought on the wolf fast and hard. Worrying—

The wolf stalked around the edge of her territory, looking for signs of intruders, but all she smelled was herself and the other-smelling two-legger who came

with food from time to time.

She dragged the hot blankets off her nest and deposited them in the corner. They might be fun to shred later, but for now, there were toys. She selected an extra large red Kong from the basket, tossing it into the air like a cat with a mouse. It bounced, and she chased its uneven rhythm across the room with joyful abandon.

Enough of that. The wolf was hungry. She sat, scratched her dark fur, and stared at the door with almost human intelligence. She thought of herself as smart, but she didn't have anyone to compare herself to.

She hoped for a visit soon, either from the food person or the dead one.

Hungry, hungry, bored.

The blanket was looking more and more tempting, and she wasn't feeling the need to resist. She stood on the blanket with all four paws, yanking the corner up with her teeth, earning herself a gratify tearing sound as the threads started to release. Those little bits would be satisfying to tear into even smaller pieces.

What she really wanted was to go out, to feel the wind sting her eyes as she ran. Chasing. Hunting.

Maybe today would be one of those days when she got to go out...

When I came to, I was surrounded by fluff and torn up bits of this and that. My wolf had not been a happy camper during her time of captivity.

I had gross morning mouth that was a combination of the stale dog breath and fresh meat. Percy didn't normally feed me meat when I was in wolf form, just dry dog food. She must have made an exception for extenuating circumstances.

I stretched, cracking my back. I was still sore from the change, but at least I didn't remember the feeling of the mandatory ones. They're faster, more intense, and covered completely by adrenaline, as far as I could tell, which is why one could go for a long time without discovering they were a werewolf, changed by force, instead of a willing like me.

I was happy to discover my key where I left it, and doubly happy to put on clothes. It was an abnormally chilly morning for the approaching summer, and people would find it odd if I wasn't properly dressed for the weather.

I wasn't up to facing anyone yet, so I decided to take a walk.

The fresh air smelled wonderful. Much better than wood shavings. I took a deep breath, still smelling them. I reached up and started picking bits of shavings out of my hair, thinking maybe there needed to be a mirror in the tack room. I'd also neglected to bring down a comb and a hair elastic, so I raked my fingers through my wild curls as best I could.

I'd chemically straightened it a few times, but the look just wasn't for me. I prefer to curl most of the time, and I'm good enough with a flat iron that I can make it stick straight, without needing a permanent solution. I caught people staring on a regular basis, trying to figure me out. Either that, or they sensed something not quite human about me. Wonder what that could be. Admit it or not, people do have a sense of the supernatural.

Percy, looking frazzled and smelling of adrenaline and anger, found me later in the day. "I got stopped by a reporter. He told me there's been another murder. Come up to the house. I'll fill you in." She sounded out of breath.

"When?" I asked, picking up my speed.

"Two nights ago, during the full moon. I've been waiting all day to tell you. It isn't good."

We hurried back up to the kitchen, where she had a tea kettle screaming for her. Tea for her, tea for me. As soon as she had the mug shoved into my hands, she filled me in.

"I think it's the pack," she stated, her eyebrows scrunched together, her knuckles turning white.

"That doesn't make any sense. How could they get inside a house during full moon?"

"They didn't. Her husband said they decided to go for a walk, since the moon was so bright. They got maybe a mile from their house when he turned to her and discovered she was gone without a sound." Percy paused to take a sip of tea. "He figured she'd gotten ahead somehow, so kept walking. Well, just a few moments later, he found her body propped up against a tree. He said her throat was ripped out, but there was very little gore, no blood left, just like the other girls. Her pulse was still beating when he called nine one one, and she was still warm."

"But no blood?" I confirmed, feeling cold fear shoot through me.

"No blood."

"That still doesn't make any sense. If her pulse was beating, that means there was still something to pump. And none of the others had their throats ripped out, just slashed."

"This was also way up north, Presque Isle. Way too far north for it to be a hairdresser doing this. It's not like a 49-year-old woman would be real competition, especially real enough completion to drive that far to get rid of. I think the wolves are sending you a message," said Percy, studying my face with troubled eyes.

I disagreed with her, but her mind seemed made up, so I kept my mouth shut. I couldn't disprove it, but it made absolutely no sense for it to be the wolves, especially during full moon when there was no human in charge of the animal's brain to point them at specific victims.

And if the weres and the vamps were both looking to recruit, that meant there was something going on in the fae world. It could be ritual. Or it could be personal.

Chapter 19: Customer Appreciation Day

My phone blared in my ear. I'd set an extra early alarm so I could get in a run before work and burn off as much full moon energy as possible. I fumbled around, finally locating it on the floor under the blow-up mattress I was now sacked out on.

Mem sat bolt upright, throwing her legs over the side of the bed.

"Go back to sleep, Mem. It's just my alarm." I stood and shuffled in the general direction of my bathroom.

She muttered something, then slid back down under her covers.

Once clothed, I jogged down the stairs and found a guest in our kitchen.

"Scott?"

He turned to me, clutching a cup of coffee. "Hey."

"Everything okay? Who let you in?"

"Percy did. Yeah, I'm fine. Just having a rough morning. I know Penny and I weren't together long, but it's really hitting me all of a sudden."

"Well, you're welcome to anything in the fridge. I'm going out on a run."

Percy walked out of the pantry armed with

breakfast items. I gave her a scowl and walked out the door without a word to her. She knew everything that was going on with Scott. He was my friend, yes, but not a first-thing-in-the-morning friend.

When I returned, everyone was up, and breakfast was being served.

"Whoa, Gretch, easy on the meat." Scott's eyes turned into saucers as he watched me pile my plate with bacon, eggs, and sausage. "Can we get some fruit over here?"

I don't know if Percy had been talking to him, but Scott was in much better humor.

I set the banana he thrust at me on the table. So close to full moon, I wasn't in the mood for anything but meat. Percy had cooked my food thoroughly, crispy to the point of crumbly bacon, dehydrated sausage, even solid yokes in my eggs. I made a face at her behind Scott's back.

Mem acted like there was nothing abnormal about my food choices. I expected to gross her out, but she never batted an eyelash. Maybe she was still in shock.

We decided to open the salon on an exclusive basis. We would go through the books, pick out our regular clients, the ones we actually liked, and invite them in for a private open house. We'd go full blown day spa, do package deals and everything. They'd hang out with us all day, we'd provide food, then we would escort them out at the end of the day. The rest of the week we'd have to play by ear.

Apparently salons all over the state were having problems with the media, and the police were finally going to help us out one salon at a time, which meant we'd get a visit either Wednesday or Thursday.

We dressed comfortably, trying to convey a relaxed atmosphere. True to the hairdresser's unwritten code, we mostly wore black.

I chose a black turtleneck tank top, but the rest was challenging as I didn't want to go monochrome. I settled on a pair of light colored jeans and black combat boots then clambered down the stairs, pretending everything was going to be all right.

Three clients arrived right off the bat. Scott stuck around to mooch food, so Hades recruited him to help direct traffic.

Tamara Bebe was a high school student. I wondered what she was doing at the salon instead of school. Percy, who was her stylist, was the one to greet her.

Right on Tamara's heels was Ray Gaboury, my client. He was a mill worker who always came for his cuts on Tuesdays. He was wearing his customary basketball shorts. In fact, I'd never seen him in a pair of pants, even in February.

Natasha the Russian was by far the most interesting client we'd ever had. She used all of us and was scheduled for Lacey-Marie. I say interesting for many reasons. The biggest one for me was she didn't seem to have a personal smell. She was always wearing perfume or body spray, perhaps to hide the fact that she didn't have a scent of her own. Another reason was she didn't have a last name, to the best of any of my knowledge. She drove the hour and a half to Isenburge from Farmington to get her hair cut and colored, and paid cash.

My theory was she's fae and she had some heavy duty glamour that even Percy couldn't detect. We never asked, so we'd probably never know.

Christine prepared the food, so Percy didn't have to cook or run around. Oh, deviled eggs! I grabbed a couple and stuffed them in my mouth before I had to be social, a mug of tea clutched in the other hand.

With my teeth clenched in a smile, I was ready to face the world. "Hey, Natasha, I love the skirt," I said, coming up beside her.

"Thanks. I made it last night." She struck a pose, one hip jutted out, modeling her new pink and black plaid school girl style mini skirt, which she'd decorated with an abundance of safety pins.

"I feel old. Thank goodness Percy is here to join me in the over 30 crowd." Natasha waved at Percy in an act of solidarity.

I didn't believe she was in her thirties, but whatever.

Ray was up by the front counter flirting with Meredith, who was trying desperately to look busy. I decided to interrupt and rescue her. At that rate, I'd never do a haircut. I would be absolutely thrilled when the day was over.

Doug showed up around midday, causing a sensation with his beastly hairiness.

I was kind of getting used to having him around. It helped that I wasn't trying to hide anything from him, like I was from Scott, who was glaring at Doug from across the room.

It wasn't like he was competition. I had a strict no human policy. Neither of them had a shot, no matter how much I found myself liking Doug.

"I've got a haircut to do," I muttered to myself, shaking my head. I couldn't keep an eye out to see if they were causing trouble with each other. I made my getaway and took my time with the cut.

Glancing up to the mirror from time to time to check on them showed me they were talking amicably enough. Hades even joined them, hopefully not to keep the peace.

The day went surprisingly well. We even managed to get everyone out safely when an officer from the local sheriff's department cruised by slowly. I didn't know if he was specifically patrolling us, but his timing couldn't have been more perfect, and I was grateful.

After we got all our clients out, those of us who remained sat down to finish up the food. Scott and Doug sat on either side of me, making an effort to get along, which was going better for Scott than it was for Doug.

Scott seemed weirdly protective of me, glancing between Doug and me, his eyebrows knit together and a hint of nerves in his scent.

Doug didn't really know anyone, not helped by the fact that he wasn't the most talkative person in the room.

After supper, Scott pulled me aside. "That dude has the hots for you," he muttered in my ear with his back turned to that dude.

"He's interested, but I don't know about the hots part," I whispered back, patting his arm.

"He's more than interested. He hasn't stopped staring at you. All day."

Doug, as far as I could tell, was interested in what I was, not who I was. I didn't want to explain that idea to Scott, so I kept it to myself.

"That guy, he's too shy to ask, but I can tell what he wants." Scott pulled away and went in search of more food.

I wanted to know for sure if Scott had a clue what he was talking about, but my investigation was going to have to wait because the alpha changer was peering through our window.

Meredith shrieked but managed to keep her plate. Everyone dropped their things and ran to look outside.

He wasn't visible but I could smell him, so he hadn't gone far.

"It was just a bear," Percy stressed, bringing everyone's attention to her and away from the darkness outside.

I took the opportunity to make for the back door. I wouldn't put it past the changer to walk right in. After all, I didn't really know him. I'd spent maybe 40 minutes with him 150 years ago. That's not much of a relationship.

I shut the kitchen door behind me and walked into the darkness. I didn't have to go far before his scent intensified. A wave of alpha magic hit me, buckling me at the knees. The whole dominant /submissive thing is not a choice. It attacks your nervous system.

I hate losing control of myself, which is something I obviously have to deal with on a regular basis. I knelt down in the dirt with my eyes averted from the changer.

His shadow, invisible in the dark, fell over me. "Stand, Maude." He grabbed my bicep, hauling me to my feet like I weighed no more than a puppy.

My legs scrambled to hold my body, knees shaking, and all I wanted to do was tuck tail and roll over.

"I've been told you're giving the pack a hard time." He let go of me, and I looked up into his glowing yellow eyes.

He's not a wolf, but fae. It's as if God, when creating the fae world, decided that there was a wolf needed on both sides, and this was his freaky fae equivalent.

He stood upright like a man, but really, there are no similarities beyond that. He wore no shoes on his enlarged dog feet. His hands, if you can call them that, are really paws with extra joints, pads and all. His short, hairy, pointed ears swivel on the sides of his head, picking up the night sounds. The barrel of his enormous body was dressed in clothing straight out of an old Hollywood western, minus the hat. Who knew where you find a seamstress to do work with such odd measurements.

I was terrified. They were bringing out the big guns on this one. He was here because *he* wanted me, not just the pack.

"I really wasn't informed of all the details when I agreed to this." I spoke through clenched teeth.

"You knew enough. You'd be cared for, treated as precious. Where else could you get that? You are not human, as much as you try to be."

"Do you think I don't know that? Well honestly, I don't have my mind made up. The whole pack thing is very attractive. I'd never have to worry about anything ever again. I'd get to be what I am. But I want to be who I am, and frankly, worrying is a good thing." I needed the worry. The worry kept me connected, human.

"I need the pack to move on soon. They don't belong all the way up here, as pure as it is." He referred to the amount of magic that Maine has managed to retain by keeping a vast uninhabited wilderness. "And you must be told, if you refuse the pack you'll never be welcome back. They may even view you as their enemy. I don't suggest refusing your place."

That got me. I snapped. "How can I submit to an alpha that I'm dominant too? You should have thought of that possibility when you bit me."

"I have to choose strong women. You know a weak one would not survive the change. I knew very well that you would be dominant. It's something we need to breed more of."

"Yeah, well, I'm no broodmare," I said, my voice squeaky, not the threat I intended to convey.

"You're not a horse, youngling. You're a bitch. Don't make any hasty decisions." He started to melt back into the darkness.

Despite flinching at his words, I stepped forward, bringing him back in focus. "Wait!"

He stopped and turned slowly.

Again, I was overwhelmed with the need to grovel, sending me to my knees, but managed not to face plant this time.

"I have a friend," I started.

"No. I choose the wolves, not you." He narrowed his eyes at me.

"Well then, will you scare him out of it?" I crossed my arms.

Don't look in his eyes, Gretchen. Don't look, he'll flatten you.

"Very well. Where can I find him?" He gave the slightest of nods.

"He's here." I tried to swallow, feeling like I was being choked.

"Bring him to me." The changer faded into the shadows without a sound.

I could feel him but was able to get back up on my feet. As soon as I was sure of my balance, I raced for the house to search for Doug.

He was deep in conversation with Scott and Hades.

"What's going on? Where did you go?" Lacey grabbed my elbow, scaring the bejesus out of me.

"The alpha is outside," I whispered.

"Like, the alpha, alpha?" she hissed back, her eyes wide as her clutch tightened,

"As in the alpha changer, the thing that made me

the woman I am today." I yanked my arm from her icy grasp and stalked towards the men.

"We need to talk." I butted my way into their conversation to stand in front of Doug.

"Whoa there, Gretch. Don't bite the poor guy's head off." Scott held up his hands as if preparing to referee. He probably thought I was upset about what he had told me about Doug earlier.

"No promises. Come with me. Now." I pushed Doug back forcefully, causing him to step back to regain his balance.

"All right. I'm going." Doug held his own hands up and started walking in the direction I'd come from.

"What's the matter?" he asked me as soon as we got away from the others, his eyes full of concern as he studied mine.

"I have someone I need you to meet. Come on." I took his hand and once again entered the darkness.

I was prepared this time when I entered the alpha's presence, steeling myself for the full blast of dominant magic. I still went down on my knees but was able to keep my attention on Doug.

Not being a wolf, he didn't feel the need to bow like I did, but he still felt the effects of an alpha male. He bristled as he shook in his sneakers. Had he been a wolf, his hackles would have been standing on end. Of course, if he was a real wolf, he'd be face down like I had been earlier.

"What's this?" asked the Alpha, crouching on his haunches to inspect his potential victim.

"This is Doug. He wants the change," I said, shuffling backward on my knees until I could stand again.

"Does he? Is he a masochist? Does he enjoy pain? Does he want to watch his friends and family die while he lives on?" The alpha stepped closer to Doug and bent again so that he was just a few scant inches from touching the man's face with his own.

"I want to be normal. I want you to fix me." Doug stood firm, his back strong and his jaw set.

"I can't do that." The alpha straightened up and rearranged his face in an expression that could only be sympathy.

"You can. I'm sick of being a freak, and you can make me normal."

For once, the alpha was speechless. As far as I knew, he always had an answer. People wanted the change to become special, to be apart from the general population. No one asked to be changed to be normal.

"You think that werewolves are normal," the alpha repeated for clarification, as if he were experimenting with the sounds of the words.

"Yes. Gretchen's normal, anyhow. She's the only werewolf I've actually met that I know of," said Doug.

"Gretchen?"

"That would be me." I raised my hand. I hadn't realized that no one told him I changed my name. I'd thought he addressed me as Maude because he was an old geezer.

"I'll think about it. That's the best I can offer you. I make my selections very carefully, and until now you've not made it onto my radar." And he was gone.

Chapter 20: Secrets

I was feeling the need to avoid all human contact. If I really wanted, I could call all my appointments and tell them I was sick or some other cop out, but the others were working without complaint, so I would as well.

The time we spent closed messed us up so badly that we were scheduling the next week or so from scratch, doing our best to work around the schedules of the clients we'd previously canceled on. Most just rescheduled for a couple weeks, but some wanted their hair cut immediately.

One such woman sat in my chair, known to me only as Mrs. Ostolski, mother of the little brat that was currently dominating Percy's attention and testing her patience.

Again, let me state: I like kids. I like them outside the salon playing and having fun. Kids inside a salon are a whole different bag of kittens. Kids in a salon, in general, are: rude, obnoxious, vile, and at times creepy. Ann Ostolski was all of the above. The child might never live to see her adolescence if she continued in her wicked ways.

Her mother was a pushover who checked on her daughter every three seconds.

"Are you all right, honey?" She used her feet to scoot my chair around to face her kid.

A moment later, "Do you need anything, dear?" And then, "Just a little bit longer, then we'll go to Burger King."

Bribe, whine, bribe, tantrum, bribe, finish. It was a very tired routine, and they were by no means the only family who followed such a script.

"I'm going for a wander. Be back in 15!" Fern peeked her head out the door of her little massage room under one side of the grand staircase, the back side of Toni's space.

We gave her a collective nod, then went back to work.

"Ma'am, just give me two minutes. Then you can go check out your daughter's cut." I yanked the chair straight so that she was facing the mirror where I needed her to be to check my work.

"Oh, I'm sorry. I didn't even realize I was moving," Mrs. Ostolski said, turning her head to look towards Percy's station.

Bull. "It's okay. It can get a little distracting in here." Using a hand on either side of her head, I turned her forward facing once more and worked quickly to finish the cut.

"Mommy, I need you to look at my hair!" Ann yelled. She was only two stations over, and Meredith wasn't being all that chatty with her client in between.

Mrs. Ostolski got up out of my chair and marched over to check her daughter's hair. Upon giving her approval, she returned to my seat where I was glowering at the wall.

Restrain the death gaze, Gretchen. The death gaze turns away money. We like money.

I yanked the cape from where it was trapped

between her back and the chair so it could drape properly once more. She shot me a dirty look in the mirror, which I ignored.

One more snip of my sheers, then I let her check it out. She nodded her satisfaction, running her fingers through it.

"Would you like a blow dry?" I asked, which she accepted with a smile.

I couldn't get them cashed out fast enough.

"I need a moment," I muttered to Percy as I rushed out the back of the salon.

I skittered to a halt when I beheld Fern standing white faced, clutching one of Lacey-Marie's blood donor bags. She held it aloft as soon as she realized I was there. We stared gape mouthed at each other for a moment before Fern gained her composure enough to speak.

"Whose blood?" she asked, her voice coming out with a bit of a squeak.

I didn't know how to answer with anything besides the truth. It was our fault for keeping the blood behind the milk, but it was our personal fridge, not the salon fridge. She had no right to be going through our kitchen.

I struggled not to let the snarl out that was lurking near my surface. "What are you doing in here?"

"I went for a walk," she said, her fingers digging into the plastic.

"People normally walk outside." I crossed the room and snatched the blood bag from her grasp.

She let it go without any resistance. "I did. I went to the barn." I could hear her heart beat faster, and the smell of her fear rolled towards me.

Oh, good.

"Why do you have a dog kennel and no dogs?" She

took a step away from me, her smell intensifying.

Did she have a clue what she stumbled upon?

"Hey Gretchen, do you think—" Hades sauntered in, in full-force god mode, "Hello Ms. Mayberry."

Well, if she didn't have doubts about us before, she definitely did now.

"What the hell is going on here?" Fern back away until she hit the counter, reaching for balance with one hand.

She darted sideways, towards the door to the garden. I dashed forward to block her path. Her eyes widened, pupils dilating, and her breath quickening.

I'd moved too fast.

"Get away from me," she whispered as her body started shaking. The scent of her fear dripped off of her, exciting my wolf, making me want to attack.

This was the third person to find out what I was in a very short time, and the first of them to show rational signs of fear.

I growled, low in my throat.

"Gretchen, back off." Hades pulled rank on me.

I cowered and exposed my throat. I hadn't known that Hades could do that. I suppose that's what it takes to be the god of the dead: supreme dominance.

"You first." Apparently talking through gritted teeth was going to be my new thing.

Hades immediately toned it down, and I was able to straighten up.

While Hades and I were finding a balance, Fern was once again trying to escape.

"Fern, please." What, let me explain? Don't run away from the crazy monsters?

"Please what? You are insane!" said Fern, her arms hugged her rib cage, fingers gripping at the fabric of her shirt as she fought to keep herself from panicking further. "My Nana told me stories. But this?"

"I'll behave myself. If you just stay the rest of the day, I promise I'll come up with something truthful to tell you." I was pulling my words out of thin air, scrambling for the right thing to say.

"She was telling the truth?" she whispered, her voice filled with wonder and the smell of fear diminished.

"Please don't mention this to anyone," I pleaded, pulling out a chair, motioning for her to sit down.

She eased into it, using her hands for balance, her eyes were slightly unfocused, as if she were deep in thought.

"Tell me about the stories your Nana told you."

"Well, she told me about men who shape-shifted into wolves and killed off the local herds when she was a little girl. She told me that they were mercenaries and berserkers. She said a few of them fought alongside Grandfather in Vietnam. She said they saved his life."

She looked up at me during that last bit, studying my face.

I took a seat opposite, letting her feel safe with the heavy table between us. "Have you heard anything about the mass killing of livestock lately?"

She shook her head. "No." She drew out the word, as if considering my point.

"I swear I haven't mauled any sheep lately. And I work very, very hard to keep myself calm and under control. That's why I drink this all the time." I tapped my travel mug of soothing tea.

"Okay." Her eyebrows scrunched together as she pressed her index finger to her lower lip with her elbow settled on the table.

"Did your Nana tell you to be afraid of people like me?"

"Actually, no. She respected the men my grandfather fought with. There are even pictures of them hanging on their wall. I just figured she meant they fought like animals to keep Grandfather alive, not that they were animals."

"Well, we're not, strictly speaking."

"Their wolves are fae." Hades interrupted our conversation. "This body," he pointed at me, "is human with fae DNA added."

Fern's focus shifted to the now glamoured god in the corner. "And you?"

"I'm all fae, m'lady." He swept a bow and flashed her a charming smile. "It's my job to keep rascals like this pup under control." He indicated me with a sweeping motion. "And also the blood drinkers. We fae like to keep our lives private, so it's in my best interest to keep an eye on them all."

I stood from my place. "We should probably get back to work. Please, will you keep our secret? You can ask us any questions you like. Anything to make you feel safe."

"Yeah, I'll try." She stood, her face betraying the fact that she was deep in thought. She moved gracefully around the room and out the door, a stark difference from the beginning of our conversation.

I glanced over at Hades, heaving a sigh of relief.

And then I smacked him hard across the face, not holding back, knowing he could take it.

"What the—" He stopped, composing himself.

"Don't you ever do that again!" I roared, just about certain everyone in the building would be able to hear me.

"I'm sure I don't know what you're talking about." He furrowed his brow, tilting his head a little to the side.

How dare he not grow a red handprint on his cheek! It made that slap so thoroughly unsatisfying.

"You pulled alpha on me." I struggled to keep my volume down.

"Sorry. I was just trying to keep you from wolfing out," he said, stepping away from me, his hands held up.

"Well it worked, so thanks." I know I didn't sound grateful, but it was as good as he was going to get from me.

I chose to go outside instead of slinking back into the salon like a naughty puppy. I ran out to my kennel and tried the tack room door.

It was unlocked, as was the kennel. How did that happen? I knew I'd locked it behind me when I left, and Percy never went in.

On my way out, I spotted something lying on the ground, shining in the brilliant afternoon sun. I knelt down and picked up the key for the tack room. Had Fern gotten a hold of the key, or was there someone else snooping around?

I locked the door and stuck the key in my bra for temporary safekeeping. I'd have to ask Fern about it later.

As soon as I got a moment, I filled Percy and Lacey-Marie in on my confrontation with Fern.

"So what should we do?" I asked, not liking any of my options.

"We tell her the truth, or as much of it as is relevant to anything she or any of the others might come across on the property. I say we just tell her about ourselves and Hades, since she got an eyeful of him," Percy purposed. "And nothing about the farm hands. Or the pack. Or the family. Or the rest of the fae."

"I guess I'll have to live with that." I heaved a sigh and leaned against the wall, feeling drained.

"Fine by me," said Lacey, shrugging her shoulders. She would have preferred not to hide at all. But for the sake of us, she did.

Some days it would've been nice to not hide, but most of the time I liked my privacy. If the fae went public, I'd be put on display, possibly muzzled. I liked being left alone, not a known oddity. Being of mixed background in Maine was enough. Let's not add to the list of things that make Gretchen stick out like a sore thumb.

"All right then, as soon as the others get out of here, we'll meet in the library. Gretchen?" Percy turned to me expectantly.

"No. There's absolutely no way I'm wolfing out in front of everyone. You can forget it." I knew exactly what she was up to. I hadn't wolfed out for Mem or Doug, and I wasn't going to do it for anyone else.

Speaking of Doug, I hadn't heard from him since he left after meeting with the changer. He'd sounded solid on his decision to become a werewolf, but maybe it was just a front, and he was changing his mind. Maybe he'd just leave with the circus and forget about me and being anything other than human.

Yeah. Right.

"All right, fine. I'm not going to force you to do anything you don't want to. I just think it would be easier to accept if there was something to show her," said Percy, throwing her hands up.

"So show her you! You're more spectacular than my wolf, and you don't scream in agony when you shed your glamour. I'll see you after work. I have a color to do." Thank goodness.

I threw myself into my work. I may even have been too friendly, if that's possible for me. Of course, I was acting. Hopefully my client didn't realize that. As long as I was doing something that distracted me, I was hoping I wouldn't stress and wolf out. Whatever impression I made, my client left a sizable tip, which went right in my bra with the key I'd forgotten to mention to Percy. Oh, well, it could wait until after we pounced on poor Fern.

I really hoped she was holding up her end of the bargain and not telling anyone, though I didn't know how good of a job we were doing at hiding. There were so many times that I'd freaked out right there in the salon, occasionally accompanied by the snapping of bones as they reshaped themselves into unhinged wolf form. I had yet to fully transform in the salon, but there had definitely been some close calls recently.

I was counting down the days to the new moon when I would be human and could stop worrying, if only for three days. Of course, I would then be more vulnerable to whatever was killing cosmetologists, but I was hoping that would all be over by that point.

I didn't want to get involved, but I still had that nagging feeling that the deaths were supernatural, fueled by how little the police were revealing to the press. Not to mention, the killer had yet to make a mistake, which meant the killer was either brilliant or didn't leave a trail the police had any capability of following. I suspected it was the latter. The circus freaks were officially off my personal suspect list, leaving me with no leads.

When we met in the library that night, I was a bundle of nerves. I'd already partly revealed myself, but I was still selfish enough to wish that Fern wouldn't be afraid of me.

Everyone was sitting down, trying to look small and safe. Fern was sitting, eyes wide, back straight, and with slightly more fear in her scent then she'd left with earlier.

I took a seat towards the back of the library, allowing Fern a clear escape route to the door if she needed. The only person not present was Mem since we hadn't told her about the meeting, and she wasn't an official member of the household. Come to think of it, neither was Hades, but he'd gone into full creeper mode in front of Fern, so we made him come.

"So, I guess you found us out. Congratulations, we thought we were hiding well," Percy started us off.

"What, exactly, is the true story?" asked Fern, her arms crossed across her chest.

"How religious are you?" Percy asked.

Where was she going with that one? This was a facts of life speech, not a conversion.

"Not at all," Fern said, her shoulders drooping slightly.

"Well, I'll skip all that and go to the bit that goes: When God created Earth and all its creatures, he also created the fae and all that goes bump in the night. You might call it a different plane, an alternate universe, we can easily travel back and forth between. We, the fae, have been coming to your earth for eons. Every once in a while, a human gets into Underhill, but I wouldn't advise looking for it, let's just leave it at: there are ways in and out."

"All right, so you're all fairies?" Fern asked.

"We're fae, but only Hades and I are pure blood," Percy clarified.

"Hades. Hades as in the god of the dead." Fern

snapped her fingers as she made the connection. Her eyes widened and flashed in his direction. "Oh, my god."

"What can I do for you, madam?" Hades asked. The smile that came with his words was less than comforting.

"Not the time, dear." Percy shook her finger at her husband.

"Of course, my love." He turned his smile to her and softened.

"So that makes you..." Fern dropped off, leaning away from her new boss.

"I'm Persephone, queen of the dead three months out of the year. It's nice meeting you, dear." Percy took Fern's fingers and squeezed them gently.

As she did so, she shed her glamour, revealing the goddess underneath.

"Oh, my! Am I missing something? Who is this divine young lady?" Mem walked in unsuspecting of what the current topic of conversation might be.

"It's just me, dear," said Percy as she let go of Fern's fingers and waved Mem in.

"So this is what you really look like? This magic stuff is quite something, isn't it?" Mem said, taking a seat next to Fern.

Fern stared at Mem like she was the freak, instead of the rest of us.

"So, how did you find out?" Mem asked.

"Uh, blood bag behind the milk. They haven't explained that yet, though." Fern fidgeted in her chair, and I could smell her sweat with nerves.

"I'm a vampire," supplied Lacey.

"I figured someone was. Does that make you a dog, Gretchen?" Fern finally turned to face me.

"I'm the bitch," I acknowledged. "Although I'm a

werewolf, not a shapeshifter, hence the accidental outbursts. Sorry about earlier." I figured my apology was better late than never.

"Uh-huh," she said.

She didn't have to agree with me. Twerp.

"And what are you?" she turned back to Mem.

"A widow," she said, crawling back into reserved mode.

"Oh, no, I'm so sorry," Fern apologized, finally losing her terrified look in exchange for one of empathy.

"You didn't know. It isn't your fault," said Mem. "Gretchen invited me to stay with her until I figure out what to do next. She's been a godsend, excuse my pun." The smile she directed at Percy didn't reach her eyes.

Percy patted her hand, then turned back to our newest employee, drawing up her glamour once more. "Do you have any questions for us, Fern?"

"Uh."

We all waited. I bet there were a billion questions floating around in that brain of hers. None of them were popping through her lips.

"Well, if you come up with any, feel free to ask us. Any of us. Just please don't say anything to the other girls. There's no need for anyone else to know," Percy said, standing and towering over us all.

"Are we really safe? Us humans, I mean?" asked Fern, raising from her chair.

"Yes," I promised. I hadn't eaten anyone in years, though she didn't need to know that last bit, or that I'd eaten anyone, period.

"All right." Fern nodded. "Goodnight, then."

Before she could make it out the front door, Amanda burst through it.

"There's been another murder!" she said without any sort of preamble. "Her name was Jennifer Tardiff, and she was from Cape Elizabeth."

"What are the details?" I asked, pulling her in by the arm.

"She was at her boyfriend's house last night, cooking supper. He was watching TV in the living room. He came in to ask a question, and she was propped up on the counter."

"That's sick and twisted," I commented.

"This whole thing is sick and twisted," Amanda corrected me, collapsing on the couch beside Hades.

I nodded mutely.

"I just thought you'd like to know. I've gotta get going." She stood up again.

"Amanda, be careful. In fact, I'd feel a whole lot better if there was someone to keep constant watch over you." I didn't betray how worried I was because, if I could, I would have kept her in my suite with Mem.

She shrugged off my words. "G'night." She left, leaving the door open for Fern.

"Whoa," said Fern.

"That about sums it up. Be safe." I watched as Fern made her way to her car.

Chapter 21: Hair Show

I hated hair shows. They're loud, full of strange smells, and brightly lit, not to mention gaudy. We'd bought our tickets months ago for the Paul Mitchell show in Portland, and I'd completely forgotten about them until Percy banged on my door at six in the morning.

"Time to get up, dear. We're already running late." Her footsteps descended the hall before I could utter a word

Mem's eyes peeped at me, and I waved at her, clambering to my feet.

I headed to the kitchen to scarf down breakfast dressed in black skinny jeans and an oversized sweatshirt. My hair was tamed into a semblance of an updo, held together with bobby pins and a generous helping of hairspray. My makeup I kept minimal, just eyeliner and mascara. I wasn't in the mood.

Meredith, Percy, Lacey-Marie, and I packed ourselves into Percy's BMW and started the two-hour trek south.

I snuggled down in my hoodie, fully prepared to sleep my way through the trip. Percy threw a crumpled up Burger King cup at me, and Lacey cranked the music, making me wish I'd brought my headphones.

Lacey usually listened to seventies classic rock, but every once in a while, to appear the age she portrayed instead of the age she actually was, she'd listen to pop and hip hop. It was one of those days.

I muttered death threats at them both under my breath, while leaning forward and sticking my forehead to the back of the driver's seat. Meredith, who was stuck in the back with me, scowled in my direction.

Hey, it wasn't my fault I wasn't feeling the morning. I'd be glad when the whole month was over and we could start over fresh.

Just sip your tea, and everything will be fine, I thought to myself. I lifted my travel mug to my lips and savored the extra bit of lemon and honey I'd added.

Lacey turned the music down, and I could hear her singing softly to herself. We didn't have much to discuss that we could all talk about, so we sat in silence, watching the world go by. I felt I deserved a gold star for not barking at the tollbooth attendant or sticking my head out the window.

As soon as Percy pulled into the parking spot, I rolled out of the car, stretched my arms up over my head, and arched backward to crack my back. When I felt like maybe my limbs might function, I stumbled after the rest of my little group.

Inside, we showed our printed out tickets to the attendant and entered the auditorium. The pounding music assaulted my ears, causing me to wince until I pulled a pair of the earplugs I used for performances out of my bag and shoved them in my ears. It wasn't perfect, but it was definitely an improvement. The flashing lights were just as harsh on my eyes as the music was on my ears. I couldn't recall the Paul Mitchell team ever coming to Maine before, but I was betting they were putting the show into hair show.

We scooted down a row near the middle and took our seats. My fingers pulled themselves into fists as feelings of claustrophobia clawed at my skin.

Lacey-Marie was twisting this way and that, looking for people she knew. Percy was absently filing her nails, and Meredith seemed to be trying to look as unassuming as possible.

A whoosh of air hit me as someone plopped themselves down in the chair behind me.

"Oh, good, you made it," said Amanda, her voice close to my ear.

I turned, and she leaned forward, propping herself on the back of my seat. The rest of Babe's Place's small staff took seats around her.

"I did. How's it going?" I asked, trying to sit cross-legged facing her. I wasn't fitting, so I settled for sitting sideways instead.

"Eh, all right." She rocked her flattened hand back and forth in a so-so motion. "Business has been kinda slow. I don't know how you guys are doing it."

"Reputation, darling, a stunning reputation. Maybe you should have applied when we were hiring." I stuck my nose up in mock snobbery.

"Ha! I'd rather sail under the radar, thanks." She leaned back and laughed.

It was a good thing I was capable of making good-natured friends to balance out the ones I couldn't maul.

"How's the morale?" I asked, tugging the conversation back to our mutual work.

"Kinda low. Gotta admit, we're shaking in our stilettos."

"You don't wear stilettos," I remarked, glancing down at her sneaker-clad feet.

"True, I wear running shoes," she retorted.

I didn't want to tell her that she probably wouldn't get a chance to run away if she were targeted.

"When's this thing supposed to start?" I glanced down at my naked wrist. "I've got us at half past a freckle."

"And you don't have freckles. Nine, I think."

"That's because it's half past it. It faded away," I insisted.

"Turn around, and behave yourself. I think something's going on." Amanda shoved my shoulder.

I turned as the lights dimmed and the music rose in a crescendo. The house lights dimmed, and the stage lights blared to life, revealing a line of Steampunk-costumed men and women. As they pranced around the stage, holding products and dancing, I wondered if they were supposed to be models or stylists. Some of them opened the bottles and proceeded to pick one of the others to goop up and twist and turn into elaborate styles.

It's actually kind of cool, I found myself thinking. Was I enjoying myself? Who'd have thunk it?

Near the end of the day, the stage quieted, and a gaggle of young-looking police officers filed in to mill around the front of the room.

"Oh, he's kind of hot," Lacey-Marie whispered to me, using a low finger to point out the object of her desire.

I poked her hard in the ribs and whispered, "You're obscene."

"What?" The smile on her face told me she knew exactly what.

I rolled my eyes and ignored her. Leave it Lacey to notice fatal attraction during a public service announcement.

"What?" she asked again, goading me.

"Never mind, Lacey, it's just inappropriate timing." I gave her an answer, knowing she'd pester me until I gave one.

She hissed out a puff of air. "Whatever."

I could live with whatever.

A whistle and a shout called our attention to the stage. Trying to quiet a room of hairdressers is like trying to quiet a room of sugar-amped five-year-olds. Not worth the effort. It took perhaps 10 minutes for it to dawn on the room full of the overprocessed that maybe they should listen up.

The announcement itself was pretty short, detailing most of the things that we had gone over ourselves, such as telling us not to talk to strangers. Of course, it was our job to talk to strangers, to be their friends, to make them feel special. It made the crazy come out in us and encouraged the crazy in strangers.

Don't be alone. Don't give out personal details. They revealed as little about the actual murders as possible. Don't tell the nice hairdressers that the police know next to nothing.

"We strongly suggest checking in with your coworkers every night. Take on a roommate if possible. I know this is tough on you, but you've really got to start being more careful." The police spokesman talked as if he actually knew what was really going on.

I knew he was full of it. I also knew that having someone with them at all times didn't mean that they'd be safe. There were no guarantees with this psycho.

After the show was over, the whole lot of us headed to Jose's bar and grill, first getting caffeinated, then a little drunk.

The nachos I ordered were piled high with cheese, salsa, olives, seasoned burger, guacamole, and sour cream, which I shared with Meredith since she hadn't planned on dinner. I skipped the coffee in favor of my customary rum and coke. Meredith chose a fruity margarita thing. It takes a lot to get me drunk, so I wasn't too worried that I'd make a fool of myself.

Lacey-Marie pouted, refusing to order anything to keep up pretenses.

Sorry, chicky, them's the breaks.

She could have ordered a drink and dumped some blood in it, but she'd been complaining earlier that her jeans were feeling tight. I'd never seen her gain even an ounce. I didn't know she could.

I found myself having actual fun. It was a good feeling, I should have tried it more often.

I'm not sure the wait staff was having anything close to a blast as we were messing things up by pushing tables together, shouting across the room, and passing food around. Hairdressers really like to eat and drink, which leads to acting the fool.

Meredith was another of the few who looked less than thrilled to be there. She kept glancing at the exit, as if expecting someone to come through and rescue her.

I shoved an extra cheesy guacamole-covered chip into my mouth. "What's up?" I asked around my mouthful.

"Nothing." She shifted her eyes away from my face.

She'd barely touched the food, and I could smell fear oozing out of her pores.

"You don't look like there's nothing up," I pushed.

She glanced at me then away again. "I don't know if I can do this. I don't know. I'm scared shitless."

Percy's head whipped in our direction.

"Oh, sweetie," she scooted her chair over and put an arm around Meredith's shoulders, "it's going to be all right."

"You don't know that! You can't promise that. If keeping this job means dying, then I want out." Meredith's voice rose in panic.

I didn't have anything to say about that other than, "Please don't quit. We need you. You fit in well with us, and your customers go home happy. You don't start drama. You're a wonderful person. Please think hard before you leave us."

I was begging, I knew that, but if begging is what it took to keep Meredith as a part of our team, then I would have gotten down on my knees.

Lacey-Marie joined in, though she didn't have anything to add for a change.

We all gave her pleading puppy eyes.

"I didn't say I was settled on leaving. I just thought you had a right to know that I might." Meredith leaned back in her seat, crossing her arms across her chest.

I smiled, shoveling another smothered chip in my mouth. Yum.

The drinks were becoming more plentiful, made obvious when rounds of toasting started.

"To those of us that have survived! May it stay that way!" A woman dressed completely in black raised her cocktail in the air, just barely keeping its contents from sloshing over the glass's rim.

"Amen to that, sister!" someone shouted.

We clinked glasses, and Lacey raised her untouched glass of ice water, pretending to take a dainty sip.

"To the girls who have died!" Another hairdresser climbed up onto her bench seat and raised her drink.

More clinking glasses.

For some un-thought-out reason, I decided to join the fun. I jumped up on my chair and raised my half-empty glass. "To Sweeney Todd."

There was a dead hush.

"May the police get to him before I do!" I threw back the rest of my drink and hopped back to the floor.

"Hell yeah!" Amanda shouted, downing her own drink.

All around, glasses were emptied.

Lacey-Marie was glaring at me.

Time for another round. "What?" I asked, taking my seat.

"You can't seriously be thinking about going after Sweeney Todd yourself." She set her glass back on the table without the pretense of a sip.

"Why not? What the hell have we already been doing?" I took a gulp of my ice water and was happy to see that Meredith was finally digging into her meal.

Lacey narrowed her eyes and leaned across the table towards me. "Well, for one thing, you can't have these women following your example."

I was one of the three women in the room who could do something about the killer without worrying about my own personal safety. Lacey had been gung-ho for figuring out who it was only a week ago. Werewolves can be killed by a clean shot to the head, but most anything else we could recover from.

The Sweeney Todd killer didn't seem like the gun-toting type.

"Why, Lacey-Marie, are you concerned for my safety?" I hissed at her, in imitation of how she was speaking to me.

"No." She crossed her arms.

"Ah, you want to come along and play." I leaned back and smiled.

She rolled her eyes at me and started poking at the ice in her glass with her straw.

I pulled my attention away from my attitudinal friend and focused back to the general conversation going on around us. It is amazing how resilient a group like that can be. Or how stupid. It wasn't like they couldn't possibly be next.

After ordering another drink, I jumped back up on the seat of my chair.

"Listen up, people. There is one option the police didn't discuss with us today: defending ourselves."

That got their attention. Once again, I had every eye on me. The police had only talked about taking precautions to make ourselves less of a target, which is all well and good, but none of those precautions had worked thus far.

"We are not a bunch of weaklings. We stand for work all day. We blow-dry for hours on end. That requires muscle. Any one of us can hold a gun, or a knife, or, hell, a pair of shears. If you've got them, you can use them against him."

I was encouraging them to take the defense, while I had every intention to go on the offense for them. There was only a week until the new moon when I would become fully human, but there was nothing preventing me from sniffing around and keeping my ears open. I'm not a cop—I didn't know procedure—but I hoped I could discern what was making particular hairdressers targets. I needed to get a gun or a knife to protect myself during my most human moments, but I had all week.

I felt a tug on my arm. I looked down at Percy. She was shaking her head at me and trying to inconspicuously put me back in my place.

I sat. "Sorry, I may have gotten carried away."

"You think?" Lacey said loudly, so I could hear her over the general thunder of voices in the room.

I'd definitely started them thinking, and with most women, thinking involves talking.

"All we need is hairdressers getting panicky and shooting random strangers on the street," Percy murmured so even Meredith couldn't hear her.

"Sorry." I shrugged off her scolding. I stood by my words that they had every right to defend themselves, if they got the chance.

The ride back home was even quieter than the ride down. Lacey ignored me, curling up in a little ball in the front seat. Percy turned the radio on low and concentrated on the road. Meredith stared out her window, avoiding the rest of us as best she could. I sat with arms and legs crossed, waiting for someone else to say something, anything.

No one did. Silence is a very uncomfortable way to spend a car ride.

I pushed the button to roll down my window and leaned my forehead against the door, letting the cold air blast my face.

After a minute, Percy rolled my window up from the front seat as she glanced at me in the rearview mirror, revealing a tinge of violet in her otherwise brown eyes. If she was having a hard time holding it together, then things were bad. Percy never lost it.

I pulled my gaze away from hers and willed her to concentrate on the road. I'm not entirely sure she needed to look at it to concentrate. I don't really know how the whole fae goddess thing works.

Hades met us at the front door, holding it open as we filed in.

"I want to talk to everyone before you head home. The others will join us shortly." He shut the door behind us and followed us into the kitchen.

Lacey beat us all there and sat with a steaming mug

clutched in her hands. She'd been drinking rations daily that usually lasted her the week. I chose to ignore it. For one formerly so proud of her body, she was becoming downright glutinous, no matter the public image she was trying to project earlier.

I wandered to the library with tea in hand and settled down with my book. If I kept going at that rate, I might actually finish it before the month was up.

I was looking forward to being human. I would pig out on all the stuff my body couldn't handle as a wolf. Like chocolate. Mmm, chocolate. The one square I allowed myself from time to time wasn't cutting it. I fully intended to seclude myself with a monstrous bar and a jar of peanut butter. Oh, and a mug of hot cocoa.

If I thought any more about it, I would drool all over my book. Being that it belonged to Percy, and not me, I should probably concentrate on the reading about silly, silly Marianne.

I couldn't focus. My mind kept wandering from the words on the page to the current circumstances filling up my days and my nights. Eventually, I set the book aside. I wasn't going to retain anything anyhow. I turned on the computer, hoping it could distract me more successfully.

I looked up Doug's mutation. There really wasn't much research out there. Hypertrichosis is apparently a rare mutation, and anything I read about it, especially in recent times, linked them to the circus. There was an entire Mexican family working as part of a regular circus at one point, and one guy working for a legitimate freak show. If that's not the politically correct term, so sorry. Along with him was scorpion boy, a guy whose fingers were fused into pincher-like hands, and another man not mentioned in the caption. The three of them were smiling, looking for all the world like they were having the time of their lives. Maybe they were.

I hadn't seen a smile like that on Doug's face, and I wanted that for him.

There was a soft knock on the door, and I turned to see Mem walking in without even a hint of a shuffle in her step, a huge improvement over the last few days.

"Hey, Mem, what's up?" I leaned back in the computer chair and swiveled from side to side.

Mem took a seat on the big couch in the center of the room. "I just wanted to check on you. We haven't talked in a few days, and I know things have been difficult. How are you, dear, really?"

I stopped swiveling. "Pissed off. But not in a wolfy way," I corrected hastily, not wanting her to worry about me wolfing out in the library.

"I can understand that. I've been a bit pissed off myself. Mad at the world. Mad at God for taking my husband away. There isn't anything Hades can do, is there?" She sounded so hopeful, and I hated hurting her, but I couldn't lie.

"No. He's just a fae. He's a very powerful fae, a king in fact, but no actual power over life and death. He kind of rules over all the creepy crawlies that go bump in the night."

She nodded, her eyes downcast and her shoulders falling. I got up from my chair and sat down beside her.

"What were you looking at?" She changed the subject before I could say anything.

"Stuff on Doug's mutation. He wants to be like me. He thinks it's gonna cure him, but mutation isn't like a disease—it's a part of him. I don't think it would work, but he got the alpha changer to consider it." I pulled my knees up to my chest, not caring that my shoes settled on the couch.

"Oh, dear." Mem scooted closer and rubbed my back. The maternal power she possessed was comforting, despite the fact that I was the elder, and I relaxed. Mem was almost as good at soothing the wolf as Percy, who relied on her power to do it.

I heard noises as more girls entered the kitchen. Hairdressers always seem to be girls, no matter their age. I excused myself from Mem, leaving her reading my copy of *Sense and Sensibility*.

I was suddenly curious about what Hades wanted to speak to us about. Surely he wasn't going to reveal himself. I took a seat on the counter beside a slightly more subdued Lacey-Marie.

"As you ladies know, I'm from away," Hades started, being the only one to remain standing.

"Florida," Toni supplied.

"Florida, right. I have access to a security team, and I've requested they come up here until this thing is resolved. I don't like how unsafe all you ladies are forced to feel, and since I can help out a little, I'm going to. You'll never see them. They'll stay outside your homes and keep suspicious people away." He crossed his arms over his broad chest and waited.

"They'll be guarding all of us?" Meredith clarified, sounding like she was warming up to the idea. She'd recently moved in with Fern, but that wasn't enough for her to feel safe.

"They will, just until the killer is caught. Then I will pay them and send them on their merry way." Hades turned his attention from our employees to us.

"Fine by me," I said, sliding down from the counter.

Lacey just shrugged, not thrilled with the idea.

Percy nodded, her face a mask of blankness.

I wondered what Hades' security team might be

made up of. Maybe I should have asked before giving my agreement. Of course, I couldn't have asked in front of the girls since they didn't have a clue what we were, besides Fern, who had remained silent the whole time.

I fidgeted as the girls hung around to chat. Leave, just leave. *Time to toddle on home, little chickies.*

It took a while, but they eventually did leave, and I swung around to fix my gaze on Hades, who was staring coolly back, despite my glare.

"What's the security team? I'm guessing they're something less than human." I crossed my arms, mimicking his stance.

It had better not be vampires. While they could certainly fight most things off, they had a tendency to kill who they were protecting, especially in bunches where they could egg each other on.

"One of my security teams from home," he answered, more vaguely than I would have liked.

"What are they, Hades?" I tapped my foot.

It was just him and me in the kitchen, so he wouldn't have to worry about any of the humans hearing. Who knew where Lacey-Marie and Percy took off to.

"A necromancer and his zombies," he admitted.

Ew. "Is that, uh, kosher?"

"They've done surveillance work for me before. The zombies act like security cameras most of the time, with their necromancer as a monitor. If anything goes down, he'll notify me. Then I can choose to call the police or deploy the zombies, depending on what the threat is." Hades didn't seem to find anything icky about it.

I rolled my lip in disgust but didn't pursue the topic. Instead, I grabbed some leftovers and headed out. I had band practice and a gig coming up.

I stopped as soon as I reached the salon.

Something stood there, completely covered in dark robes and veils. The only thing visible were black eyes and some red-tinged skin.

Percy dashed down and greeted him. "Welcome, Bob! Let me show you to one of the guest rooms. Gretchen, would you please notify Hades that his security team has arrived?"

I took me a moment to move. This was just too weird, even for me.

Chapter 22: The Festival

Despite staying out late to rehearse with the guys, I submitted to being dragged around the Isenburge Garden Festival, a fair disguised as a celebration of spring, and yet another event to get our minds off things. I wasn't too keen on the idea, seeing how the last one turned out. I was really hoping we wouldn't come across anyone suspicious there, or any funny smells that needed investigating.

Doug discovered our plans and latched on to me. Not that I minded. Much better than walking by myself since Percy had Hades, and they looked at things with an entirely different perspective than I did.

Not that Doug and I shared a point of view—on the contrary—but he was fascinated by how I experienced things and still hadn't let go of his desire to be changed.

Lacey, of course, couldn't come due to the whole sun thing. It's hard to dodge around, even with a parasol.

The salon was in a state of flux as our clients were starting to call to volunteer not to come in. I think they were afraid the killer would jump from stylists to them. The pattern was far too set for that, but I supposed it was better safe than sorry. Either way, it was horrible for business.

Despite being in my human form, and having layered on the clothes, the animals were able to sense the predator emanating from me. They might say hi to a dog, but there's something about a werewolf that animals are instinctively terrified of.

Doug had no such problem. Despite his odd appearance, most of the animals would come over and give him a curious sniff as long as I stood well back.

We paid our entrance fee around lunch time but opted out of food for the time being.

"We'll meet at the pulling ring around four. The girls should be here by then." Percy glanced down at her watch, ready to sync up.

I held up my empty wrist, as did Doug.

"Well, you could just ask someone, couldn't you?" Percy balled her fists on her hips, elbows jutting out, " Or check your cell phone."

"Didn't bring it. If I remember, I will," I promised.

"I'll remind her." Doug followed up my promise with one of his own as he placed a hand on my shoulder.

"Good. Have a wonderful time, kids. Oh, Doug, do you have to work tonight?" Percy asked before letting us split.

"No, I got out if it, thanks to Sabrina." Doug smiled, revealing white teeth that were slightly crooked on the bottom.

"Lovely. Then you'll get to see Chaos Theory perform tonight. See you later!" Percy took Hades' elbow and steered him away.

Doug grabbed my arm gently. "You're playing tonight? Why didn't you say anything?"

I shrugged. I hadn't thought to mention it.

He looked hurt, and I couldn't think of anything to

say to fix it.

"Let's go look at animals." I slid my arm through his grip until his hand landed in mine.

I was surprised how natural it was to do so. I hadn't really felt anything either way towards him, except protective. Come to think of it, why did I feel protective? Why should I care if he wanted to be a wolf?

Huh.

"Okay. Where first?" Doug intensified his grip on my hand as if I were his lifeline.

Perhaps I was. I didn't know how much time he spent out in the normal world. This very well may have been the first festival he'd ever attended.

"The sheep." I tugged him in the direction of the sheep barn. I wanted to skip the whole rides thing as I tend to puke when spun.

People gave us a wide berth, staring at Doug as we passed by. If only they knew it was me they should avoid. I smiled and pulled myself in closer to him, matching his stride. A woman of color and a hairy man —how shocking!

Doug gave me a look and pulled away, just a little, so we were walking the way we had been before.

"Do you need to make us more a spectacle than I already am?" he muttered at me.

I was caught.

"Sorry. I was just embracing the weirdness," I muttered back, sniffing as a waft of fair food blew past.

"Well, don't." He let go of my hand and sped up his pace, pulling ahead of me.

"Sorry." I caught up and tried to take his hand again.

Again, he pulled away from me. I hadn't realized how personally he took things. Or maybe I did. He was going to the extreme to get rid of what made him outwardly different from the rest of humanity.

Of course, if he hung around the fair long enough, he was bound to run into some other woolly mammoth mountain men that tended to populate the state in the mid to northern regions. He wasn't as abnormal as he thought. He just cared about it more. I mean, yeah, they didn't grow hair down to their eyelids, but they got pretty freaking close.

"Sheep barn's over there." I pointed.

He glanced at me, then followed the line of my finger.

Not thinking, I walked into the barn and right up to one of the pens.

The giant rams sheltered there were climbing over one another trying to get away from me. Gee, was I popular. I seemed to have that effect on everyone and everything in the last few minutes. I backed away, bumping into Doug, who blocked my escape route.

I turned so I could watch where I was going, not bothering with an apology. My plan was to wait at the entrance. It didn't work. I was upwind to the sheep, and the entire barn blazed into a panic.

I left the entrance and ran around the outside to the opposite end where I endured the mouthwatering scent of sheep, and they couldn't smell me. I watched Doug squat down in front of the lamb pen, sticking in a couple fingers. He waited a moment or two and was rewarded when an especially curious black lamb with a white splotch on its forehead wandered over to take a nibble.

A smile replaced his scowl, and he was, for the most part, left alone with the sheep he was making friends with. He wouldn't be making friends with any animals if he was changed. He'd be a critter pariah like me.

It was about 20 minutes before he made his way over to my side of creation, stopping at every pen to say hello.

"Are you still mad at me?" I asked when he approached.

"No." He gave me a small smile.

I nodded and offered my hand again, which he took. I would have to work on compromising a bit on things. He was shy, wanting to blend in. I was just so sick of hiding all the time. Not as much as Lacey-Marie, mind you, but I did have the distinct advantage of being able to go out in daylight.

The cows were less concerned by my presence, and as long as I didn't approach, they pretty much ignored me. For some reason, the cow barn was packed. There were people jostling us all around, and none gave Doug a second glance.

He started to relax and enjoy himself.

I did as well. The sheep were the only ones to have such an extreme reaction to me, and I knew better than to go anywhere near the horses. Horses are smart. They'd know exactly what I was. Most horses are not afraid of dogs. Most that I had encountered had wanted to squish me to a bloody pulp. If Doug wanted to get friendly with the ponies, he'd have to head in alone.

"Feeling hungry yet?" I asked when another whiff of deep fried food wafted towards me.

"Always." Doug tugged me towards the good smells.

I knew exactly what I wanted. There's always a booth with spicy bratwursts on hot dog buns with nearly burnt onions and slathered with mustard, which were mouthwateringly divine.

I was about to join the line and expose Doug to a

whole new world of overpriced foods when someone knocked into the back of me, which in turn shoved me into Doug, who stumbled.

I turned with a snarl and beheld Greg, the jackass who I'd kicked out of the salon a couple of weeks ago. I recognized his smell before I even got a lock on his face.

He clutched a large woman in too-tight clothes around the waist, close to his side. I glanced at her three-inch roots exposed above the box blond, and my snarl intensified. I hate bad hair.

"Hey look, babe, the freak's gone and got the ugliest fuck that would have her." Greg threw his head back and laughed.

My bones cracked, and my face began to warp. Yet another pair of contacts down the drain. This just wasn't my month.

It took every bit of not inconsiderable muscle that Doug possessed to pull me back. He grabbed me by the shoulders and looked right into the amber of my eyes as he spoke softly to me.

"Easy, Gretchen. He's not worth ripping to shreds. You've got other fish to fry." His hands slid up from my shoulder to caress either side of my face, forcing me to look back into his.

Greg leaned in our direction. "Don't go breedin' and make more of ya."

Doug's expression was forced into relaxation, but I could see his muscles twitch as Greg the lummox grabbed him from behind.

"Hey, I'm talkin' to ya, dickwad."

Doug ignored him, keeping me focused on him and trying to get me to relax.

The stench of a group of people stopping to gawk surged my adrenaline. I had to get ahold of myself. I sucked in deep, slow breaths, imitating Doug's, closing my eyes and paying only attention to his thumbs sweeping gently along my cheeks.

Another presence entered the gathering rabble.

"Watch your mouth." Hades' words were full of angry authority. I could feel his glamour drop. Once again, he was drawing the attention off of me by exposing himself.

Doug moved his hands into my hair and pulled my face down to his shoulder, so that all I could smell was him, then wrapped his arms around me.

"There are children present," Hades added. "If you're going to make a scene, do it somewhere besides a place full of families."

People started moving, and the scent of Greg and his trash blew away. How Hades knew he was needed, I'll never know.

I remained wrapped up in Doug until he pulled away.

"Are you all right?" he asked, studying my eyes.

I reached up and plucked out my ruined contacts, letting them fall to the dirt. I nodded.

"Good, let's get some food in you. The line's gone." He kept an arm around my shoulders as we approached the booth.

"I take it you had some history with that jerk?" the vendor asked.

"Yeah," I said with a sigh.

"Well, I just thought I'd let you know that he's the freak, not you. What can I get for you folks today?" he asked, leaning his bulk over the counter.

"Two extra spicy brats," I said, surprising myself with how normal my voice sounded.

It was a good thing the moon was on her way out, or things might not have turned out so well.

"Good choice. I just put some on the grill a few minutes ago." He picked up two sizzling sausages and placed them in lightly toasted buns. "They're on the house." He held up his hands when I offered up the cash. "And tell the big scary guy he gets one too."

"Thanks!" I gave him a genuine smile.

"Yes, thank you," Doug repeated, then squirted mustard onto our sausages.

We found a grassy spot out of the way of the general flow of traffic and enjoyed our meal. It was nice, sitting there basking in the afternoon sun and watching all the different people pass by. We sat with our legs outstretched, paper plates balanced on our knees, arms propped back for support, close enough to lean against one another.

I wondered if turning Doug into a wolf would ruin his effect on me. What kind of wolf would he be? A submissive? I couldn't imagine so. There were definitely moments that belonged to a more dominant personality.

Why was I even considering it? I was dead set against changing Doug. Wasn't I? I felt safe with him, but as long as he remained human, we could never have any sort of romantic relationship. I found myself wanting that from him. I'd gotten so used to having him around, I didn't particularly want him to leave.

"Do you have to leave to go help your band pack up?" Doug asked, his tone mellow.

I shook my head. "Nope. We finished last night and parked the van in Austin's garage so nothing would get stolen. They'll stick the instruments in just before they leave. We're meeting up here."

"Good. I'm having fun."

Fun, seriously? It was fun keeping me from going psycho in public?

"You're awfully quiet," he commented, sitting so still it was if he were a piece of furniture instead of an actual person.

"I'm relaxed." I tilted my face towards the sun, reveling in the warmth spreading over me.

"Well, that's good. Are you ready to get up and look around some more?"

I was growing fond of his soft French accent.

"Did you grow up in the circus?" I asked, not quite ready to give up my spot.

"Yes, not Treats and Freaks, but in circuses. Both my parents were, um, hairy people, or so my mother tells me. My father didn't stick around."

"Do you talk to her often?"

He'd have a hard time keeping in contact with her if he was changed. The differences are too obvious to someone who knows you well.

"Not really. We're both on the road. She'll send a postcard occasionally, but that's mostly it."

Doug got to his feet and offered me his hand, which I took, letting him pull me up.

"How old are you?" he asked.

"Really old." I dusted off the seat of my jeans, then wandered over to one of the many trash bins to deposit my plate.

"No, really. How old?" he tried again.

I started walking away. "You don't want to know."

"Yes, I do." He rested a hand on my forearm, stopping me.

"One hundred and eighty something. I think." I was a little fuzzy on the dates.

"Wow. You are old." His voice held a joke, but I didn't laugh. "Are you sure you're all right?" He sped up to keep pace with me.

"I'm fine. Let's go look at the crafts."

We spent a lot of time in the rustic barn-like building displaying paintings, drawings, and photographs. Some were beautiful. Some were obviously done by children. Many had ribbons hanging off of their frames.

There was one in particular that stuck out to me. A close up of a wolf's face, its eyes appearing almost human. The tag underneath revealed that it was painted by a 16-year-old boy named Jason. I don't think it was meant to look like a werewolf. Those were probably just the kind of eyes he knew how to do. I found myself thinking it was too bad the painting wasn't for sale. I would have bought it.

As soon as we made it back outside, my hackles rose.

There, waiting in a group for me, was the pack. Could a girl catch a break? Was this entirely necessary?

"Good afternoon, Gretchen. We heard your band was performing tonight, so we're here to show our support," Kaine said as soon as he spotted me. He looked out of his element dressed in jeans and a t-shirt instead of his button-down and jacket.

"Kaine." I tried not to let displeasure color my voice as I stood my ground.

"And this must be the human." Kaine turned to my friend, casting a critical eye over him, a sneer lifting one corner of his lip. "Doug, if I'm not mistaken."

"You're not." Doug tightened his grip on my hand, though the rest of his body remained relaxed.

Neither of them held out a hand in greeting, which was just as well as Kaine would have turned it into a dominance contest that Doug couldn't have won.

"We're meeting up with friends. Enjoy the show." I squeezed Doug's hand in return and started to walk away.

Kaine's hand flew forward, hitting my shoulder. I hadn't realized he was that close. I should have been paying closer attention.

"You are not my alpha. Now excuse us. We have somewhere to be." I stepped around him and pulled Doug with me.

"Not yet," I heard Kaine say.

I didn't stay to hear what he'd follow that up with. We'd agreed to meet Percy and Hades, and we were running late. Then something occurred to me. I turned back to the pack.

"Who told you where I was?" I certainly hadn't mentioned my gig to them.

"The perky dead girl. I called your cell, and she answered." Kaine smiled at me, more aggressive than happy.

Damn that girl. She had no right to answer my phone. Especially when I had left it in my room.

"Come on." I kept my grip on Doug's hand, keeping myself from submitting to my wolf. "Remind me again why I'm friends with her?" I muttered to him as we walked away.

"I don't know," he answered honestly.

I took it little, blonde, and flirty wasn't his type.

We found a spot on the bleachers downwind from the gathering draft horses and close enough to the way out that I could beat a hasty exit if the breeze changed.

Percy and Hades were early as well. We moved from our spot to join them, still downwind but not as close to an escape route.

"Thanks," I said to Hades as soon as my butt hit the bench.

"No problem. It's amazing people like that make it through high school."

Now what did Hades know about high school?

"No kidding," I said. "Oh, the brat vendor says you're welcome to a freebie. He was pretty in awe of you."

"At least someone is. I seem to be losing my touch with you ladies," said Hades, only half joking if his scent was anything to be trusted.

"Aw, come on, Hades, we're all in terrible fear and awe of you," I said, somewhat more brightly than I felt. In fact, it was downright out of character.

Hades raised a dark eyebrow.

We turned our attention to the team of Belgians pulling a sled full of cement blocks, their muscles straining against the straps of their harnesses, moving the sled forward. The momentum of the startup allowed them to ease up only a little as they worked in perfect harmony with their driver, a straight up old New England farmer complete with overalls. They made good time around the edge of the arena, managing not to knock over any of the orange cones that were arranged in a pattern.

I happen to like watching things like that. I wondered if I could pull the load. I wasn't about to go out and try, but that didn't stop the wheels from turning.

We watched the entire competition, which was won by another pair of Belgian geldings, a strawberry roan, and a bright chestnut with a flaxen mane and tail. I like horses. They just don't like me, so I deal and just watch from a distance.

The sun was sitting low in the sky when Doug and I made it to the back entrance of the fairgrounds to meet up with the guys. Austin's white van was already parked with the back and side doors open.

Not thinking, I grabbed a huge amp and lifted it,

instead of pushing it on its little wiggly wheels like I should have done to avoid suspicion. I was thinking of not getting grass and dirt stuck in there. Doug saved me by running around the other end and shoving down.

"Let me help you with that," he said.

"I've got it. Thanks for the reminder, though. Could you get my duffel? It's the green one." I jerked my head back towards the van, where my duffel of equipment waited.

"Sure, of course." He left me to retrieve it.

The white gazebo we would be playing in was empty of all but the sound guy. We'd managed to wrangle the tech from Club North to do sound for us, being that he had a night free. He nodded at me in greeting, mostly focused on checking all his buttons and switches.

The guys followed me quickly. And they had help.

The pack was carrying the less expensive equipment, and some of Austin's drums, while the guys carried their more treasured toys. I really didn't like them getting so chummy with my friends. I could feel the subtle threat in the action.

Mark's fire-engine-red mohawk dazzled with a fresh coat of color and razored sides. I was pretty happy with how the color was lasting this time around. It had been through several days, and hopefully several washings. Red tends to run away screaming, unless of course you don't want it, then it flat out refuses to go. Mark was in charge of his own razor blades, probably a daily process for him.

Austin's head was freshly buzzed down to a quarter inch, while Scott's had grown out to about a quarter as well.

Aw, they were twinsies. How precious.

I eyed Kaine and his lackeys and managed to keep

my mouth shut.

"We wrangled in some volunteers. If you just go get Lola, we'll be just about set." Mark set his guitar down on the white painted board floor of the gazebo.

"Great," I said, trying to sound truthful.

I grabbed Doug's hand and headed for Percy's car.

"Are they dating?" Austin asked Scott innocently.

I didn't hear the reply as I hurried to get out of hearing distance. Such a conversation could get very interesting, I'd wager, but not so interesting that I wanted any part of it.

The sent of wolf hit me with a breeze. I turned, but couldn't see him. It was the one they'd made their emissary, Quintavious. The pack appeared to be especially interested in Doug. Had the alpha sent them to watch us?

It wasn't like Doug and I were actually dating. I had to keep reminding myself it was not a possibility the entire day. No, no, no, no, NO!

I dropped Doug's hand, trying to be casual about it.

"Something wrong?" he asked.

"No. Yes. I don't want to talk about it." Not with him anyhow. I'd unload it all on Lacey-Marie later.

"Oh." He lagged a for a bit, then caught up. "Did I do something wrong around your friends? I know I'm not the most socially conscientious guy—"

"No, nothing like that. I'm just feeling a bit psycho today. I'm glad you're here." Exceedingly glad. I might have lit into Greg otherwise.

"Yeah, I noticed. Is that normal?"

"Uh." Was it normal for me to start wolfing out every five minutes? "No." I usually have my wolf on a short leash, except for those days when the night was bright. I seemed to have slipped my collar. Was he worried he'd become a maniac if the alpha decided to change him? Perhaps I should have lied.

"Good. I like being with you, but you can be a little scary."

It didn't matter how tame I may have appeared. He should always have a healthy fear of the wolf.

We made it to Percy's car. "Yeah, I know. I really can't help it. It's been a stressful month." I had one of Percy's keyless remotes in my pocket, so I waved my foot under the back, popping the trunk.

No violin. I looked under the blanket, digging down to the spare tire, then started tearing the car apart.

"I'm absolutely positive that I put my violin in the trunk. Where the hell is it?" I hopped into the trunk to dig some more, hoping it had just been pushed farther back into the emergency blankets.

"Ah, Gretchen? What are you doing?" Doug held the trunk open as I frantically shoved the back seat down and crawled through.

"Shit, shit, shit! It's not here. It's not anywhere! Where is it?" my performance outfit hung from the garment hook in the back seat, but no violin.

"Gretchen, you're um—"

"What?" I turned around and snarled at Doug.

"Fuzzy," he finished.

I ran my tongue over my growing teeth, and the pain kicked in. Double and triple shit!

Suddenly, Doug went flying sideways and was replaced by Quintavious, who reached through the trunk, grabbed my leg, and dragged me out.

I started wolfing out faster, and I roared, my fangs inches from his face.

"Gretch, easy." Doug pushed the were out of his way and placed his hands on my shoulders for the second time that day.

He was too late. I could feel it. A loud snap

punctuated with snarls escaped my body.

"Get away from me!" I roared, pulling away from Doug's soothing hands.

He didn't listen, pulling my face into his shoulder again. He was breathing calmly and evenly. Not at all what I would expect from someone who was afraid of me from time to time. He kept one hand in my hair, massaging my scalp, the other made slow circles between my shoulder blades, down to my lower back and back up.

"It's okay, *ma colombe*. You're going to be fine." His voice was as soothing as his heartbeat and hands.

Concentrating on making my breaths match his, I relaxed little by little and brought my arms up to hug him back. There was another snap, and I groaned in pain. He continued to hold me as the fur and extra bits of teeth receded back to wherever they came from. It was quick and far too unsettling for it to happen twice in one day.

As soon as Quintavious knew I'd calmed, he dragged Doug from my clutches. "What the hell is wrong with you? Do you have a death wish? Do you realize she could have ripped you to shreds?" Gone was the peace keeper. After all, a submissive were was still more dominant than a human.

I squirmed my way between them and shoved Quintavious back. "Leave him alone."

"She won't hurt me," said Doug.

I didn't want to hurt him, but if he kept taking chances like that, appreciative though I was of him, he was going to end up dead. That's how a wolf works. I didn't say anything, just tugged on Doug's shirt and went to find Percy.

She was waiting for me at the gazebo, carrying my violin case.

"You looked busy, so I retrieved it for you." She held it up, not knowing the disaster she'd almost caused.

"Thanks. Don't ever help me again." I snatched Lola and stalked away, leaving Doug to explain.

My boys were still surrounded by weres. Quintavious hadn't reappeared to enlighten them about my latest episode.

"There you are," said Scott, slinging an arm around my shoulders. "We were wondering where you'd wandered off to with the hairy guy."

"His name is Doug. We went looking for my violin. I had a minor panic attack when I couldn't find it, and here I am." I wiggled away.

"Ok—ay." He let his arm drop back to his side. "Well, you should probably get changed, so we can get going on sound check."

Right, changed. Back out to the car I went. At least I knew my stage costume was still there. I picked it up and hiked over to the bathrooms halfway across the fairgrounds. I was grateful they had bathrooms and I didn't get stuck changing in one of the bright blue port-a-potties.

I had several layers: a tight black long sleeve shirt as the under layer, a loose bell sleeved shirt, and the black and red corset over the top. Hey, I wanted to look warm. It was expected that people get cold when the thermometer drops, so I had to follow conventions to avoid suspicion. Knee-high buckle-infested boots and black skinny jeans completed the look. I'm a creature of habit, and people recognize the costume. I pinned and teased my wild curls into a Mohawk to rival Mark's, pinning in some red extensions and weaving them in. Makeup, hairspray, all done.

I marched out in much better spirits than I entered.

I had needed the time alone and managed not to get pissed off by any of the obnoxious teenagers who haunted the festival after school hours. They needed to watch their mouths. This was a family event. Of course, it was almost dark, and the families had a tendency to leave, making it a young person haven.

I tuned up and plugged in, just in time for sound check. Mark smiled at me, and I grinned back. Yep, I was in much better humor.

We worked well with the Club North sound guy. I wondered if we could talk him into doing gigs with us on a regular basis. It's so much better when you can use just one sound guy, instead of suffering through some of the hacks available at some venues.

As final dark descended, we jammed in preparation for our show to draw in the crowd. There were five sets of wolf eyes, besides my own, glowing throughout the crowd. I hadn't thought about the glow. Our eyes are reflective, just like real critters. Of course, mine wouldn't be too bad, as we had lights shining in our direction.

When we were satisfied with the size of the crowd. Mark made our introductions, and we began playing in earnest, my computer set up with the sound guy to record everything. We'd pick through it later and see where we could make some improvements. The sound guy was familiar with my software and was perfectly happy to fiddle with it along with the sound board.

With adrenaline zinging through my system, I played more were than I normally would in public, managing to pull my attention away from the glowing eyes staring back at me and pouring myself into the music. There were spots in a couple of the songs where we each got a chance to improvise and show off. I took full advantage, reveling in it.

When we finished the set and went about breaking everything down, a guy in his forties with a neatly trimmed beard approached us.

"I'm Blake Adams." He held out a hand to Mark, who shook it. "You guys have a great sound. I've been hearing your name thrown around a lot lately, so I came to check you out, and I'm glad I did. I own a studio down in Portland, and I'd love it if you'd came and recorded an album with us." He shook hands with each of us in turn with a firm grip.

Mark looked around at us, taking in our matching grins. "We'd love to. How can we get in touch?"

Blake pulled out his wallet and handed Mark a business card.

LAST QUARTER

Chapter 23:
Drinking with Werewolves

We finished breaking down and found ourselves surrounded by the pack.

"Congratulations, Gretchen, that was a great show. And a chancy one." Kaine referred to my near wolf out moments before the show.

"Thanks, I'm fine now." I could keep the wolf muzzled, at least until I got home.

"We'd like to invite you and your friends to join us for some drinks."

Werewolves in a crowded bar. That didn't sound smart. "Sure. You guys up to going out?" I turned to my boys.

Austin shrugged, and Scott didn't say anything at all.

"Yeah, sure. Sounds great," Mark said, flipping down the clasps on his guitar case.

I wound up my cords, using Velcro strips to keep them organized before storing them back in my duffel. I had a surprising amount of equipment for such a petite instrument. I relinquished it all to Percy, who waited just out of earshot.

"We're going out for a drink," I muttered

"Is that wise? You smell positively canine," she

muttered back, searching my eyes with concern.

"Wanna come and hold my leash?" I invited.

"No, no. I'm sure Doug can manage you without me there. Besides, Hades and tequila aren't a good mix. Unless you're trying to make a bomb." Percy waved me off. She wasn't one to get drinks anyhow. In fact, the hair show was the first time she'd been out with actual drinks in over a year. She usually ordered lemon water.

I waved and turned back to the kerfuffle I may have created.

The wolves were looking convincingly young and innocent. It was almost scary how well they pulled it off. I did all right, managing to fool customers and friends alike into thinking I was really 24. They were a whole different pan of cupcakes. If I couldn't smell what they were, I'd never know. They were so much more in control than I, keeping each other in check, and Kaine had the whole pack to balance him out.

I was a dominant wolf without a pack. And though I'd found some balance with Percy and Lacey-Marie, they lacked the doggy social skills, or whatever magic is involved in forming a pack. Maybe I should have gotten a dog for mental health purposes.

I stopped Percy to grab my cash and ID from my purse and let her cart the rest away. I didn't have any workable pockets, so I stuffed everything down into my bra.

"Mr. Wolfemin, will you be joining us tonight?" Kaine asked.

I hadn't been aware of Doug's last name.

"If you're sure you don't mind me tagging along." Doug shrugged, looking uncertain. He knew what they were, despite their disguise as normals.

"Not at all. And if you're willing to stay out late

our, ah, boss would like to have a word with you."

Very well done, slipping in the alpha changer into the conversation without betraying what he was.

"I'll definitely be there then. I hope it's business we'll be discussing?"

The pack closed in around Doug, and I tensed. I had a feeling it would be more than a conversation taking place later on. I didn't like being cut off from him. I wasn't a member of the pack, so apparently I didn't have a say in the matter.

"So, you know all those guys?" Scott asked, pointedly not looking at my face.

"Yeah, they're kind of family." I stared at the group surrounding their potential new member.

"Right. Family." Scott stalked off.

Why was he so angry? I'd already told him that Quintavious was my brother, hadn't I? Apparently he didn't believe me. Whether they were my pack or not, they were all family. We had the same father, after all, in a loose sense of all being bitten by the same fae.

"Hey, Austin," I called across the small crowd.

"Yo!" He waved.

"Can Doug and I catch a ride out to the bar with you?"

"Sure. Help me drag the rest of the gear out to the van, and we can get going."

"Of course."

First I had to extract Doug from the midst of the pack.

"Hey, we're getting ready to leave. Can you finish your conversation at the bar?" I asked, planting myself at Doug's side.

"Of course, my lady." Kaine took my hand and kissed my knuckles, all the while keeping his eyes on mine.

I yanked my fingers from his grasp, adding a little dramatic flair by wiping them on my pants. "Doug. I was talking to Doug." I took his arm and gave him a small smile. "Are you ready?"

I was using him to push the point home that I didn't belong to Kaine, who just smiled at me like I was a precocious child rebelling against him.

"Yes, I'm ready." Doug's smile was even bigger than Kaine's, and I could hear his heart race with excitement, which didn't bode well if the alpha turned him down.

Being a wolf has its positives and negatives, and I firmly believe that if one has the chance to remain human, they should hold on to that existence with a death grip. I walked away brooding over the change of events, hauling gear, mindless of the fact that I shouldn't have been able to lift most of it so easily.

Doug followed me, toting some lighter things. His smile had disappeared, my mood rubbing off on him.

"What's the matter?" he asked, shifting his armful into the puzzle of equipment.

"Nothing. I'm fine. It's just been a long day."

His shoulders slumped with disappointment. "Would you rather go home?"

"No, I think it would cause less trouble if we just go. I can't afford to tick off the pack tonight." I rearranged some amps so the big plastic bins could fit in without too precarious a balancing act.

"So the pack's leader seems to be in love with you." He couldn't have brought up a sorer subject. His statement was innocent enough since he didn't know what it meant if a wolf carried a torch for someone.

Wolves are very loyal to their packs. They're even more loyal to their mates. From what I've picked up over the years, divorce between were-couples is unheard of. There were the occasional cases of death and dismemberments, but those were rare and far between. The bond is on a primal level, chemical, and it's a solemn vow. Wolves also pair up quickly when they find someone compatible. I think it's a survival thing, as there aren't so many women who've been changed. The males have to snatch them up before someone else does. It's yet another reason I have problems with relationships and commitment. I'm fully aware that if I make any sort of commitment to a mate or a pack, it will be instantaneous and eternal.

I wasn't ready for forever, not with Kaine, no matter how badly I wanted a family.

"Who's riding shotgun?" Austin saved me from having to come up with something else to say to Doug.

"Me!" I pasted a smile on my lips and darted for the passenger side door.

"Where do I ride?" Doug asked, glancing at the van's two seats.

"In the back with the junk. As long as Austin doesn't get pulled over, we'll be fine." I opened the door and hopped up into the seat.

I hated seat belts and all they represented, but I clipped mine in just the same. The whole 'you must wear a seat belt because it's the law' thing really irked me. It's just another way for someone to tell you what to do when it doesn't affect them at all. Besides, even if we did get into an accident, it wasn't as if I could get hurt badly enough to die. But Doug could.

I hopped back out. "I changed my mind, I'll ride in the back."

Doug had already settled himself in amongst the equipment. "No, I'm fine back here."

"Sit in front," I hissed quietly at him, proving my temper was still too close to the surface.

"Fine, okay, I'll sit in front." Doug held up his hands in the defensive position and scrambled up to the front of the van.

I found a good spot between an amp and the bass drum.

"All set back there?" Austin asked, turning the key in the ignition.

"Yep. I'm comfy."

The fairgrounds were close to Bangor, so I wouldn't get jostled around too badly, especially with Austin on his best behavior behind the wheel to avoid attracting any police attention. There were plenty of things to hide behind if we had the misfortune to be pulled over, but we made it to the bar without mishap. We had the good fortune to be the first ones to arrive, which meant the pack would have to join me, instead of me joining them, giving them the wrong message.

Kaine had mentioned that the alpha would be around at some point, and I briefly wondered if he would show up at the bar, or if there was some preordained place where he'd meet with Doug and me.

I felt a little like an overdressed bar skank, compared to the blue jeans and sweaters all around. The hair and makeup didn't help my case, as they were intended for the stage, not for a night out on the town.

Being the most aggressive of my little trio, I fought my way through the crowd to the bar. The bartender was a big guy in his early thirties, dressed in a black wife beater-style tank top to best show off the tattoos on his biceps. Both his ears were gauged, and he obviously made a slather and bic a part of his daily routine.

"Two beers and one Captain and coke," I sang out as soon as his attention wasn't quite so in demand.

"Be right with you." He looked me over, his eyes

roving over my costume and lingering on my face. "You look familiar." He set the beers down in front of me, then proceeded to mix my drink.

"I'm here every once in a while, and my band plays around. We played the festival tonight." I used a swinging hand motion to explain my getup.

"You're the chick who plays the weird looking fiddle." He set my drink in front of me.

"Electric violin," I supplied, trying to figure out how I was going to carry three drinks.

"You guys are good." He crossed his arms over his broad chest and smiled with a nod.

"Thanks, I've had about 150 or so years of practice, and the guys were playing together before I joined up."

I decided to tuck one of the glasses between my arm and my body, carrying the other two in hand. I was about to walk off when I remembered to pay. Sheepishly, I reached into my top and pulled out my wad of money and plopped some bills down on the counter before tucking the rest away again.

"Beer for you, rum and coke for me." I set my prizes down on the table and slid down onto the seat next to Doug.

"Good girl." Austin raised his drink to me, then took a swallow.

We were soon joined by the pack and the rest of my boys. We were a rowdy bunch, but no one wolfed out. I was especially proud of my deceptively convincing humanity.

As the noise level grew, I found myself with an opportunity to talk to Doug without anyone paying attention. "So the alpha—" I started.

"Yes, I'm scared shitless." He shrugged his shoulders and pursed his lips tight between his teeth.

I was surprised by Doug's uncharacteristic cursing.

"Are you having second thoughts?" I asked hopefully.

"Not at all. He's just intimidating, and I don't like what he does to you." Doug slid down in his chair so his shoulder blades came to rest on the back. He looked totally at ease with his feet stretched out under the table and crossed at the ankles. I envied him.

"How can you just throw everything away?" I leaned towards him, trying to convey the full weight of my worry to him.

"Throw what away? I have nothing, Gretchen."

"Don't be an idiot."

"I'm not. I want this. Besides, who are you to talk?"

"I was a sex slave, you ass! I thought becoming a were would be an escape. It wasn't. I'm still the same girl. I'll always be. Plus the fact that I have to live with being the murderer who massacred dozens of innocent people."

"Innocent? Listen to yourself. One moment you're a slave, then next you love your captors." He shifted upright.

"They didn't deserve to die. I didn't have someone to tell me what I was signing up for. It's a lifetime membership to a life that never ends."

"Sounds pretty great to me. Besides, I know you don't really hate it."

"I accept it, and sometimes I enjoy it, but if I had a chance to take it all back, I would. Life is full of choices. I made a bad one. Don't make my mistake." I was getting riled up, and I could feel my wolf pull closer to my surface.

Doug wasn't perturbed at all. "It's my mistake to make, and I don't think it will be a mistake. Besides, you could use a friend."

I could, yes. "I have friends."

"Yes, you do, but wouldn't it be nice to have someone who could understand you?"

He needed to stop making sense, or my defenses would break down.

I didn't reply, and his smile grew. He obviously knew I was done arguing.

If he was that set on being changed—and when it came right down to it, it was his choice—then I wouldn't stand in his way. I would support him. I would be there for him. And that would make all the difference. When I was changed, I had no one. I would be his someone.

"Are you done trying to talk me out my decision?" Doug asked.

I nodded, drumming my fingers on the sides of my glass.

Scott took the seat to my other side. "How's it going?" he asked.

"Fine," I lied, getting up. I just couldn't take his mournful looks.

Maybe that made me a terrible friend, but I'd known Penny for longer than he had, and I still found it easier to deal than he did. Yes, I was sad she was dead, but shit happens, like death. I'd been dealing with it for years, and I didn't know how to respond to people who hadn't. Especially someone like Scott who was depressed about it one moment and hitting on me the next.

Kaine followed me out. I couldn't shake the guy.

"What?" I turned on him as soon as we made it outside.

"Just out getting some fresh air. It's a little cloy in there with all the scent going on."

I nodded in agreement, though I didn't believe him.

"What's up with you and the hairy guy?"

"Absolutely nothing." I found myself wishing it were a lie.

"I don't think it's nothing to him. You need to stop leading him on." Kaine ran a calloused hand over his stubble-covered face.

I stood tall, trying to out-intimidate him. "That's none of your business."

"You are my pack. It is very much my business. And even if the alpha decides to change him, he won't be."

That startled me a little. "Why not?"

"Because his genetic code is no good. We want to strengthen the pack, and his mutation indicates a weakness in his blood."

I didn't believe that for a second. Who cared if a werewolf was hairy? "That's bull." My pulse picked up tempo.

"Oh? Ask the alpha. He's very picky about who he changes. He's not a vampire to bite purely for the thrill of it. He chose you specifically for your strength. Apparently he didn't take into account your stubbornness."

"If you object to me, why do you insist on pursuing me?" I snarled.

"You're hot, babe, and your genetic code is excellent. I think you'll settle down after mating. You might actually be satisfied."

I growled at him, "Not a chance, buddy."

It was time for me to go back inside. I didn't know if I was going to last for a meet-up with the alpha changer. I found myself saddled with the intense desire to go home and lock myself away, but I resumed my seat between Doug and Scott instead. I'd take both their company, in any temperament, to Kaine's any day.

Even if I chose to stay with the pack, there was no way I was mating with that guy. He was a good leader, but terrible with women. I couldn't imagine that the ladies in the pack liked him. Respected him, perhaps, but like? No way.

I was presented with a terrible smelling shot, tossed it back, and turned to Doug.

"Are you absolutely sure of your decision?" I asked.

"Oh, no. I thought we were done with that." He leaned away. I could tell he didn't want to argue.

Neither did I. "We are. I'm just thinking you might want to get a bit smashed. From what I remember, the bite hurts like hell. If he really is going to change you, then a were constitution will kill any hangover possibilities."

"Werewolves can't get drunk?"

"We can, it just takes a lot more all at once, the whole metabolism thing. We burn through alcohol really fast."

"Really fast what?" Scott asked from my other side, obviously feeling good.

"My metabolism," I supplied, blinking innocently.

"I don't doubt it. I've seen you eat before, and I've never seen you drunk."

"And you never will, I promise." I let an impish smile grace my features.

"Aw, come on, I think you'd be fun. Loosen you up a bit."

"That doesn't really sound like a brilliant idea to me. You didn't drive yourself here, did you?" I could drive him home, then run to wherever the weres were meeting.

"'Course I did."

"I'll get him home. Our boss really wants to talk to you tonight." Quintavious interrupted our conversation.

I nodded. If he was the one to normally deal with the humans, then I supposed I could trust him not to wolf out on Scott. Huh, I almost liked the guy. I hadn't been prepared for that.

I ordered a round of shots for everyone and a double for Doug. Mine tasted a little better than the first one I'd sucked down.

He was more than a little sloshed when Kaine appeared once again behind us.

"Time to go," he said. "I'll take you to the alpha."

Kaine's vehicle wasn't as nice as I'd expected. Perhaps he hadn't been as wise with his investments as I'd gotten other people to be for me over the years. It was a rental, and I wondered how the rental place would like the obvious dog smell that it would be returned with.

We didn't drive too far out of town, just enough away from people that no one would hear the screaming. Doug and I got out as soon as the car stopped, but Kaine remained in the driver's seat.

"He wants to see the two of you alone. He isn't going to hurl, is he?"

I looked at Doug, who did look a little off.

"Nah, he's just prepared." I was pretty sure his ill look was more from nerves than alcohol. "Uh, are you going to give us a ride home?" I hated to ask, but I didn't really want to carry Doug back to the caravan if he passed out.

"Of course. I'll be right here enjoying my music." Kaine turned up his radio, and I shut the passenger side door.

"Ready?" I asked, purely for the need to say something.

Doug just nodded.

"I can smell him. Follow me."

The scent of magic and wolf caused me to stumble. Doug caught my arm and kept me moving.

We found him sitting on a boulder, looking bored.

Bored or not, he still had the power to make me crumple. Down on my knees I went. My upper body disobeyed my will, and once again I was face down in the dirt.

Doug wasn't faring much better. He couldn't feel the alpha's influence, but the alcohol was having a similar effect. I shoved a hand out to keep him from tipping over.

"Thanks," he slurred.

"Welcome, children. I'm mostly here to speak with Doug. As he is your friend, I thought you should be here. Is that acceptable, Maude?" The alpha climbed to hind feet, still awkwardly clad in boots as if to fit in with human imaginings.

"It is," I whispered into the dirt.

"Good. You may rise."

I hurried to do his bidding, knowing there was no way I could have stood had he not demanded it.

"I have come to a decision. I will change you. I find your condition pitiable. However, you will be condemned to the life of a lone wolf, as the pack has spoken of their unwillingness to take you in. I must warn you, I don't know what effect the magic will have on your particular abnormalities, and it will hurt. Are you willing, human pup?" The alpha towered over Doug, his eyes glowing creepily in the dark, as I'm sure mine were.

"I want it. I don't care if I'm part of the pack." Doug swallowed his fear and stood tall.

Bravo for him. Despite my apprehension of his

decision, I was proud of him.

"Good. I let all my children choose the location where I bite as it will scar." The alpha grinned. and I was truly creeped out. The guy had way too many teeth.

"Where were you bitten, Gretch?" Doug asked, looking at me instead of the teeth.

"Here." I lifted my left arm and indicated a spot just below my armpit. The scar was hidden beneath clothing, but I could feel it with the alpha so close.

"Bite me there." Doug rolled up his sleeve.

I shook my head. "Better rip that. You don't want it falling down over the wound later." I stepped up to Doug and lifted his sleeve to my teeth to tear it, ripping it until it split up to the shoulder seam. I'd use it to bandage the wound later.

I stepped back, allowing the alpha space. He took Doug firmly in his arms, lifting him and pressing his body against his massive barrel of a chest, just as he had done with me so long ago. He pinned him there with one alien arm and held Doug's left arm up with his free hand.

The alpha looked me in the eye, and I immediately glanced away. I couldn't watch him bite Doug or meet the alpha's stare.

I turned my back when Doug screamed as the alpha's grotesque teeth ripped into his underarm. I winced in sympathy but kept my position.

Doug's scream escalated in volume and pitch, and I was forced to look when the alpha beckoned me with a yip.

I caught his body as he dropped to the ground, finally passed out from the pain.

"How long will he be like this?" I asked, lifting my friend in my arms.

"A couple of days, probably. It varies. Take care of my pup. I'll check on him someday."

I wasn't sure if I'd understood him. He had made it very clear that the pack wanted nothing to do with Doug. Why did he want me to look after Doug if he wanted me to be a full member of the pack?

Chapter 24:
Life or Death

I carried Doug over my shoulder to the car, where Kaine stood waiting. Kaine went so far as to open the back door so I could shove Doug in feet first, then follow him in.

My hand against Doug's forehead revealed a raging fever. I hadn't filled him on the little fact that not everyone survives the bite. It burns you with a fever so hot that you could die as your insides cook themselves. There was no point. It wouldn't have changed his mind.

I tore his ripped sleeves into strips and bandaged the bite as tightly as I dared. I didn't want to get blood all over Kaine's rental. Had it been a normal bite, I'd have been forced to take Doug to the hospital, but being as it was, I was taking him straight to Percy. She was bound to have some kind of herbal or magical goodness to at least make him comfortable.

I propped Doug's wounded arm up in the air with my shoulder, keeping it immobile. I didn't know what the chances were of him bleeding out, not being a medical expert, and I didn't want to take any chances.

"How's it going back there?" Kaine asked as we coursed down the road.

"I have no idea." I hadn't been conscious for my change, so I had no clue how 'going well' looked.

"Is the blood flowing or seeping?" he asked.

I tipped my head to look at the bandaged covered wound. "I think it's oozing."

"He should be fine. If it isn't gushing, then most of the saliva will stay inside to work its magic. Otherwise, the fever will kill him."

No shit, Sherlock.

"I'm not a bad man, Gretchen." Kaine watched me in the rearview mirror, and I met his eyes, staring him down. To look away would be to admit his dominance over me. As much as it irked him to do so, he looked away first, having to watch the road.

Free to turn my attention back to Doug, I was happy to see that he had yet to break a sweat. It was magic versus body chemistry. Sweat would cool a fever, which would halt the transformation. This was just theory and conjecture on my part. I didn't really know how it all worked. My research had been mostly speculation, not having any contact with the pack since my own change.

There was no way Kaine was driving the speed limit. I had to keep from sliding from side to side as we wound around corners and swooped over hills.

"We going back to your home?" Kaine asked, taking the turn for my road.

"Yeah, thanks."

Doug's blood seeped through the bandage and soaked into my top. I pushed my hand against it, hoping to keep as much blood in him as possible. I didn't care about my outfit, just the fact that blood did more good inside a body than out.

The tires made a different noise as Kaine turned the car onto our paved driveway, which was smoother than the public road.

Lacey-Marie met us at the front door, her nose

fluttering in response to the scent of Doug's blood. Her eyes opened wide, and her pupils dilated. I saw her take a deep breath and hold it, trying to keep the scent of blood at bay. A paper cut, or a cut from someone's sheers, she could deal with, especially with the house's peculiar type of help, but the amount of blood that stained both my and Doug's clothing was too much for her.

"Percy!" she shrieked as soon as she got the door closed behind us. She backed away, taking quick, shallow breaths as she retreated, her fists clenching and releasing.

I stood in the entryway, one arm under Doug's knees and the other around his shoulders, cradling his burning body to my own. It was uncomfortable, but I was unwilling to put him down.

Out of the kitchen ran not Percy, but Fern, Meredith, and Toni. I hadn't realized they were around, else I'd have carried Doug directly up the stairs. I couldn't imagine this was going to go well. Fern knew about us, and as far as I knew, she had kept her mouth shut. Percy and Mem dashed in right on their heels.

Great, a party.

"Can you get him to the attic?" Percy asked, rushing over and peeling back his eyelids.

"Yeah, if someone can pull the cord. Probably not Lace." I glanced in the vampire's direction who didn't have much visible cornea left, her tongue snaking out to lick her lips hungrily. "She's not taking the blood too well."

"I'll get it," Fern volunteered, separating herself from the group.

I was shocked. She seemed pretty freaked out when she discovered us, but the bleeding man in my arms didn't phase her. Maybe she just performed well under pressure?

"All right, it's upstairs in front of my room." I started for the foot of the stairs and moved up them carefully, not wanting to jostle too much.

Fern ran up ahead, and I heard the thud of the stairs falling, followed by a soft string of swears. I'd forgotten to warn her how easily the ladder released once the trap door was pulled.

I ran up the unsteady ladder into my favorite hideout. If the girls followed us, they would be fully exposed to everything we were. From the clatter coming from behind me, there would be no avoiding it.

"Whoa," Meredith gulped upon pulling the string connected to the light in the ceiling, revealing the open area.

It spanned the entire length of the mansion, and it was full of stuff we'd collected over the years, plus spell books, and the herbs hanging from the ceiling. I was seeing it with them, though I knew exactly what to expect.

I wondered how Toni had gotten away with staying out so late. Percy must have invited all the girls over for drinks. It had to be at least one in the morning.

Fern hurried ahead of me, looking around for a clean surface. "Where are you going to put him?"

"If you guys could clear off the big table, that would be best." I jutted my chin the direction of Percy's big old oak work table.

She got busy setting things on the floor and scattered chairs. The others joined in as soon as they were finished gawking.

"Why didn't you bring him to the hospital?" Meredith asked, eying the blood-soaked strips.

"Doctors can't help him. All we can do is make him comfortable until the change is complete." I laid

Doug on the table and held his arm in the air, scarlet staining my hands and darkening my sleeves. Kaine had said it was okay for it to ooze, but now the blood trickled out at a pretty steady rate. The sodden t-shirt bandage probably needed to come off, but I was leaving that to Percy.

She made it up the ladder carrying a basket of things from the basement. She looked around at all the girls, then at Hades, who was also carrying a basket.

"Shut the door, would you, hun?" she asked, setting her basket on the floor next to the work table.

Hades knelt by the hole in the floor, pulled the ladder up, and secured the trapdoor.

"Girls, I'm afraid there's not time to dance around the issues here. You're going to see things that may frighten you, but I'm going to ask you to put that fear aside because I need your help. I'm afraid I can't work as I am." Percy took a deep breath then released her glamour. The power shone over her in the poorly-lit room, until she lit the kerosene lamps with a flick of her fingers.

"So, what happened?" she asked, ignoring the gasps of the girls.

"We met with the alpha changer tonight to get Doug bitten."

"He did it, then." She laid a hand on his forehead, then felt for the pulse in his neck, nodding grimly.

"That's the idea. He'll be like me if he lives. Kaine said oozing blood is okay. Anything more than that is bad because the saliva will run out with it. I've been keeping his arm up, but he started bleeding pretty good after we got inside."

"All right. Let's get these rags off him, get him cleaned up, and I'll see if I can stitch him up." Percy picked up a pair of sewing scissors. "Toni, there's distilled water in that jug over there. Pour some in the electric kettle, and plug it in, would you? Gretchen, keep his arm elevated for me." She began cutting away the sodden cloth, releasing more blood. The coppery scent tickled my nose, and I fought my predator instinct that wanted me to put him out of his misery.

"What can I do?" Meredith asked, stepping up to the table, hands clenched behind her back.

"Open my basket, and hand me things when I ask for them," Percy answered, completely absorbed in her task.

I watched, fascinated, as she exposed the wound, carefully peeling away more of my sad looking bandage. It looked like a ragged dog bite, though much larger than your average pooch's maw. In other words: Doug's arm was a mess. I don't know how she'd keep it clean long enough to stitch one ragged side to the other.

I came to fully appreciate the fact that I too had been unconscious for my change.

"There's a list of herbs right on top. If you could gather the jars from the shelf over there, everything should be labeled." She addressed Meredith.

"Sure." Meredith didn't move

"Meredith, are you all right?" I asked.

"Uh," she said, looking less than all right. "Hades, Percy, what are you guys?" She looked from one to the other, as they were both in full fae mode.

"Ever heard the myth about Persephone and Hades?" I asked her.

She nodded.

"It's not a myth."

She stumbled back a couple of steps, then started loudly rummaging through the jars. I thought she was taking it quite well.

"Wait, what?" Meredith paused in her search.

After swallowing the excess saliva that hungrily pooled in my mouth, I explained. "Myths, fairy tales, and some horror stories have some basis in reality." The piercing whistle of the kettle saved me from having to explain further.

"There are measurements next to each item. If you'd put them in the wooden bowl, then Toni can pour the boiling water over it all. Mem, there are clean bandages in the plastic drawer set. Bring some to me." Percy turned her lavender gaze on Mem, who was patiently waiting for instructions.

They all kept moving, hopefully not thinking too hard on what they were willingly participating in. While the herbs and bandages sat steeping, Percy became the subject of much scrutiny.

"So, you're like a goddess?" Meredith asked, watching her through the rising steam.

"Yes, though that bit is a little fictional. I'm just a fae." Percy said, giving the bandages as stir.

"She's the queen of the land of the dead." Hades supplied what he probably thought was helpful information.

"Yeah, I'd forgotten about that part," Fern gulped.

"So, Gretchen, is that your real name? Are you a goddess too?" Toni asked, watching the goings on with great curiosity and without the smallest scent of fear.

"It's been my name for a very long time, but I used to be called Maude. I didn't think it fit me, so I changed it. No, I'm not quite fae."

"She's a werewolf," supplied Fern.

If I had thought things were going well, my perceptions were dashed as the girls backed away from me in a hurry, and the tang of fear rose to frenzying levels.

"Oh for heaven's sake, I'm not going to bite you or anything. I didn't do this to Doug. The alpha changer did." I rolled my eyes in Percy's direction, and she grinned at me.

Great, she thought it was funny that the girls were terrified of me. That's so nice.

"Seriously, ladies, I'm housebroken." I leaned towards the steam to muddle their scents.

"You were changing, weren't you? That day, when that guy was being an ass?" Toni asked. Her voice lacked its normal volume.

"Uh, yeah, but I got a hold of myself, and now it's all good." It's all good? It wasn't all good. I held less and less control every day. I was supposed to be gaining control with the new moon just days away.

It got quiet as Percy used one of the bandage strips to wash away the gore that coated Doug's arm.

Maybe it isn't that bad. Maybe the blood just makes it look worse than it is.

I glanced down. Nope, it really was just as bad as I thought. No imagination required to amp up the adrenaline.

Percy, seemingly unimpressed by it all, kept her composure professional. She didn't bother with latex gloves—the magic would kill any bacteria she might spread—and I had a feeling she was using a fair amount of her own. She even skipped the plier-like instruments that doctors used to keep the needle clean and used her own fingers to sew with the curved needle. The thread she used looked like silk and smelled like flesh.

I didn't want to know where she got thread made of skin.

"Oh gross, gross, gross!" Meredith looked away, suddenly becoming squeamish.

Mem and Toni looked on with interest. I assumed they'd had the opportunity to see stitches performed before on people they cared more about.

Fern was at the other end of the room, collecting gauze and more clean bandages.

"I'm thinking it would be good if he didn't get dehydrated," Toni said, touching Doug's forehead.

"You're correct. Would you go pour a cup of water and get a dropper out of the glass cabinet?" Percy kept her eyes on her work.

"So what is Lacey-Marie?" Meredith asked, staring at the rafters.

"Work now, questions later," said Percy.

Hades was guarding the trapdoor like a dog with a favorite bone. We would have to make sure the girls would keep their mouths shut about us before we could let them go. So far, they were handling our revelation well. Greek and Roman gods didn't have the best of reps. Werewolves were considered outright monsters, but there was no question that vampires killed people in any of the stories. I suppose it was a good thing that Lacey had run away from the smell of Doug's blood.

Toni rejoined us at the table, bearing a glass of water and a dropper.

"Go ahead and give him some. Gretchen, you'll have to pry his mouth open for her. We don't want to accidentally drown him, so only a squirt or two at a time. I don't know how well he'll be able to swallow," Percy continued, repairing the extensive damage.

With the hand I wasn't using to prop up Doug's arm, I shoved a couple of fingers in his mouth. His jaw was clenched like a steel trap, but I managed to jam my index finger into the little space in the back with no teeth, then squished my thumb in with it. It took some doing, but I opened my pinched fingers in his mouth, forcing his jaw open.

Toni was ready with the water dropper, squirting in a small amount of liquid as soon as she saw Doug's teeth separate from each other. At my nod, she repeated it, and we waited.

The liquid sat on his tongue for a moment, then I tilted his head back, my fingers still in his mouth, and he swallowed.

"More," I commanded, wanting to get as much liquid into him as we could while I had his jaw pried open.

Toni obliged, and again I tilted his head back, forcing him to swallow.

Percy tied off the thread and cut another length to work on another section of damage.

It was very slow going, and the girls were helpful, but I wanted Percy to hurry. I wanted to know that everything was going to be okay. With Doug. With the girls.

Meredith started pacing, wringing her hands and muttering. She was the one who worried me the most. Toni seemed like a level-headed woman, but Meredith was unpredictable. She did as she was told and was, for all intents and purposes, a good girl. There was just something, maybe just her youth, that put me on edge.

Why was I more willing to trust the older women? Age did not always come with a ready supply of wisdom.

After what I considered to be a satisfactory amount of water had been squirted into Doug, I waved Toni away.

"Thanks." I extracted my fingers from his mouth and touched his hairy cheek with my fingertips. So far, there were no signs of the magic doing anything about the excess hair. I had some extreme doubts, as I had voiced to him, but I hoped something would happen, for his sake.

I honestly didn't care what he looked like under all the fluff. I'd grown accustomed to his appearance. His hair was shorter than when I had first met him. I found myself wondering what Ulysses thought of his new cut.

Doug hated his condition, hated the stares it drew. All he had wanted was to be normal, at least on the outside, to not be considered a freak. Of course, by attempting the change, he was becoming a true freak. Like me. I wondered how much he had really thought about it.

My research on the condition hadn't been as thorough as I would have liked, so I didn't know if there were any medical side effects to the mutation besides the hair. Maybe I would ask him after it was all over. Right now, he just needed to stop bleeding and survive.

The blood that Percy wiped away as she worked became less and less. Was that because her stitches were keeping it in where it belonged, or because he didn't have much left?

"Gretchen, you can set his arm down now." Percy set her supplies on a clean white towel and wiped her hands on another.

"Are you sure?" I continued clutching his arm.

She patted my hand and smiled reassuringly. "Yes, dear."

"I have to pee," Meredith announced, heading for the trapdoor.

Hades blocked her path.

"Gretch, why don't you take her?" Percy suggested.

"Fine." I could use the escape for a couple of minutes, even if it was only for guard duty.

Hades knelt down and opened the door, sending the ladder crashing to the floor below.

"I'll go first." I didn't wait for an argument. Meredith wouldn't get the chance to run away. Not that it mattered if she tried. I was faster.

I ran down the ladder as if it was a staircase, having plenty of practice and the coordination, and waited at the bottom, as Meredith descended at a much slower pace. When her toes touched the hardwood floors, I steered her towards my own suite, as it contained the closest bathroom. I didn't think there was a chance she'd try to jump out the window.

"Come on in," I invited, holding the door open for her, mentally thanking the house for keeping my room in its place. "It's the door on the left." I took a seat on my armchair, too nerved up to care about the blood I was probably depositing on the upholstery.

Were we bad people for keeping our friends prisoners? I hoped not, and I hoped they understood.

I heard the toilet flush, then the sink run for a few seconds before Meredith reemerged. She seemed to be in no particular hurry to go back upstairs. I can't say that I blamed her. The atmosphere was intense. Instead, she wandered over to the shelving I was seated next to.

She pulled a picture down for closer inspection. "Is this you?" she turned the photo around.

A big soft-eyed wolf stared trustingly back at the camera.

"Yes." I decided the simple answer was the best one.

"Whoa." She replaced the photo and took down one of me and Lacey-Marie running together.

I surmised the exclamation was for the size of my wolf in comparison to my petite friend, who was wearing a pink sports bra and running shorts.

She put that one back as well and continued looking. I had no old photographs—these were all from the past 10 years or so.

"So, is Doug going to be all right?" Of all the questions she could have asked, that wasn't one of the ones I'd been expecting.

"I don't know. I hope so." I fidgeted with the seam of the cushion I was seated on.

"Me too."

"Do you need anything else while we're down here, or are you ready to go back up?"

"No, I'm good."

I pushed myself up out of the comfy oversized chair and escorted her back to the ladder.

Percy was applying herbal-smelling goop and a bandage.

"How is he?" I asked, rushing over.

"He's breathing. I think if he makes it through the rest of the night, he'll be fine." Percy stepped back from the table, again wiping her hands on a clean towel.

"How much night is there left?" There were no windows in the attic through which to view the night sky.

"A couple of hours. You should get some rest. You all should. The salon is open tomorrow to select clients, but we are open. Feel free to crash in the extra bedrooms." Percy finished up her application and stepped back to examine her work.

I was surprised there wasn't a mad dash for the ladder. Instead, everyone stood around in a daze.

"What about Doug? Shouldn't we move him?" I stared at his prone figure. Where to? The guest rooms were being occupied.

"Where do you want him?" Percy asked, rolling up

her tools in the remaining towel and placing them in her basket.

I wanted him wherever I could keep watch over him, but Mem still used my room

"I'll sleep in the library," Mem volunteered. "Just give me a couple of blankets, and I'll be just ducky."

"In my room, then," I decided.

"Will you sleep, or stay awake to watch him?" Percy asked.

Was it a trick question? She'd told me to get some sleep, but I bet Doug needed some extra attention.

"Hades will put him in your room, but only if you promise to get some rest. I'll bring you some supplies. If anything happens, you come get me right away. Understood?" Percy directed.

I nodded.

"Good, if you'd help me get cleaned up, that would be wonderful."

While we were talking, the others had filed down the stairs.

When I finally got a chance to schlep into my own room, I found Doug already tucked in on one side of the bed.

I quickly stripped down to my underthings and threw on a set of navy blue pinstriped pjs. Getting under the covers without jostling the invalid was a bit of a challenge, but I fell asleep as soon as my head hit the pillow.

I would wish I'd gotten more sleep.

Chapter 25:
Fight Night

I woke up to Percy seating herself on Doug's other side just as the sun was rising. Pushing up carefully, I watched as she gently unwound the bandage from his upper arm, revealing the scabbed over bite that looked remarkably less angry than I expected. Better yet, Doug was still breathing, and it no longer felt as if I were lying next to a lump of lava. His human smell was dull, replaced by the more pungent smell of wolf.

He had made it through the night. He was going to live.

"I'll take out the stitches tonight. In the meantime, we'll notify his friends of his whereabouts. I'm sure they're worried sick about him." Percy applied more goop and a new bandage.

I groaned as I glanced at my alarm clock, a whole three-and-a-half hours of sleep. Peachy.

"Coffee?" I questioned.

"I suppose," Percy relented, not liking the combination of me and caffeine.

"Yay!" I made a point to bounce extra carefully when propelling myself out of bed. Doug didn't even utter a moan.

If I kept moving, maybe I wouldn't realize how stressed and tired I was. I grabbed an outfit from my closet, then proceeded to fall asleep in the shower. The water felt so warm and wonderful, and I'd only sat down to let the water beat on my back for a moment. There was banging coming from my bathroom door, rousing me once again.

"Coffee's on!" Lacey-Marie's muffled voice filtered through the door.

"Thanks, Lace. I'll be down in a minute."

I glanced down at my stubble-covered legs and decided they could wait. I'd be wearing pants and boots anyhow. How did I come to live in a house of early risers? Lacey-Marie never rose early. She could always be depended on to be the last one downstairs in the morning. Why did she have to go and change her routine on me?

I stood under the spray for another minute, then forced myself to turn off the water and get out. My clothes sat waiting for me on the counter, and I pulled them on before I was fully dry. Shivering, I scrunched the water out of my hair with a towel, then threw in silk drops. It's the only stuff that will allow me to get a comb through my mass of curls. They weren't super tight, just wild and thick.

Today was destined to be a straight hair day, so I plugged in my flat iron, got out my goops and sprays, and began blow-drying with a huge round brush. When I finally finished I studied the effect in the mirror. Not quite right. I pulled the hair around my hairline into a loose angel braid, which was sort of like a French braid except only hair from the very edges is included. Including all my hair in the back, I pulled the top strands down so they cradled the sides of my head, and pinned the bulk of the braid up underneath. It's a simple updo that's always pretty on long hair.

I poked in my contacts before slapping on my makeup, taking care to hide the dark circles under my eyes, and stepped back to take a look at the whole effect. It would have to do. I wanted coffee.

When I made it down to the kitchen, I found out why Lacey had become an early riser. It was just us three girls and Hades.

"So. What's going on?" asked Lacey, sipping her mug of microwaved blood.

"I just thought it would be good to have some time before the humans come with questions." Percy handed me a steaming mug.

I raised it to her in a salute, then took a taste. Mmmm... Caffeine, sugar, cream, and a hint of cinnamon.

"How's Doug?" Lacey fidgeted with a napkin.

"All right, I think. Percy?" I looked to our wise leader.

"He's going to be fine, though I doubt you bled so much."

I looked down into the spiraling top of my drink. "Yeah, I doubt that anyone would have gone through that trouble for the life of a whore, no matter how much I brought in."

"Well, I'm glad you survived. I kind of like having you around." Percy walked around the table and slung an arm around my shoulders, squeezing me affectionately.

I glanced over at Lacey and her shiny red mustache. "So what do we tell them about our little blood sucker?" She licked the liquid from her lip and grinned.

"Nothing, if we can help it. Vampires don't exactly have a good reputation." Percy came to rest on her husband's knee.

"Neither do weres. How come Gretchen gets the grand revelation, and I get locked in the closet?" Lacey gave a pout to beat any three-year-old.

"Well, there's the whole thing where we think it may be your vamp friends who are draining hairdressers," I pointed out.

"Yeah, well, nothing's been proved."

"It will if I ever get near another crime scene." I set my coffee on the table and crossed my arms.

"Oh, go chase a rabbit." She rolled her eyes at me.

I rolled mine back.

There was a clamor coming from the stairs, signaling we were about to get some company. Fern was the first to burst into the kitchen.

"Do we tell them about Lacey-Marie?" she hissed, grabbing the coffee carafe and pouring herself a mug.

"It's been voted down," said Lacey, her features going from pouty to grumpy.

Ah, mornings.

"Okay." The petite redhead took a seat on my left.

Meredith and Toni burst in, making a mad dash for the coffee maker.

"Should I make another pot?" Percy pondered the bottom of her mug.

I drained my own. "Yes."

"No more for you, young lady." Percy put down her own mug and grabbed mine, demoting me to herbal tea. She refilled the coffee maker, then set a kettle on the stove to boil.

"Young lady? How old are you, Gretchen?" Meredith asked.

"Younger than Percy," I stated with a smug grin.

"She's 181. Ish." Lacey got up to rinse out her mug before the rest of the room could guess its content.

Meredith's mouth gaped open. "Holy crap."

I scowled. "Thanks a bunch, Lace."

"No problem, grandma." She smirked at me,

dancing across the kitchen to peruse the fridge.

"So, how old are you?" Meredith addressed Percy.

"We've lost count," I supplied helpfully. I couldn't be the only one getting picked on.

"Well, the myths about us were told thousands of years ago. Add a few, and you might get our correct ages." Percy settled her hand against Hades' shoulder.

Somehow, we managed to skip the age question in regards to Lacey-Marie. Thank goodness for small favors.

I checked on Doug after breakfast. As he was still out cold, I went to work.

I had my first client in my chair when the bell over the door rang.

"Good morning. How can I help you?" Meredith wandered out from behind the desk to greet the pack. She had seen them at the fair, but she didn't know what they were.

"You can't help us, little lamb, but Gretchen can," Kaine said, brushing past her.

"Oh." Meredith stepped out of the way, looking in my direction with concern.

Individually, the pack were not threatening men to look at, but all together with rabid expressions on their faces, they looked far from safe.

"Mrs. Peterson, would you mind letting Percy finish your cut? She'll only be a few minutes." I stepped between my client and the menace stalking towards us.

Mrs. Peterson, a frail looking woman, scuttled out from behind me and straight to Meredith, who offered her a cup of my herbal tea from the cozy-covered pot.

"Time's up. If you don't wish to cause more of a scene, you'll come with us." Kaine grabbed my upper arm, his claw-tipped fingers digging into my bare flesh.

"I'll come. Just give me a moment to wrap things up." I jerked my arm from his grasp.

Kaine nodded. He wasn't used to being disobeyed, but he didn't really have a choice. I planned on staying in control of the situation.

I approached Mrs. Peterson again. "I'm so sorry about this, ma'am. There will be no charge for your cut. If there's anything else we can do for you, let us know." I nodded at Percy, who nodded back.

I raced upstairs to grab my cell phone and check on Doug once more. He was resting peacefully, so I left him with only the smallest bit of worry I could spare for him.

The pack had a limo waiting outside, which we all piled into with Quintavious in the driver's seat.

"Where are we going?" I asked.

"North, away from people. Drink?" Kaine held a flask out to me.

"No. Thanks."

Kaine was sitting so close to me that our knees touched. I didn't want this. I didn't want any part of it. Maybe if it had been a different pack, and maybe if I'd been included all along, who knew? They had no claim on me, beyond being in the same building when I was changed.

"Where are you taking me?" I asked again.

"I just told you, north. We'll be meeting up with the rest of the pack and the alpha changer. You will be my mate, little Miss Maude." He ran a fingertip down the side of my face, his claw scraping my chin as he pulled away.

Uh-uh, no way. "No, I won't."

"We'll discuss this in front of witnesses." His breath tickled my ear, and I shuddered.

"Fine." I crossed my arms and shifted as far from

him as I could in the confined space with three other people besides Kaine and me.

Kisa and Dirk, the mated couple, were huddled close while Jacque sat staring at me. Quintavious kept his eyes on the road, as he was the only wolf in the front seat.

If there had been a way to resolve everything with my friends present, I would have taken that route, but as it was, there were innocent humans about, and I couldn't risk them getting hurt. Funny, I was willing to risk my friends but not clients.

The car slowed after an hour, and the unpaved road crunched under the tires for quite some time after we turned down some kind of logging road.

The smell of alpha was so intense that I could barely stand when Quintavious stopped the vehicle and opened the door. I managed to stumble out before falling to my knees. The alpha stood waiting for us in the middle of a semicircle of weres.

"Rise, children," he commanded, raising his massive paws.

I climbed slowly to my feet, difficult even with the command given.

Kaine, standing beside me, moved to grab my arm.

"No," the alpha's voice was a low rumble like thunder.

Kaine withdrew his hand as if burned.

"Maude, is it your desire to be separated from Kaine's pack?" the alpha asked.

"Yes." I hoped the one word answer was enough.

"And Kaine, you wish to keep Maude as your mate despite the fact that she is more dominant?"

"The pack needs her. And she is not more dominant."

I snarled at that.

"I think the lady is begging to differ," the alpha said with a chuckle, then turned to address the pack. "Here is how it's going to be: Maude and Kaine will fight for dominance. If Kaine is the victor, he will claim Maude as his mate and a permanent member of the pack. If Maude succeeds, then she walks away from the pack, instead of claiming it."

We bowed low to the alpha, showing our acceptance.

I was being given a chance at freedom. If I didn't take it, then I deserved to be condemned to be Kaine's mate.

"Strip, and wolf," the alpha commanded as he signaled the pack to create a ring around us with a turn of his finger.

It was nearly new moon, so we weren't at our strongest, yet neither of us complained.

I wandered to the edge of the clearing to change. I hated turning my back on the pack, but I had to trust that the alpha would keep them in control. I pulled my shirt over my head, unzipped my dark wash jeans, and began wiggling free. The fact that my underwear came with them was of little consequence as they'd be coming off anyhow. I knelt down with my pants around my ankles to loosen the buckles of my boots. All that was left was my bra, which I unhitched and let fall with the rest of the pile.

Taking a deep breath, I welcomed the wolf into the forefront of my mind. I'd need her to be more in control then I'd ever let her be before. There was no room for human qualms, just raw wolf instinct. My muscles creaked, and my bones cracked as different areas expanded and contracted. I watched, slightly cross-eyed as my snout grew out of my face.

Oh, did it hurt. The farther it was from the full

moon, the more it hurt.

My scream of pain took on a deeper tone as my throat reshaped itself. My muscles felt like cold rubber bands as they stretched. I barely comprehended the deep-throated roar that meant that Kaine was having just as hard a time as me. Finally, the adrenaline kicked in, the snaps and creaks rapid-firing, and I lifted my muzzle to the sky and howled.

The pack howled as well, though in support of Kaine and not at all for me.

I scratched as my fur continued to grow out of every follicle, itching almost as much as it hurt, until it was over.

I turned to face Kaine across the circle, neither of us looking away. To do so would be to admit submission to the other. Deciding it was as good a time as any to get the fight over with, I attacked, my lips pulled back from my teeth, aiming to get a grip on his shaggy throat.

We reared up and clashed with such force that it would have been enough to knock the air out of my human body, but in the body of this 400-pound beast, it was nothing.

I managed to get a mouth full of his scruff as he fastened his teeth into my shoulder. We tore sideways, our combined momentum bowling us over each other a couple of times.

His claws found purchase first, and he thrust forward, getting a better grip on me and shaking me with enough force to throw me a couple of feet.

My turn.

I let him get close before catapulting myself up and over, grabbing his ear as I went. Tasting blood, I bit harder and ripped, the slickness of his blood caused me to lose my grip and serving only to piss him off.

Again he shook and flung me. This time I let him charge me while I planted my feet and crouched. I was the bigger wolf, and therefore harder to move.

The impact of his hit slid me over the dirt of the forest floor but allowed me to get a good grip on his neck. Still not his throat and still not a fatal bite, but my best so far. It was my turn to shake. I clamped my jaws tight, not wanting to accidentally let go, and shook him with all my might.

Shaking its prey is part of how a dog kills in the wild. With enough force, a dog can snap the neck of its opponent. Kaine thrashed as I shook him, gaining purchase once again, twisting away, leaving me with a mouth full of fur and managing to toss me a couple feet.

We backed off, getting a lock on each other's eyes once more, and I knew how to win. It was a dirty trick, and it gave me no small thrill to use it, even though I thought I could win without it. I dropped my eyes and rolled over onto my back, signaling my defeat and my acceptance of his dominance. I even went so far as to curl my tail up between my legs. I think I got the drama queen flair from Lacey-Marie.

He dropped his head and kept an eye on me, wagging his tail.

All I had to do was wait as he trotted over, lowering his muzzle for me to lick.

I lunged up and grabbed his throat instead of kissing him, rolling him underneath me and digging my teeth still deeper, cutting off his air supply. He whined, but I didn't let go, squeezing my jaws together and holding fast as he fought to get out from under me. I just had to hang on until he ran out of air.

It didn't last all that long. I felt his pulse weaken until he stopped moving. I didn't let go until the alpha came over and touched my head with a heavy paw.

Letting go of my prey, I crawled backward on my belly, whining softly as his dominance rolled over my every nerve.

Kaine had fought like a wolf. I had fought like both an animal and woman. I gave a doggy smile and bounced to my feet. I'd changed back without a wince. I was going to enjoy this moment on my own two legs.

I spat Kaine's blood out of my mouth and wiped my lips on my bare arm. "I want out of the pack. I want nothing to do with them ever again. I will not be forced to be anyone's property." I straightened my shoulders and stalked over to the limo.

Quintavious followed me, tossing me my clothes before shutting the door. I dressed quickly as we drove, knowing I was going to be sore later on. The sun didn't even set before I got home. He came around again and opened my door as soon as we pulled up to Olympian's Salon and Day Spa. He kept his eyes downcast as was appropriate behavior around an alpha.

"Congratulations, you earned it," he said before flying back down the driveway.

Hell yeah, I did.

Chapter 26:
It's a Date

Bruised, bleeding, and downright exhausted, I marched my butt up the stairs and turned on the hot water in my tub. As steam rose, I added just enough cold water to make it bearable. I wanted a bubble bath but instead added a menthol and lavender soak with Epsom salt. It would sting at first, but my joints would appreciate it in the morning.

Doug was still sleeping like the dead, so I hoped I could moan and groan without bothering anyone. I assumed that Percy had seen to it that Mem got her own room or made it back to her house.

Just as I sank into the hot bath, the door burst open.

"So are we celebrating or commiserating? Either way, I have wine!" Lacey-Marie balanced herself on the edge of my clawfoot tub, holding out a bottle for my inspection. Cabernet Sauvignon, my preferred grape. Lacey was a white wine girl, so I was touched that she'd considered my taste.

I sank lower in the water, wishing I had gone the way of the bubble. "Celebrating. Good choice."

"Percy will be up in a minute with a corkscrew and some glasses." She set the bottle on the floor. "You look like hell."

"Gee, thanks." I glared at her with tired eyes, then admitted, "I feel like it."

"So, what happened?" She swirled her hand through the water above my feet.

"The alpha refereed while Kaine and I duked it out. I kicked his ass." I was still feeling smug about the fact.

"Celebrations all around!" She threw her hands in the air, sending water cascading everywhere.

"I figured by the noise," Percy said from the doorway, juggling three glasses and the corkscrew.

She took position on the edge of my tub by my arm and accepted the bottle from Lacey in exchange for the glasses.

I waited, holding my glass as Percy popped the cork.

She filled our glasses, set the bottle aside, and raised hers. "What shall we toast to?" she asked.

"Freedom." I touched the rim of my glass to Percy's, then Lacey's.

"To freedom, indeed. Congratulations, by the way." She tilted her glass again in my direction before taking a delicate sip.

Toasting complete, we settled in to drink and laugh. It had been a while since we'd had some good old-fashioned girl time.

A moan from my bedroom and footsteps jarred us from our revelry. I jumped up as Percy leapt across the room and slammed the door.

"Naked girl in the tub! Naked girl in the tub! Naked girl, get back in that tub!"

I was pretty sure Percy's first two exclamations were aimed at either herself or Doug. The last was definitely for me, as I was about to climb over the edge. I sank back down into the soothing hot tub, splashing water over the edge, not having the energy to disobey, nor the inclination.

Lacey jumped up as the water soaked into her jeans along with a splash of wine. "What the hell, Gretchen!"

Mmmm, wine. I took another sip.

"Drink up, ladies, I'll be back in a bit." Percy set her glass on the floor. "Nobody knock that over." She pointed to us each in turn.

"I'll try and restrain myself." I sank up to my chin in the water and took another sip.

"No problem." Lacey-Marie regained her seat.

"Good. I'll be back." Percy edged out of the bathroom, so as not to reveal too much to Doug, and closed the door behind her.

Being very naked, as Percy had pointed out, I let a good deal of the water out of my bath.

"What're you doing?" Lacey asked, scrubbing uselessly at her pants with a dry washcloth.

"I want bubbles. Will you pass me that bottle?" I waved my hand in the general direction of my bubble bath.

Lacey located it and went so far as to open it for me.

"Thank you." I turned on the water again and poured until I was satisfied with the foam.

Leaning back, I let the water run over my feet, I wanted to sleep more than anything, but my friends were determined to celebrate.

"Doug's awake," Percy announced, reentering the bathroom.

"So I heard. How's he doing?" I pulled the bubbles up towards my chin, covering the floating bits of my body.

"Fine. A bit sore under the arm and hungry. I sent him down to the kitchen to go bug Hades." Percy picked up her glass.

"Good. And Mem?"

"She's gone home. She felt it was time. Her students showed up and volunteered to help her out at home. I think she'll go back to school soon. Those kids are doing her wonders. I talked to her for a bit after you were dragged out." Percy drummed her nails on the porcelain as her glamour dissolved. "Ah, that feels better."

Having never worn a glamour, I didn't know how it felt, but I'd guess it's stifling. I wondered what it did to her senses. I supposed there would be plenty of time to ask later. Right now there was wine and bubbles.

"Will the pack be heading south soon?" Percy asked.

"I'd assume so. Technically this is my territory, and for a pack that I am not associated with to remain on it for a prolonged period of time would be considered a challenge for seizure. I don't think Kaine has any desire to stay in the area, no matter how much he probably hates me at the moment."

Percy nodded at that. "Makes sense to me."

"So how was work after I left?" I asked.

"Rather dull. Word got around that you were dragged out. We had to cancel your appointments, and people started calling to cancel with the rest of us. Apparently, there's a rumor is going around that it was the cops who took you." Percy hitched up one leg to sit on the edge of the tub and lean against the wall.

"I don't think Mrs. Peterson will be back," said Lacey-Marie, not helping my current state of mind.

"Well, that's just wonderful, isn't it?" I let the sarcasm in my voice drip before asking, "Have any of the other salons called?"

"Not yet, but I bet you'll get a call from Amanda tonight. She'll spread around whatever you tell her is the truth." Percy was trying to reassure me, but I didn't know if my reputation was salvageable. Once a rumor runs rampant through salons, it kind of sticks, whether it's fact or not.

"Why don't you finish up your bath, then come down for supper." Percy kissed my forehead and stood.

"Yes, Mommy." I leaned my head back against the edge of the tub and closed my eyes.

"Don't get all wrinkly. You'll make me lose my appetite." Lacey-Marie rose as well and followed Percy out the door.

Maybe I'd get my room to myself for the first night in forever. It was a comforting thought as I was feeling less than magnanimous about my personal space.

When I made it down the stairs dressed in jeans and a sweatshirt, everyone was halfway through their meals.

"Your plate's in the microwave. It should still be warm." Percy waved her empty fork.

I found a chair next to Doug and dove into my lamb-based shepherd's pie. Dinner turned out to be a quiet affair. I had freed myself from the pack, but there was that little issue of a free-range serial killer still on the loose weighing heavily on our minds.

I helped clear the dishes and was getting ready to go back up the stairs when Doug caught my attention.

"What?" I asked, wanting to sleep, not talk.

"What are you doing tomorrow afternoon?" he asked, staring down at his feet.

"Nothing that I know of. I think I lost most of my clients today."

"I was, um, wondering if you'd like to go do something with me?"

"Sure." Was he asking me out on a date? It sure sounded like it. I couldn't remember the last time I was asked out by someone other than Scott.

"Great." He looked up, smiling.

"Um, how should I dress?" I asked.

He shrugged his shoulders. "Like you always do, I guess."

"Okay." Well, that was awkward.

I wandered out of the kitchen in a little bit of a daze. I had a date with Doug. There was no way I was getting sleep any time soon, so a run seemed like a good idea.

Lacey-Marie was back in the kitchen, so I tried to recruit her. "Feel up for a run?"

"Nah, not tonight. I think I'm just going to take it easy." She dug around in the fridge, emerging with one of her 'juice packs,' emptied about a quarter cup into her mug, and shoved it into the microwave.

"Still hungry?" I'd never seen Lacey eat as much as she had during that month.

"Yeah, just a little."

I watched as she turned, exposing a little skin under her tiny tank top that was no longer lean and muscular. In fact, she had a little bit of a pooch. If I hadn't seen her drink so much at home, I'd think she was indulging on the side.

I shrugged my shoulders. "Fine, I'll go all alone. All by myself."

"You'll be fine." She gave me a look that said I was being a big baby. Apparently I wasn't as good at manipulation as she was.

I trudged back upstairs, grabbed running gear, tossed off clothes, dressed, and used my dash down the stairs as a warm-up.

Maybe it was a good thing I was going alone. It would give me a chance to think of what I'd done, of what I'd become. On second thought, maybe it wasn't such a good thing that I had time to think. I didn't want to regret any of the recent decisions I'd made.

The wolf inside me wanted to escape, to feel the wind in her fur, but I wanted to stay as human as possible. It was almost new moon, and I had the control. Had it been closer to the full moon, I might not have been able to resist. It's an alpha thing, and that's part of why it was important to have a pack. The submissive wolves can resist the furry call at a better rate and can help dim the rage of their alphas, which meant no killing sprees unless it involved cute little cottontails.

I had no such support network. My month's work had made sure of it. I didn't want a pack, just a family, at least for the time being. But it would be nice if I could rely on Doug to keep an eye on me, help me soothe the savage beast, if he hadn't lost the touch. I wondered what Doug's wolf would be like.

I ran deeper into the woods, avoiding branches as I made my way over the uneven ground. It felt good to be free, to not have to worry about the pack or fae politics. My focus shifted to the killer, in spite of how much I wanted to push him from my mind.

I was winded when I made it back to the house, so I walked a few laps around the perimeter of the property until I felt comfortably tired.

Now just keep your mind blank, Gretchen, and you'll get to sleep. I chose to crash on my cot in the barn. I didn't know where Doug was staying, but I wanted to avoid any uncomfortable pillow talk.

Why had he asked me out? Probably to get me to help him get in touch with his wolf. He'd need the guidance I never received.

I pulled off my sweaty clothes, leaving them on the floor to fester until morning when I'd make sure they made it down the laundry shoot in my bathroom. Old pjs folded up in the trunk, just waiting for such an occasion, called my name, so I pulled them on and curled up under the blanket, wishing I had brought my book down and was asleep within moments.

To say the next day dawned bright and early was nonsense. I woke up around five a.m., so it was definitely early, but I wasn't seeing the whole bright aspect. I had gone to sleep early the night before, but couldn't I have at least slept in a little? I squeezed my eyes shut in a useless attempt.

Nope, not tired. I sat up and stretched, searching around for some clothes. Finding none, I threw on my workout clothes and made the hike back to my room, where Doug was fast asleep on my bed. On top of the covers.

Weirdo.

Now, to take a shower without him walking in on the naked girl in the tub—or shower, as the case may be. I did my best to keep quiet, wolf-like and all that, but being that we were closer to being more human than wolf, I stubbed my toe, managing to grunt instead of swearing. The water cooled, then flashed to scalding. I made it a quick shower, lathering up and rinsing as rapidly as I could.

I decided it was safer to shave my legs outside the shower, so dressed in a fluffy purple towel, I foamed up my legs and proceeded to get rid of the jungle. Perhaps they would even stay that way for a day or two, instead of just a few minutes. There's no point in shaving around the full moon. You're gonna be hairy no matter what.

My day was nearly empty. After my little knock-down-drag-out episode two days prior, my clients were making themselves scarce. I had one client. You can count that on one hand. With one finger. One client.

How depressing. She had a slot first thing in the morning. Then I got to deal with tedium until afternoon. I hunted down breakfast first.

Lacey-Marie, beating me to it, was perched bleary-eyed and bunny slippered, on her favorite counter spot. The scent of cinnamon in her blood wafted my way, which I found oddly appealing.

"Morning," I mumbled, cracking an egg into the cast iron frying pan that lived on the stove.

"Mmhmm." Lacey sipped her breakfast with a smile on her face.

I added three more eggs and a couple strips of bacon for flavoring. Breakfast of champions, that. Some toast and a small chunk of cheese, and I was a happy pup. The good thing about living in Percy's house was things like bread were always freshly made, so I cut two thick slices, popped them into the toaster oven, then got the butter out of the fridge. Real butter, no chemically saturated margarine in that house. No, sir.

The smell must have permeated through the ceiling because Doug stumbled into the kitchen sleepy-eyed and disheveled.

"Bacon and eggs?" I offered, grabbing the bread out of the toaster oven.

"Smells good." He took a seat in my chair.

I grimaced and flipped the eggs over. I always sat in that chair or on the counter with Lacey-Marie, who had finished the last drop of her blood and was rummaging around in the fridge. I plopped the mess of protein onto a plate and set it in front of him before starting all over again for myself. A newly changed werewolf needs to eat. I'd rather wait than see what would happen if he didn't.

Screw cooking. I put some milk, raw eggs, protein

powder, and yogurt into the blender and whirred it all together. I don't need to cook my eggs, and I was starving.

I was drinking directly from the blender when Percy and Hades made their entrance. We were one big, happy, dysfunctional family.

Percy and Lacey-Marie both had full schedules for the day. With only one client, I didn't feel the need to impress, so I threw my still damp hair into a ponytail.

It was a simple trim and only took me about 10 minutes. Upon finishing and cashing her out, the girls descended.

"So, I hear you have a date tonight," said Meredith as she slid onto the stool that I just vacated.

"Uh, yeah, sorta." I edged away, only to be blocked by Toni on the other side.

"Oh, honey, it's definitely a date." She tapped one wildly painted nail on the desk.

Apparently, they didn't have a healthy fear of wolves.

"I guess." I stepped backward and was headed off by Fern.

"How long has it been since you've been on a date?" she asked.

A very long time. My dates didn't tend to end well. "A while," I said, thinking they didn't need to know about the dead men littering my past.

"Well, what are you going to wear?" asked Meredith.

I looked down at my outfit, indicating it by pointing.

"Oh, no, no, this won't do." Meredith plucked at my sleeve, shaking her head in disapproval.

"What's wrong with my clothes?" I looked down at my boot clad feet.

"It's a date. You're supposed to look your best."

I crossed my arms under my chest and planted my feet firmly apart. "I'm supposed to dress like I normally do."

The girls looked at each other, surrounded me, and herded me to the stairs.

"Hey! Don't you guys have work to do?" I pleaded.

"I think we might have a spare moment or two," said Fern, pushing from behind with a surprising amount of strength for such a little thing.

I let them push and pull me toward my bedroom, knowing they wouldn't give up. Toni shut and locked the door in an effort to slow down any escape attempt or to prove a point, I wasn't sure which. She then raised her face toward the ceiling and sniffed loudly. "I detect the faint scent of man."

Immediately, there was a row of woman in front of me with arms crossed, looking intimidating instead of silly.

"He slept in here. I slept in the barn," I defended with my hands up, palm out.

"Right." Fern walked right up and sniffed my shoulder. "I suppose we'll have to believe you. Now, where are your clothes?"

There was no way she'd be able to smell anything on me, even if I had slept with Doug. Besides, I'd taken a shower.

I led the way to my closet and turned on the light. The vultures descended on my clothes, chattering loudly.

"This maybe, definitely not that," and, "Oh, that's pretty!" They finally settled on a form-fitting cowl neck short sleeve red sweater, a pair of my customary black jeans, and a pair of black ballet flats.

"You tend to tower in your clunky boots." Meredith handed the shoes to me, and I was ushered into the bathroom to change as they stood guard just outside the door.

I contemplated jumping out the window but resisted the urge. When I was dressed, Meredith tamed my hair with a curling iron, Toni went at my claws, and Fern my toes.

"There's absolutely no point in nail polish," I complained loudly when Toni pulled a bottle of red that was a close match to my sweater from her pocket.

"So? You can't have nice claws for one day?" Toni yanked my hand toward her and started her job with a base coat procured from the same pocket.

"Well if I change, which we will since I want to supervise Doug's first, it kind of goes away while running around." I submitted my hand to her, somewhat enjoying the attention.

"Again, so?" she said, blowing on the clear coat then starting on my other hand.

Fern picked up my makeup case and advanced. She was a masseuse—she wasn't supposed to do makeup.

"Hey, gimme that," I grabbed the eyeshadow brush from her and tried to apply while Toni grabbed for my hand.

Fern grabbed back. Woman can be dangerous critters. I gave up and sat meekly. I didn't want to end up with mascara down on my cheekbones. They finished at an astonishing pace and stepped back to admire their work.

"Now you're presentable," said Meredith.

Wow, thanks. What happened to the shy girl we had hired?

"Where are you going?" Toni wanted to know.

"Not a clue."

She smiled. "Fine. Since you don't have any plans for the rest of the day, We're going to hunt down the man and see if he's ready to go."

They disappeared in a moment, giving me a chance to inspect their work. My makeup was a little more natural than I tended to go, but it wasn't out of place. I wandered back to my bedroom and picked up my Austen novel, attempting to catch up on my reading.

There was still the date itself to get through. I glanced down at the red polish on my claws, so expertly applied, and smiled. I had friends. Human friends. I used to be able to count on one hand how many full-blooded humans knew what I was and stuck around. If they could accept me, then I could as well. I felt content for the first time in a long time, sitting there curled up in the sunny spot on my bed, reading.

My tranquility didn't last long. I heard the pitter-patter, clatter, thunk of the girls once again gaining the top of the stairs. They didn't even bother knocking, just burst in and piled on the bed around me.

"So we found Doug," Meredith said, "and he's getting ready. He'll be waiting out front for you in 15 minutes."

"But you're driving," Fern added.

"Yeah, he doesn't want to take the RV to the coast," said Meredith.

"Hey, I don't think you were supposed to mention that!" Toni shoved the younger woman playfully.

Meredith shoved back. "Yeah, whatever."

It seemed she was picking up my attitude. Great, now I'm a bad influence.

"The coast?" I asked tentatively. It was still a little cold for swimming, which would mean the beaches would pretty much be abandoned.

"Uh-huh. Sounds like a romantic walk on the

beach. So what is Lacey-Marie?" Meredith stared me down, her fists balled up and balanced on her hips. She even tapped her foot.

Apparently Fern had kept the information to herself.

"Uh." Right, think of something intelligent to say to the way-too-curious woman.

"Oh, for goodness sakes, I'll tell them," said Fern, not being able to hold out any longer. Traitor. "Lacey-Marie is a vampire. She drinks the blood donor bags behind the milk."

"Nasty." Meredith wrinkled up her nose.

Toni just nodded as if this made complete sense. Maybe it did. I hadn't had to deal with finding out there was something else out there in a very long time. There was plenty I probably didn't know about, but then I was aware of the idea.

They chattered, and I listened, contentment welling up in me once again. That is, until Toni checked her watch.

"Up! Time to go." She pushed me gently, trying to hurry me toward the door. I grabbed my keys and wallet from the stand and again let them herd me, this time down the stairs where Doug sat waiting in the salon.

"Ready?" Doug stood, his fingers tucked in the front pockets of his jeans, shrugging his shoulders up and back, his plain black t-shirt pulling tight.

"Yeah, I hear we're taking my truck." I pulled away from the pack of girls and took his arm.

"Yes, is that all right?" He opened the front door for me, shutting out the sound of excited squealing behind us as we exited.

"Sure." I dug my keys back out of my pocket and climbed into my old pickup. "Where to?"

"Head southeast, towards the coast," he directed, buckling in.

I couldn't see any marked difference in him since the change, except maybe in his confidence, and the amber eyes of course. I couldn't remember, but I would guess the claws came after the first change. I could see the wolf in his eyes fighting to be free.

If one was with a pack, and it wasn't new moon, it was guaranteed that you would change right away. The pack magic drew it to the surface like metal to a magnet. But this was just the two of us, and I supposed my wolf wasn't enough to pull it out alone.

I hadn't changed right off—not until the moon was full and I had to, and I had been completely alone. From what I had gathered, the alpha and the pack had abandoned me right after I was bitten. The alpha changer had been biting strong females in hopes to strengthen the packs he had begun, that didn't necessarily mean the packs wanted us.

Small talk kept us busy during the long drive, neither of us saying anything of consequence. I was thinking it wasn't a stupendous start to a date, but it was better than uncomfortable silence.

Doug directed me from a map in his lap, which he angled so I couldn't see the area he had highlighted.

"So, I'm guessing you want to try changing?" I pulled into the parking space closest to the woods. I could see the ocean directly ahead and woods on either side. There would be plenty of places to hide if we ran into any errant hikers.

"Yes, I didn't want to do it alone."

And there it was, the reason he'd asked me on what I had thought was supposed to be a date. He wanted me to act as his alpha and teacher.

"Of course, that's..." I struggled for the right thing

to say. "Safer."

"Maybe, maybe not." He came around the truck, closing my door for me.

"Um… We should probably change somewhere off the path, in the woods."

"Yes, of course." He grabbed our packs out of the bed of the truck and returned to my side, to hand me my bag, I thought.

Instead, he leaned in and kissed me, softly, hesitantly. When he pulled away I pulled in a breath of surprise.

"I thought—" I started but was stopped when he kissed me again, this time with more enthusiasm.

I leaned into him as his arms folded around me in one of his comfortable hugs. He still had the ability to keep me calm, even as he sent my head spinning. Interesting. When the kiss ended, I buried my face in his shoulder.

He squeezed me and chuckled. "Let's go." He stepped away and took my hand.

Right, time for me to get a hold of myself and take charge. I lifted my nose to the wind and, smelling a complete lack of unwanted company, led him away from the path and up into the thick tangle of Maine woods.

Woods in Maine are dense, mostly evergreens and a few birches and lots of thorn covered ground-hugging bushes.

We hiked for perhaps half an hour before finding a spot secluded enough to appease our needs. Again, I scented the wind, making sure we were alone. I found a good clump of bushes to strip behind and let Doug find his own hiding spot. I remained clothed and instructed Doug to change first, if he could.

I waited for the screams to start, but there was

nothing except a very human growl of frustration.

"Okay, sounds like I'm gonna have to go first. Stay there, no matter how loud I scream." I knew it was going to hurt. We were bordering on the new moon, and the change was going to come hard and slow. I usually avoided it so close, but I didn't want Doug to have to wait a week before trying it out.

I stripped off my clothes and stowed them in my backpack, then shoved it all into the underbrush, piling partly decayed leaves on top. I pulled on the wolf, my skin feeling like it was ripping apart. I felt every strand of fur pierce through my pores, starting out like splinters being slowly extracted. My bones splintered like muffled gunshots, reforming themselves. I spit out blood as my teeth grew and split my gums. When my adrenaline finally kicked in, I felt as if I were going mad.

On fours instead of twos, I searched out Doug. I found him naked and human, crouching in his hiding spot. At least naked for him was different than it was for me. There's not much risk of a sneak peek with that much hair involved.

Having thought that my wolfing out would spur the magic in his blood into action, as it worked that way in a pack, I sat staring him in the eye, pondering the best options. Pissing him off didn't seem like the best solution, but nothing else was coming to mind.

I rolled my lip at him. Change, damn it!

He reached a hand out to pat me, and I seized it in my teeth, shaking him like a rabbit.

The change came on him so strong and fast that he didn't have a chance to scream before he was howling. As soon as he had four paws and a tail, I let go and stood back. He turned to me, crawling, before turning onto his back at my feet, offering me his soft belly.

I yapped playfully, then ran full tilt into the woods. I heard him scramble to his feet behind me, then his body crashing through the underbrush. I finally got a good look at him when we reached a clearing that someone had used for camping recently. His overabundance of hair translated into a beautiful, long-coated wolf that looked like it belonged in Maine, or maybe Alaska. Shaggy or not, he made one gorgeous *Canis*.

He crouched down as if to spring at me, and I took off running. If anyone was going to do any pouncing, it was going to be me.

We reached the water faster than I thought, so I waited for him, lying down instead of using the butt-up-in-the-air pose he had used on me. As soon as he got close enough, I leapt up and onto his back. I outweighed him only a little, and we had a good tussle before he took off running with me in close pursuit.

He was exuberant in his play, and I was glad I'd agreed to come out with him for this—not to mention the kiss that had preceded our hike.

I might just end up with a pack after all.

NEW MOON

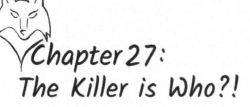

Chapter 27:
The Killer is Who?!

We spent the night in wolf form, roughing it in the woods. We'd had the good luck of avoiding hikers and were only forced to return to our clothes when the hidden new moon took over the next morning.

I stumbled back to my hiding place. The amount of noise Doug was making fighting through a patch of wild blackberry bushes assured me he was close behind.

The first thing I did after yanking on my underwear was pull my hair up into a pony. At least it hadn't grown like it does when the wolf takes over. I glanced down at my bare legs speckled with just the barest hint of stubble, and I smiled. There were definitely advantages to wolfing out around new moon, even when it hurt: no excess hair.

As I was yanking on my pants and flats, I heard a muffled yelp from Doug. I pulled my sweater on as I ran over. He'd gotten his pants on by the time I got to him, but the rest of him was still a shock. Don't get me wrong, he was still a hairy fella, but normal hairy, not sideshow hairy. He stood with his arms held out in front of him, inspecting the visible skin. He was pale—the formally excessive hair never gave him a chance to tan—but his half Hispanic heritage kept him from being pasty.

"Wow," I said, slowing my pace.

"Yeah." He held his arm out to me, and I let my hand land on it, inspecting the newness of it. "Do you think it's permanent?" He took his arm back and shuffled through his bag for a shirt.

I hated to disappoint him, but I didn't. Not exactly. "Maybe."

He gave me a look that said: details, lady.

"Ah, well, closer to the new moon you'll probably look like this, but I'm willing to bet big bucks that as the full moon approaches you'll be more like before."

His huge white-toothed grin was not the reaction I expected.

"Are you all right with that?" I asked, taking a seat on a fallen tree.

"Anything is better than being the wolf boy full time. I get to be normal, at least sometimes. Thank you."

"For what?" I hadn't felt as if I'd done anything, besides exist for him to find.

"You gave this to me." He pushed the items he'd discarded to find his shirt back into his bag, then sauntered over to pull me to my feet and into a hug.

"You're welcome," I said, muffled by his shoulder. I pulled back and touched his bearded cheek. "Maybe you should shave when we get back, to celebrate."

"Hey, yeah! Oh, do you think you can drop me off at the circus? They should be packing up right about now, and I want to get my RV from them and say goodbye." He picked up his pack and followed me back to where my bag waited.

"Sure."

"Besides, I want to show them all my new look." He grabbed up my pack as well.

We made it back to my truck in good time, and I

dug my key out, then tossed my bag into the bed with his.

While in wolf form, we hadn't been intimate. If I slept with him, it would have been a signal to my wolf that I had chosen him as my mate, and I was pretty sure I wasn't ready for that. I wanted to get to know him a lot better before I made that kind of decision. Besides, Percy would want a wedding, and I couldn't ruin that for her. After all, wolves only mate once. I liked Doug, a lot, but come on, relationships take time.

During the ride back, our conversation was more animated. He asked me questions about Chaos Theory, specifically about my violin playing. He didn't ask me anything about my human days, and I got the feeling that he really didn't want too many details, not yet, not until he knew me better and wanted to share things about himself. I wondered how he would feel about me when he really grasped what I had been, as a human, as a monster.

We didn't make any stops, and I was dropping him off at the circus within what felt like no time at all. I would have liked to have gone out back with him to see the reactions of the twisted ringmaster and Sabrina. My desire for a shower outweighed that wish, and I made it back to the mansion right around sundown.

I parked my truck and walked in around back to find Percy and Hades sipping decaf at the kitchen table.

"Well, well, the wanderer returns. So how was the date?" Percy got up to give me a hug.

"Great! Doug had a little trouble wolfing out so close to the new moon, but me being me, I managed to piss him off enough to spur him into it." I grabbed Percy's mug and took a sip. I found it a little cool, but still good.

She huffed at me then poured herself another mug. I knew she loved me.

"And," she spurred me on, wanting to know if I'd taken things a step too far.

"No, we're not mated. I'm holding off until I'm absolutely sure." I smiled over the rim of my mug at her as I took another sip.

"Good for you. Marriage isn't something to rush into," said Hades.

"You mean like you did?" My snort betraying my unbelief.

"Daddy would have killed him otherwise, and I was young and impressionable," Percy said.

"Yeah, how old were you?" I was pretty sure her young and my young were two very different things. She still considered me a pup.

"None of your business." She set her mug down with a thump.

I just smiled in response and searched out the hard boiled eggs I knew were in the fridge somewhere.

"They're in egg salad form now. Just slap it between a couple pieces of bread." Percy read my mind.

Changing is hungry business, burning excessive amounts of calories, which is why you'll never see a fat were, unless they're really submissive and the forced change is the only exercise they get.

"Chocolate?" I asked, opening and shutting cabinet doors in quest of a sweet treat.

"Cabinet above the fridge." Percy pointed.

I stretched up onto tiptoe and felt around in the cabinet until my hands settled on a bar of dark chocolate flavored with chili. This was my personal stash, which Percy hid in different places while I wasn't fully human so I couldn't give in to temptation and make myself sick.

I set my sandwich fixings to the side, peeled back the wrapper on the chocolate, and took a big bite, closing my eyes in bliss. The rest of the bar could wait until I finished my sandwich, but I would enjoy the nuances until that first bite of egg salad.

"Lacey upstairs?" I asked around the melting bite of chocolate.

Percy shrugged and settled back down next to her husband.

I grabbed up my meal and a big travel mug of milk and headed for the stairs, ending up in a closet before I landed on the correct door. I had so much to tell my best friend. We'd been a little distant over the last month, but the wolf wouldn't get in the way for three whole days, at least until sundown the day after the new moon.

I clomped up to Lacey-Marie's door, figuring the shower could wait until after a bit of girl talk, and rearranged my meal so I could knock. I could see a sliver of light coming out from under the door, so I figured she was in. I gave her a minute to yell or come to the door before letting myself into an empty room. Her bathroom and closet doors were both wide open, so I took a bite of my sandwich and sat down on one of her couches to wait. She'd probably stepped outside for a cigarette.

Strange, I hadn't seen her on my trip in.

I finished my dinner while waiting on her couch, then started to get irritated. I clomped back down the stairs to the kitchen.

"Has Lacey headed down this way?" I asked, thrusting the door open.

Hades and Percy gave identical head shakes.

"Well, her light was on and she didn't answer my

knock, so I went in to wait and she never showed up." I set my empty mug in the sink.

"You've only been home for half an hour, dear." Percy set her own empty mug next to mine.

"Maybe she went out for dinner," said Hades, tipping his chair back on two legs.

Percy's head and mine whipped in his direction.

"What do you mean?" Percy asked, not sounding like she really wanted to know.

"She goes out for dinner sometimes. Haven't you guys noticed the scent of blood on her?" He set his chair back down, looking from one of us to the other.

"No," I drew out the word. "She always smells like blood from the donor bags. Stale."

"No, not just blood, fresh blood and death. Your girl's been feasting." He crossed his arms over his broad chest.

I clenched my fists. No way. She couldn't be the killer. Could she?

"Are you sure?" Percy asked the hard question.

"Yes, I thought you guys knew she took living blood." Hades' expression became worried. "You didn't know?"

"Go check her clothes. I guarantee you'll be able to smell it on them."

"Shit." I felt like throwing up.

"What?" Hades threw his wife a worried look.

"Lacey-Marie is Sweeney Todd." Percy's face bled free of her emotion until her features were an empty mask.

"Shit," I repeated, sprinting out through the back room, into the salon and over to our little museum. I started grabbing old barbering razors off the wall, throwing them on the ground as I went.

We had a lot, and a total of six looked like they had

blood on their blades, and there was one missing.

I skipped a third "shit," and made for Lacey-Marie's rooms again. Percy was hot on my heels with Hades in tow.

"It's not one of your girls. I'd know. I'm having them watched, remember?" Hades promised, which was only a very small comfort, under the circumstances.

Lacey-Marie was still going to kill whether she was one of ours or not. I slapped her closet light on and found a black trash bag in the corner. I opened it enough to see the bloodstained clothing concealed within.

New shoes. She'd acquired a lot of new shoes, and jewelry, and clothing lately. She wasn't good enough with her money to afford most of it. She was taking trophies from her victims, along with the thrill of the blood on the razor blades.

What were we supposed to do? We couldn't call the cops. They didn't stand a chance against a vampire.

I started throwing things around, looking for something, anything, that would indicate who her next victim might be. I tore out of the closet, finding the others staring at me.

"Trash bag full of bloody clothes in the corner and a closet full of stolen trophies. Damn it! This freaking house, Percy, seriously?" I threw down a pair of shoes in disgust and sat on her bed, trying to will the tears back into their ducts.

"She's your best friend. We could only see what we wanted to see." Poor Percy was just as at a loss as I. She had a tendency to try and see the best in people. Good for making friends, bad for seeing reality. And to top it all off, she had built a house that could think for itself and protect its inhabitants.

I picked up a pretty journal that lay open on Lacey's bed stand that I hadn't seen there before. The page had a name and an address:

Alice Glowa
1493 Augusta Rd, Sydney, ME.

That had to be her, the next victim. I flipped back to the beginning of the month and glanced through. Penny Yeaton, Catherine Materna, Heather McKay, Jennifer Tardiff, Lisa Viola, and Joslin Webber all had their own pages. Each detailed the evenings Lacey-Marie had made appointments with each, how she had followed them back to their homes, and what she had taken from them.

I handed the journal over to Percy without a word and stalked out of the room. If I drove fast, maybe, just maybe, I could get to Alice's house before Lacey had a chance to kill.

"Gretchen!" Percy yelled from the top of the stairs. "Don't! You can't! She might kill you!"

"Might?" Hades interrupted. "Will. Gretchen, don't be stupid. You can't beat her like this. Just wait. Let us come with you."

I didn't stop to listen, just jumped in my truck and laid rubber peeling out of the driveway. Turning my police scanner on, I ignored the speed limit. Maybe I should have stolen Percy's car instead. It was faster.

I had to try. Better she kill me than an innocent. I'd killed before and probably deserved to die. And this was the only time of the month that it would be easy for her.

The scanner hissed and scratched, and I slammed on my breaks. The police were feeling awful chatty. Good for me.

I had to stop for gas, which sucked, but I couldn't afford to break down, then jumped onto the highway in Bangor and floored it, weaving my way through the minimal traffic.

Thank goodness it was midweek and it was only workday traffic and not shopping traffic. It thinned out as I gained distance from Bangor. I hopped around the roadways a bit, avoiding cops and trying to stay headed in the right general direction. It was a long drive, and I knew that Lacey could run faster than my truck and that she'd left before I'd gotten home.

It took me a while to find the right house when I finally located Augusta Road in Sydney. Having forgotten my cell phone, I had to turn around a couple of times. I jumped out at mailbox 1493, which stood in front of a cookie cutter white farmhouse. I raced around, trying to find how Lacey would have gotten in, if she were there. I couldn't see anything, though there was a light on the second floor as well as the kitchen and living room.

I could see a middle aged man and woman flitting around the kitchen. Alice's parents, maybe? I didn't have time for the niceties of knocking, so I burst through the front door, much the shock of the man and woman who were indeed Alice's parents.

"Hey, lady!" the man shouted as I beat my way up the carpeted stairs with no time to explain.

The door that had the light on behind it was locked. I backed away from it, leaning back for balance as I kicked it once, twice, to knock it off its hinges and reveal my best friend cradling an unconscious girl, an unfamiliar smell in the air.

Lacey-Marie pulled her face away from the girl's neck and giggled. "There's my little accomplice! She's good, want some?" she held the unconscious girl out to me as blood spurted out of her slashed jugular.

Great, the vampire had gotten high off the drug-filled blonde girl she was drinking. That made the situation about 10 times more dangerous.

Wait, accomplice? My mind raced back to the full moon after which I had woken with the taste of meat in my mouth. I'd helped her kill someone.

"Lacey, stop. You're going to kill her." I held my hands out, remaining as still as possible.

The girl's parents came puffing up behind me. The woman shrieked and crumpled. Her husband was too shocked by the scene before him to catch her.

"So?" She bent her head and drained what remained. No wonder she had been gaining weight, drinking that much fresh blood in such a short period of time. It only took moments to drain a full-grown person, though a vampire typically didn't, unless they were starving.

She dropped the girl's corpse and sashayed over to me, patting my cheek with a blood-drenched hand. "Loosen up, Gretch, I'm just killing off the competition."

"You bitch." I slapped her, not thinking.

"Hah! I wouldn't do that if I were you, mutt." She caught my hand on the backswing and licked it.

"You're disgusting," I said, my teeth gritting as soon as I got the words out.

"You love me."

"Mosquito," I insulted her, like everything was normal. It was a desperate attempt, and it didn't work.

She laughed as she yanked my head to the side and giggled into the gurgle of blood that spurted when she sank in her fangs and tore away a mouthful of flesh. She chewed the piece of my neck for a moment, then spit it out and bent to drink the hot gush of my blood.

Pain shot from the wound throughout my body as I thrashed and screamed. Within moments, I lost control of my limbs, and my screamed turned to a gurgle.

She was killing me. My best friend was killing me. My eyes rolled in the direction of Mr. and Mrs. Glowa.

"Run, get out of here. She won't come after you until I'm gone," I wheezed out as the drag of Lacey's mouth on my neck threatened to knock out my air supply.

Lacey wanted my blood too badly to let go.

Mr. Glowa, hearing me, grabbed his wife around the waist and dragged her away. He moved quicker when the adrenaline kicked in, overriding the shock of seeing his dead daughter lying on the floor. They'd probably gone for the police, and I hoped that Lacey-Marie would be gone by the time they got there.

I became lightheaded. Blood loss will do that to you.

We weren't alone for long. The smell of death permeated the room so strongly that even with my human nose I could smell it.

"Come, child." Kern, the patriarch of the New York family of vampires, used one finger to lift Lacey's chin from my neck. "You've had your fun. Now it's time to come home."

Lacey kept her grip on my hair and arm. "She's still got blood."

"She'll empty on her own. Come." Kern disentangled his protégé's fingers from my hair.

I didn't have any strength left in me, so I crashed to the floor. My shoulder bounced against the hardwood, sending my blood splattering around the room. I could feel it draining away with every quickening heartbeat. Vampires have venom in their fangs, which causes one's heart to beat until there is nothing left to circulate, unless they licked the wound to cover it with their thick saliva. Such a thing wouldn't do a thing for the gouge in my neck.

The heat left my limbs as I watched Lacey-Marie's blurry back with Kern's arm around her shoulders leave through the broken doorway.

My eyes closed, and I lacked the energy to open them again. This wasn't so bad. Lacey was leaving. My death wouldn't be useless. I sank into the darkness, content.

$$\text{)(} \bullet \text{)(}$$

I woke with a groan, lifting a shaky hand to feel the side of my aching neck. My fingers connected with smooth skin. I felt sunshine somewhere around my feet, so it must have been late afternoon.

Doug grabbed my hand to keep me from moving around any more. "Percy!"

"Thanks," I said, as I became more aware of my surroundings.

"No problem. I'm glad you're awake." Doug smoothed the hair away from my forehead and planted a loud kiss there.

"Gross," I said.

"I don't think you mean that. Your neck is all healed up, by the way." He straightened back up.

"How?" I touched my neck again, feeling around for a scar.

"Hades, god of the dead, remember? Apparently he stuffed enough of your blood back into you for you to survive. All Percy had to do was keep you alive until the moon came back."

"Cool." I tried to sit up.

"Don't you dare, young lady." Percy appeared in my field of vision with her hands on her hips.

I sank back to my pillow.

"How long have I been out?" I asked, reaching my hand out for the water again.

Doug held the bottle to me, and I snatched it from him, taking a good long drink. It hurt, but I was so thirsty.

"Easy, pup. You've been out for about four days. You're nowhere near one hundred percent, so you're not getting out of that bed." Percy took the bottle from me and set it back on the nightstand.

"What if I have to pee?" I asked, trying to be practical.

"Either I, or one of the girls, will accompany you." Percy was taking her role as mother hen seriously.

"The girls are here?" I tried once more to sit up.

Doug slid an arm around my shoulders, and Percy rearranged my pillow so I could at least pretend to sit up. I sighed a little as Doug eased me back onto them. Maybe this whole being waited on hand and foot thing wouldn't be too bad. Except for the peeing bit. I really preferred to do that alone.

"Yes. I called them as soon as we found out about Lacey, and I sent Hades after you. Lacey must have just left when he got there. We haven't found her yet."

"She's probably in New York City by now. I'm pretty positive that Kern showed up."

"She better be gone. I'd kill her otherwise," Doug growled.

"None of that. Lacey's mine," I growled back. As the alpha, I had first dibs on Lacey-Marie's life. I wasn't quite sure what I'd do if I did get my paws on her, but I'd have plenty of time to think about it while I lay in bed.

"I'll go tell the girls she's awake," said Hades from his position in the doorway. "Welcome back, Gretchen."

"Thanks to you, I hear." I smiled at his retreating back.

He raised one hand as he went, brushing off my gratitude.

It was only minutes before I was mobbed by Toni, Fern, and Meredith. They were all talking at once, and I couldn't follow any of it. I was happy I could count on them. We'd asked a lot of them over the past couple weeks, and they'd stood their ground.

They confined me to my bed for several days, and though I managed to go to the bathroom by myself, I was rarely alone.

I fantasized about how I would take revenge on my best friend, but when all was said and done, she was no longer in my territory, and there was nothing I could do. Instead, I turned my attention to the new relationships I'd developed with the girls and with Doug. This was what was worth living the rest of my life for. Revenge would be a momentary pleasure which could only hurt me. I was done with letting anyone control me. I was ready to live a new life.

Epilogue:
A Full Moon Later

The shift during full moon had returned me to complete health. In fact, I felt amazing. I don't know what Hades did to me, but I felt powerful. The wounds on my neck had completely disappeared, without even an ache left behind.

I stood in front of the mirror rearranging my mess of curls out of my face and off my neck. The heat of the day that radiated throughout my room didn't dampen my giddiness in the least. Doug was taking me out on a date, bowling. We had spent the full moon together in wolf form, but as we couldn't remember it, we wanted some quality time.

I'd overheard Doug talking to Robert and referring to me as his girlfriend. We hadn't had any sort of discussion on the matter yet, but there was no denying the growing bond between us. I was attempting to be careful, to take things slowly, but animal instincts pushed to be set free, to claim what was ours.

"Down, girl," I muttered to myself as I dabbed lavender oil on my pulse points. I wanted to enjoy getting to know the amazing man who had strolled his way into my life. It was harder with the moon in the sky, but so far I'd been successful in muzzling my wolf's desires.

I dashed out into the hallway and nearly collided with the man in question.

"Slow down, *ma columbe*." He chuckled and folded me in his arms, burying his nose in my neck.

A rumble reverberated out of him, and I pulled away, straightened my clothes, and bit my lower lip. I tried to subtly clear my nose of his scent and bring my heart rate down to normal. "Uh, are you ready to go?"

"Yes. Is this okay to wear?" He motioned at his jeans and t-shirt. Even a few days after the full moon, he was still pretty hairy, though not quite to his former level. He'd trimmed his beard close to his jaw and neatened the edges. I thought he looked handsome. Before I could stop myself, I reached up and ran my fingers through his neatly brushed hair until my fingers met at the nape of his neck. We stepped into each other, and our lips pulled together like a pair of magnets.

I felt his heart speed up and his scent change. I quickly pulled away as my body echoed his. "Yeah, you look great. We should probably go." I turned and pulled him by the hand through the house and out the door.

Damn wolf trying to make decisions without me. Not that I was against them, I just wanted to be cautious, while she wanted to throw herself into things.

Once we got out into the soft evening air, I was able to relax. We climbed into my truck and headed out, my mind swirling over the past couple of weeks.

Lacey-Marie had called my phone, but I'd handed it off to Percy. I was still beyond enraged about what she had done. Percy had tried to refuse it, but I walked away. I listened from outside the kitchen as Lacey tearfully apologized for everything.

She had moved into an apartment of her own. Well, sort of her own. It was situated in a building that belonged to Kern, which meant that she was back under his watchful eye and protection. She said she wanted to talk to me, that she'd call back again. I walked back in the room and took the phone from Percy's hand and hit the end call button, then blocked her number.

The news stations were broadcasting stories about Bigfoot sightings, and there were new photos circulating of tiny winged people that the internet was attempting to tear apart for proof of photoshop. Problem was, if it was photoshopped, it was a professional job. Percy took one look at the picture the evening news had flashed across the screen and drew a sharp breath. They weren't faked.

There were websites created for meet-ups to hunt for proof. Some people were excited to look for something magical. Others were growing suspicious of everyone around them.

We arrived at the bowling alley just as the sun sank into darkness. Doug grabbed my hand, and we strolled in together to claim some shoes and a lane. A poster was hung up at the front counter: "How well do you know your neighbors? Are they reclusive? Do they look or behave strangely? Beware: they might not be human. Always be aware of your surroundings, and report any odd instances to this hotline." A 1-800 number was blazed across the bottom in red and on tabs that were a little over half torn away.

I narrowed my eyes at the poster, then tore it from the wall, balled it up, and tossed it on the counter with my shoes. "On second thought, we should go see a movie." I tugged Doug back out, not caring that we had already paid for our game.

"Gretchen?" Doug questioned, his eyes glimmering with concern.

"It's starting. Hades warned me a war is coming. I think it might be right around the corner."

Acknowledgments

I've got a pretty good list of people I want to thank for making Beauty is the Beast possible. First, to my editor, Stacey, for all the hard work you've done. There is no way I could be publishing this without you. Seriously, you are amazing, woman!

To my cover artist, Mirella Santana, who did such an incredible job with this cover (It's gorgeous, isn't it?!) I hope to do lots of work with you in the future.

Next to my beta readers: Casey, Roxi, Melissa, and Cheryl. Thank you so much for taking time out of your busy lives to read through and give me thoughts, opinions, and corrections. You guys are great!

A big thanks to my sister-in-law Kate, your werewolf drawing is beautiful, which is why I keep sticking it everywhere.

To my family: my parents, my husband Devin, my girls Autumn and Hadassah, and my brother Josiah (for marrying Kate, ha!)

To my reader group, Zamboni's Pack Lair, I can't wait to hear what you think!

A big hug to my writing group, The Nomadic Guild of Scripturients. You've been with me for this entire journey and I can't thank you enough for that. (Note to Heather: I do NOT breathe too much, I just like commas!) An extra thanks to Asher for having read the rough draft that I scribbled all over and still giving me some great notes!

To my former co-workers: Sabrina, Lacey, Dawn, Renee, Amanda, Angela, Jen (both of you), Julie, and Michelle. I drew a lot from my work experience for this book, so in a way, you helped shape this story (just saying the things on the page that we all wanted to say out loud from time to time).

And to my readers. I hope you loved the beginning of Gretchen's journey, and I hope you'll be back for more!

Dear Reader,

Thank you so much for exploring what if with me. Gretchen has been on my mind since way back in '09 where this very book started as a NaNoWriMo project. That first draft was a mess. I tore it to shreds and meticulously Frankensteined it into the novel you just read.

I'm so excited to be sharing Beauty is the Beast with you in its final form.

Loved it? Hated it? Please leave a review on Amazon and Goodreads. It can be as simple one-liner or as lengthy as you wish, it's all appreciated!

If you'd like to keep in touch, there are a few places you can find me:

Social media & on the web:

Facebook   Instagram

Twitter   Blog/Web

If you want to keep up with all the latest news you can sign up for my newsletter here:

And join my Facebook group, Zamboni Pack's Lair, here:

Please don't be a stranger, and keep an eye out for more adventures with Gretchen!

Lots of love,

Jen

About the Author

Jen loves books. Reading them, writing them, reviewing them, and collecting them. (She claims it's not hoarding)

Urban fantasy is the name of her game, and being a mom is her day job. She also is a licensed cosmetologist, though she no longer works in a salon.

She lives in the boondocks of Maine with her husband, 2 tiny tornadoes (girls), 2 dogs, 3 cats, and 1 vocally insistent cockatiel.

To learn more, check out: jenniferzamboni.blogspot.com

Gretchen's
Anti-Werewolf
Tea

Ingredients*

· 1/2 cup Chamomile
· 1/3 cup Lavender
· 1/8 cup + 2 tsp
  Mint of Choice

Instructions

Mix thoroughly & store
in a lightproof container
for up to 6 months.

Prepare a Cup

Place 1 TBS of tea in a
steeper. Using boiling water,
steep for 4-7 minutes
Add lemon & honey to taste.

Enjoy as needed!

*Individual Cup Ingredients
· 1.5 tsp Chamomile
· 1 tsp Lavender
· 1/2 tsp Mint

Bookmark instructions:

Carefully remove
from book, fold in
half, & tape edges.
Enjoy your bookmark!

Made in USA - Kendallville, IN
43200_9780692042847
03.26.2022 1420